T0325513

Rogue Sentinel
By Tom Wither
This edition published in 2019

Popular Press, is an imprint of

Pike and Powder Publishing Group LLC
1525 Hulse Rd, Unit 1   1 Craven Lane, Box 66066
Point Pleasant, NJ 08742   Lawrence, NJ 08648-66066

Copyright © Tom Wither
ISBN 978-0-998059-35-8
LCN 2019948981

Bibliographical References and Index
1. Fiction. 2. Espionage. 3. Action

Pike and Powder Publishing Group LLC All rights reserved
For more information on Pike and Powder Publishing Group, LLC,
visit us at www.PikeandPowder.com & www.wingedhussarpublishing.com

twitter: @pike_powder
facebook: @PikeandPowder

ROGUE SENTINEL

A Novel

By

Tom Wither

For Donna, who came into my life
when the time was right for both of us.

FOREWORD

Even as the Islamic State believed itself the beginning of a world dominating Islamic Caliphate, the U.S. and its coalition partners were working to undermine and destroy its savage and brutal subjugation of the people trapped within its territory in Iraq and Syria.

Many operational successes have been publicly lauded over the years by the U.S. led coalition against the Islamic State, known as Combined Joint Task Force Inherent Resolve (www.inhrentresolve.mil). Others, due to the need to maintain military secrecy about means, methods, and techniques, never will be.

This story is intended to honor those whose names and deeds will never be known publicly, and will always be considered the 'quiet professionals' within the intelligence community and the U.S. Special Operations Command – *Libertate sapienter et fortiter servatur.*

CHAPTER 1

Present Day - Somewhere in Jordan

The electronic ring of the Ericsson CM-200 cell phone was shrill and metallic, a ringtone chosen specifically to convey urgency and require immediate attention. The phone lay on a small light-colored ash end table, marred by scratches and cigarette burns across its surface. The wide base of a white plastic tumbler half-full of iced tropical fruit punch was surrounded by a fine line of moist condensation in the reading lamp's light.

The tumbler was halfway to the man's mouth when the cell phone began its electronic screeching, and he hesitated in mid-movement, his dark brown eyes flicking to the phone, deciding whether to take a quick sip or answer. His prominent nose, strong and slightly upturned at the end, dominated his face, and beneath his angular cheekbones, the edges of his thin-lipped mouth turned down slightly.

He flicked his eyes around the room in mild frustration, scanning the spartan interior. The living room had white painted walls dulled and yellowed by regular sun exposure and the chain smoking of the previous occupant. The stale smell of burnt tobacco still lingered faintly. Before him, an ancient leather couch lay a threadbare Persian rug in the center of the room. The couch's dark upholstery, with its deep creases, heavily worn seat cushions, and missing rear wooden feet added to the room's shabbiness.

The sun had fallen hours ago, and he had drawn the heavy drapes as the last orange rays of the sun caressed the walls. Like the living room, the house itself was small, with only three other rooms: a simple kitchenette with a stove, sink, and tiny refrigerator/freezer, and two small bedrooms. Given his job, it would not do to live in a more ostentatious home, and living in one of the poorer sections of the already humble town offered several advantages.

Duty won out in his decision process, and the man leaned to the left from the deep recess of an armchair covered in dark brown fabric to place the tumbler back on the table. As he did so, the light from the reading lamp splashed across his face, highlighting brown skin tanned further by the strong Middle-Eastern sun. His beard, placed in sharp relief by the lamp, was closely trimmed, as he felt befitted a man two years shy of thirty. He wore it as a cultural and religious necessity, but he secretly preferred to be clean-shaven. There were so many people these days who viewed a man of Middle Eastern descent wearing a beard with suspicion, and when he did travel internationally—which was not often—he took the opportunity to shave it off.

The Ericsson CM-200 was one of the few 'flip' phones still in production, and he flicked it open without conscious thought, or bothering to check the caller ID. It could only be one man.

"Al-Amriki?" the voice at the other end asked in Arabic. Akeem was not the brightest of the faithful, but his use of the sobriquet also proved that the man had not received an unexpected call. He was, as far as he knew, the only man born in America serving the true jihad with the Islamic State of Iraq and Syria.

Others had tried, but most had died during the rigorous training, or had not gotten past the exacting background check conducted by ISIS sympathizers in either the Syrian or the Iranian governments. Those few determined to be spies for the infidels were killed, their decapitated bodies left to rot where they fell, and the videos of their executions mailed to the American Embassy in Amman or Riyadh as warnings not to try such foolishness again.

Al-Amriki may have been born in the States, but his mother and father taught him Arabic at a young age, primarily so he could study the Holy Qur'an in its native tongue, and that fluency served him well now as a senior planner of the jihad. "Of course," Al-Amriki answered, mildly exasperated. "Is it going well?"

Al-Amriki could hear Akeem breathing over the line. His breathing was fast and a little labored, which introduced unexpected pauses in his speech.

"It is, my friend. We blocked the ground floor fire exits before we began, and with the lobby entrance blocked, the apostates and infidels are trapped in the hotel with us."

"Allah be praised," Al-Amriki responded somewhat dryly. "How many have you sent to Paradise?"

"At least twenty so far."

Al-Amriki's eyes shifted to the muted television at the other end of the Persian rug. It was nothing a techno-geek would brag about, just a cheap satellite receiver paired to an inexpensive twenty-four-inch Samsung LCD flat panel with built-in speakers, all of which was resting on an inexpensive particleboard stand with a faux oak veneer. The black RG-6 cable connecting the receiver to the small satellite dish ran behind the drapes and through the nearest window, cracked open just enough in spite of the day's heat.

"The television cameras are not focused on the lobby entrance yet, and all the video is being shot from a distance. I can see the flashing lights of the police cars along the road; I think it's Diplomatic Street," Al-Amriki told him.

"Can you see the bodies of the policemen?" Akeem inquired. "Mohammad cut them down from the second story windows when they first arrived."

"No. The man on the anchor desk isn't saying much either. He keeps referring to an 'incident at the Hilton Hotel'. Are you learning anything from the scanners?"

"Yes," Akeem replied. "The local police have called for military units, as we expected, but they won't arrive for thirty minutes or more. In the meantime, the local police commander has ordered the hotel block cordoned off and anyone who leaves the hotel arrested."

Al-Amriki nodded grimly. "It seems Allah is with you tonight."

"Yes, but..." Akeem hesitated.

"Go on." Al-Amriki told him.

"The hotel manager, an infidel western swine, triggered a recording that's playing over the hotel public address system. I'll hold the phone closer to one of the speakers..."

Al-Amriki heard some rustling and then another, male voice growing louder.

"...stay in your rooms. Attention please. All guests of the hotel are in immediate danger. Lock yourself and your family in your room immediately. Let no one into your room. Block the door with furniture if you can. Wait for uni-formed police instructions, and stay in your rooms..."

Akeem came back on the line. "The message keeps repeating and we don't know how to stop it. The infidels and apostates are hiding in their rooms now. Abu and Muqtada have been patrolling the hallways on the floors, knocking on doors claiming to be the police..."

"Has that worked?" Al-Amriki asked.

"Only a few have actually opened their doors. All were sent to Allah for judgement."

The grim look on Al-Amriki's face deepened, and he shook his head. "This was not how it was supposed to be. You've only killed a handful. Do you think you can lure more out?"

Akeem thought for a few seconds. "I don't think so, Al-Amriki. We may get a few more, but the gunfire will make those that remain more suspicious."

The mention of his name occasioned another thought. "You are contacting me as we discussed?"

"Yes. The manager's phone line in his office, to the electronic relay set up in the apartment a few blocks away."

Good. Al-Amriki thought. *That relay connects to three others in different countries. The American NSA will never be able to track one call through all that noise. Besides, I'll have this cell phone dismantled and dumped as soon as this operation is over.*

"Listen, my brother," Al-Amriki said, his tone soft and reassuring, "I think we can still achieve the goals of this operation."

Akeem listened intently, saying nothing. Al-Amriki was the pre-eminent engineer within ISIS, rumored to advise its director of operations, Akil Badr al-Bukara.

"You must challenge the Qatari forces directly. They conspire with the Western Crusader nations, and give them and the cowards in their military safe bases and succor. You can hurt them badly. Find another phone in the hotel, and call Al-Jazeera's office in Al-Dofra. Wait a moment."

Al-Amriki got up from his chair and found the folder with his notes for the operation. Scanning them quickly, he found the sheet with the listing of Al-Jazeera offices throughout the Middle East. Since Al-Dofra was Al-Jazeera's headquarters, the number was at the top of the page. He read off the phone number to Akeem.

"Tell them you are Holy Warriors for the Islamic State and that no government or people is beyond the Caliphate's reach."

"Gladly." Al-Amriki could hear the pride filled smile in Akeem's voice.

"Tell them that each Holy Warrior of the Caliphate is worth 10 Qatari soldiers. Then, praise Allah, you and the others must prepare for the Qatari forces."

"We will, Al-Amriki." Akeem intoned solemnly.

"Fight them at the entrances. Forget the infidels in the rooms."

"But we should kill them..." Akeem interjected.

"No!" Al-Amriki interrupted. "You will kill the infidels, but after you deal with the Qatari forces! Make a stand at the entrance and when they come in, set fire to the hotel. Let the warmongers, infidels, and apostates burn."

Al-Amriki knew the Hilton Hotel in Al-Dofra catered primarily to westerners, particularly U.S. military members and government contractors. Although owned by a wealthy Qatari, with two Americans as senior managers, the hotel staff was predominantly Indian and Pakistani, since both were cheap labor sources in the Emirate, and most of them were Hindu, Buddhist, or Catholics. It was one of the more compelling reasons for Al-Amriki to select it as a possible target for ISIS, and likely why it had been approved.

"We shall kill them all for the glory of Allah. They shall burn on earth and then burn in hell after they are judged by Allah." Akeem said fervently.

"Yes, you shall." Al-Amriki replied solemnly. "My brother, your deeds and the deeds of your men shall resonate throughout the world tonight. You will also know Allah's peace and boundless favor."

"Allah is truly beneficent. Allah be praised," Akeem responded.

Al-Amriki could visualize the man bowing his head. "I envy you, my brother. I wish I could be there to join you on the journey."

"You have done so much for us. Without your training and knowledge of the infidel, we would not be able to seek Paradise this night. Allah has been kind to you and you shall see him when He chooses, my brother."

Al-Amriki hung his head, the phone pressed to his ear and his eyes closed. "May Allah be with you all tonight as you complete His work."

"Allah be praised, and peace and blessings be upon His Prophet, Muhammad. May the Prophet guide our hands this night."

The line went dead and Al-Amriki began to disassemble the burner cell phone. His hands worked nearly without thought as he watched the television feed from Al-Jazeera. Once the phone was in pieces on the table, he again sipped his juice, waiting patiently. It took nearly twenty minutes, but the live video was soon reduced to a small square image in the corner of the screen as the network switched over to the live feed from the set.

The anchor, a man whose grooming was as impeccable as any movie star's, was speaking, and Al-Amriki used the remote to turn up the sound.

"...we have a man on the phone who claims to be the leader of the people currently occupying the Hilton Hotel and holding the guests hostage." The anchor folded his hands and addressed himself to the caller.

"Sir? Can you hear me?"

"Praise be to Allah, I can..."

"Can you tell me why you are occupying the hotel and what are the condition of your hostages?"

"I was told I would be speaking to a Muslim. Are you a Muslim? Do you believe in Allah and his One Prophet Muhammad, blessings and peace be upon him?" In spite of the call being routed across phone lines and then re-transmitted over the satellite link as part of a television broadcast, Al-Amriki clearly recognized Akeem's voice.

The anchor was obviously surprised by the line of questioning, and he chose to answer the question, in spite of his training to be an objective journalist.

"I am a Muslim, sir, yes. Would you please tell us why you have occupied the hotel?"

"We have taken this festering den of opulence and inequity, this shelter of the Crusader's army's, in the name of the Islamic State."

Al-Amriki could see the newscaster trying to ask another question but Akeem kept talking without pause.

"This vile place where the crusaders drink alcohol and carouse with the lowest of whores, will be destroyed. All those within are condemned to the lowest levels of hell for their lack of true faith in Allah, along with their apostate attendees and the infidels of all kinds who chose to serve the crusaders."

Akeem paused to take a breath and the anchor managed to slip in another question.

"Sir, can you tell us about the people inside? Is anyone hurt?"

"All those we have found are being judged by Allah even now. I have sent no less than five infidels to His justice since we began this operation against the allies of the Great Satan."

Al-Amriki saw the newscaster's mouth drop open. He had clearly not expected a direct admission that his caller had actually killed people, and his surprise cost him a chance for another follow-up question. The pause gave Akeem a chance to continue.

"Since the battle is now joined, I invite the weakling security forces of this tiny principality of the greater Caliphate to attack us. We shall send them to Allah for judgement! Each jihadi of the Islamic State is capable of defeating 10 Qatari apostates! This place is the stepping stone for the forces of the jihad to reclaim this province from the corrupted leadership of the Emir, the puppet of the American Satanists..."

Al-Amriki saw the anchor reach up to touch his ear as Akeem's voice suddenly cut off in mid-sentence. The producer had undoubtedly decided the content of the interview had outweighed its usefulness as a newsworthy event. Akeem, in the emotion of the moment, had gone farther than he had instructed, but the effect was the same.

"We will have one of our most senior reporters continue the interview with the caller, and return now to live video from outside the Hilton Hotel."

Al-Amriki looked carefully at the fresh image from the video feed, tuning out the anchor's continuing monologue with the help of the mute button on the remote. He estimated the Al-Jazeera camera location as being more than one-hundred meters from the lobby entrance, and it seemed peaceful enough, except for the obvious presence of two bodies lying on the stone pavers in front of the police cars, their red and blue flashing lights reflecting off the building.

The Hilton Hotel in Al-Dofra was a large complex, dominated by a single oval tower rising more than twenty-four stories. The tower, designed as a layer cake of pale concrete and glass, was the primary target, since it held the guest rooms. An attached four-story rectangle on the tower's north side held a mini-mall and spa, and another larger rectangle on the southeast side housed the conference center. The hotel complex sat on the edge of the Persian Gulf, and the large marina a block to the south was intended as the escape route for Akeem and his men.

Al-Amriki knew that was out of the question now. He had always known the responsiveness of the Qatari authorities would dictate whether Akeem and his men would escape or become martyrs, and the delay in killing the guests had made escape impossible. Fortunately, Al-Amriki had ensured that Akeem had chosen men who wanted martyrdom, and were not too experienced. After all, why send experienced men to their deaths, when you only needed cannon fodder for a relatively low-gain mission?

The lobby entrance on the west side of the hotel was visible on the current camera shot Al-Jazeera was broadcasting and, based on Al-Amriki's memory of the overhead imagery he had studied when planning the operation, their camera was located on the far side of Diplomatic Street, just northwest of the hotel's complex of buildings.

Unconsciously leaning forward to get a better view, Al-Amriki could see through the clear glass of the automatic doors leading to the lobby, thanks to the darkness of night and the brightly lit interior of the hotel. He could see the furniture Akeem's men had stacked up against them. Al-Amriki could also just barely discern the shape of a body lying on the floor to the left of the doors.

He was surprised that Al-Jazeera was still broadcasting this live, and then silently cursed himself for a fool. Stabbing the remote again with his thumb, he put the satellite receiver in record mode. Whatever happened next, he would have a record of it.

The Al-Jazeera video feed switched to another angle, the view centered on a small parking lot next to a set of tennis courts. Al-Amriki was sure that they were the courts at the Four Seasons, across the access road, just west of the Hilton Al-Dofra complex.

Al-Amriki saw heavily armed men boarding three armored Foxhound urban assault vehicles. Born from the harsh lessons the British learned operating out of Camp Bastion in Afghanistan, the Foxhound was a four-wheeled, heavy-duty troop carrier, designed to protect a six-man crew from small arms fire and the sudden devastation improvised explosive devices could cause. Although box-shaped, and weighing more than eight tons, the FOXHOUND had a V-shaped undercarriage to deflect blast damage, and could race to or away from a threat at more than seventy miles per hour.

The three Foxhounds appeared to be painted in desert tan camouflage, and the men boarding them were fitted out with the standard fare for entry or assault teams: body armor and assault rifles. The rifles looked like a mix of Heckler & Koch MP-5 submachine guns and Colt Firearms CAR-15 assault rifles.

Al-Amriki glanced back at the disassembled cell phone on the side table next to the chair, then back at the television feed. The Foxhounds were pulling out.

Al-Amriki leaned back and began to reassemble the phone. He could at least try to warn Akeem about what was coming. As he snapped the battery back in place and reached for the SIM chip, he glanced back at the television.

The three Foxhounds were moving out of the Four Season's parking lot and turned right on Diplomatic Street, accelerating quickly. The SIM chip slipped from between his fingers and dropped between his thighs. Looking down and lifting his right leg, he found it, snatching the tiny plastic-coated chip off the fabric of the chair. He tried twice to fit it into the phone's exposed backside, and in his haste, he kept having trouble slipping it into the slot.

He risked another glance at the Al-Jazeera broadcast and stopped assembling the phone. Al-Jazeera had switched back to the original camera feed, and Al-Amriki could see that the three Foxhounds had turned right off of Diplomatic Street and were heading straight for the glass fronted lobby entrance. Al-Amriki expected them to stop, and the men to dismount for entry, but the Foxhound's drivers had other plans.

The three armored vehicles raced down the short access road towards the lobby entrance, the Al-Jazeera camera zooming in to track the action. The lead vehicle made a short arc around the small decorative fountain to the left, while the other two arced right, decelerating slightly. The lead vehicle rammed through the plate glass framing of the lobby entrance without pause, smashing into the furniture and blasting it clear of the now-shattered entryway. The driver slammed on the brakes, slewing the wheel to the right to skid the vehicle into a halt, its armored left side facing the building.

The two trailing Foxhounds followed, with the second vehicle hitting a point just to the right of the first Foxhound's entry wound, widening the hole. Once in, the second armored car angled right, its driver stopping the armored behemoth's front bumper just shy of the left edge of the first Foxhound's front bumper. The third Foxhound followed suit, but hitting left of the now wider opening in the lobby facade, its driver turning right to bring its right bumper to the leftmost edge of the first Foxhound's left rear bumper.

Al-Amriki was impressed. In seconds, the Qatari forces had managed to eliminate Akeem's barricade, enter the hotel, and create an overlapping 'U' shaped armored barrier with their vehicles for the assault element to use as cover.

The Qatari troops exited the Foxhounds quickly, using only the doors on the Foxhounds facing the interior of their improvised barrier. Al-Amriki watched them and knew instantly that Akeem and his men would be dead sooner rather than later. The Qataris showed excellent discipline and their movement bespoke well-trained commandos or police special tactics units.

Weapons up and tracking, four of the Qataris established overwatch positions behind the armored Foxhounds, covering the interior of the hotel lobby as members of the predetermined assault teams formed up in two-man elements alongside the interior of the armored box made by the Foxhounds and prepared to move out.

As Al-Amriki watched, the partially reassembled phone momentarily forgotten in his lap, two of the Qatari commandos opened fire at someone in the lobby. Al-Jazeera unexpectedly cut away to an exterior view, and Al-Amriki could see flames licking at a few of the second story windows facing Diplomatic Street. As he continued to watch, two of the windows blew outward, and billowing clouds of black smoke began to pour out of the burning building.

Without warning, the video cut off, replaced by the image of the well-groomed male anchor in the studio talking to the camera. Al-Amriki reached for the remote and unmuted the sound.

"...we apologize to our viewers, but the commander of the Qatari Special Forces has requested that we not endanger his men by broadcasting the ongoing operation to retake the Hilton Hotel from the Islamic State forces that have claimed to..."

Al-Amriki muted the sound and disassembled the cell phone again. As far as he was concerned, the operation at the hotel was over. Akeem and his men would be dead by the end of the next hour. The Qatari Special Forces were obviously well trained and the entry team was probably being reinforced with additional commandos now.

The Qatari soldiers would clear the hotel floor by floor, seeking out Akeem and his small band while evacuating the hostages. Akeem and his men would surely die as martyrs as they recklessly attacked the commandos, each jihadi sure in the knowledge that he would see Paradise.

Tomorrow, the international news would focus briefly on the bold attack by ISIS against the west, and then attention would turn to profiles of the dead hotel guests and the capabilities and courage of the Qatari commandos.

Al-Amriki rose from the chair and walked past the small kitchen into the bedroom at the end of the short hallway. The bedroom was sparse, with a spare double bed on a steel frame bookended with oak head and footboards at each end. There were no shelves or wall hangings, only a mismatched night table of particleboard with a maple veneer and a small closet.

Al-Amriki made a beeline for the night table and picked up one of the items that seemed very out of place in the predominantly low-tech house. The iPhone X was far sturdier than its slim and seemingly fragile case and screen would lead someone to believe. Al-Amriki always thought its weight surprising for such a slim device.

He tapped the twelve-character pin code to unlock it, and typed in the phone number from memory. Another trip through electronic relays established by Islamic State sympathizers in Jordan and Syria, and he heard the call being answered.

"Yes?" The male voice that answered was calm and precise, deep and mildly gravelly. His English was unaccented.

"You saw?" Al-Amriki inquired.

"I did. You did not tell me he would be calling a news outlet."

Al-Amriki frowned. "No, that was not part of the original plan. He called me for advice as things changed, and I suggested he attribute the event to the organization and challenge the home team to a game." The allusion was simple enough for Akil, as football fan, he never missed the World Cup.

"That suggestion has obviously produced at least one of the preferred outcomes. What about the people at the location? How many were hurt in the stadium?"

"Only twenty or so, based off what Akeem told me. Many others were able to find shelter and avoid the storm. The resultant fire may harm others."

"I expected, based on your assurances, that more would be hurt in the storm's initial fury." Al-Amriki could hear the disappointment in Akil's voice.

"Yes," Al-Amriki told him, blowing out an exasperated breath, "there was an unanticipated recorded announcement. It allowed people to seek sheltered areas. I'll bear that in mind so that I can better advise you for future weather events in similar locations."

"Please do. Overall, you are to be commended for your evaluation of the storm's impact." The satisfaction in Akil's voice was unmistakable.

"Thank you, Sahib."

"When will you be ready to give me your next set of predictions?" Akil asked.

"I'm reviewing the material now. Perhaps in four to five days. It will be the largest storm yet," Al-Amriki promised.

"Good. I look forward to hearing from you again."

The line went dead, and Al-Amriki turned the iPhone off before returning it to the night table. He left the bedroom, and headed back to the card table in the corner. It was not a mahogany conference table in an underground bunker, but you did not really need much more than paper, something to write with, and a thick, chocolate brown document folder to plan operations for the jihad against the unbelievers in the world.

Al-Amriki slid off the retaining elastic band holding the document folder's large flap in place, and withdrew a thick sheaf of documents. He had printed all of them on the laser printer nestled in the corner, a seven-year old HP-600 color multifunctional that still worked surprisingly well. Doing so meant connecting his Toshiba Satellite S70T laptop directly to the printer, something he did only when new information came in via the usual method. In any event, he preferred working with the hard copy, in spite of the advances of the digital age – paper could be burned quickly after all, and that was simpler than the complex hours long wiping procedure he executed on the laptop every week.

Placing the overhead imagery in the center, he carefully studied them. The six photos from various heights above the target gave him the varying perspectives he preferred. Around the photos he arranged the other information – observed information about the guard force, apparent shift change times, and some photos taken at ground level of the various entry points and security measures. The last thing he laid down was a hand-drawn diagram of the facility, with the suspected locations of certain areas penciled in.

Now that he had his intelligence before him, he took the last two items from the folder. The yellow legal pad sat at his right hand, and he began to study the materials in front of him, making notes with his preferred fine-tipped blue pen and writing questions that would eventually become intelligence requirements he would pass on to Akil for action.

Hours passed while Al-Amriki worked, and after he had misspelled the same word three times in a row, he realized he was too tired to continue. Leaving everything where it lay, he walked to his bedroom, where a glance at the brass-colored wind-up clock on the night table next to his bed told him it was after 1 A.M.

Al-Amriki disrobed quickly, removing his brown ankle-length tunic, called a Thawb, before dropping the long-sleeved garment at the foot of his bed in an untidy puddle. His Sirwal undergarment quickly landed next to it. After relieving himself and taking a brief sponge bath of cold water, he crawled into bed.

He did not burden himself with worry that he had not yet found a way for ISIS to attack the facility, and settled himself comfortably. Before sleep took him, Al-Amriki resolved to perform two Salāts in the morning to make up for missing the late evening prayer time as he had worked.

Two minutes later, he was fast asleep.

CHAPTER 2

Lieutenant Commander Shane Mathews let his eyes wander over the terrain. The grassy slope fell away sharply toward the water, and the sun glinting off the steady ripple of the Pacific Ocean waves would have been dazzling if he were not wearing his favorite pair of polarized, impact-resistant Ray-Ban sunglasses.

His training and experience meant that he evaluated the terrain before him in ways most people did not. He looked for places of cover and concealment, and overwatch positions for snipers, assessing the risk to his team if he had to defend the crest of the hilltop he sat on—at least that was his first evaluation.

His second was much more in keeping with the moment. The sun that glinted off the waves shone from a bright blue sky dotted here and there with puffy white altocumulus clouds, and the light offshore breeze caused the bright green grass covering the hill to sway back and forth in a pleasing pattern. The air temperature was a comfortable seventy-six degrees, and the low humidity common to the San Diego shoreline made for another gorgeous day on California's southern coast.

Mathews tore his eyes from the ocean view, and looked down to admire something even more beautiful. Kristen had agreed to spend the weekend with him in San Diego before he could finish asking her the question. A few minutes ago, she had snugged her arms around him and laid her head on his chest to enjoy the view.

Mathews knew he was lucky. Kristen worked in the reception area back at his duty station and was part of the base security team. Smart and capable, she was twenty-nine, with shoulder length blonde hair and dark brown eyes, and he could not help but notice her impish smile and athletic figure when he was first assigned to the 152nd Joint Special Operations Unit.

She was part of the team that surreptitiously monitored and evaluated prospective assignees to the unit and, while Mathews thought Kristen was beautiful from the moment he met her, he tended to approach attractive women cautiously, having learned early on that it was more important to have a woman of good character in his life, than one that was just a pretty face. He kept his first interactions with her polite but professional while he waited for his final security clearance, knowing that if the attraction were mutual, he would find a way to get to know her better.

A few weeks ago, after being in the unit for nearly six months, he had run across her one afternoon at the indoor firing range. The shooting lanes at the range allowed him to evaluate her shooting skills (and her butt) without being too obvious, and he took the chance to ask her about her sidearm. Her choice of the Walther P99 chambered for .40 S&W for its stopping power, reliability, and built-in safety mechanisms was solid in Mathews' opinion, and spoke to the professionalism she brought to her job.

She was an impressive shot, able to place rounds wherever she needed to, even under simulated stress. She had challenged Mathews to a single magazine shoot off on clean 50-foot police silhouettes. First, they ran in place for three minutes, which was intended to simulate a chase or running toward an objective. The activity elevated their heart rates, making the sight picture harder to hold during each shot. When they safed their weapons and reeled the targets in, each of them scoring the other's target to ensure fairness, he had bested her by only five points, and grudgingly admitted to himself that he had probably gotten lucky.

As they finished their range practice, field stripping their weapons to clean them on the rear table, he asked her to dinner and she agreed. During the meal, he was pleasantly surprised to learn she had a Bachelor's degree in criminal justice with a minor in psychology, and was well on her way to a dual Masters in business administration and criminology. The next day, he also learned the hard way that she could kick his ass in racquetball, as she beat him in three straight games at the base's athletic center.

Over the last few weeks, his days were filled with training, and when she was not on duty, his nights were spent with her. They cuddled on the couch in his small on-base apartment watching movies, talking, making dinner together, and trying unsuccessfully for the first two dates to keep their hands off one another.

It had even gotten to the point where he now had trouble sleeping when she was not next to him. Wrapping his arms around the pillow when she worked the mid-shift just was not the same as feeling her warmth and smelling her hair and skin during the night.

She looked up at him and saw he was looking at her. Her smile was broad and reflected genuine happiness. "Whatcha looking at?" Kristen asked.

He smiled in return. "You're more beautiful than the San Diego bay."

She stretched up to plant a kiss on his lips. "You aren't too bad yourself."

"Thanks." Mathews smiled, still enjoying the lingering taste of her lips.

"Enjoying yourself?" Chambers asked.

Mathews smiled at her again. "Of course. It's a beautiful day, and I've just enjoyed a terrific lunch with my girlfriend. You?"

"Yes," she smiled in return, thinking this was a good time to ask. "How are you feeling?"

This again. Mathews knew she was going to bring it up. He brought her out here to get away from the base, and forget about duty, obligation, and recent events for a while. He needed not to wake up angry every morning, especially when he walked into the team area. Sam's desk still sat there empty, waiting for him to choose a replacement from the pool of candidate personnel files waiting in his computer for review. His smile fell, but not too far. He knew she was asking because she cared.

"I'm fine." Another kiss.

She was not buying it. "Honey, it's not your fault."

OK, fine. We'll have this conversation. "Yes, it is. I was his commanding officer."

"But..."

"But nothing," Mathews cut her off, his tone sharpening a little as his smile disappeared. "He was my responsibility."

"You can't..."

"Yes, I can." Mathews insisted. "My team, my men. I take them into combat and it's my responsibility to bring them all home again."

Chambers pushed off him a little, and straightened up, sympathy in her eyes. "Honey, you can't hold yourself to that standard." She put a gentle hand on his chest and rubbed. "You are not God."

Mathews shook his head. "No, I'm not, but you don't just ignore the

16

responsibility. I'm an officer and in the teams, you lead from the front, at home or overseas."

Chambers knew where he was coming from, but he was not listening to her. "Honey…"

Honey, you are starting to piss me off. Mathews cut her off again, his voice taking on a distinct angry edge. "Kristen, when you become an officer in the Navy, you're taught to look out for the welfare of the men and women you lead, on and off the battlefield. When you become a SEAL, you're expected to lead from the front. You're taking men into combat and you better be damn sure you bring them home again!"

Mathews found himself leaning towards her, his face inches from hers, the last few words still echoing in his ears. She recoiled and took her hand off his chest, and he was sure he saw her eyes starting to water. He had not intended to yell at her, but she just would not let it go.

Mathews looked away from her in the awkward silence. "I'm sorry." He felt her move and looked back. She was packing the remnants of lunch into the sacks, and sweeping up the crumbs off the blanket. He reached out to touch her and she shrugged him off.

Surrendering to the fact that he had wrecked their idyllic lunch, he helped her pack in silence. When she rose, he touched her arm gently, genuine sorrow in his voice. "Kristen, I'm really sorry. I didn't mean to yell at you."

She looked at him. Her face was set and her eyes dry. Mathews had never seen her mad before.

"Look," Chambers said hotly. "I care about you. I know you're sorry you yelled at me and I also know you weren't really yelling at me." Chambers paused to let that sink in. She could tell from the look on Mathews' face that he was not getting it, and that cooled her temper a little.

"No, I didn't mean to yell at you." Mathews responded. "It's just that talking about this isn't going fix it. I was responsible…"

This time, she cut him off. "Yes, you were."

"Why don't we just take a drive?" Kristen said in a flat voice, the anger evident.

What the hell is she mad about? She doesn't understand. If she wants to take a ride, that's fine. Maybe we can work this out later. "Sure," Mathews answered. "We can drive through San Diego and out across the Coronado

Bridge. The view is terrific. I only saw it a couple of times while I was stationed here."

He helped her fold the blanket, and Chambers handed it to him to carry as she hefted the sacks with the lunch leftovers. As they walked back to the rental car, he tried to reach for her hand to hold it, and she pulled out of range, not entirely ready to forgive him for yelling at her.

They were almost to the rented silver Ford Fusion when the iPhone X in his pocket warbled. Chambers stopped before he did. It was the 'work' phone's distinctive ringtone. Mathews pulled the phone from his pocket, tapped in the six-digit code, and then hovered his thumb over the button. The two-factor authentication was a safety measure built into the phone by the technical wizards at NSA. From the outside, the phone may have looked like a standard issue iPhone X with a Mophie battery pack, but its internal configuration, software, and encryption were anything but standard.

Mathews tapped the button to accept the call, and held the phone to his ear, only to hear a sexy female electronic voice repeating 'Going secure' until the call connected. When the sexy voice stopped, he said. "Mathews."

"This is Simon."

"Yes sir?"

"I'm sorry, but I have to cut your leave short. I need you back here immediately."

Given recent events, Mathews' first question was automatic. "My people?"

"Your team is fine. I've got a mission for you."

"Understood, sir. It will be a few hours at least. I'll need to check out of my hotel and rebook my flight."

"We've already called your hotel and booked your tickets. The ride home is on Uncle Sam. You and Ms. Chambers have tickets waiting at the San Diego airport for the 1400 flight. Once you arrive in Phoenix, have a taxi take you to the General Aviation terminal. The G280 will be there for the last hop."

"Got it." Mathews was none too pleased that the Colonel knew whom he was with, but it did not take a nuclear physicist to make the connection. He and Chambers both had to file leave forms, and the forms had a space on them for where you would be on leave, and since the Colonel approved them both...

"Anything else sir?"

"Not until you get here." Simon told him. "Safe flight."

The line went dead.

The Gulfstream G280 completed its approach to Runway 10 at 140 knots and began to flare out in preparation for landing. The jet was liveried in white and nothing else. Most unusual for an aircraft, it did not even have a serial number on the fuselage to identify its country of origin, provide it with a radio call sign, or use to communicate with air traffic control. Its radio call sign was chosen from a randomly changing pattern of words and numbers – standard operating procedure for the U.S. military.

The main gear of the G280, whose call sign for this mission was LEGION-61, touched down gently at 125 knots. As soon as its nose wheel touched the pavement, the engines reversed their thrust while the wing flaps split to deform the airflow over the wings and add more braking power.

Mathews looked over at Chambers. She was sitting to his right, and had softened enough since their argument in San Diego to reach over to hold his hand during the flight while she read a novel on her iPad. Mathews gave her hand a gentle squeeze, and he felt her thumb slide along to the top of his hand in response. He still needed to make up for yelling at her, but at least he knew he was partially forgiven.

Mathews glanced out the window to his left, marveling as usual at the barren appearance. The airstrip was in an area devoid of human habitation in the desert southwest. The closest town or houses were two hundred miles away; in fact, there was no sign at all of human habitation other than the airstrip, its east-west oriented twin, the control tower, and one enormous hangar.

As soon as LEGION-61 reduced speed to a rate fit for driving instead of flying, it turned left onto the taxiway designated "Charlie" and began to move toward the hangar. The hangar was at least two thousand feet long and wide— large enough to allow eight 747s to enter wingtip to wingtip and be swallowed whole. Deep enough to hold another eight 747s, it rivaled the Boeing assembly plant in Seattle in interior floor space.

When it reached the hangar, the G280 stopped, and after a moment, the center set of three monstrous doors guarding the contents of the hangar began to open. They stopped when the gap was ten feet wider than the sixty-foot wingspan of the G280.

LEGION-61's pilot increased his throttle slightly until the thrust of the engines overcame the aircraft's inertia and it began to roll forward into the opening. When the plane was moving, he reduced the throttle to idle. The aircraft continued to roll into the hangar where two men with lighted wands began to guide it toward its parking space along the right side of the hangar near the monstrous doors.

After the G280 parked and the whine of the engines had faded, the male cabin attendant popped the seal on the passenger door, swinging it into the cabin and securing it to the bulkhead. Once he had the door secured, he pressed a button to extend the stairwell from the interior of the fuselage, just below the door.

Chambers released Mathews' hand to put away her iPad, and unbuckled her seatbelt. Mathews unbuckled as well and followed her toward the G280's door, knowing full well that she had just slipped into 'work mode' now that they were back at the base. No outward signs of affection until they had some privacy and god help anyone who was not a personal friend making a comment about her and Mathews being on leave together.

Waiting near the base of the aircraft's flight stairs were a man and a dog. The man wore a uniform that was a variation on military battle dress uniform: black, not camouflage green or brown, and adorned only with the rank insignia of a full bird colonel in subdued black and a cloth nametape spelling 'SIMON' sewn over the left pocket. The dog sitting alertly to his immediate left was a jet-black ninety-seven-pound German Shepherd named Zeus from whose collar hung a metal tag in the form of an Air Force master sergeant's stripes.

Chambers stepped lightly down the flight stairs from the jet, with Mathews right behind her.

"Welcome back, Ms. Chambers, Lieutenant Commander," Colonel Simon said, nodding to each of them. Since he and Simon were both indoors, military protocol did not require that Mathews salute, and Chambers was a civilian.

"Thank you, Colonel. I know you need to speak to the commander, so if you'll excuse me..." Chambers said. Without waiting for a response, she snatched her overnight suitcase off the ground and headed off deeper into the hanger.

Mathews watched her leave, knowing that the next time they had some private time she would bring up Sam's death again. He really wished she would just drop it.

Simon gave him a minute, incorrectly assuming that Mathews deserved a few seconds to admire the way she moved, since he had cut their leave short. Once she was out of earshot, he broke into Mathews' thoughts.

"You've got good taste, Mathews."

Mathews' looked at Simon, expecting to see a lecherous grin, but finding only a fatherly look of understanding on his face.

"She's a great girl, sir."

"Yes, she is," Simon agreed, "You'd do well to keep her, if she lets you."

Mathews grabbed his overnight bag and put his mind on his duty. "What's the mission, sir? Is my team waiting for us?" Mathews asked, taking the opportunity to give Zeus a scratch on the head. Zeus was a trained Military Working Dog, and naturally cautious around strangers, but Mathews had been in the field with him during Operation Juno, and he and the dog were old friends now.

"I'll explain a little while we head to the briefing." Simon said as he turned to lead Mathews deeper into the hanger, and Zeus slipped out from under Mathews' hand to follow his master. "You need a stop at the head?" Simon may have been Air Force, but like any member of the military with years of service under his belt, he knew naval slang too.

"No sir, thanks." Mathews answered, quickening his step to keep up with the pace Simon set.

Simon did not start talking right away, probably because of the proximity of the other people in the hanger. Despite being assigned to the 152nd JSMU, known informally as the Wraiths, for nearly six months, Mathews took the chance to look around the enormous hangar, still impressed by its contents.

The smell of lubricants and aviation fuel mixed with diesel exhaust permeated the air, and sounds of aviation mechanics talking and air-powered tools echoed across the cavernous interior. The rear corner of the G280's hangar housed a medium-sized two-story office building for the maintenance office block, the lower half surrounded by a steel cage that contained engines and other oversized aircraft parts.

Directly in front of the two-story structure, in the direction of the parked G280, lay a parking pad the size of a 747, with large yellow fire extinguishers welded to wheeled hand trucks placed at intervals. Mathews remembered standing there in formation with his team for a rare visit by the president and the secretary of defense a month ago.

Parked along the remaining part of the hangar wall were two KC-46

Pegasus refueling tankers; another G280, a virtual twin to the one he flew in on; and two longer-range G550s. Four sleek and deadly looking F-22A Raptor fighters near the hanger doors added sex appeal to the row of aircraft.

Rounding out the collection of aircraft were a set of four AH-64E Apache Guardian attack helicopters, four Boeing 747-400s, and two C-17 Globemaster III cargo aircraft along the far wall, each one parked with its nose pointed toward the center of the hanger.

Maintenance personnel were working on various aircraft, and, as he watched, one female Air Force loadmaster gestured at the base of a C-17 Globemaster III as her male counterpart used a forklift to maneuver a pallet of gear towards the loading ramp leading into the aircraft's massive cargo box. Mathews wondered briefly if the gear was for his next mission, but did not ask, knowing that Simon would fill him in soon enough.

The general led the small group toward the back of the hangar. Zeus kept pace between Simon and Mathews as they approached the rear wall. There were two large areas of the floor offset to the right of the rear wall's centerline marked by thick yellow lines. The stenciling formed two large yellow squares, one within another, and the portions of the hangar's floor within the two squares were composed of steel grating instead of reinforced concrete. In the gap between the squares were the words, "WARNING – KEEP AREA CLEAR" in two-foot-high letters, repeated at intervals all the way around the perimeter. At each corner of the outer squares were unlit red lights, embedded in the floor.

Mathews knew the massive cargo elevators could easily allow one of the 747-400s with its more than 200-foot wingspan to park on it with room to spare, and led to the next level down where depot level maintenance of the aircraft and team equipment could be carried out without interfering with on-going flight or minor maintenance operations on this level.

Mathews continued to pace Simon and Zeus, walking obliquely past the aircraft elevators and a freight elevator capable of holding two enormous jet engines to what appeared to be a more conventional passenger elevator. The passenger elevator, encased in a small concrete box to house its electronics, cabling, pulleys, and counterweights, sat solidly behind two guards in desert camouflage. Both men currently on duty wore body armor, and carried AR-15 rifles.

As Simon and Mathews approached, the two guards came to attention and allowed them to enter the elevator. The elevator had a larger interior than normal, and could hold twenty people or so. The extra interior space came in handy when teams, fully kitted out for a mission, and often dragging heavy equipment with them, headed for the flight line on the hanger level. It was well lit and finished in burnished steel to help it resist damage and dents from unintentional impacts from squad sized weapons, heavy packs, and MILSPEC hard cases.

Mathews recalled Simon telling him about the base's history when he was first assigned to the Wraiths. The complex itself was a refurbished nuclear weapons assembly, a storage and handling facility taken over by the Department of Defense from the Department of Energy after the last nuclear weapons reduction treaty took effect.

Simon removed his ID badge from his pocket and waived it near the elevator controls. A soft chime, accompanied by a green light on the panel, indicated the elevator was active, and the colonel pressed the button for Level 7.

The nine-level deep facility, built underground to limit radiation leakage or damage to the surface environment in the event of an accidental detonation, was ideal for repurposing as the base for the Wraith teams, and provided a secure location for their operations. The Corps of Engineers expanded the surface facilities to accommodate the unit's small air force and converted the original first two levels into maintenance facilities for the aircraft.

Mathews knew the layout of the levels by heart, and thought the design well considered, with aircraft operations and maintenance on the first two levels, and the remaining lower levels offset from them below ground for safety and security. The passenger elevator they rode in was the only elevator offering access to the deeper levels of the complex.

Mathews watched the floor indicator as they descended. Kristen worked on Level 3 when there were new assignees or VIP visitors to the base. That level was the 'showplace' administrative area that also held a small security detachment and some temporary quarters for visitors and people awaiting their final security clearances to work for the Wraiths.

Level 3 also held the main base security office, Kristen's usual duty post, the command post, and the security armory. Levels 4 through 6 housed the officer and enlisted quarters, a multi-level Base Exchange & Commissary, and an indoor park.

The facility redesign even allowed natural light to shine down through the triple armored glass and aluminum structure that made up the ceiling of the offset housing and security sections that started at Level 3.

The setup always reminded Mathews of living inside a huge Embassy Suites hotel, or something out of the 'Zion' sets in the Matrix, a movie he had loved as a kid, but with much more greenery and a more pleasing decor than the steam punk vision in the film. The need to avoid prying eyes was addressed by the application of a special polymer to the exterior of the glass structure of the ceiling. The polymer reflected a small percentage of sunlight at all times to keep spy satellites and their imagery analysts guessing, while allowing natural light in, and at night, it kept all the interior lighting of the core area from being visible to the outside by closing an integrated set of steel shutters that also provided physical protection in the unlikely event that the base needed to be locked down.

Levels 7, 8, and 9 were the operational levels. Vertically aligned with the hanger level instead of the levels housing living spaces, they provided secure facilities for the main armory for the teams, the 152nd JSMU command post, operations planning offices and conference rooms, and team administrative areas.

As the elevator continued its descent past Level 6, Simon finally felt it was safe to talk.

"You won't be taking your team along on this one, Shane."

"Sir?" the tremor and mild uncertainty in Mathews' voice involuntarily betrayed his concern about his ability to lead after the death of one of his men, but Simon did not seem to notice it as he focused on elevator's floor indicator. "We're sending you in solo against the objective," he continued. You'll be going undercover."

Mathews considered that. These kinds of missions were not unheard of in special operations, but they were usually the CIA's job. Mathews had been recruited into the 152nd JSMU to lead Wraith Team 4, a group of very capable Tier One operators drawn from across all the services.

Team 4's recent success against a man who had made significant strides to rebuild and reinvigorate Al-Qaeda, including making some successful strikes on the United States, had proven his abilities as a team leader and earned his entire team promotions—by presidential order no less. Running solo missions into denied areas was not something he expected to be doing, but it was not outside the realm of the expected, in spite of the increased risk.

Mathews felt the elevator come to a halt on the seventh level. Simon waved his badge at the reader in the elevator again, and the doors parted smoothly. Simon headed out the door with Zeus hot on his heels. Mathews hefted his bag and followed. The walls in all the operational levels were constructed straight out of some standard issue military base interior decoration manual. Light brown paint above the dark chair molding gave way to chocolate brown sound dampening carpet below the molding, and the floors were covered in cream-colored carpeting. Framed photos of military aircraft, cargo drops, parachute jumps, tanks, and other similar scenes were hung every few feet.

Mathews trailed Simon and Zeus down the hallway and in through the door labeled 'Conference Room B'.

"Take a seat, Lieutenant Commander." Simon invited in him with a wave. He made another gesture towards Zeus, and the dog settled himself on the floor obediently.

Mathews dropped in the seat, glancing at the dog. "He looks like he's all healed."

Simon looked at Zeus, who had opened his muzzle slightly to pant, his gaze moving between Colonel Simon and Mathews, obviously alert and attentive.

"Yes. I'd forgotten you hadn't seen him since Operation Juno. He healed quickly. The vet is very pleased."

"I'm sorry he got hurt, but he was really brave out there."

The corners of Simon's mouth turned up slightly. "I'm proud of him. He's as courageous as he looks."

"If I have to go back in the field with a K9, I want him with me," Mathews assured him.

Simon turned back to Mathews, slightly chagrined at the thought. "I appreciate that, but I'm not sure I want my buddy getting shot again."

"I understand, sir." Mathews assured him.

Simon touched a control, and the lights dimmed. "Let's get back to why we are here," Simon told him, starting to tap on the keyboard embedded in the conference table.

"Aye, aye, sir." Mathews turned his attention to the large LCD screen across from them.

Simon logged in and brought up his e-mail, and the item at the top of the inbox queue caught Mathews' attention.

"That looked like Mr. Cain's e-mail address at the CTS." Mathews observed.

"It was. He sent the intel package over for the operation this morning. General Crane cleared it with the Pentagon and the CIA Chief of Station a few minutes before I called you back from leave."

Counter-Terrorism Support, located on a secure compound near the NSA on Fort Meade, was the intelligence and operational support center the Wraiths worked with. In fact, Cain's team had helped Mathews and his team of commandos out of more than one narrow escape, and provided all the tactical intelligence and fire support they could use during capture or kill operations against that Al-Qaeda lunatic a few months back.

"One day I'd like to go out to the Fort on temporary duty and meet the man," Mathews stated.

Simon nodded as he double-clicked on the attachment to the e-mail to open it. "That's a good idea. Once you're back from this mission, I'll set up a couple of TDY trips to the Fort. The team leads can go out in two waves. You can lead one, and Major Kline can take the other out. It will be a good opportunity for the team leaders to meet Cain's people and see how they do things."

"That's great, sir," Mathews said. "It would be better to take the team NCOICs along as well."

"Fair point," Simon agreed, seeing the Power Point logo pop up on the screen as the presentation software loaded. "I'll make arrangements for them too. We've got enough travel funding left this fiscal year."

As Mathews watched, Simon clicked past the boilerplate classification slide reminding anyone viewing the briefing that it contained TOP SECRET// CAPTIVE DRAGON classified information, as well as the subsequent title slide, bearing the unit logos for the 152nd JSMU. Mathews always thought his unit's logo was pretty cool.

The logo was taken from a still image of three Wraith operators, wearing their full winter kit, which conveniently hid their features, immediately after being inserted onto a snow-covered mountaintop by a dark gray camouflaged CV-22B Osprey sporting the large black 'W' emblazoned on the left vertical stabilizer. The image spoke to the Wraith's ability to operate effectively in the harshest environments anywhere on Earth to accomplish their assigned mission, using some of the most advanced equipment a modern soldier ever carried into battle. The masked faces and armored bodies also represented the Tier One operator's surrender of identity to serve on an elite team for the larger purpose of defending the United

States from its enemies. The Osprey symbolized the mobile nature of the force, and the 'W' on its tail was a subtle reference to the team's informal name.

Simon clicked again, and the title slide was replaced. "This is your target," Simon began. "We're calling him Objective FULLBACK. The cover name for this operation will be ROGUE SENTINEL."

Mathews studied the slide. The biographical information in the column to the right of the grainy black and white image told him that FULLBACK was twenty-eight years old, and a senior 'Engineer' for ISIS. Known as 'Al-Amriki' within ISIS, FULLBACK was responsible for planning major ISIS operations, including the attack on the hotel in Qatar a few days ago.

Mathews recalled the news reports. They seemed to match what he was seeing in the bio: eighteen dead, six wounded. Some of the casualties were Qatari cops, but most of the dead were civilians in the hotel, including eight Americans, all of whom were in Qatar to finalize the details for a cellular telephone service upgrade as part of a joint venture with the German telecom giant Siemens. The deal was purely to support Qatar's growing civil population, and none of the eight had even remote ties to the U.S. military or government.

As Mathews continued reading, he saw that the intelligence community tied FULLBACK to two other operations: the killings of U.S. oil company employees and their families in Riyadh and the suicide bombing at the Karnak Temple Complex in Egypt, both in the last year.

"How confident is the IC that this guy is responsible for all of these?" Mathews asked. He did not see any sourcing or footnote information on the attacks.

"Very," Simon answered him. You can read the CONOP once we're done here. All the intelligence reports are listed in the appendix. Based on what I saw when I went through it, most of the reporting is HUMINT from DIA – they seem to have a source in ISIS that is well placed and reliable. I also spoke to Cain. He tells me NSA managed to get recordings of a phone call made by one of the jihadi SOBs who hit the hotel in Qatar."

"How'd they manage that?" Mathews asked, not really expecting an answer. NSA never talked openly about sources and methods, even to the rest of the intelligence community. Sources could be compromised or blown if they became known, and more often than not people died as a result – something that bastard TRAVELING JUDAS apparently never learned when he was an NSA contractor before he fled to Russia.

"Cain told me the State Department and FBI were given a copy by the Qatari ambassador here in the U.S. Since American citizens were killed, our Qatari friends have elected to share everything they learn during their investigation. The Qatari cops managed to recover the record of the call after they checked the call logs for all the phones in the hotel. They focused on a call made from the manager's phone during the event, and discovered that it was used by one of the terrorists in the hotel. A quick request to the local phone company, some electronic wizardry, and the Qataris had a recording of the call itself. Since 9/11, the FBI shares everything like this with the intelligence community."

"Nice." Mathews observed.

"What else do we know about FULLBACK?" Mathews asked.

Frowning, Simon clicked to the next slide. Cain had not thought to include a translation of the term 'Al-Amriki', but Simon did a quick Google translate search when he was reading the package. Mathews scanned the slide as it came up.

"Wait a minute!" Mathews exclaimed, turning to look at Simon. "He went to school in Pittsburgh?"

Simon nodded. "Yes. Carnegie-Mellon. He studied chemical and structural engineering. Graduated summa cum laude."

"So, he's an AMCIT?" an incredulous Mathews asked.

Simon nodded again, chagrined. "Yep. An American citizen. After he graduated from CM, he did his graduate studies in Adana, Turkey, at Cukurova University. The FBI did some interviews with some of his friends here in the States who stayed in touch with him, and they told the agents that while he was in Turkey, he started to express a lot of interest in jihad. Shortly thereafter, he broke contact with the friends he had back here. That's when we think he joined ISIS."

"How long ago was that?" Mathews inquired.

"Nearly three years now. The details from the FBI interviews are in the intel appendix too."

Mathews shook his head slowly from side to side, coming to grips with this new twist, and wondering just how the rest of this briefing was going to turn out. He liked Simon as an officer, and when he came on board with the Wraiths, Simon told him the teams were not assassins. If that was about to change, Mathews needed to know now. It was time for a carefully worded question.

"Sir, I think I need to know exactly what this mission is about. What are my orders regarding FULLBACK?" Mathews' tone was flat and direct, his interest intense. Maybe he could balance the scales for Sam's death?

"Lieutenant Commander, your mission and orders are specific and very well scoped. You will attempt to locate FULLBACK and set up long-term surveillance to develop pattern of life intelligence to support a capture operation. You'll see that in writing in the CONOP, and in the execution order once General Crane signs it."

Mathews blew out a breath. "Sir, this man is an American citizen who has joined ISIS and is planning operations that have resulted in the deaths of American citizens. We've killed one man doing that with a drone strike. Isn't that an option here?"

"No," Simon replied. "For several reasons. His house is located deep inside the borders of a friendly nation, and there is no way we'd get a drone through hundreds of miles of their airspace without permission or detection. We don't want to risk the chance that an ISIS mole in the government or military might tip FULLBACK off, and this presents an opportunity to develop actionable intel for a successful capture operation. Since this man is not a tactical battlefield threat, capturing him presents the opportunity to interrogate him and potentially capture any exploitable materials we might acquire during his capture."

"Papers, cell phones, computers..." Mathews said, trailing off.

"Yes," Simon agreed. "The usual. You alright with this mission, Mathews?"

"Yes sir," Mathews responded with a tinge of eagerness in his voice. "If we get that far, what about the capture team? If he resists..." Mathews trailed off again, hoping for the right answer.

"If he resists," Simon said, "the usual rule applies. Team members will defend themselves with lethal or non-lethal force as needed."

Mathews nodded once, satisfied. "Roger that, sir. Just one more question."

"Shoot." Simon told him.

"Where is he?" Mathews asked, eager now to know where his quarry was.

Simon clicked once more and the next slide came up. A map on the left side, and three overhead images, probably from a satellite, took up nearly all the room on the slide.

"Jordan."

CHAPTER 3

Mathews finished placing the last of his clothes in his favorite travel bag, made of heavy duty tan canvas trimmed with chocolate colored leather, checked his toilet kit to be sure he had full bottles of soap and shampoo, and tucked it in the travel bag as well. The bag lay on the queen-sized bed in his cramped bedroom, and he took a few moments to duck into the adjoining bathroom for a quick look in the mirror. He had skipped his last haircut a couple of weeks ago to lose the hard-core military look, anticipating his leave with Kristen, and he looked a little shaggy.

Ordinarily he would head for the base barbershop now that he was back, but since he was heading out on an undercover mission, that was out of the question. He would shave only once every few days for good measure. Maintaining a healthy stubble would further distance himself from looking like a military man. There was nothing he could do about his western features, but his cover should take care of that.

The last six hours had passed very quickly. He and Simon had finished getting through the briefing slides with another ten minutes of review and discussion – the remaining slides were devoted to nothing more than additional overheads of the little town in Jordan where they believed FULLBACK was hiding. In sum, they provided nice overviews of the town from various angles, but the notations from the National Geospatial Agency pointing out some of the major features like the town square and main road were unnecessary in Mathews' opinion, since they were apparent to the naked eye.

He spent the next two hours in Colonel Simon's office, buried in the concept of operations for the mission and the background information in the CONOP's intelligence annex. Overall, the mission was simple and straightforward, but the intelligence package supporting FULLBACK's presence in the town was a bit thin.

The two DIA reports were from a source the lead-in paragraphs said was reliable, but only one of them reported FULLBACK's presence somewhere in the town. The report from the NSA about the attack on the hotel in Qatar was interesting, but was only composed of the transcript of the terrorist's call to FULLBACK during the attack. The annotations in the report were clear that the Qataris provided the transcript, and that NSA's only action on it was verifying or amplifying the Arabic translation and sending it out to all the relevant organizations like the CTS.

Mathews had never read anything like it. FULLBACK's exhortation to the terrorist in the hotel to sacrifice himself by fighting with the Qatari cops was bad enough. The disappointment the murderer exhibited because he could not kill more of the civilians staying in the hotel was maddening, but FULLBACK advising the evil bastard to burn down the hotel to kill the hotel guests and then die fighting the Qatari military was downright infuriating. Unfortunately, the NSA report did not corroborate FULLBACK's location in Jordan, since the Qataris had been unable to trace the call beyond the Qatari managed international telephone exchange, and FULLBACK did not reveal his location during the call.

Mathews knew by the time he finished reading the transcript that finding FULLBACK would be worth the effort and time in the field. He had to be captured or killed, American citizen or not. The son-of-a-bitch had joined a terrorist organization, one avowed to spread its form of strictly conservative Islam across the globe and kill as many innocent people in the United States and other countries as needed to achieve that goal. Al-Amriki had chosen to become an enemy combatant, and enemy combatants are legitimate military targets.

In this case, given FULLBACK's intelligence value, capture was preferable, but it was the more difficult, risky objective to achieve. Assuming the intel from DIA was solid, Mathews knew he still might spend a week or more in the country trying to find FULLBACK; then if he found him, several weeks or months more watching him covertly to develop what the intel pros called a 'pattern of life' – that would be the toughest job of all.

Learning everything about how FULLBACK lived his daily life—when he rose in the morning, ate, slept; where he traveled to, if at all; and if he had a guard force or support team nearby—would be a grind. Especially because it had to be done covertly and solo.

The goal of this kind of long-term observation was to find something FULLBACK did during his regular routine that might make him vulnerable to capture. Ideally, that meant identifying something he did in a predictable, relatively isolated place where a capture team could set a trap with no hope of escape for the target. FULLBACK's daily life would dictate nearly every detail of the where and when for the capture, depending on how social the man was, where his house was, and any number of other factors.

If they captured him at his house, that introduced several immediate concerns, foremost the potential for collateral damage to any immediate neighbors, or the possibility that one of his neighbors might play good Samaritan and try to help as the capture team bundled FULLBACK into a vehicle. The goal was to grab the bad guy, not to end up shooting an innocent local or police officer.

Mathews smiled wanly at the thought of the actual capture. Since he was already in the country, he would likely be taking actions to enable the capture team's approach to FULLBACK and perhaps even lead the team itself, since he would have the advantage of long-term knowledge of the area. Mathews resolved to do everything he could to minimize or eliminate collateral damage during the capture, in keeping with standard operational practice and procedure.

During the execution of the plan, the possibility that FULLBACK might die during the capture op would really be in his own hands. When the capture team approached him, Mathews would ensure that they did so in a way that would minimize Al-Amriki's ability to respond with force.

If the team's cover or concealment was blown, FULLBACK might have a chance to grab a weapon and open fire on the team. In that event, Mathews knew the Wraith rules of engagement as well as any team commander: if the target objective was a threat to the life or safety of an innocent civilian or a team member, lethal force would be employed without hesitation, American citizen or no. Mathews would not allow him to harm one of their own or an innocent bystander.

The mental image of this bastard Al-Amriki's chest blown apart with gunfire if he resisted appealed to Mathews. It would balance the books in some small way for the deaths of those men and women in the Hilton in Qatar, and for Sam. Men like Al-Amriki and their predilection for violence as the preferred means to achieve Islamic State rule throughout the world were the reason Sam was dead...

Mathews shook his head. Killing FULLBACK was not his mission. Even so, Mathews knew that if FULLBACK resisted, three rounds to the head or chest from one of the team's suppressed M-8 assault rifles could do hideous damage to a person, well beyond the abilities of even a Level One trauma center in the States. Out in the 'sticks', with the nearest hospital one hundred miles away in Zarqa, in central Jordan, death was a virtual certainty if FULLBACK decided to resist capture.

The lack of nearby medical support from non-Jordanian sources caused Mathews to make a mental note. If the capture operation came to fruition, Mathews would have to request medical support deploy as part of the capture team, in case a team member or FULLBACK was wounded.

All of the men assigned to the Wraiths were cross-trained as combat medics, but two men on each Wraith team were fully trained Air Force pararescuemen, known as PJs. A PJ's core mission in combat was to parachute in from a MC-130J COMMANDO II aircraft or fast rope down from a CV-22B OSPREY behind enemy lines, stabilize downed aircrew members suffering from traumatic injuries, and extract them. If the capture mission resulted in casualties, the PJs would be able to stabilize FULLBACK or their fellow team members long enough for a MEDEVAC flight to a trauma facility in Europe equipped to treat them.

Mentally docketing the MEDEVAC issue for later, Mathews headed back into the bedroom, and let his eyes roam over it, checking to see if he had forgotten anything. The furniture was government standard bachelor officer's quarters, with oak wall units for shelves and neutral floor and wall coverings throughout. Kristen had suggested that he paint the white walls, and maybe get a throw rug to brighten the place up, but he had not wanted to expend the money or effort on a place he viewed as a temporary home.

The one concession he had made was buying the queen-sized bed from a former team commander who was rotating back to the Pentagon. It fit in the room with only inches to spare on one side, but once Kristen started sleeping over, it had become a necessity. The government issued double bed just wasn't roomy enough for two people, especially when they 'actively recreated' as she referred to it. Kristen would have preferred a king-sized bed, but that simply was not possible in the room. When he was promoted to Commander in another year or so, he would qualify for larger quarters, but for now, they would need to make do.

Mathews cocked his head to one side, and smiled. That was the first time he had thought of Kristen being in his life in the long term, and the idea seemed very nice to him. Looking at the face of his trusty black Casio G-Shock watch, he resolved to be sure to see her before he had to leave.

Deciding that he had packed everything he needed, he zipped his bag and hefted it before heading out into the living room and pausing, letting his eyes could roam over everything briefly for his usual pre-deployment check.

The thirty-gallon fish tank in the corner was already seeded with the long-term feeding pellets his Red Wag Platys liked to attack, and he knew without asking that Kristen would check on the fish every couple of days for him. The forty-eight-inch LCD television was off, and he had programmed the DVR to record his favorite shows for the next three months. It was a pity he would not be able to use his Slingbox while he was gone. Streaming his shows across the Internet to Jordan would have been a nice way to stay connected with home, but it would be an operations security violation, and it could get him killed.

A quick look over the low breakfast bar into the kitchen confirmed that he had left the refrigerator door closed this time. Leaving it open during his last month-long deployment had resulted in spoiled food, a smell that took two gallons of bleach to eradicate, and a six-hundred-dollar check to the base logistics office to replace the old, Uncle-Sam-provided refrigerator and its burned-out motor. The white trash can's lid was still propped open from his last trip down the hall to the main trash chute before his leave with Kristen, and the sink was devoid of dirty dishes and pans since he had not had time for a meal since his return.

As always, the pre-deployment check reminded Mathews of helping his Mom and Dad check the house before leaving on summer vacations when he was a teenager. The similarity of the actions in his quarters made him briefly nostalgic for those simpler days and the anticipation of the fun and adventure that lay ahead in Orlando, the Grand Canyon, Yosemite, and the beach with his parents.

Making sure his small living space was ready for his sudden TDY signified a departure from the safe and comforting confines of the base, his friends and teammates, and now, Kristen and her warmth. Ahead lay adventure, and a danger that he had trained long and hard to deal with.

Once he walked out the door, it would be time to transition into his 'mission' mindset, and when the first of his flights to Jordan left the ground, he would literally move at five-hundred miles an hour towards a mission goal he would need to accomplish completely on his own. He would not be able to call for help and have it arrive in minutes, nor would supporting fire rain down from the sky seconds after he requested it. Moreover, he would have no one but the locals to talk to, none of whom he would be able to trust or confide in.

Others might be frightened at the prospect, but Mathews knew his training and experience, first as a SEAL and then as a Wraith Team leader, would get him through this mission, and that knowledge gave him confidence.

He also found himself, in an odd way, looking forward to being in the field alone. It would be good to leave the responsibility of leading a team behind for a while. Sam's death had been so sudden, so unexpected. Knowing his team was safe here at the base and he was the only one risking his life for a while gave him some peace of mind. The added need to put his entire focus on FULLBACK would be a welcome change from thinking every so often of how he had failed his friend and teammate.

Mathews turned his back on his quarters and its safety, put his hand on the doorknob, and walked out into the corridor, letting the door click shut behind him.

After a short ride in the elevator to Level 9, Mathews emerged, bag in hand, made a 90-degree left turn, then another to the right, and continued down the arrow-straight 200-foot-long corridor that led to the team armory, passing key card secured doors marked "Ops Plans" and "Team Areas" as he went.

At the end of the hall was a machined steel vault door, eight feet high and wide, and three-feet thick. It sat open, exposing the inner steel cage door of what looked like a shiny jail cell. If fact, to Mathews' eyes, it looked just like the vault door setup in the main branch of the Chemical Bank his father used to take him to as a boy to deposit his allowance money.

Mathews knew it was originally used to house the nuclear weapon triggers and 'physics packages' when the DoE managed the complex, and the six-inch diameter pins sticking out from the inner beveled edge were hardened and tempered steel guardians of the Wraith's armory.

Mathews approached the closed inner steel cage door without breaking stride, grinning at the sight of the man in Army-issued camouflage and a brown tee shirt that stretched at the seams to contain his solid physique behind the bars.

"Lieutenant Commander Mathews! Nice to see you again sir." Master Sergeant Williams was one of the nicest men in the unit to work with, in Mathews' opinion. Williams, an Army Ranger, was always cheerful and accommodating, one of those people in the military who had the words, 'happy to be here, proud to serve' ingrained in his DNA.

Williams was also one of the best hand-to-hand combat instructors Mathews had come across in his time with the Wraiths. Only average height, Williams was an African American raised by a neurosurgeon and his psychiatrist wife, who nonetheless choose to leave Duke University to enlist in the Army after 9/11. When Mathews had asked him why his parents, given their backgrounds, had not insisted he finish college, Williams said he told his parents that he was more than capable of fighting his nation's enemies and getting a college education at the same time. Moreover, he had proved it by earning his bachelor and master's degrees in night school, in spite of one tour in Iraq and two tours in Afghanistan while on active duty.

Williams was barrel chested and solid from his fitness regime, which included three-mile runs six mornings a week, followed by alternating days of Tony Horton's P90X Extreme program and full contact Krav Maga in the base gym.

"Good to see you too, Master Sergeant Williams." Mathews said as Williams opened the inner steel cage door before offering his hand to the young Lieutenant Commander. Mathews shook it, and went right to business. "What do you have for me?"

"This way, sir." Williams motioned him inside and shut the inner door before leading Mathews into the rear of the spacious vault. Mathews could see the racks of cleaned and ready M-8 assault rifles, H&K MP-5 and MP-10 sub-machine guns, and Benelli M4 semi-automatic shotguns resting in their wall mounted racks, as well as the crates of ammunition, grenades, and high explosives stacked deeper in the vault.

Stopping at one of the worktables near the entrance, Williams indicated the single pistol laying centered on a tan cleaning cloth on the table. "This is your weapon, sir."

Mathews shook his head as he lay his bag on the floor next to the table,

and said sarcastically, "At least I'm going in loaded for bear on this one."
Williams grinned at the comment and said, "Colonel Simon's orders were very
specific sir. One pistol only, along with the support and ISR equipment."

"I know." Mathews replied, lifting the pistol from the cleaning cloth and
examining it.

The weapon was a brand-new Sig Sauer P226, chambered for .40 S&W.
The pistol was matte black, and its solid, one-and-a-half-pound weight felt reassuring in his hand.

Mathews pulled the slide back and visually checked the chamber, ensuring it was empty, and then glanced down through the center of the handgrip,
verifying that there was no magazine inserted. He cycled the action several times
to ensure it functioned smoothly.

"Has anyone touched this other than you?" Mathews asked pointedly.

"No, sir" Williams replied. "I took it out of the packing material an hour
ago. It has never been used, and the shipment it came from was part of a buy one
of our cover companies did. It can't be tracked through transaction records to the
government or DOD."

Mathews gave the pistol a closer look. He could smell the gun oil and
cleaning solvent. "You cleaned and oiled it?"

"Yes, I also test fired it and checked the sights. It's factory fresh."

"Good," Mathews said, thumbing the slide release and feeling as much as
hearing the reassuring snick of the slide snapping forward to close the chamber.
Holding the P226 in a two-handed grip, he pointed the muzzle at the far wall
and focused on the sight picture the tritium-coated sights gave him. After the
hundreds of hours he had trained to handle small arms, Mathews lined the three
green circles up in a straight horizontal line without conscious thought, feeling
the pistol's balance and the position of his fingers on the handgrip. The balance
was a little heavy to the barrel side, but that was normal with the absence of a
magazine in the weapon's grip.

Mathews relaxed and let the weapon fall, then raised it twice more in
quick succession. Satisfied with the two-handed feel, he shifted to one hand, first
left, and then his dominant right hand to be sure he could handle the weapon
with either hand alone if needed.

Mathews nodded, "Feels good," he said, and then put the pistol back on
the cloth before asking, "What kind of rounds do you have for me?"

Williams replied, "One sec." and headed into the depths of the vault, returning less than a minute later with two fifty-round boxes of ammunition.

Williams hefted one at time, showing their labels to Mathews before placing them on the table next to the pistol. "One box of Glaser Safety Slugs, and one box of standard FMJ rounds."

The Glasers were good for low penetration work, shooting targets in an urban environment where a building's walls would effectively cause the round to break up and lose penetrating power, whereas a jacketed round such as the FMJs would punch through masonry and interior walls easily, potentially killing innocents.

"No light loaded rounds for stealth work?" Mathews asked with an arched eyebrow.

Williams looked mildly surprised. "I didn't pull any, since the Colonel didn't say you needed a suppressor."

Mathews thought a moment. "I want a suppressor in the shipment, just in case, so give me a box of light loads to go with it. I'll talk to Simon before I leave. If he doesn't approve, you don't have to put it in the package. Do you have an already threaded barrel for the Sig?"

"Yes, sir." Williams replied, heading back into the depths of the armory for the items.

Simon and Mathews both knew that there was no way Mathews could waltz into Jordan carrying a pistol and ammunition, especially given his cover identity. Once Mathews was satisfied with the weapon and his ammunition, Simon would see to it that it was sent to Amman, and Mathews knew better than to ask just how Simon would accomplish that. In fact, due to the circuitous route Mathews had to take to get to Jordan, the weapon would actually make it into the country before he landed at the Queen Alia International Airport. He would retrieve it at the pre-arranged pickup point, along with the other gear he would need, after landing.

"Here you are, sir," Williams said when he returned, laying the suppressor, box of light loaded .40 S&W rounds, and threaded barrel on the table.

"Good." Mathews reached into his travel bag, pulled out his Emerson CQC-7 combat knife, and placed it near the pistol and ammunition. "Please make sure that ends up in the gear package too."

"Good luck charm?" Williams asked with a flash of intuition.

Mathews nodded. "Never gone on a mission without it. It was a gift from the chief of my first boat crew when I was assigned to SEAL Team 3."

"I'll put it in the hard case with the pistol and everything else."

"Thanks, sergeant," Mathews said, extending his hand.

Williams took Mathews' hand and shook it firmly. "Good luck, sir."

Mathews nodded his appreciation, let himself out through the inner door, and headed back down the corridor to the elevator.

The senior NCO who served as administrative aide to General Crane knocked on Colonel Simon's office door, and opened it without waiting for a response, ushering Mathews in. Simon was expecting him. At a wave from Simon, Mathews made himself comfortable in the black Herman Miller chair before the colonel's desk. Simon touched a switch, and a set of heavy security bolts slid home, securing the door so they would not be interrupted.

Simon's office on Level 8 was not nearly as palatial as General Crane's office just down the hall in the command suite. Mathews knew that much like Simon's, the general's office had thick walls and carpets to aid in sound absorption, and the simulated cherry wood furniture and the Herman Miller chairs gave the room the ambiance he had come to expect in a senior officer's working office. The two officers shared the adjoining conference room, but the general had exclusive use of the bathroom and shower attached to his office. Simon had to use the men's locker room two doors down the hall. Rank had its privileges after all.

"Where's my buddy Zeus, sir?" Mathews asked, noticing the empty dog bed in the corner where Zeus usually lay.

"He's at the base vet for some follow-up X-rays," Simon answered before moving on to the mission at hand. "You all set?"

"Yes, sir," Mathews answered. "I'm packed and Master Sergeant Williams and I have gone over the armament. I asked him to include a suppressor and some light loaded rounds in the package."

Simon leaned back in his leather desk chair and gave Mathews a hard look. "Do you really expect to need them?"

"No sir, but you know the drill. I'd rather have them and not need them..." Mathews trailed off.

"...than need them and not have them," Simon finished.

Mathews nodded. "Yes, sir. I'm going to be completely alone out there, and if I need to recon the objective personally, there are all kinds of advantages to having a silenced weapon."

Simon sat still a moment, considering Mathews' line of thinking. In spite of what Hollywood may portray, a silenced weapon had multiple uses beyond killing someone quietly. A silenced round could shatter glass or strike metal to make a noise distraction, or be used to shoot out street or building lights to create shadow if an operator needed to move from one point of concealment to another.

"Approved," Simon told him. "I'll pass that on to Master Sergeant Williams. It will be in Jordan when you are. Are you satisfied with your cover identity?"

Mathews turned it over in his mind one more time. "Yes. I think it's solid. It's very plausible and the locals shouldn't give me a second look," Mathews said, adding quickly with a smile, "as long as I'm friendly and respectful enough."

There was a quick double knock on the door, and Simon touched a switch behind his desk, electronically releasing the security bolts locking the door.

The visitor heard the 'snick' of the bolts sliding back and opened the door. It was Kristen. She had changed into one of her 'work' pantsuits, this one in steel grey, with a blue silk blouse beneath an unbuttoned jacket. Mathews knew the reason she always left her suit jackets unbuttoned was to give her quick access to her Walther P99, secreted in the small of her back, not show off her figure. She was carrying a sealed manila envelope.

"Sir," Chambers said, ignoring Mathews and addressing herself to Simon. "I have the travel and identity documents you requested from the National Cover Office."

The NCO was a relatively new creation within the federal government, created specifically to create and manage cover identities when needed and authorized under existing law.

"Excellent," Simon replied, rising from his chair and checking his watch. "I need to speak to General Crane. I'll be back in a few minutes." Simon exited the office and shut the door behind him. He was obviously giving them a few minutes alone together. Mathews was due to leave in less than thirty minutes.

Mathews looked a Kristen. She was pointedly staring at Simon's 'I love me' wall, scanning the photos of him during previous assignments, his military citations, and Simon's college diplomas without really seeing them.

"Honey..." Mathews said gently, expecting her to take advantage of the few minutes of privacy, not stare at Simon's career history.

Kristen looked at him. "I don't think you should be leaving on this assignment."

That threw him off. "Why?" Mathews demanded. He was not expecting his new girlfriend to be giving him career advice this early in the relationship.

"You haven't dealt with Sam's death..."

This again? Now? "Why do you keep bringing this up? Sam is dead! Life goes on! This is the kind of mission I've trained for, and I'm more than capable of handling it!"

Chambers recoiled a little at the venom in his voice. "Shane," she pleaded, "I don't want you to go out into the field like this. You've told me how it's bad for an operative to have his attention divided when he's in the field, and I don't want to..." her voice cracked and she stopped. Her control slipped and tears welled at the corners of her eyes.

Mathews wanted to hold her, but his anger overcame his reason. He stepped closer to her, his face red. "My mind is on the mission! I am not dwelling on Sam or what happened to him! He's gone and I can't bring him back!"

Chambers gathered herself and met his angry tone. "You can't even see it, can you? All you've done since he died is brood and blame yourself! I'll bet you're even looking forward to this mission as a nice break from being responsible for your men!"

Mathews was surprised at her for knowing what he was thinking, and his denial died on his lips. Chambers saw him pause and she plowed on.

"I'm right, aren't I? One of the things you told me on our first date was how proud you were to lead your team, to be responsible for the welfare of some of the best and bravest men you had ever led into combat! Now one of them dies suddenly and you're just leaving them behind."

She said the last sentence in a softened tone, but Mathews looked at her with stony eyes.

"My men are my concern, not yours."

Chambers stared at him in the shared silence, but for once in their relationship, he could not understand what her problem was. Accusing him of abandoning his people was way out of line, especially for somebody in a support role, and that look on her face that expected him to see that she was right... "I think this discussion is over."

Motioning to the manila envelope she still held, he asked in a flat voice,

"Is that for me?"

She tossed the envelope on Simon's desk. "Yes, Lieutenant Commander," she responded, brushing past him and continuing sotto voce, "You need to find someone else to feed your fish."

Mathews turned to watch her walk out of Simon's office, stunned that this argument had soured their relationship in the space of a couple of minutes. He stared at the closed door, part of him wanting to rush after her and say whatever he needed to repair things between them, the other part of his mind kept his feet rooted to the floor, remembering that Simon would be back in a few minutes. The mission comes first. Service before self.

Mathews stood there, seeing her in his mind's eye walking farther away from him, probably seeking a quiet, private place to let her feelings out. He looked at his watch. Fifteen minutes until wheels up, and Al-Amriki was waiting. First Sam dies because of these terrorist bastards, and now I'm going to lose a woman I care for because another terrorist is out there and it's my job to hunt him down? Al-Amriki is going to be shot during the capture op if I have anything to say about it!

Mathews blew out a breath and tried to release his anger. He had to stay and do his best to at least project calm, or Simon might send someone else on this mission.

As if on cue, Simon opened the door and came in. "Did Ms. Chambers give you the packet?"

Mathews gathered his thoughts quickly. "No, sir. She just left it on your desk. She didn't want to break operational security."

Simon studied Mathews for a minute. Whatever their goodbye was like, the kid sure hid it well. Simon nodded, and then tore open the packet, spilling its contents on the desk.

"I appreciate her professionalism. OK, let's do the True Lies bit."

In spite of his youth, Mathews got the reference to the film where the character is outside his home after returning from an undercover mission to Europe and started emptying his pockets to leave his real identity behind. He laid his Military ID, driver's license, and all his credit cards on Simon's desk.

Simon picked up the items from the manila envelope one at a time and handed them over.

"Connecticut driver's license, passport with Jordanian visa, two letters of introduction from the University of Jordan's Archeology Department..."

"What will happen if someone calls the department head?" Mathews asked pointedly.

"You should be fine," Simon replied, "You're using the name of a graduate student your age from the University of Chicago who has been corresponding with a Professor Yousef in the University of Jordan's Archeology Department via e-mail and webcam for the last six months. The prof in Chicago is actually an NCO asset who helps establish potential backstories for agents. Cain asked the NCO to send us a good university cover background this morning, and they responded with their usual speed."

Mathews arched his eyebrows, impressed at NCO's foresight and rapid response, and then Simon dropped the other shoe.

"Having said that, the letters are for show only. Try not to use them with the police or a government official that might be tempted to check. Any serious investigation might lead to questions you can't answer about the University of Chicago's campus and its programs."

"Something to bear in mind," Mathews observed without trying to sound too pessimistic.

"Do you have the basics memorized?" Simon inquired.

"Yes," Mathews nodded. "It's actually not going to be difficult for a Navy man."

Simon grinned. "Good. We hoped that would help." Simon snatched the last object off his desk. "This should help keep any of the Jordanian ladies at bay," Simon said, holding it out.

Mathews took the gold wedding band and stared at it a moment without smiling at Simon's attempt at humor before slipping it on his left ring finger. Kristen would have had a field day with this – if we were speaking. He did his best to keep the sadness off his face when he looked up to face Simon again.

"Anything else, sir?"

Simon looked him over, mistaking his sadness for trepidation. "I know you've never run a solo mission before, but remember, this is just a recon mission. Keep your head down among the locals. Be friendly, but not overly so, and stay situationally aware. If you feel you've been compromised, head for the Embassy and ask for the Marine security force commander. I spoke to him this morning, and his name is Master Gunnery Sergeant Tobin. Tell him the code word is

'Tabasco'. He'll get you a secure line to me and we'll work on a way to get you out of Jordan safely."

"Fair enough sir. What about the Chief of Station?"

"Her name is Sally." Mathews waited a few beats for more, but Simon's look spoke volumes about why he did not know her last name.

"Sally what?" Mathews asked to draw out the explanation.

Simon frowned. "She wouldn't tell me. CIA station chiefs have become notoriously cagey since the TRAVELING JUDAS leaks a few years back. She promised whatever cooperation you needed, but would not tell me anything but her first name – if it really is her first name."

"Spooks," Mathews replied with mild disdain. Well, the woman's ass was on the line out there, so if she wanted to be coy about her identity, he would have to assume she had good reason for it and not press for specifics. "Anything else, sir?"

"No. Let's get you to your plane."

Simon led the way out of his office and to the elevator core. The two men rode in silence up to the hanger level, and when the doors slid open, Simon started walking him to the plane. Mathews could see Williams waiting by the G280. A quick scan around the hanger for Kristen brought back his anger and sadness from their argument in Simon's office – she was not there to see him off. He kept his feelings off his face, and kept pace with Simon.

"Try to relax and enjoy the flight," Simon advised him, his attention on the waiting G280 and his mind on the responsibility of sending a young man into a denied area alone.

"Your gear will be offloaded at Houston," Simon continued, "inventoried as one sealed package for shipment to Amman, and put onto a scheduled C-17 flight to Jordan. The Globemaster III should arrive nearly twelve hours before you get there. Marines from the embassy security detachment will transport the package to the embassy. Your equipment gets separated out and taken to the drop point after your gear arrives at the embassy. You remember what the car will look like?"

"Yes, sir. An old tan Range Rover, white tags, license number 69854. It will be parked on the south side of Sheraton Hotel in Amman, in the lot nearest the Arab Medical Center, and the long-term rental papers will be in the glove compartment. Photos of the Range Rover and parking place are on the phone."

Using the word 'phone' triggered a thought, and Mathews exclaimed, "Shit!" as he reached for his back pocket. Simon stood still, understanding immediately, and held his hand out. Mathews handed him his government issued iPhone X with a hangdog look.

"Get your head in the game now, son!" Simon admonished him sternly. "Where's the mission phone?"

Mathews hefted his travel bag and pulled the old iPhone 6s out of a side pocket. The technical wizards at NSA had added the same encryption package to the slim Mophie battery case that fit this version of the well-known phone, and it was pre-loaded with a simulated set of contact phone numbers and e-mail addresses, corresponding accounts, and photos that supported his cover. Moreover, the older iPhone would not draw the attention of the shiny new iPhone X and better fit his cover as a modestly paid university graduate student.

"Right here, sir. I had intended to give my phone to you in your office. Sorry sir," a chastened Mathews responded.

"Look son," Simon told him, deciding a fatherly advice approach was best right now, "you need to get your game face on now, especially if you want to come home to her in one piece. Got it?"

Given their last conversation, Mathews was not sure she would be there to come home to, and took a second to look around the hanger interior, hoping she might have come out to see him off. Damn. There was no sign of her, but for now, that was none of Simon's business.

"Yes, sir." Mathews resumed the walk toward the plane. As they approached, Master Sergeant Williams met them and reached out to shake Mathews' hand again.

"Your gear is all packed and loaded," he told the young officer as the G280's right engine began to whine. "I used tamper evident tape to seal it, so you can be sure it's exactly the way I packed it."

Mathews returned the man's handshake and nodded his thanks, not trying to speak over the high-pitched scream of the G280's starboard engine igniting. Mathews turned to shake Simon's hand again and the Colonel clapped his shoulder as a parting gesture of good luck.

Mathews turned and climbed the boarding stairs into the G280, dropping his travel bag in an aisle seat, since he knew the cabin attendant would not insist that he stow it, and sat in the window seat beside it.

In minutes, the male cabin attendant had retracted the flight stairwell and Mathews could see the ground crew pulling the chocks away from the wheels. Once the ground crew was clear, he heard the G280's left engine spool up, and the aircraft began to roll toward the parting hanger doors.

Mathews kept his eyes out the window. Simon and Williams were well back from the aircraft, holding their hands over their ears to protect them, but no one else seemed to be watching. The men and women in the hanger went about their business of servicing or repairing aircraft, oblivious to the departure of the single business jet. He kept scanning the hanger, hoping to see just a glimpse of her, but to no avail. Kristen had not come to see him off, not even disguising it as a visit to the hanger on official business.

Mathews' heart sank as the G280 slipped through the gap in the open hanger doors, revealing the barren dirt and scrub of the high desert, the runways, and the tall control tower. The relative emptiness of the surrounding miles mirrored his feelings as the plane taxied into position and then hurtled into the sky.

Letting out a disappointed sigh as he felt the wheels retract into the fuselage, he forced himself to focus on the mission, and he pulled out the iPhone 6s, unlocking the screen and double checking the information about his cover identity's reason for traveling to Jordan.

As he worked his way through the e-mails from the fictitious friends and colleagues, the satellite images of the town Al-Amriki was hiding in (cleverly disguised as images saved off of Google Earth), and the pictures of the Range Rover that he needed to recognize, his thoughts kept drifting. First Sam dies, and now a woman he was sure he was beginning to love had just left him because of his devotion to his duty and responsibility. The death of terrorist like Al-Amriki would balance the scales for both those losses nicely.

Back in the Wraith Base control tower, Chambers watched the G280 shrink to a speck in the distance, her back to the duty controller who had probably returned to reading the novel on his Nook. As the sleek white jet faded from view, she closed her eyes against the tears of anger and sorrow that threatened to spill down her cheeks.

CHAPTER 4

The road arced right in a gentle curve, and Al-Amriki turned the wheel to the proper angle without conscious thought. Picturing the map in his mind, and recalling his last trip along this route, he was sure his current trip into Islamic State territory would be a straightforward one, though risky, especially since it entailed a small amount of subterfuge committed against both the Jordanian and Syrian authorities.

He had packed carefully this morning for the long drive, taking the expensive leather two-suiter from under his bed, along with a small black leather satchel. He drew from the closet a very expensive gray suit made from Super 170 wool that practically glowed, even in the early light. Knowing he would not likely need to wear it, he nonetheless packed it carefully into the two-suiter along with a light and airy white Thawb he fully expected to need, two changes of underwear, and toiletries.

With the two-suiter ready, Al-Amriki put the expensive and heavily encrypted iPhone X into an inner pocket of his light gray Thawb, and slipped his feet into a pair of comfortable black leather sandals before visually checking to ensure that the top of an expensive silver Mont Blanc pen protruded from the chest pocket of his Thawb. It was a gift from his mother upon his graduation from high school, and a reminder of everything good that had happened to him since he had left the United States, he never traveled without it.

The last thing he did was re-check the Jordanian passport laying on the bed next to the packed two-suiter. It was in surprisingly good shape, given the use it got. He leafed through the pages quickly, his memory flicking through images of the cities he had visited in the countries each entry stamp signified. Damascus, Riyadh, Kuwait City, Al-Dofra, and even one entry and exit from the United

States, dated eight months ago. Today would see another entry and exit from Syria.

Al-Amriki slipped the passport into his inner pocket next to the iPhone and hefted his bags off the bed. A few minutes later, with the doors of the small house locked, the two-suiter in the back seat of the old blue Hyundai and the black satchel on the front passenger seat, he started the car's engine and drove off. It was three hours to the border post.

"Ah, Doctor Hafiz!" the guard at the Syrian side of the border with Jordan greeted him. "How good to see you." As usual, Al-Amriki's eyes slid over the border post, checking for signs of untoward alertness from the security detail. He could see none and, judging by the guard's casual attitude, in spite of the precision with which he wore his uniform, Al-Amriki guessed that the officer of the watch was enjoying his midday meal well away from his guards.

"It's good to see you as well, Saladin. As-salaam alaykum." Al-Amriki replied.

"Wa alaykum assalam," the border guard said as he approached Al-Amriki in the Hyundai. Al-Amriki could see Saladin's eyes automatically checking the car and roving into the rear passenger compartment. The avarice in his eyes at the sight of the expensive two-suiter laying on the back seat was tough to miss.

Al-Amriki handed the man his passport without being asked, and Saladin barely glanced at it before taking out his stamp and inkpad, laying the passport on the hood of the Hyundai to stamp it on a blank page.

"It still surprises me that a Doctor such as yourself does not buy a nice German car for these road trips," Saladin observed as he authorized Al-Amriki's entry into Syria.

"I should move my practice closer to Amman, so I can take on more patients, but I cannot leave my current patients without a doctor. Many were my father's, you know."

Part of Al-Amriki's cover for these trips was that he had moved from Amman out to the distant reaches of Jordan to care for his father's patients as soon as he graduated medical school in Amman. The implication he left unsaid in his conversations with the various guards at this checkpoint was that his elderly father had ordered him to return, having paid for the young man's education. It was a cultural issue they all understood, but never spoke of, and it helped solidify in their minds that 'Doctor Hafiz' was still taking orders from his father and therefore was not yet a man in their eyes, making him seem like a person unworthy of scrutiny as a threat.

"Besides," Al-Amriki continued, "the WHO does not pay much for these consultations, and I'd rather have a reliable car for the long trips from Korea than a German machine that would be expensive to repair after driving a few thousand kilometers on the roads in Jordan."

Saladin nodded thoughtfully. "I can understand that," Saladin replied, handing over Al-Amriki's fake passport.

"Also, I give a great deal of money each year to the local Mosque in Zakat. My father insists that I donate from my earnings at least as much as my education cost. He says it is important to remain humble. Allah has allowed me to be very fortunate."

Al-Amriki had yet to say this to any of the guards, and it was the second layer of his cover – that of very pious Muslim. Yet another item of information to keep the guards from giving him too much scrutiny.

"I think your father is a very wise man," Saladin told him with utmost sincerity, trying to keep his own disappointment in himself out of his voice, inwardly ashamed that his zakat was only the minimum that was required.

"How long will you be in Syria this time?" Saladin asked.

"Only overnight. I will see patients this evening and tomorrow in Damascus. One of the WHO physicians had a death in the family and had to head home immediately. They will have a replacement available tomorrow afternoon."

As Al-Amriki finished speaking, an ancient white Nissan Sentra pulled up behind him. Seeing the car waiting, Saladin waived him forward. "You are a generous man Doctor Hafiz. Safe journey."

"Ma'a as-salaama," Al-Amriki said, rolling up the window and driving past the checkpoint.

The sun would not set for at least two more hours, and Al-Amriki was grateful for the air conditioning in the old Hyundai Avante. The temperature in this part of eastern Syria regularly reached the mid-90s, and while rainfall never exceeded 10 millimeters in the month of May, resulting in a very arid climate for the region, the cool air circulating in the car was far better than being exposed to a hot wind for the entire eight-hour drive.

An hour later, a single two-lane ribbon of asphalt stretched before him into the distance, still lit by the reds and oranges of a sun low on the horizon behind him and sinking steadily. His grip on the wheel was relaxed as he drove, and his thoughts wandered a little. He had already memorized the route to avoid carrying a marked map that might betray him, and he still had many kilometers before him to travel.

Al-Amriki knew that under normal circumstances, driving from western Syria into Islamic State controlled territory in the eastern half of Syria was unwise, to say the least. The border between the two was not marked in any way, beyond the burned-out hulks of the odd tank, armored vehicle, or four-wheel drive truck or other civilian car left behind after one battle or another, scattered randomly along the roads leading east.

Moreover, the soldiers of the Syrian army were likely to shoot first and ask questions later, especially if you were driving anything other than a Syrian military vehicle – most of which were of Russian manufacture. Civilian vehicles, often used by the ISIS jihadis for concealment of improvised explosive devices or as troop transports, often approached Syrian lines or encampments. As far as Al-Amriki was concerned, he was taking enough risk being a lone male in a car. If he had the misfortune to come upon a Syrian army convoy or outpost unawares, the Syrian troops would immediately assume he was a suicide bomber and likely open fire—one of the many reasons he kept these trips to an absolute minimum. It was never wise to venture into a war zone alone.

The armed men of the Islamic State's corps of jihadis would stop a car in their territory to question the occupants. Being anything but a Muslim left the male occupants two choices: accept the Islamic faith before two witnesses, or immediate execution by gunfire as an infidel.

Apostates—those who had ceased to follow the Islamic faith and were foolish enough to admit it to the ISIS jihadis—were given one chance to recant their apostasy, and if they refused, they were arrested and taken to the nearest town square under ISIS control. After Friday prayers, called Jumu'ah, they would be stoned to death for their crime in public.

If there were women or teenage girls in the car, things could go well or very badly. If a woman or teenage girl was Muslim, had dressed modestly, and the man driving could prove he was her relative, they were allowed to drive on unmolested.

If the women were dressed immodestly, her male escort had to purchase the proper garment from the jihadis for an exorbitant fee. If he could not afford it, the woman was forcibly stripped and then whipped for her immodesty while her male escort was verbally chastised by the jihadis before he was allowed to leave with his 'sharmuta' or whore. If the male could not prove he was related to the woman or had her eldest living male relative's permission to travel under the driver's protection, the result was the same, except instead of just being whipped, the woman would likely be raped as well.

Al-Amriki knew that thievery was also common among some of the less disciplined of the jihadis, as was rape of all non-Muslim women, married or not. One married western female reporter discovered this fact, to her horror, when she tried to surreptitiously cross into ISIS controlled territory one night with her Syrian camera crew, foolishly assuming that being a married woman and a member of the media would protect her.

Al-Amriki had not heard of any ISIS encounters with pre-pubescent children in this part of Syria, and suspected that most people were wise enough to keep their children away from an active battlefront. Those that had strayed with their parents into border areas often found themselves joining the jihad in one form or another.

Young Muslim men, fifteen years old or more, were often 'drafted' into the jihad by the ISIS fighters. Teenage girls and unmarried women who practiced Islam were sometimes forcibly taken from their parents or male relatives by ISIS fighters to become the wives of courageous jihadis fighting for Allah in Syria or Iraq. These 'conscripted brides' were an important part of the expansion of the Caliphate, especially since it could not rely solely on the steady but light stream of young Muslim women from the west.

Al-Amriki knew that the young women from the west, often inspired via Internet videos and the more radical Islamic discussion groups to join Allah's jihad, found more than they may have bargained for when they gave themselves to the Caliphate. These young women tended to trickle into occupied lands rather than arriving in a rising tide of immigrants. Some would even bring less-committed girlfriends along, which helped, but not enough.

Once they arrived in ISIS occupied lands, the committed would willingly submit themselves to their new husbands, some of whom were twenty or more years older than they were. The less committed who had traveled with their more steadfast girlfriends or sisters were taught and disciplined as firmly or as gently as needed, in the end also dutifully serving in safe homes in ISIS controlled areas of Iraq and Syria. Both groups of women would give birth to the next generation of jihadis, raising and training the children in accordance with their husband's instruction while they dutifully remained in the home where they belonged.

With Damascus now nearly two hours and one hundred and sixty kilometers behind him, Al-Amriki took his eyes off the road for a moment and glanced at the black leather bag known all over the world as the sign of a medical man, and a satisfied smirk curled his lips. This was his sixth trip with this cover, and it had worked splendidly so far.

Another half a kilometer later, as he crested a rise in the road, the last remnants of the smirk faded as he spied the unexpected ISIS checkpoint on the road ahead. Al-Amriki could see eight men and two four-wheel drive Toyota Land Cruisers blocking the road about two hundred yards ahead.

The eight men carried the ubiquitous AK-74 Kalashnikov rifles, and were dressed in standard foot soldier garb: off-white or brown Thawbs, with Sirwal pants of various neutral colors beneath them. Six of the men also wore green or tan tactical vests festooned with grenades and the dull brass of extra ammunition or AK magazines. All of the men wore keffiyeh in various colors, and three wore them across their faces, leaving only their eyes showing.

Al-Amriki thought quickly, taking his foot off the gas pedal and letting the Hyundai's inertia carry it toward the makeshift roadblock while he considered his options. Running the roadblock was not an option. The eight jihadis would hose the car with gunfire and he would end up in a flaming wreck. Stopping and heading back was not a viable alternative either. They would probably chase him down, and the flaming wreck option would be in play again. Even this close to his destination, it was not likely that these men knew who he was, and stopping would entail a delay that would likely be intolerable to who he was meeting with.

Seeing no other choice, Al-Amriki touched the Mont Blanc pen for good fortune and continued to let the Hyundai glide toward the makeshift roadblock. Once he was within twenty-five yards, Al-Amriki saw two of the men train their weapons on the car, and his heart stopped. It took serious effort on his part not to mash the brake pedal to the floor, knowing that maintaining the car's forward momentum would help him have a fighting chance to accelerate quickly out of the kill zone if they did open fire.

After a tense few seconds, he was close enough to the roadblock that one of the bare faced, vest wearing jihadis standing in the road on the driver's side of the car held his hand up imperiously. Al-Amriki stopped the car and rolled down the window half way, doing his best to keep his hands in view as much as possible.

"Who are you?" the jihadi demanded.

"Doctor Hafiz," Al-Amriki replied, starting in on an improvised cover story for what he was doing heading into Islamic State territory in Syria. "I am—"

The jihadi interrupted him. "Show me your passport, now!"

Perplexed, Al-Amriki hesitated, and the jihadi's assault rifle came up. "The passport!" he demanded again, pointing the AK-74 muzzle at Al-Amriki's head.

Al-Amriki reached slowly into the pocket of his Thawb and withdrew the passport, keeping his eyes locked on the jihadi's. If he was going to die, he would see it in the man's eyes before he fired. Grasping the passport firmly, Al-Amriki held it out of the half open car window.

The jihadi took it and lowered the AK-74 rifle to open the passport, his eyes reading the information page and comparing the picture to Al-Amriki's face.

The jihadi contemptuously tossed the passport back through the window into Al-Amriki's lap. "I have been ordered to tell you to continue down this road and turn left in four kilometers. Others are waiting for you."

Al-Amriki was confused, but held it in check. The original meeting site was supposed to be another ten kilometers farther down this road. Clearly, Akil was taking additional precautions, including not telling him everything about the meeting location.

The jihadi motioned with his rifle, waving 'Doctor Hafiz' along, and Al-Amriki wasted no more time, accelerating clear of the roadblock. A few minutes later, he turned left and kept driving. Six kilometers later, he saw another roadblock ahead. This one was different from the one he had just encountered, and surprisingly enough, those differences actually made him much less nervous about approaching it.

The vehicles this time were three late model Land Rover Defenders, fitted out with black roof racks, front high intensity light kits, and rear racks for extra fuel cans. All three were painted desert tan, and the men near them were not the garden-variety jihadis he had just encountered. They were dressed in Iraqi or Syrian army camouflage, and the weapons they carried were a mix of AK-74s and RPK light machine guns. A couple of men even carried Russian SV-98 sniper rifles slung on their backs. Even their gait and stance on simple roadblock duty bespoke professionalism and military training.

Al-Amriki again kept his hands in view, gripping the top of the Hyundai's steering wheel as he covered the last fifty meters to the roadblock at less than fifteen kilometers an hour before rolling the window down again. One of the men wearing Syrian camouflage approached the car.

"Al-Amriki?" he inquired.

"Yes."

"As-salaam alaykum," the man in the camouflage replied. "Akil is waiting for you. Park your vehicle over there," he said, gesturing toward the left side of the road, "we will drive you to Akil's location."

Al-Amriki nodded, and turned around to park where the man indicated, then exited from the vehicle, leaving his two-suiter and the doctor's medical bag in the car.

The man in Syrian camouflage was waiting for him at the rear of the Hyundai. Al-Amriki knew what this was, and raised his arms, holding them out to his sides. The jihadi frisked him expertly, removing his pen, passport, and iPhone from his Thawb and placing them on the trunk of the Hyundai. He then withdrew a portable metal detector from his right thigh pocket of his camouflage utilities to scan Al-Amriki's body.

The metal detector remained silent, so the jihadi returned it to the large thigh pocket of his utilities, and picked the iPhone up off the trunk, thumbing the round button near its base and noting that the lock screen displayed.

Frowning, the jihadi pressed and held the button on the right side of the case. When the 'Slide to Power Off' screen appeared, he used his thumb to initiate the shutdown, and watched the phone as it powered off.

"Store all of this in your trunk, Al-Amriki. Do not turn the phone on until you are twenty minutes into your return trip," the jihadi ordered in a harsh tone.

Al-Amriki nodded, returning to the driver's door to reach inside and trigger the trunk release on the key fob still inserted into the ignition. After the pen, passport, and phone were secured in the Hyundai's trunk, the jihadi motioned Al-Amriki to follow, and Al-Amriki dutifully trailed along behind him.

Al-Amriki understood why the jihadi insisted that the pen, passport, and phone remain in the car. Pens could be weapons in close combat or disguised single-shot pistols, and modern passports contained smart chips holding the bearer's personal information, providing the opportunity to place microminiaturized parts that might turn it into a GPS locator. Leaving the phone behind was obvious, since all modern smart phones had location and tracking capabilities built into them. They undoubtedly did not want Al-Amriki to know where he was meeting Akil.

As they neared one of the Defenders, the jihadi escorting him made a radio call. "Is he clear? No tails?" he asked, turning to watch Al-Amriki closely.

Al-Amriki looked back, forcing a calm expression. He must have missed the surveillance team watching his approach. Al-Amriki mentally chastised himself for being too casual about this mission after clearing the Syrian border and not employing good counter surveillance techniques. Akil obviously had. If he had allowed a group of infidels to follow him to the meeting with Akil, the punishment for the oversight would have been swift, and he would stand before Allah for judgement moments after his execution.

"Understood," the jihadi said a moment later, reaching out to open the rear door of the Defender, and motioning Al-Amriki to board.

Al-Amriki did not hear the reply himself, and he looked more closely at the jihadi. He could just barely discern the body-colored molded earpiece lodged in the man's left ear. Al-Amriki knew these men were not run-of-the-mill jihadis, but the earpiece took his assessment to another level.

"Former Republican Guard?" Al-Amriki probed, tying the man's Syrian camouflage and the earpiece together. The Syrian Republican Guard was a division of mechanized troops that guarded and occupied Damascus, securing it for the Assad regime and acting as a counterforce to the country's regular mechanized and armored forces. Assad purportedly secured the loyalty of the Republican Guard's senior officers with large payoffs funded directly from the country's oil wealth. This man was likely one of the Republican Guard's highly trained junior officers whose loyalty belonged to ISIS now.

The man nodded once, gesturing again to the open rear door of the Defender.

Al-Amriki clambered into the Defender's right rear seat, taking note of the overly thick doors and glass that bespoke the level of gunfire the car could withstand, and made himself comfortable before fastening the seatbelt. When he looked up, he saw his escort holding out a blindfold in the form of a knit ski mask with the eyes sewn shut. With a resigned smile, Al-Amriki took it, and pulled it over his head.

Al-Amriki felt the Defender roll to a stop, and his former Republican Guard escort dismounted. He had tried to get a sense of where he was being taken, but the driver had cleverly taken the precaution of driving in several circles, both counterclockwise and clockwise before setting off, which completely disoriented him. The best he could estimate was that the trip had taken twenty minutes and, from the bumps in the road for the last five or so, that they were not on a main or even side road.

The sound of the door opening next to him was followed by a sudden tug on the top of his head as the knit ski mask was removed. Al-Amriki blinked a few times to clear his eyesight in the orange and reds of the approaching sunset. Then he unfastened his seatbelt before clambering out and looking around.

The Defender sat near an old and apparently abandoned one-story building along the rusting rails of a train track. Al-Amriki studied the building briefly, noting its plain exterior primarily consisting of corrugated sheet metal walls and a roof, which likely made it unbearably hot during the day. It appeared to be about fifteen meters long, and perhaps five deep, mounted upon on a low platform near the tracks.

The building's construction did not speak to anything other than haste and low cost in its manufacture. It had no windows and only one door that faced the railroad tracks and the dirt track beyond. His escort in the Syrian camouflage motioned him toward the structure and Al-Amriki walked toward it, his mind still working to discern its purpose.

As he crossed the railroad tracks and he glimpsed the faded yellow bodies of three Mitsubishi earthmovers, their driver's cabins and heavy chassis pockmarked with dozens of bullet holes, he finally figured it out. They were at an abandoned phosphate mine, one of the dozen or so in this part of Syria long since abandoned due to the ongoing jihad and the actions of the so-called 'Syrian Resistance' fighting against the Assad regime. Crude oil was a far more lucrative commodity to smuggle than mining and processing raw rock for phosphates.

Al-Amriki could hear indistinct male voices coming from inside, and mounted the low steps to the building's door. As he approached the door, the voices became more distinct. One he recognized as Akil, the other was unfamiliar to him.

"Are you certain?" Akil asked.

"Yes," replied the unknown man's voice. "The assault on the dam is ready and we have enough of the holy warriors in reserve to hold it against the Iraqi apostates."

"What of the Americans and their cowardly drones?"

"I am deploying nearly one hundred men with SA-7s, and six of the SA-8 mobile missile launchers we captured from the Syrians. We will swat the drones out of the sky, along with any aircraft that approach the dam."

Al-Amriki stepped on a loose board outside the door and it gave off a loud squeak, interrupting Akil's conversation.

"Al-Amriki?" Akil's voice called out.

"Here, Sahib," Al-Amriki replied, opening the door without waiting for a further invitation.

Akil crossed the floor to greet him. The man's smile was wide and genuine. Al-Amriki always thought that Akil looked less like a senior leader of ISIS and more like a man who should be selling fresh melons in a market. He was of medium height, with skin browned by the sun, deep-set brown eyes, and straight white teeth. He was dressed in a simple brown Thawb covering him from throat to ankle, and his cheeks were full, matching the extra fifteen kilos he carried, and his hair was hidden beneath a black turban.

Although he might look like a fruit seller, Al-Amriki knew otherwise. Akil had spent most of his twenties as an officer in the Iraqi Republican Guard, and his thirties as part of the Iraqi resistance to the American occupation. He joined Al-Qaeda's cell in northern Iraq once the Americans doubled down on their commitment to helping the Iraqi government deal with the insurgency by leveraging help from Iraqis that wanted a self-sufficient nation.

Rumored to be present at the meeting where Abu Bakr al-Baghdadi formalized the creation of the Islamic State of Iraq and Syria after the integration of the Al-Nusra Front organization in Syria, Akil rose rapidly to become the Islamic State's head of military operations. He had taken notice early on of Al-Amriki's skill in planning operations outside of the Islamic State's sphere of military influence, and had been one of Al-Amriki's mentors in ISIS.

Al-Amriki greeted Akil with the traditional three kisses. "I am sorry to have interrupted you, I can wait outside..."

"Of course not," Akil told him. "You are a trusted brother of the jihad and your work has helped expand the Caliphate while striking fear into the unbelievers and misguided Shi'a. This is one of our senior field commanders, Ghalib."

Al-Amriki locked eyes with Ghalib and he could feel himself being evaluated. Where Akil resembled a portly fruit merchant, Ghalib was much more menacing. He was taller than average, with strong Arab features, bushy eyebrows, and a full beard. He moved economically, but the breadth of his shoulders and depth of his chest spoke of a man accustomed to the kind of physical training elite military units underwent, and he wore a black combat uniform with an Islamic State flag embroidered on one shoulder. 'Ghalib' meant 'Victory' in Arabic, and it suited him.

Unlike Akil, Ghalib did not approach him for the traditional three kisses. In fact, while Akil might have used the opportunity to stab a man face-to-face, Ghalib seemed more like a man that would take pleasure in crushing the life from anyone who displeased him with his bare hands.

"Al-Amriki," Ghalib said, his voice sonorous and measured, "Akil has told me of your great skill in planning our overseas operations."

"I'm pleased to be of service in the jihad against all the unbelievers," Al-Amriki answered. "Akil—"

"Are you?" Ghalib interrupted. "Why Akil trusts you I do not know. You are an American, and as such should never have been allowed to join our cause."

Al-Amriki felt the chill in his words despite the warm air in the room. No matter, he had encountered men like Ghalib in the armies of Allah before.

"I serve Allah, and His just war against the infidels alone. If Akil orders it, I shall join whatever battle he orders..."

"Peace," Akil said to both of them. "Ghalib, I have seen this man's mind at work and it is truly Allah's guidance that shapes his plans for our victories."

"Indeed," Ghalib said skeptically, eyebrows arched.

"Yes," Akil confirmed. "I found him working with a group of our brothers in Erbil. His skills and knowledge have been proven by men I knew from my time in the Republican Guard under that lunatic Saddam. He is truly Allah's gift to our cause."

Ghalib did not appear impressed, or less skeptical, but he did nod. "As you say, brother, but I will not fully trust him until I see his commitment to

Allah's cause with my own eyes."

Akil looked directly at Ghalib, his eyes narrowed. "That is not your concern," he said flatly, "Al-Amriki has proven himself to me, and has planned many operations that have resulted in the deaths of hundreds of unbelievers in many countries."

Al-Amriki felt Akil was exaggerating, but said nothing, accepting his leader's praise in silence.

"It is unfortunate that his last plan was not so successful," Ghalib observed acidly.

"Yes," Akil confirmed, "but it was not through any fault in the plan that I or my other advisors can detect."

Akil turned to face Al-Amriki. "In fact, I have decided that you are to be known within the Caliphate as a Senior Engineer of the jihad." Akil smiled warmly. "You will now advise me on a level equal to my other operations planners, and your focus will continue to be on overseas operations, as befits your proven expertise."

Al-Amriki was surprised by the promotion. "You are most kind Sahib, but surely there are others..."

Akil waved away his protest, coming forward again to clap him warmly on the shoulders. "You will do what no others can, and as an American, you will eventually become an idol for others in your country. In a few weeks, our Information Ministry will arrange to conduct videotaped interviews with you to help our recruitment in the infidel states of America and Canada."

Al-Amriki had been surprised at the sudden promotion, but he was positively shocked at Akil's intent to have him give interviews. The Islamic State's Information Ministry leveraged every element of social media on the internet to spread the word of Allah, recruit new jihadis, and disavow western lies and propaganda about the Caliphate.

Akil saw the shock on his face and asked, "What are you concerned about, my brother?"

"I do not know how effective I will be if I am in Paradise, Sahib. Such exposure will make me a primary target for the Americans and their Satan spawned drones."

"And you are afraid," added Ghalib.

"Only of not being able to serve Allah in this war as our Caliph and Akil require!" Al-Amriki retorted hotly.

Akil shook his head. "Do not concern yourself with such things. The men who make these videos are adept at hiding your face and voice, for the very reasons you stated, yet they also manage to make the videos inspiring. They will highlight your courage for your countrymen, encouraging the bravest of them to join us here, or better yet, conduct martyrdom operations in your misguided homeland."

Al-Amriki considered that. "I will help them all I can," he said, nodding.

"Good," Akil responded. "Now it's time for you to share with us the details of your new plan."

"Yes Sahib. In the name of Allah, the Most Merciful, and bearing in mind the Caliph's requirements," nodding to Akil, "I have narrowed the list to four targets that meet our needs."

"Only four?" Akil asked pointedly.

"Yes," Al-Amriki told him. "I initially considered fifteen in all, throughout the Middle East. Eleven of them are not viable targets."

"Why not?" Ghalib demanded.

Unshaken, Al-Amriki replied, "Six did not present the possibility of a large number of casualties – their locations were too small for the minimum number of deaths the Caliph required, or they had recently cut staff due to local conditions of either civil unrest from political issues or actions of the jihad. Three were eliminated due to the projected response time of American forces..."

"The Americans are cowards and cannot stand against us." Ghalib stated flatly.

"With respect, I must disagree," Al-Amriki said, making his point by looking unflinchingly into Ghalib's eyes as he spoke. "They are well equipped and trained, and it would be most unwise to meet them on a battlefield without preparation. More importantly, for this operation, the presence of the Marine rapid reaction force within thirty minutes flying time would leave our brothers undertaking the mission outgunned within an hour if they were discovered."

Al-Amriki turned to look at Akil. "The Caliph desires this operation succeed to show diminished American influence in the region. It will fail if their devil-spawned Marines are able to kill our brave fighters."

"I agree," Akil told him, "go on."

"The last two were eliminated because they are not centrally located in a major population center."

Akil nodded, thinking. "Your reasoning seems sound to my mind," he said after a moment's thought, shooting Ghalib a look of warning. Al-Amriki was proving his competence, and it was time Ghalib recognized it. "Continue," he ordered.

"Yes Sahib." Al-Amriki licked his lips before continuing. He would remember to bring some bottled water on the next trip.

"The four that remain meet all the criteria. I am especially pleased with the location of each. They are all in the heart of a city with more than three hundred thousand people. Using the publicly available imagery, I've also identified potential entry points—"

"How did you do that?" Ghalib demanded, deciding Akil's look of warning was irrelevant. No matter how infatuated Akil was with this man, this 'Senior Engineer' still needed to prove himself, as far as he was concerned.

"It is actually quite simple," Al-Amriki told him with a smile. "I used the street-level view of the area provided by Google Earth, and I simply 'walked' around the target location."

"Excellent," observed Akil with a smile.

"Yes, but it is not enough."

"Explain," Akil said, his expression changing to confusion.

"The date and time stamps on the ground level and overhead images are between six months and a year old. Committing the lives of the brothers training for this mission on those photos alone would be folly."

Being the military operations planner, Ghalib understood first and his estimate of the younger man's worth grudgingly rose a couple of notches. Perhaps he was all Akil believed him to be. "What else do you need to know?"

"Several things. I need recent photos of the four target buildings from all angles, and the photographs must include the street approaches. Video would be good as well."

"Surely that is not all," Ghalib observed.

"No. I also need reliable information about any guard patrols, actions that are repeated every day, and any other activities that might interfere with our operation."

"I know exactly what you need," Ghalib told him, his tone that of a man who had just heard the obvious. "There are trusted men who provide us with similar information about the Syrian and Iraqi apostates. Surely Akil knows of some men who can do similar things for Al-Amriki?"

Akil did not bother telling Ghalib that he had done such things for Al-Amriki before, and he was secretly pleased that his new Senior Engineer of the jihad had offered proof of his abilities in front of Ghalib. He needed them to work well together in the future. The Caliph had plans for the Islamic State that would require the services of both men.

"I do," Akil said confidently. "Tell me what four places they must go to and exactly what you need."

Al-Amriki told him. Akil removed a small notebook from his Thawb and took some hasty notes as Al-Amriki spoke. Ten minutes later, Akil put the notebook away.

"You will receive the information as we get it, via the usual means."

"Thank you, Sahib," Al-Amriki said, "once I have it, I will complete the plan and seek your approval. Are the brothers assigned to this mission prepared?"

"Not yet. They continue to train and improve their skills as warriors."

"What else would you have of me, Sahib?" Al-Amriki asked.

"Nothing. You have done well so far. Return to Damascus and spend the night before heading back to Jordan." Akil took him by the arm and led Al-Amriki toward the door. When they were out of earshot, he continued.

"Spending the night in a modern hotel room rather than that shack you live in now should be a pleasant change, yes?" Akil asked.

"Yes," Al-Amriki agreed, thinking of the amenities the hotel offered compared to cooking his own meal this evening and falling asleep with only satellite television and internet radio for entertainment.

"In addition to appointing you to a new position in Allah's jihad, the Caliph has decided that you are to be compensated for your hard work." Akil told him.

Al-Amriki's eyes grew wide, "But Sahib..."

Akil shook his head, silencing any argument. "No objections. You have served the Caliph and Allah well, and the Caliph is generous to those who serve as you do. Besides, it is better that the wealth from the oil fields we have captured go to the faithful doing Allah's work than some infidels in the west, or apostates or unbelievers in Iraq."

"As you say," Al-Amriki replied, bowing his head slightly.

"My guard will see you back to your car. I will send you the account information where we will deposit funds on your behalf."

After Al-Amriki was gone, Akil rejoined Ghalib.

"Are you more impressed now?" Akil asked as he turned, hearing the single door open again. Another of Akil's men, this man dressed in Iraqi camouflage, his AK-74 slung over his shoulder, entered and walked toward the two men unbidden.

"Yes," Ghalib said grudgingly, "but I still do not trust him."

Akil nodded knowingly, looking at the bodyguard's approach. "Nusrat?" he asked when the man was three paces from he and Ghalib.

"We are following him, Sahib," Nusrat replied.

"Good. If he encounters trouble, see to it that he is protected."

"Yes Sahib.

"Good. Al-Amriki is very valuable to the Caliphate. Also, report anything that seems strange or suspicious."

"Of course, Sahib." Nusrat assured him. "I will report to you immediately."

Akil nodded, dismissing the man, who left without another word.

"You watch him?" Ghalib asked with an arched eyebrow.

"Of course, particularly when we meet face-to-face. Al-Amriki is very valuable to the Caliphate and his skills are sorely needed."

"I see," Ghalib said, dismissively, unconvinced the American was worth the effort.

"It is as much for our protection as his." Akil assured him.

"Yes," Ghalib reluctantly agreed, "the Americans sometimes surprise us. Should they discover him, and follow him to us..." Ghalib trailed off, the implication clear.

"If they discover him and try to follow him to us," Akil responded, "then we will determine if he was merely careless or lured back by the unbelievers. If he was careless, forgiveness would be warranted given his service to Allah."

"If he was lured back?" Ghalib asked.

"He will die by scaphism for his betrayal," Akil replied without a moment's hesitation. The words came out flat and with no room for compromise as he used the term describing an ancient Persian method of execution.

Ghalib considered that for a moment, looking at the door Al-Amriki had left through a few minutes before. Death by scaphism saw the victim stripped naked and placed in a hollowed-out tree trunk, with only the head, hands, and feet protruding. Next, the victim is force-fed milk and honey until they soil themselves. Last, their exposed skin is coated in honey to help attract insects, just before the log was floated on a pond. The pungent scents of excrement and honey would attract insects within hours. They would eat and breed within the victim's skin and the pain would begin. Gangrene would follow quickly, but death from a combination of starvation, dehydration, and shock often took two weeks or more if the victim was young and reasonably healthy.

"If he betrays Allah and the Caliph, I'll help you prepare the tree trunk," Ghalib said, savoring the mental image.

CHAPTER 5

Mathews stood still on the corner of Princess Basma Avenue in Amman's hot afternoon sun. He withdrew the iPhone 6s from the front pocket of his tan khakis while shifting the travel bag slung over his left shoulder to a more comfortable position.

He felt a bead of sweat run down the side of his face and wiped at his forehead with his free hand, flicking the moisture away. He would have preferred to avoid walking in the heat of the day, but having the taxi drop him off several blocks away allowed him to continue his counter surveillance routine while stretching his legs. He had been cooped up on planes or airport terminals for the last thirty-six hours.

After paying the taxi driver in Jordanian dinar, Mathews took a moment to breathe in Amman's air with its mix of smells: cooking food, car exhaust, and heated concrete and steel, all edged with the taste of the desert. Inhaling deeply, he began walking along the side streets west of the avenue, moving in the general direction of the Sheraton Hotel at a leisurely pace, turning right and then left at intervals, forming a zigzag path. He stopped at random points near larger stores or shops with large front windows, using them as mirrors to study his back trail. He even doubled back twice as an extra precaution.

After traveling nearly eight blocks on his circuitous route, Mathews was reasonably certain that he was not being followed, unless it a very large team was doing it, in which case he was already screwed. Feeling his heartbeat quickening from the uncertainty and excitement of the moment, he quickened his pace for the last block, moving directly towards the heavily trafficked Princess Basma Avenue and stopping at the corner where Zahran Road crossed it. He took a long look at the tower of the Sheraton Hotel on the far side of Princess Basma, wishing he could have run three or four miles after he arrived.

The G280 he boarded at the Wraith Base had taken him only as far as Denver, where he joined the mass of other travelers in the terminal, checked in for his coach class seat, and boarded an overnight flight to Paris.

After arriving in Charles De Gaulle International, he waited nearly ten hours, alternately napping in the imitation leather chairs of the terminal, watching CNN's international broadcast, or listening to the music stored on his 'new' iPhone. When the battery level dropped below fifty percent, Mathews recharged the iPhone from a wall socket to ensure he would not be short of battery life before the next series of flights.

The next leg of his trip took him to Rome and, after a four-hour delay, he finally boarded a flight to Athens which, after a two-hour delay on the ground, eventually took off for Amman.

Mathews was rested and alert, having slept as often as possible during the flights. He would have preferred to have a solid eight hours under his belt, but the naps and the surge of adrenaline he was working on since the Airbus A320 touched down at Queen Alia International Airport were keeping him sharp.

Satisfied that he had a minute or so before the traffic signals changed, he rested his thumb against the button near the base of the iPhone. The phone accepted his thumbprint and unlocked. Tapping the photos icon, he scrolled to the photo of the empty parking spot in the lot.

The lot itself was just across Princess Basma Avenue, and adjacent to the Arab Medical Center. The medical center was directly opposite from the Sheraton across Zahran Road, and Mathews glanced up from the phone to look across the street, using the images on the phone to orient himself, cross-checking the buildings to be sure he was in the proper place.

The paired dual carriageways that formed Princess Basma Avenue were thick with afternoon traffic, and Mathews glanced briefly at the small group of Jordanian men and women gathered around him at the corner. Some of them were also looking at their smartphones and tapping away or talking on them, or just watching the lights and waiting to cross. A couple of them even had the telltale white ear buds dangling from their ears, listening to music or a caller.

Seeing nothing suspicious in the small crowd around him, Mathews returned his attention to the iPhone for one last check. He flicked through several images in rapid succession, looking up for a few seconds to ensure the pedestrian crossing signals had not changed, and comparing the images with the Sheraton at his one o'clock on the far side of Prince Basma, and the Arab Medical Center at his eleven o'clock.

Satisfied that he successfully matched the images of the buildings on the iPhone with the expected location of the tan Range Rover in the parking lot, he re-locked the phone. The pedestrian crossing light shifted to green, and he crossed Princess Basma a step behind the small crowd. Once across, the other men and women split apart, some heading further along Princess Basma, and a few waiting at the corner to cross Zahran Road towards the Sheraton Hotel. Mathews kept walking, angling left and stepping over a low concrete curb into the parking lot near the Arab Medical Center.

Mathews surveyed the lot, focusing on the portion he expected to see the Range Rover in, and immediately spied it. The lot itself was unsecured, lacking even rudimentary traffic barriers or security guard. Mathews expected the lack of security was the primary reason for choosing it as the drop point.

Mathews strode purposefully towards the two-ton Range Rover, eyes alert and sweeping the lot for anything unusual. He looked for vehicles that seemed out of place, occupied with the engine running or positioned near the exits to block a car trying to leave the lot, or for people loitering in the immediate area that seemed unusually wary or watchful. Seeing nothing, he turned his attention to the car.

The passenger seat visor was half way down, and he noticed that the left rear tire's dust cap was missing. A brief look in the rear windows showed him one large and one smaller sealed cardboard box, both resting on the rear seats, secured in place with the seat belts.

Mathews looked around the lot one last time, before committing himself. Still no signs of surveillance on the lot, and no other people anywhere in the lot. He took a deep breath and opened the driver's side door. Once he saw the small white sliver of paper trapped between the door and the doorframe flutter to the ground, he relaxed a little.

There were three telltale signs: the visor position, missing dust cap on the tire, and the piece of paper were all expected, assuring him that the car had not been touched since the four-wheel drive vehicle was parked.

Mathews slid in behind the wheel and popped open the central console. The keys were right where he expected them to be according to the simulated e-mail from Professor Yousef. The engine caught immediately, and he took a few moments to adjust the mirrors and look around the car.

Mathews thought this Range Rover was in decent shape, especially for its age. The odometer told him it had done one hundred and twenty thousand kilometers. The cream-colored leather interior was in good shape, although it was obviously well used and could have benefited from a few hours of leather cleaner and elbow grease to freshen it. The radio and cruise control buttons on the polished wood steering wheel also showed their years, the white accent paint on the etched symbols nearly worn off, with only some traces of white in the deepest part of the grooves for each symbol.

Mathews listened for a moment, and studied the dash. No idiot lights, and the engine made a steady rumble. Even better, Mathews could feel the cool breeze emanating from the air vents. He smiled slightly; taking a few seconds to adjust the climate control to a level he thought would be comfortable. Functioning air conditioning was an unexpected but welcome luxury.

Mathews examined the GPS, grateful that the UK-built Range Rover was already set up to use English instead of Arabic, and then used the dash controls to input his destination.

While the system worked to calculate the best route and arrival time, Mathews opened the glove compartment and rifled through the paperwork inside. All of it appeared to be written in Arabic, but he could guess at the purpose for each of the documents. The registration was obvious because of the license plate number in one of the blocks. The second was probably the insurance card, based on the phone numbers on it, and the last item, in the form of a letter from the university's letterhead, was undoubtedly his permission to use the vehicle.

Stuffing the documents back into the glove box, Mathews fastened his seat belt, and backed out of the spot. He exited the lot and began following the GPS unit's female voice directions to Ar-Ruwayshid. The digital readout next to the moving map told him it was a little over two hours away.

An hour and a half later, Mathews was glad the techs had loaded nearly thirty hours of music on the iPhone. The English language Bliss 104.3 FM out of Amman had faded about a half hour and seventy miles ago, just as the last part of 'Here Comes the Rain Again' by the Eurythmics was ending.

The phone sat upside down in a cup holder playing Pink Floyd's 'Dogs of War' as the miles continued to roll by. As long as he kept the phone in that position, Mathews thought the little speakers at the base of the phone sounded pretty good. He made a mental note. The Pink Floyd song was a cute touch by the tech geeks back at the base, and he would need to stop by and thank them when he got back. He stole the occasional glance in the rear-view mirror for a tail, but the last car he had seen passed him ten minutes ago, heading toward Amman. At this point, any tail he might pick up would stand out like a sore thumb.

Mathews could see from the moving map on the Range Rover's GPS display that Highway 10 was an arrow straight ribbon of asphalt running right down the middle of the roughly rectangular section of Jordan that was wedged between Saudi Arabia to the south, Syria to the north, and Iraq's Anbar region to the east.

Out the windshield, the highway was bordered by nothing more than the reddish clay and chocolate brown colored sand on either side of the black strip of pavement, and that uniform landscape was only broken at random points by stretches of black volcanic-looking rock fields that were sometimes small blemishes and other times two-hundred-yard-long irregularly shaped tracts.

Mathews reached under his sunglasses and rubbed his eyes briefly before stealing another quick glance at the GPS. The white path superimposed on Highway 10's green stripe was straight and unwavering, with no symbols for gas, food, or lodging anywhere on the moving map. The digital readout next to it informed him that he was still forty miles from Ar-Ruwayshid, and thinking back to the overhead imagery he had studied before leaving, he knew not to expect much when he got there.

Ar-Ruwayshid was effectively a weigh station in the deep desert, a loose collection of mostly single-story buildings less than fifty miles from the Jordanian/Iraqi border, and less than thirty or so miles from either Syria or Saudi Arabia, if you were willing to strike out across the barren landscape to the north or south. The town itself was barely two miles in length astride Highway 10, with most of the homes and shops clustered south of the highway and no more than a mile away from it.

To the north was a small Jordanian Air Force base, its lone runway used more by the old AH-1F Cobra attack helicopters as a sighting reference on their patrols or sanctuary during bad weather than by any fixed wing aircraft stationed there. Mathews recalled from his briefing material that Jordan had bought Cobras from Israel in 2014 to improve its airpower in the eastern desert since the rise of the Islamic State, a sale both nations declined to comment on publicly.

The last notes of the Pink Floyd song faded from the iPhone's small speakers, and Mathews wondered what would play next. As the song clicked over and he heard the first notes of another oldie, 'Every Breath She Takes' begin, Kristen's face swam into view in his mind.

Mathews shook his head. He should have found Kristen before he left, and tried to apologize again for snapping at her. The memory of the angry, hurt look on her face when she left Simon's office caused his heart to constrict. A man should not have to choose between a future with someone special and defending the nation he loves.

Frustrated, Mathews slammed his fist into the center console of the Range Rover as he shifted position in the driver's seat. The impact bounced the phone out of the cup holder and onto the passenger floor, where the song just kept on playing.

He blew out a breath, angry that what he enjoyed the most, being one of his nation's elite warriors and hunting down those who would harm innocents, was getting in the way of something else he wanted badly to be a part of his life: a wife and family. His instructor's admonition during SEAL training, 'this isn't a job, it's a lifestyle and a commitment' rang in his ears, the implication clear: the nation, your unit, your team, and the mission come first.

Since he met Kristen, he thought he deserved to enjoy the fruits of his hard work, sacrifices, and dedication over the last few years, just as any person might. Sam's death had brought that desire into even sharper focus, a harsh reminder of the risks and realities in his chosen profession.

When he wasn't sleeping during the flights and while the waiting in the terminals for the next plane, Mathews' argued with himself. Mathews was a soldier, not an assassin, and when he first joined the Wraiths, Colonel Simon had been very clear that the Wraiths would abide by all the precepts of the Law of Armed Conflict, or suffer punishment under the Uniform Code of Military Justice. He believed in that ethos, but even so, he wanted payback for Sam.

Murdering Al-Amriki in cold blood was out of the question, but Mathews' experience told him that more often or not, when confronted with capture, these self-styled 'holy warriors' would rather die than be taken away in hand cuffs.

It wasn't murder if the target chooses to die, right? Mathews told himself.

The simple answer to his dilemma then was to find a way to be a part of the capture team, and if Al-Amriki even looked at a weapon within reach, he could kill him. As a weapon of his nation, faced with an immediate threat from the objective, Mathews could and would kill Al-Amriki where he stood, and be justified in doing so to protect the members of the capture team, intelligence bonanza be dammed.

And after Al-Amriki was dead, what would he do? Mathews asked himself. Get on a plane and head home – but to what? More importantly, to whom? He enjoyed being a member of the Wraiths, and taking the fight to his nation's enemies, but the bunkroom on a ship, or even his quarters at the base, were still very lonely places during the days and nights between missions or deployments. Frowning as he considered that, Mathews also recognized that one day, there would be no more orders to go on missions, to deploy to another country and take the fight to his nation's enemies.

Kristen's appearance in his life had erased that loneliness, and shown him a glimpse of a future beyond the secret world of special operations. He had dated girls in high school and college, of course, but all of those relationships were much more casual. He had not treated them poorly, that was not the kind of man he was, but it was much more of a 'let's have fun' situation than an 'I might want to marry her' kind of thing. Mathews was proud of the fact that most of those relationships had ended pleasantly, but there were one or two that had ended in tears and recriminations.

Kristen was the first woman he had been involved with where spending time with her was something he looked forward to every day. He spent every spare hour he could with her, talking and just enjoying her company. Even sharing the simple things, like watching a movie or television, was sweeter when she would cuddle up against him. Remembering the feel of her warmth along his side triggered the memory of her lips against his, and how nice just kissing her felt, followed almost immediately by the unpleasant thought that their kiss on the hill in San Francisco might have been their last.

The blare of a horn tore Mathews out of his unexpected melancholy. Mathews refocused on the task of driving, seeing that he allowed the Range Rover to drift into the oncoming lane by a few feet. He turned the wheel sharply, putting the big four by four back in its proper lane, and waved his apology to the driver of a green Toyota sedan as they passed one another.

Adrenaline surged in his veins and Mathews swore aloud. If he kept letting his mind drift back to Kristen and losing focus on the mission, he might end up dead. He glanced at the GPS again, angry with himself, the music from the iPod adding to his frustration. Less than twenty miles to the town where a dangerous terrorist was hiding, in a foreign country with no backup, and you are sitting in a car during a long drive pining for a woman! Pull your head out of your ass, Mathews!

Mathews shook his head. He needed to save thoughts about his love life, or potential lack of one, for after the mission. He pulled over quickly, stopping the Range Rover before unfastening his seat belt, and reaching over far enough to snatch the iPod off the floor in front of the passenger seat. A few taps on the iPod, and silence reigned in the Range Rover's cabin as he dropped the phone back into the cup holder.

Refastening his seat belt, Mathews checked his mirrors, and accelerated away hard. The next several miles passed in silence as he seethed. The focus of his anger drifted from his own inattention, to the piss poor timing of this mission, to despair over how his last few minutes with Kristen had played out – he wished that he could call her and work things out...

The desert scene around him continued to roll past, ten miles speeding by in a blur as his thoughts drifted back again to his last few minutes with Kristen, trying to think of a way to repair things with her after his return from the mission. The mission, Mathews! he chided himself, forcing his eyes to the surroundings.

Mathews could see the low rooftops scattered to the south of Highway 10 in the distance and knew it was time to 'get his mind right,' as one of his old instructors used to say. If he did not start keeping his attention on the mission at hand, he might never get the chance to work things out with her, and that in itself was just as motivating as finding this bastard Al-Amriki and stopping him.

Mathews eased off the accelerator and let the Range Rover coast as he reached the outskirts of Ar-Ruwayshid. As the speed dropped below fifty miles per hour, he scanned the road ahead, looking for roadblocks or any unusual police activity. Seeing nothing, he held the Range Rover at forty miles per hour, and glided around the forty-degree bend in Highway 10 that marked the western edge of Ar-Ruwayshid.

The line of buildings on either side of the highway was uniformly desert brown, broken at irregular intervals by one or two bleached white structures.

Most looked to be one story and unkempt. Some, probably the abandoned ones, had white- or green-colored graffiti of Arabic lettering on their sides. The graffiti reminded Mathews of one of his biggest disadvantages on this mission; one he, Simon, and Cain thought would be addressed by the cover identity he was using: his Arabic was rudimentary at best.

In fact, most of the Arabic he spoke came directly from his training as a commando. The routine polite phrases and other words he knew—'Halt', 'Hands up', 'Drop it', and 'quiet'—were not likely to help him during the mission's initial stages, and Mathews was pretty sure he was not going to use them at all if he came face-to-face with Al-Amriki. Fortunately, although English had no official status in the country, it was the defacto language for banking and commerce, as well as university level classes. He would find out in a few minutes if that would be enough to get by.

Three quarters of a mile into the town, Mathews spied the right hand turn he was looking for, and turned south, heading down what passed for the other main road in Ar-Ruwayshid. Another mile later, and he saw a Jordanian man dressed in a white Thawb standing beside an ancient Peugeot 405, whose red paint had faded under the Middle Eastern sun to the point of looking chalky and pale pink from bumper to bumper.

Here we go. Mathews braked the Range Rover, touched the button to lower the driver's window and leaned out with a friendly wave. "Mr. Obeidat?" he asked the man.

"Mr. Forrestal?" Obeidat asked in return, his English thickly accented, stepping forward to offer his hand. Obeidat was an older man, in his early fifties, Mathews guessed, clean-shaven, with bright, dark brown eyes under slim brows. His thick black hair showed no signs of gray, and his skin was a tanned leather that only a person born to these latitudes could acquire.

Mathews put the Range Rover in park and clambered out, leaving the engine running as a precaution. He met Obeidat two steps from the waiting Range Rover and shook his hand. "I hope I haven't kept you waiting?" Mathews spoke slowly to help the man, not knowing how used he was to hearing an American speaking English.

"No, no. I came after your university called and told me what plane you flew on."

Mathews smiled, for two reasons. Firstly, Obeidat was obviously not fluent in English, but he assumed the man timed his arrival to how long it would take Mathews to drive from Amman, and appreciated him making the effort. The second reason was that National Cover Office seemed to be doing a good job backing up his cover.

"Shokran," Mathews said, thanking Obeidat.

Obeidat waved his hands dismissively. "It is no trouble. You are a guest in my country and I rent houses to researchers from America and Great Britain for ten years now."

"My school has paid you, yes?" Mathews asked.

Obeidat's smile was wide, "Oh, yes. In euros. If you want to stay longer, you ask. No trouble. Follow me, I show you the house."

Mathews nodded and thanked the man again, and Obeidat turned and walked towards his Peugeot. Mathews returned to the Range Rover and settled himself, fully comprehending Obeidat's generous offer of staying longer. The exchange rate from euros to Jordanian dinar was to Obeidat's advantage, and Mathews guessed the National Cover Office had paid out a little more than usual this time, hoping to garner a little extra consideration from Mr. Obeidat.

Obeidat's well-used Peugeot coughed to life after two tries, and he waved unnecessarily for Mathews to follow him. Mathews smiled and waved in return, growing more confident in the security of his cover by Obeidat's behavior and overall 'feel'. The man was undoubtedly exactly what he appeared to be – an older man earning money by providing rental homes for archeological post-docs from various western universities, which was just what Mathews' cover as 'Dr. Forrestal' portrayed him as.

Up until the rise of the Islamic State, archeological post-docs were a regular presence in Jordan, and small teams of them usually descended on the eastern portion of Jordan at random intervals to survey the ancient Assyrian or Babylonian structures that could still be found in the desert sands. Many of them used Ar-Ruwayshid as a staging point in the eastern panhandle of Jordan for daylight forays out into the deeper desert, which gave Mathews an ideal way into the town to search for Al-Amriki without standing out too much.

Mathews trailed Obeidat's Peugeot by a couple of car lengths, scanning the passing rooftops and buildings for any signs of Jordanian police or military presence. Obeidat drove slowly, and Mathews could see the buildings starting to thin as they moved farther from the center of Ar-Ruwayshid. A little shiver of apprehension traced its way down his spine as the spacing between the buildings went from ten feet to thirty, in the space of a few hundred yards.

Caution was the watchword here, Mathews thought. If this was a setup, there was scant cover or concealment options. Mathews kept scanning his mirrors and the area around the roadway for signs of anything out of the ordinary. Obeidat did seem genuine, but being situationally aware at all times was the best practice in the field, especially as he approached what would be his local base of operations.

Obeidat pulled left across the road and stopped in front of the last house before the trackless desert that stretched into the distance. Mathews' eyes followed the road, which went from paved to a featureless dirt path beyond Obeidat's Peugeot, the layer of asphalt stretching itself thin and surrendering to the desert's depth and majesty in a gravelly layer of pebbles in less than one hundred feet.

Mathews pointed the Range Rover across the road and parked in front of Obeidat's car, then joined Obeidat on the short path to the small house.

"This is good house," Obeidat told him.

Mathews considered the outside briefly. Calling it 'weather worn' would be generous. Like most of the houses he had seen on the drive through town, it was single story, on a plot of bare desert about twelve hundred feet square that was pockmarked with ruts and gullies —xeriscaping was not really an issue amongst the people of Ar-Ruwayshid. They were far too poor for such things and besides, the nearest home and garden store was in Amman, or maybe Zarqa.

The exterior walls were a uniform adobe color, and at close range, Mathews could see they were faded and pitted from the inevitable sand blasting that happened when strong winds blew across the hot desert. As they approached, Mathews thought they were either concrete or cinder block with an exterior coating of some sort of thick faux finish.

Obeidat beckoned him closer. "The house is not as big as those in America, but I've tried to make it comfortable for guests." Mathews could see that the older man was trying to soften what he perceived as the inevitable disappointment Mathews was about to experience.

"I'm sure it will be more than comfortable," Mathews told him reassuringly. As a Tier One operator with the SEAL teams and now the Wraiths, he had spent nights in muddy ditches, swamps crawling with poisonous snakes and spiders, and buried under a snow shelf in the Russian arctic. He even spent a few days hiding in a makeshift blind in the Saudi desert once. As long as there was a bed and running water, the house would be as good as a luxury hotel.

Obeidat produced a key from somewhere in his Thawb and unlocked the door, and Mathews trailed him inside, looking quickly through the crack between the hinge side of the door and the frame to see if someone was waiting in ambush.

The house was plain, but surprisingly well furnished. Mathews and Obeidat stood in the large common room that dominated the front portion of the house. It held two medium-sized easy chairs covered in faded orange leather, a low table, and a couch upholstered in saddlebag-colored leather, all resting on a thick Persian rug that showed its age in the slightly frayed edges and faded colors in its geometric patterns. A small window-mounted air conditioner rattled away.

Mathews walked across the rug and peered into the kitchen. It was cramped and tiny. The only appliances were a small refrigerator and an electric stove, both of which looked like units more fit for a dollhouse than a home with people in it. He glanced at the brand names and, not recognizing them, guessed they were European and intended for apartments. The sink was the dominant feature of the tiny counter, and its interior was rust streaked in places. Two small cabinets flanked the window over the sink, and the sunlight streamed in practically unabated by the thin curtains.

"I plugged in the refrigerator a few hours ago," Obeidat called from the common room.

Mathews opened the small unit's door and felt the cold air, pleasantly surprised to see a case of bottled water on one shelf and a plate of food.

Mathews heard footsteps behind him and turned as Obeidat approached.

"My wife insisted that you have some food available after your long journey,"

"Is that Mansaf?" Mathews asked. The traditional Jordanian dish, made of lamb cooked in fermented dried yogurt sauce, served with rice and flatbread, it was traditionally served to guests in Jordan.

"Yes," Obeidat told him, "My wife is proud of her Mansaf recipe." Mathews was not a lamb eater, and hated the pine nut garnish, but told Obeidat as sincerely as he could, "Please thank her for me. I appreciate her making me feel welcome. Shokran."

Obeidat smiled, seeming genuinely pleased, and Mathews let the fridge door swing shut as he continued his inspection. A short hallway ran past the kitchen and one side of the great room, bisecting the house left of center, and Mathews walked into it, feeling the air temperature rise. The air conditioner in the great room obviously was not powerful enough to handle the whole house.

The hallway was unadorned, just painted walls and three doors leading off it. Mathews checked the rooms quickly. The door opposite the great room opened onto a modest but clean bathroom with a tub equipped with a shower head, a commode, bidet, and sink. The door to the left of the bathroom led to a small bedroom with a twin bed and a closet. The door to the right of the bathroom was a larger bedroom that was obviously the master suite. The bed looked to be queen-sized, and there was a freestanding air conditioning unit in the corner, its vent pipe leading to the room's small window. Lying on the bare mattress was a neatly folded pile of bed linen and a clean blanket.

Mathews returned to the Great Room, where Obeidat was waiting expectantly, a look of concern on his face.

Mathews smiled at him. "This will be fine, Mr. Obeidat. I'm sure I'll be very comfortable here."

Obeidat looked immensely relieved. "Shokran. I am glad of it."

Mathews assumed the water was not safe to drink, given the case of bottled water in the fridge, but he had two other questions. "May I ask where the power comes from?"

"Power?" Obeidat looked at him quizzically for a second, not understanding the term, then he puzzled it out. "Oh! Electricity. Yes, it comes from the station near the Air Force base to the north. When I was a child, we had to make due with portable generators at each home, until the government built the airbase. Since it needs electricity, they built a generator station and sent it here as well."

Obeidat spent another few minutes showing 'Mr. Forrestal' the water and electricity cutoffs, the latter so he could use the portable generator attached to the house in case the electricity from the generator station was cut off.

"Will you need me to introduce you to some of our local desert guides, Mr. Forrestal?" Obeidat inquired as he handed 'Mr. Forrestal' the key. Mathews smiled slightly, assuming that the man was doing his best to drum up some work for some of his friends.

"No thank you," Mathews replied. "My thesis is based on the growth patterns of the ancient cities in the desert. I'll be conducting surveys of some of the known dig sites and attempting to correlate them with the available carbon dating work and anthropological studies..."

Obeidat waved his hands. "I never went to university Mr. Forrestal, such things are..."

Mathews smiled again, holding up a hand. "I'm sorry, Mr. Obeidat, I tend to slip into 'professor' mode when I talk about my work. I'm just going to try to determine in what order each ancient site was built."

"That seems an impossible task." Obeidat opined.

Mathews managed a chagrined look. "Yes, it may be, but if I can make any progress towards learning what order, it will make a small contribution to the field."

"Well, I wish you luck."

A few pleasantries later, Obeidat was back in his Peugeot heading toward the center of Ar-Ruwayshid.

Mathews went to the Range Rover and started unpacking it. Six trips later and he had it all in the house. Along with some local clothing, he had picked up canned meats, fresh vegetables, milk, and three cases of water from a grocery store on the outskirts of Amman. With the fridge well packed, he snagged a bottle of water from the cold case Obeidat had left, and headed back into the common room. The two boxes from the shipment lay stacked on the Persian rug near the center of the floor.

Mathews headed into the bedroom and retrieved a mini-CQC-7 folding combat knife from his checked bag, then returned to the Great Room. He examined the seals on the smaller box and saw no evidence of tampering. He unfolded the mini-CQC-7, using its razor-sharp blade to slit the seals, and opened the box.

The black shell of the Pelican 1150 milspec case was a welcome sight. It was watertight, crushproof, and dustproof, guaranteeing the integrity of its contents. Mathews extracted it and popped the latches. Master Sergeant Williams had carved out individual slots in the charcoal-gray foam padding for the Sig Sauer P226, ammunition boxes, and the silencer, as well as a snug slot for the full sized CQC-7 combat knife and its sheath.

Working quickly, Mathews pulled the CQC-7 combat knife from the case and clipped the sheath onto his pants at the small of his back, then reached for the Sig. He pulled the slide back to ensure the chamber was clear and thumbed the magazine release. Catching the empty mag with his left hand and laying the pistol aside, he pulled the box of light loaded .40 rounds out of the Pelican case and began loading the magazine.

Once the magazine was topped off, he withdrew the silencer from the Pelican case and screwed it onto the Sig's threaded barrel. With the silencer securely in place, he slammed the magazine home, and touched the slide release with his thumb. The slide slipped forward with machine precision, and he engaged the safety. From now on, the pistol would always be within arm's reach.

Closing and re-latching the Pelican case, Mathews slid it aside and examined the seals on the larger box. They appeared intact as well, and again, the mini-CQC-7 slit them open with little effort. The Pelican case inside this box was a fuller-sized 1780 transport case, nearly four feet long, two feet wide, and fifteen inches deep, and after two unsuccessful tries to remove it, Mathews found himself forced to cut the box away to free it easily.

Discarding the remnants of the cardboard box, Mathews popped the latches and looked at the components resting inside the foam cutouts. Assembly would take nearly an hour, and the first thing he reached for was the compact toolkit stored vertically in the lower left-hand corner of the foam. Once assembly was finished, he would need the Dell Latitude 15 Rugged Tablet he knew lay in the deepest level of the three layers of foam to complete the programming.

Mathews sat back a moment. He took a long pull from the water bottle and then set to work. An hour later he was finished and reached for the Latitude 15, now laying exposed in the base of the case. It booted up in less than a minute, and he brought up the control software, testing the communications link.

Satisfied, Mathews rose from the floor and headed for the kitchen, sudden hunger overtaking him now that the initial work was done.

Mathews suddenly remembered that he needed to check in. Damn. Withdrawing the iPhone 6s from his back pocket, he unlocked it with his thumb and brought up the texting app. Surprisingly, the signal meter on the phone showed four bars in the upper left-hand corner. He was not expecting that in a remote town like this, but given that a normal cell tower signal was good for nearly twenty-two miles, one cell site could easily cover the entire area around the town and much of the nearby desert.

In spite of his fluency with modern technology, Mathews was very much a hunt-and-peck texter. He held the phone with his left hand and tapped away with his right index finger, taking advantage of the word prediction capability built into the phone.

Hi Uncle Dave. Finally made it to my new assignment. The flights were long, but I managed to catch some sleep along the way. I'll be getting some rest tonight and starting in on the survey work tomorrow. At least I've got some nice toys to use this time. Take care, and tell Aunt Emily I miss her.

David Cain sipped his iced tea from his favorite spill-proof mug, the one with the NSA seal on it, his eyes glued to the computer monitors in front of him and grimaced suddenly from the bitter taste. He had forgotten to add the artificial sweetener he preferred, and he chided himself for his inattention as he unscrewed the mug's lid, pulled two yellow packets from his desk drawer, tore them open, and let the white powder dissolve in the liquid before securing the lid again.

The Counter Terrorism Section, known within the DOD as the CTS, was experiencing a relatively low-key afternoon. Cain took another sip and let it flow over his tongue, appreciating the effect of the artificial sweetener, and then tilted his head to look past his computer screens to survey the watch floor from the slightly raised platform at the rear of the CTS operations floor.

The CTS operations floor was more than thirty feet long and nearly fifty feet wide, a considerable improvement over the organization's first watch floor. The décor was sleek and modern, with solid black steel and glass furnishings instead of the usual government issued oatmeal-colored walls and cookie cutter cubicles. Five ultra slim, six-foot-wide LCD monitors mounted on the far wall displayed various video feeds, with the CTS logo on the center monitor, on a black background.

Created by the NSA graphic arts division, the Earth's eastern hemisphere viewed from space sat off center to the left, centered on the Middle East. Flying above it were an RQ-4 Global Hawk, designed for aerial surveillance; an MQ-9 Reaper firing a precision guided missile, and a reconnaissance satellite.

The RQ-4 and MQ-9 usually flew from forward bases under the command of theater military commanders. When Mathews and his fellow Wraiths were in the field, Cain and his CTS watch team used them to provide constant surveillance over an area before the team headed out to the objective, as well as fire support during operations, if needed. The satellite represented the global reach and intelligence that came into his operation center.

Each of the three elements represented the different facets of the CTS mission to provide what was formally called within the DOD 'persistent intelligence, surveillance, reconnaissance, and combat support missions focused on America's adversaries.' At the bottom, in gold lettering, were just three letters: 'CTS'.

Cain had always appreciated the subtle message the logo communicated. The fact that only people cleared for the CAPTIVE DRAGON security compartment could understand its meaning always caused a mischievous grin that belied his professionalism when he looked at it. He was a career intelligence officer with twenty-two years in the 'community', and keeping secrets within the bounds of the law and his oath to serve his country was second nature.

Cain shifted his gaze and surveyed the area between himself and huge LCD monitors on the far wall. The work area for the liaisons from the various intelligence agencies sat before the monitors. Each of the nine desks were laid out in a saw tooth pattern, starting with the drone operator's desk, with its specialized multiple displays and radio links, on the far left, currently under the watchful eye of Air Force Master Sergeant Emily Thompson. The line ended at the FBI desk at the extreme right side. All were manned; the dual computer monitors at each desk showing various Intelink websites or intelligence reports the desk officers were reviewing. A great deal of intelligence information flowed into this room, all accessible with a few mouse clicks by the watch officers.

Cain's computer blared the 'Star Trek' red alert klaxon without warning, and he reached for the speaker volume to turn it down a bit, but not before Thompson and a few others on the watch floor turned toward the sound in mild amusement, smirks on their faces as they looked at him.

Cain ignored them, seeing the humor in the moment, and letting the brief smile slide off his face quickly. He had set up the sound effect to warn him whenever Mathews sent a text. The technical wizards at NSA had reprogrammed the iPhone Mathews was using to send text messages to a special phone number auto-routed to a dummy account that would forward both incoming and outgoing messages as needed to this computer. Cain had put himself on a floating schedule to be available during daylight hours in Mathews' time zone, and all the other watch leaders were already briefed about Mathews' mission so they could cover if needed.

Cain clicked a couple of times with his mouse to bring up the message and read the text from Mathews. Smiling, he reached for the 'Grey Phone' and dialed a number from memory. Colored either in grey or an almond color depending on the manufacturer, the grey phone was a secure, entirely separate telephone system used exclusively by intelligence organizations, and cross-connected to similar secure systems serving the special operations community.

"Simon."

"Hey buddy. It's Dave. My nephew just texted me." Cain told Colonel Simon.

"Good. Everything OK?" Simon inquired.

"Ops normal from what I can see. No duress phrase in the message and he reports that he's ready to use his new toy in the morning."

"Good. Looks like the hunt is really on then. Think Mathews will find him?"

"If FULLBACK is in that town, he should find him. The guy has to leave his house at some point, or send body guards out if he has them," Cain told him.

"If FULLBACK has body guards, it will be tougher."

"One thing at a time," Cain advised.

"Yeah," Simon agreed. Like Cain, he had been serving his country for decades, and knew that being patient, especially when sending the 'kids' out into the field, was a requirement. Mathews was one of the best Tier One operators they had ever recruited into the Wraiths, and Simon knew he was their best shot at finding him.

"You'll call me?"

"The moment he reports in again," Cain assured him. "I'll be spending the next few nights here while this gets started. The senior watch officer has orders to wake me whenever Mathews contacts us."

"Same here. I'll be sleeping within reach of this phone until he's out of denied territory."

Cain was sure he would. Simon really cared about the people he sent into the field.

"Talk to you later," Cain said before hanging up.

Once the phone was back in its cradle, Cain rose, and walked off the elevated platform toward the drone station.

"Emily?"

Thompson turned when he called her name.

"Yes, David?" Cain insisted on being on a first name basis with everyone on the watch, unless there was a general officer or a member of congress visiting. He felt it made for a close-knit team, and so long as everyone remembered that there really was a chain of command, the more informal atmosphere helped keep communication between team members flowing freely in a crisis.

"Your friend Mathews just checked in. He wanted me to tell you he misses having you watching his back."

"Where is he this time?" Thompson asked.

Cain hesitated. Technically, Mathews' mission was a need-to-know matter, but Thompson held the same CAPTIVE DRAGON special access program read in that he did, and she knew full well the risks every Wraith team member took when they went into the field. Moreover, as his lead drone operator, she just might end up covering the capture operation for FULLBACK, if things got that far.

"He's in Jordan on a surveillance mission."

Thompson looked concerned, but only briefly. "Well, Jordan is a friendly country, so if his cover gets blown, he should be alright."

"He should be," Cain assured her, choosing not to explain just who Mathews was supposed to be surveilling.

"Good," Thompson said, "My husband is still looking forward to meeting him. Especially after I spent all that time with his team chasing that SOB Aziz."

"I'll let you know when he's headed back. Maybe he can get out here TDY on the way home."

"Thanks." Thompson told him as he turned and headed back to his desk. Once Cain settled himself, he started typing.

Good to hear from you, nephew. Aunt Emily says hi, and hopes you can drop in on us after you're done with your survey work for the university. Glad you got some sleep during the trip. I talked to your Uncle Simon today – he says hi and hopes you enjoy the sights. Let me know if you need anything.

CHAPTER 6

Al-Amriki rose before dawn, stretching in the pre-dawn darkness before swinging his legs out of the bed, standing up, and heading for the bathroom to urinate. Once he was finished, he began to wash, ensuring that he met all the requirements of the Wudu by washing his face, arms, head, and feet, before dressing in a sand-colored Thawb over white Sirwal pants. Most of the men in Ar-Ruwayshid seemed to prefer the colors, likely because they lived in a warm climate, and Al-Amriki felt it was better to blend in.

Once dressed, he went to the central room and laid out the woven prayer mat his parents had given him when he turned fifteen in the center of the floor, and stood at one end, facing south towards Mecca. He began to pray, adding three extra rakats during the entire SalÇt, to make up for missing the Maghrib prayer time during his return from Syria.

When he was finished, he rolled up the prayer mat, returning it to its storage cabinet before walking into the kitchen to fix himself a breakfast of yogurt and fruit, followed by black coffee. After his second cup of the cardamom-flavored beverage, called 'sada' throughout Jordan, it was time to get to work.

Al-Amriki left the dishes in the sink for later, and took a quick detour into the bedroom to take the special iPhone, slipping it in a pants pocket. On the way toward the front door, he scooped up several USB memory sticks lying on the planning table, putting specific ones in different pockets of his Thawb. The table was still covered with the plans for the next operation, and left them as they were, assured that in this sleepy little desert town, the inhabitants held no surprises for him. None would enter his house uninvited, focused as they were on their own lives and respecting each other's privacy as was proper in this culture. With the memory sticks safe in his pockets, he left the safe house, locking the door behind him.

The morning sun was well above the horizon, and Al-Amriki paused for a few moments to enjoy the feel of the sun's warm rays on his face before starting his morning walk. Al-Amriki preferred his morning walk over the afternoon one – the heat of the desert in the afternoon could be unpleasant, and the cooler mornings in the new morning's light reminded him of the few summers his parents had taken him to the beach as a young boy.

Ar-Ruwayshid seemed to be as busy as the town ever got, being so far out in the desert, away from Jordan's larger towns and cities. Al-Amriki encountered a few older men as he made his way north then east at a steady pace, greeting those he passed with a raised hand and a pleasant 'Peace be upon you'. He thought it a pity that the people of this town were so poor, but they had limited opportunities. Ar-Ruwayshid was a weigh-station on trade routes between Baghdad and Amman, one modern transportation had made obsolete with cargo hauled by tractor trailers that could make non-stop trips between the two capitals.

From his brief talks with some of the shopkeepers, he had learned that all the children attended the small primary school in town, and when they were high school age, they moved west to live with relatives during their high school years. Those that had no relatives in western Jordan bought or borrowed high school level textbooks and studied on their own or with the help of their parents so that they could apply to a good university in Amman.

Those who did not seek higher learning were destined never to leave the town, instead learning the best way to raise sheep and chickens in the arid climate, or run the small number of shops that served the town's basic needs. All their commerce lived and died by the meager 'archeological tourist' trade and the local population's need for menial services.

Continuing his way east, Al-Amriki spied the steel latticework of the tower in the distance, just to the north of Highway 10. The white, vertical poles of the cellular antennas were the most prominent, reflecting the morning sun strongly, and arrayed in a single three hundred and sixty degree circle about forty meters high. The three microwave radio antennas were above them, red colored mesh antennas shaped into shallow bowls that enabled the local telephone switch's ability to route phone calls across long distances.

One of the microwave antennas pointed north towards the airbase, providing a dedicated link for the Jordanian military to use. Al-Amriki presumed that at some point, the Jordanian government would lay fiber optic cable out to Ar-Ruwayshid, finally rendering the ancient microwave communications system obsolete, but given the small population of the town, he supposed the government had not thought it cost effective yet.

Nearly ten meters below the cell antennas were the white, octagon-shaped flat panels of the government-provided long-range wireless internet service, with enough gain to allow anyone within two miles of the town that had a wireless adapter on a computer, iPad, or cell phone the ability to connect to the internet.

Al-Amriki expected that some of the young men in Ar-Ruwayshid would no doubt find inspiration and purpose in many of the jihadist videos on the Internet, watched mostly via older model cell phones, iPads, or computers handed down to younger brothers after being purchased in one of the cheaper markets outside of Amman or Zarqa by their older brothers. He shook his head at the dismal prospects for such young men, wishing that Allah had blessed them with greater fortune than could be found in Ar-Ruwayshid.

Al-Amriki returned his attention to the side road he was walking along, maintaining his leisurely pace, to work his way farther north along the side road until he reached the east/west expanse of Highway 10. Checking both directions for traffic, he crossed Highway 10 quickly, and turned right to walk against the westbound traffic flow, making sure to stay close to the shoulder.

A few children were on the far side of the highway, playing football on a small patch of open ground between two houses. Watching them for a moment, he had to admire their foresight in stationing one child near the edge of the open ground closest to the Highway while the other children chased the white and black ball around the small pitch, trying to kick it between two green plastic trashcans serving as markers for the makeshift goal.

The owner's wife did all the cooking, and the older boys and younger girls would wait on the customers as needed. The man's oldest daughter, now in her early twenties, spent her days in the university in Amman, her education paid for by her family's business.

Al-Amriki knew the owner, Rashad, very well, and as usual, he was greeted personally when he entered.

"Peace be upon you!" Rashad said in a booming voice.

"And you, my brother." Al-Amriki responded with a smile and a wave.

"Would you like tea?" Rashad inquired as he always did.

"Yes, please," Al-Amriki told him, "but may I use your facilities first?"

"Of course, of course! Your tea will be ready in a moment," Rashad told him, shouting an order into the kitchen.

Al-Amriki worked his way between the plastic tables, moving right to the single bathroom Rashad made available to his guests. Once behind the locked door, Al-Amriki moved purposefully, but without haste.

He removed the cover from the toilet's tank, and flipped it over. Glued to the underside of the tank was a small black felt bag, no more than three inches long and an inch wide. Using two fingers, Al-Amriki reached inside and withdrew a small plastic zip lock bag, then grasped both flaps of the seal and pulled them apart.

Reaching into his right front Thawb pocket, he withdrew one of the USB memory sticks. Handling the memory stick's silvery exterior carefully, he dropped it into the plastic bag, being sure to keep the bag and the memory stick away from the open toilet tank.

He quickly resealed the plastic bag, rolled it tightly, and then slipped it into the open end of the black felt bag, before flipping the toilet tank cover over carefully and replacing it.

Al-Amriki flushed the toilet for show and washed his hands carefully, before exiting the bathroom and returning to his table to find the ceramic cup and a pot of tea and honey waiting. He sat on one of the green plastic chairs arranged around the table, poured the tea, and added a generous amount of honey before stirring it and taking an experimental sip.

Rashad came over, smiling in his usual good-natured way. "How is your tea, Sahib?"

As was the case with servers the world over, Rashad had asked his question in the midst of a sip of tea, and Al-Amriki needed to swallow quickly to answer him.

"It's excellent. Your wife does wonders even with tea."

Rashad smiled very broadly. "Thank you. Can I offer you breads or fruit as well?"

"No, thank you. Just the tea, and then I must go. I have some shopping to do and then I must continue my work on the engineering details for the new water pipes."

"How much longer do you think it will be?" Rashad asked.

"That will be up to the government, my friend. Bringing water from the desalination plant will still take years even after we decide the routes for the piping. If Allah wills it, it should not be more than a year or two."

"Allah be praised and thank you for all your hard work," Rashad said enthusiastically.

"Shokran, and thanks be to Allah," Al-Amriki said, rising to shake Rashad's hand. He sat for a few more minutes, sipping at his tea until it was gone, then left after leaving a half dinar coin for the tea next to the mug.

Once past the makeshift outdoor patio, he stopped at the edge of the highway and knelt to adjust his right sandal. Standard tradecraft when servicing a dead drop like the one at the little café would be to leave a chalk mark or some other physical indicator that the drop had been loaded, but this one was handled differently.

Al-Amriki removed his right sandal and pretended to remove a stone from it. It did not really matter which sandal he did anything to, so long as he did something with his shoes. Somewhere nearby, someone was watching him and looking for the signal. His training told him not to look around and he forced himself to keep his eyes on the sandal while he removed it, fiddled with it, and replaced it before continuing his walk. As long as he made it to the little café within fifteen minutes of its opening, he knew someone would be watching for the signal. He also knew that whoever it was would not approach the café in any way until he was well out of sight, and perhaps longer than that.

Straightening, Al-Amriki continued east. The temperature was rising with the sun. He had more dead drops to fill before noon, and it was important that he get the answers he needed quickly. He had to finish the planning for the next operation for the jihad against the west.

Mathews finished the oatmeal and apple slices he had fixed for breakfast and rinsed the small bowl in the sink. He had slept for nearly ten hours; the fatigue of the long trip and the stress of the initial arrival having worn him out more than he had expected.

He had thought he would be awake most of the night, and settled himself comfortably at the kitchen table, the silenced Sig Sauer within reach, as he played solitaire on the ruggedized Latitude tablet. Three games in, his eyelids had slid shut and his head had fallen far enough forward as he dozed off that he decided lying in the bed was a better option. Placing the Sig on the bed next to him, his right hand resting on the grip, he put his head on the pillow. Sleep claimed him seconds later.

Wide awake now after two cups of coffee and the oatmeal, he made a quick trip to the bathroom, and looked around the rented house to check for anything that appeared out of place before heading outside. The Range Rover's interior was already warm, even this early in the day, and the engine started without protest, its low rumble reassuring.

Mathews performed a quick three-point turn, and backed the four-by-four up to the front door of the house to block the view of any casual passersby. The rented house was far enough from the other homes that the chance of being observed was minimal, but he believed being prudent was a wise course of action, especially since his life might depend on it at some point.

Opening the upper part of the rear lift gate and dropping the lower half, Mathews re-entered the house. A few minutes later, he brought out his 'new toy' hidden beneath a spare sheet he had found in a cabinet in the bathroom, along with a half-full backpack. The backpack held the ruggedized tablet, along with spare food, water, a first aid kit, and extra ammunition for the Sig, which was now tucked safely in the small of his back, next to the CQC-7 combat knife.

The sheet-covered object went into the rear of the Range Rover, but did not fit completely until he folded the rear seats down. The backpack sat on the passenger seat, with the seatbelt woven through the loops of the shoulder straps to hold it securely.

With the house locked up, he drove off, turning south and heading into the desert along the dirt path, checking the rear-view mirrors as he drove. By the time he had reached the three-quarter-mile point, he had seen nothing suspicious, and pulled off the dirt track and braked the Range Rover to a halt.

Mathews let the engine idle for a few minutes while he watched his mirrors, waiting to see if anyone might have followed him. Satisfied, he killed the motor and exited the off-road vehicle. He opened the upper and lower halves of the rear lift gate, and carefully removed the sheet covering the RQ-11C Raven III drone. Mathews hefted the twelve-pound drone out of the back and placed it carefully on the ground, admiring it.

The Raven was not a sleek and sexy aircraft; in fact, it looked like a pint-sized boogie board laid on its edge, with wings and a tail glued onto it. With its nearly six-foot wingspan, and an advanced pair of lithium battery packs, it could stay aloft for more than twenty-four hours at its most efficient cruising speed.

Moreover, because of its shape and relatively small size, the Raven was stealthy, with a radar cross section smaller than a bird and camouflage paint scheme applied top and bottom to reduce its visual signature. The forward third of the nose, taking up nearly eighteen inches of the drone's four-foot length, was detachable, allowing for the installation of 'mission kits' for a variety of purposes. It was the perfect surveillance platform for this kind of mission.

Mathews went over to the passenger side of the Range Rover and retrieved the backpack, laying it on the fold-down portion of the lift gate, before extracting the Latitude tablet. He broke the screen lock with a few taps on the touch sensitive screen and brought up the command and control application for the Raven, which appeared to a casual observer to be the icon for the system-monitoring program for the tablet. The initial giveaway that the software was more than it appeared was the prompt for fingerprint identification, signified by a fingerprint symbol less than a quarter inch in size that appeared in the upper right-hand corner of the display.

Mathews stroked his thumb across the sensor at the upper right of the tablet's water-, sand-, and shock-proof protective case, adjacent to the symbol on the display. The application accepted the biometric proof of his identification and opened immediately.

Turning to look at the Raven, Mathews tapped to bring up the master command display. It appeared at the bottom of the application as a long double ribbon of symbols that turned on and off basic functions. He quickly tapped the main power, camera, radio transmitter, GPS receiver, and diagnostics check.

The upper left of the application showed an artificial horizon, along with speed, altitude, and heading ribbons along the left, right, and top of the horizon, respectively. The upper right showed a live feed from the drone's high definition camera, mounted in the ISR nosecone that Mathews had fitted last night.

The signal meter in the upper left corner of the application showed the maximum six bars of signal strength, which was no surprise, since the drone's transmitter sent its encrypted signal out over a five- to six-mile range, depending on the terrain. Mathews knew from his familiarization briefing about the Raven that the onboard system was smart enough to monitor the local wireless spectrum, searching for less utilized channels and choosing one, lessening the chances that some techno-geek might notice the increased bandwidth usage by an encrypted signal and start asking the wrong questions.

The encryption was state of the art, and for this mission the algorithm and variables employed were only in use by this drone, Mathews' Latitude tablet, and CTS in the event of an emergency, not that Cain or his people could get the signal from the drone nearly eight-hundred miles from the closest American military outpost.

Below the artificial horizon and camera feed was a moving map, with the drone's current location and the waypoints for the search pattern that Mathews had programmed last night. Tapping once to make the moving map window appear to slide 'up' underneath the artificial horizon and camera view windows, he tapped again to display the drone's diagnostics. All systems were green, and the batteries were fully charged.

Tapping again to clear the diagnostic display and bring up the master command display, he tapped the engine start button. The Raven's single pusher propeller immediately came up to idle speed and stabilized.

Mathews looked at all the displays again, tapping to bring the moving map back and checking the direction of the first programmed waypoint in the search pattern. Satisfied, he tapped another button on the master command display. He had fifteen seconds.

Walking over to the Raven, he hefted it with both hands and pointed himself and the nose of the drone in the proper direction. In a few seconds, he heard the pusher propeller's sound pitch higher, and knew the Raven was ready.

Mathews jogged three steps forward over the uneven ground, and used a one-handed throw to launch the Raven III into the air. The microprocessor on the Raven judged the airspeed sufficient to maintain flight and immediately began an optimal climb to its patrol altitude of one thousand feet.

Mathews watched the drone for a few seconds as it climbed away and then returned to the tablet computer. A few quick taps and a longer look at the camera satisfied him that the Raven was off on its first mission over Jordan.

Mathews put the control program into background mode with a couple of taps, and the software minimized itself to the tray in the right-hand corner, appearing as an innocuous system performance icon. If something untoward or unexpected happened to the Raven while it was on patrol, the tablet would send a quick text message to his iPhone via the Bluetooth radio.

Locking the screen and putting the tablet back into the backpack took only a few seconds, and a minute later, with the rear closed and the backpack returned to the passenger seat, Mathews cut a sharp U-turn and headed back into town.

Keeping a wary eye out for anything unusual, he drove only as far north as the intersection with Highway 10 and pulled off the road, turning off the motor and exiting the Range Rover with the backpack. He used the remote to lock the four-by-four and started walking east.

Mathews' needed to get his search underway for FULLBACK, but he had decided last night that he needed to spend a day getting more familiar with Ar-Ruwayshid than he could from just looking at imagery, and it would probably be good to be seen in the local shops buying a few supplies. Doing so would give him the opportunity to share his cover story with some of the local shopkeepers as he 'prepared to visit several locations in the desert east of town'.

Mathews smiled at the incongruity. Being stealthy was his usual stock in trade, and normally he and his team of commandos hit a target and melted away within minutes, leaving as little evidence or 'residual presence,' as the military termed it, as possible. This mission was a departure from that. His cover required a certain amount of visibility in the proper places, but not so much that he might garner the attention of the commander of the military base or the district commander of the Jordanian National Police.

Mathews stopped walking, suddenly remembering that he had not thought about Sam's death since he had arrived in town. That didn't seem fair, especially after how it happened. Not now. He needed to stay on mission. He began walking again, shaking his head slightly. This was not the time to think about Sam. He needed to keep his head in the game and stay focused on the mission.

Moving east, he saw what looked to be a small shop, based on the canned goods and sundries displayed in the window of one of the town's ubiquitous run-down buildings. He put on his friendly 'Mr. Forrestal' face, and opened the door.

Mathews' eyes roved over the interior quickly, and he could see that while the shop was cramped, it was more orderly than the outward appearance of the building suggested. Neat rows of low shelving held all manner of canned goods and packaged foods, while several cases of bottled water and juices were neatly stacked along the walls. Mathews surmised the owner was used to doing business with travelers, since the hand-lettered signs above the cases displayed prices in Iraqi dinar, Jordanian riyal, and European euros.

A clean-shaven man rose from a small table in the corner where an old CRT television was perched to greet him with a friendly wave.

Mathews acknowledged the man in his best Arabic. "As salam alaykum. Sabahul khayr."

The man smiled broadly and responded in English. "Peace be upon you as well, my friend. Good morning."

Mathews smiled in return and extended his hand. "Good morning. Please excuse my poor Arabic. I have tried to study the language, but I have no gift for it."

"No, no," the man replied, his English heavily accented but understandable as Mathews concentrated on it. "I am Youssef."

"Ben Forrestal. I'm out here doing an archeological survey. My university arranged for me to rent a house from Mr. Obeidat."

Youssef's eyes lit up, sensing the opportunity to sell more than he might normally. "Ah, yes. Welcome to Jordan. Has Obeidat offered you Mansaf? His wife makes the best Mansaf in all of Jordan."

Mathews smiled at the man's civic pride, "Yes. He and his family were very kind to me, thank you. I was hoping to purchase a few things for some of my longer trips into the eastern desert. May I look around?"

"Of course, of course. Please. If I do not have what you need, I can order it from my cousin in Amman."

"That's very kind of you," Mathews said, reaching out to shake the man's hand again. "It's no trouble?"

"No, no. I do this for many students in the past who come to our country to study the old ruins. If you order in the evening, it will be here in the morning. If you order in the morning, it can be here in the afternoon."

An hour and a half later, Mathews' pack was bulging and ten pounds heavier from the fresh oranges, sealed foil packages of tuna and salmon, and freshly baked pita bread from the shelves of Youssef's little store. Youssef, after seeing what he had selected, and how much, had even pressed him to accept a cup of coffee. The coffee would naturally lead to conversation, so Mathews had deferred for now. Youssef offered to prepare a package of fruits and other items for him every two days that he could stop by for.

Mathews took the opportunity to look in on three other little shops as he wandered through town, and spent a few minutes introducing himself with his cover name and making small talk. The first, a grocery and sundries store much like Youssef's, carried a lesser variety of merchandise. The second was exclusively a home improvement store, the closest thing to a Home Depot he was likely to find out here. And the last was a shade-tree mechanic with a good selection of tools and floor jacks, who reluctantly admitted that he could do little for the Range Rover if it broke down.

Surprisingly, Youssef and the other owners had not pressed him for details about his purpose in Jordan. Youssef had preferred instead to talk about the chances for the Jordanian national team to win the World Cup in the coming year, while the man running the pseudo-Home Depot wanted to spend time talking about the British fascination with cricket, which Mathews could not help him with. The shade-tree mechanic just wanted to talk about supercars and whether or not he had seen the latest season of the new 'The Grand Tour' car program on the Internet.

Mathews came away from all these visits with the impression that the average citizen of Ar-Ruwayshid was more likely to be worried about their day-to-day lives than anything he might be doing. While hardly unsurprising, Mathews was pleased to see that the people of Ar-Ruwayshid, most of whom were likely practicing Muslims, were the kind of innocents he swore to protect and defend when he joined the profession of arms, and he resolved that any surveillance or capture plan he implemented would minimize or eliminate any risk to them.

Back on the street, he worked his way east toward what the shade-tree mechanic described as the 'computer store', crossing Highway 10 to the south side of the road and keeping his eyes open for a hand-painted sign over a single-story building. He spied it another twenty yards east, and while the Arabic lettering was incomprehensible, the symbols of a lightning bolt and a computer at either end marked it as his destination.

Mathews walked in and greeted the owner using his rudimentary Arabic and, as had become the norm on his little walking tour, the owner shifted to English immediately.

"Welcome, sir." The man was thickly bearded and mildly overweight, with a hawk-like nose and thick brows, his white Thawb wrinkled and smeared with dust from the open desktop computer he was leaning against when Mathews walked in. Unlike the other shop owners, this man's English carried only a trace of accent, and Mathews guessed he was university educated.

"Hello," Mathews said, walking forward to offer his hand. The man took it hesitantly, after wiping his hand on his Thawb, leaving another dusty smear on it.

"Sorry," the owner said.

"Please think nothing of it," Mathews replied, expecting that the man was mildly embarrassed that his hand was not clean. "I'm beginning an archeological survey out in the eastern desert and I've been stopping in to the stores here in town as I learn my way around."

"Ah," the owner replied. "I see. I am Abbud. I regret that I don't have the kind of equipment you are probably used to at your university..." Abbud seemed embarrassed again, and sweeping his eyes throughout the interior, he could see why. The store seemed to consist mostly of the little repair area Abbud was working at when Mathews walked in, one display case with a few memory sticks, and a few boxes of CDs. On top of the display case were two computers, both of which were at least seven or eight years old, and probably not worth more than $200 each, assuming they even booted up.

Mathews waved away Abbud's discomfort and smiled. "Thanks, but I brought a tablet with me." Thinking quickly in an effort to eliminate the man's embarrassment, he added, "I was hoping you could order me portable hard drives in the five-hundred gigabyte to one terabyte range. I didn't bring any spares to store the photographs I'll be taking."

Abbud's face lit up at the opportunity for an unexpected sale and thought a moment. "I can have them delivered from Zaqat or Amman in a day or so, but I don't think I can get drives with such small capacities. These days, the more widely available standard size is three terabytes."

Mathews knew the truth of that, but pursed his lips to appear unsure about purchasing such a large capacity drive. To give himself a moment, he slipped the backpack off his shoulders and let it rest on the floor.

Hoping to make a sale, Abbud offered, "What kind of camera are you using? I might be able to get you additional memory cards for it instead."

"A Nikon Coolpix AW300." Mathews responded without hesitation. The new Nikon was a four-hundred-dollar waterproof and shockproof digital point and shoot that was less than five inches long, three inches high, and only an inch thick. "It takes SD type memory cards, but I'd prefer high capacity SDXC cards if you can get them."

Abbud went back to his work area, retrieved an iPad from his desk, and started tapping. After a few minutes and some apparent delays from the wireless network, he said, "I can get you either one hundred and twenty-eight gigabyte or two hundred and fifty-six gigabyte SDXC cards." Abbud looked up and did some fast math in his head. "I must ask sixty dinar or seventy-two euros for the one hundred and twenty-eight gigabyte cards; and one hundred and twenty dinar or one hundred and ten euros for the two hundred and fifty-six gigabyte cards."

Mathews thought about it, and decided to haggle a bit, knowing the man was probably padding his profit a little. "Can you get me two of the one hundred and twenty-eight gigabyte cards for one hundred and fifteen euros?"

Abbud responded without hesitation, "One hundred and twenty-five euros."

Mathews was ready as well. "How about one hundred and twenty?"

Abbud nodded. "I shall order them now and you can pick them up tomorrow."

Mathews reached into his pocket to pay the man. "I can pay you now."

"La, la," Abbud responded quickly in his native language before switching back to English. "No, my friend. I take you as a man of your word, and I will only accept payment after you come to pick up the cards."

"I appreciate that, but I will likely be in the eastern desert tomorrow and I would not want you to be in debt to your supplier."

"It is no trouble," Abbud assured him.

Abbud waved off his entreaties, even when Mathews insisted that he did not want Abbud in debt for his customer, and gave up when Abbud insisted that it was his pleasure to accommodate a guest in Jordan.

Mathews hefted his backpack again; slipping the straps over his shoulders again, shook hands warmly with Abbud, and thanked him before heading for the door. He opened the door to leave, and turned to give Abbud a friendly wave goodbye. When he turned back, a bearded Arabic man in his late twenties or early thirties stood on the other side of the door, obviously waiting for him to exit, studying him intently.

Mathews' eyes widened slightly in surprise, and then he smiled slightly and said, "Asif, shokran," apologizing and thanking the man for waiting, and he headed out the door. The young man entered Abbud's store and closed the door behind him, and Mathews continued east down the street, spying what appeared to be a café with an awning-covered group of plastic tables outside. Crossing the street, he headed over, thinking it might be a good time to get some local coffee.

Abbud greeted his new patron with a large smile. "Good morning, Sahib. Peace be upon you." This man was one of his best customers, a regular that often came in to purchase laptops and had a standing order for ten USB memory sticks every week. Today was his normal day to pick up the weekly order.

"Peace be upon you as well," Al-Amriki replied.

"May I offer you coffee?" Abbud asked genially.

"Thank you, no. I have a number of errands to do today for my company."

"The planning for the water project goes well?" Abbud inquired as he bent down to find the box he usually kept the man's memory sticks in after they arrived. Like the others in the town that knew about Al-Amriki's fictional water project, Abbud hoped the improvement would see Ar-Ruwayshid's fortunes rise.

"Yes, it does." Al-Amriki thought quickly. "Were you able to make a sale to the westerner?" he asked, gesturing toward the door.

"Ah, yes," Abbud told him. "Another university student studying the ruins in the desert. He needs SD memory cards for one of his cameras."

"Oh," Al-Amriki said. "Did he happen to mention what university sponsored him?"

"No," Abbud told him. "Obeidat usually rents one of his houses to the various universities when they need them. You might ask him if you don't run into the westerner again."

"I'll do that," Al-Amriki said, his mind moving along at lightning speed. "Perhaps I will have that coffee Abbud. You were generous earlier, and it occurs to me that we have not had a chance to talk about your son lately. Is he still at school?"

"Yes, he is," Abbud told him, obviously proud of the young man. "Let me go into the back for a moment and make you a fresh cup and we can speak."

While Abbud busied himself with the coffee pot and cups in the rear of the store, Al-Amriki took a long look out the window. The westerner was sitting at an outside table at Rashad's little café across the street, a few doors up, poring over what appeared to be a map and sipping the strong Arabic cardamom-laced coffee that Rashad liked to make. He watched him carefully for several minutes until Abbud returned with their coffees. The westerner never looked up from his work, or glanced back at the store even once as Al-Amriki watched him.

Mathews adjusted his position on the unforgiving and mildly unstable plastic chair and kept his eyes downcast. One of the plastic chair's legs had worn smooth enough over time that it was a quarter inch too short, and he had to sit in a particular way to keep it steady.

Mathews reached for the coffee again, still stunned by what happened. He literally walked into FULLBACK as he was leaving Abbud's store and it had taken every ounce of self-control he had to try and cover his shock, hoping the smile and polite words had covered his momentary surprise.

At least he thought it was FULLBACK. Aside from the sheer luck involved in such an encounter, he still was not completely sure it was Al-Amriki. His mind had raced as he walked across Highway 10, body on auto-pilot and mentally flipping through the photographs from the intelligence briefing, checking and re-checking them against the face of the man waiting for him to leave Abbud's computer store.

Sitting at the café, and doing his best to keep the front door to Abbud's store in sight with only his peripheral vision, he tried to decide on a course of action. Verifying it was FULLBACK was the first step, but he could not risk going back into the store while FULLBACK was there for any reason. Al-Amriki had just seen a western face in a store he frequented. For obvious reasons, he also could not return and give Abbud the third degree about the man that walked in as he was leaving.

Mathews toyed briefly with the idea of tailing the man himself, holding him at gunpoint in an alley to verify that his face matched the photos he had stored in the encrypted memory on his iPhone, and shooting him; then banished the thought from his mind. He had already decided he was not a murderer.

Instead, he pulled a 1:10,000 scale geological survey map of Ar-Ruwayshid and a section of the desert to the east out of the backpack, now propped on one of the empty chairs next to him and unfolded it across the table. He pretended to study it while he sipped his coffee and thought.

When nothing came to mind immediately, he went back to the basics of his training and began considering his available assets. Suddenly it occurred to him exactly what he could do without confronting or tailing FULLBACK. For show, he finished his coffee, waved at the café's proprietor to get his attention, and asked him for more coffee. While he waited, he rearranged the backpack and the map.

He moved the map aside and stood to pluck the backpack off the chair, laying it shoulder strap side down on the table, and unzipped the two cargo compartments, withdrawing a book from beneath the foil sealed tuna packets in the larger compartment.

Leaving the backpack where it was, he laid the map out over it again so that the lower third of the map lay propped up on the backpack, and completely covered the unzipped cargo compartments with about eight inches of map hanging past the openings toward him on the table.

Next, he opened the book, making a small show of looking for the proper page, and then laid it on the upper part of the map, ensuring that the map would not blow away in a sudden gust of wind or strong breeze.

The proprietor returned with his coffee in a small pot and he thanked the man as he poured. Mathews sipped, then used the small pot and coffee cup to hold the map in place by positioning them at the loose corners.

Once he had the map fixed in place, Mathews used one hand to withdraw the Latitude tablet from the second compartment, tapping quickly to open it and bring up the command application for the Raven. A quick check of the moving map showed it nearly a mile east, nearly to the end of the third leg of the twenty-leg photomapping mission he had programmed into it last night.

Mathews looked at the moving map and located the little blue dot that represented the tablet computer's position, based off its reception of the available GPS satellite signals. He tapped the end of the fourth preprogrammed leg for the drone and dragged it to the little blue dot. He had to move it twice to get it right where he wanted it, then he double-tapped the end-point to bring up a card with detailed instructions for the adjusted navigation point.

Clearing the previous instructions on the card, he selected 'Orbit' and '200 Yard' from the dropdown menu for the radius of the orbit, then 'Full Motion Video'. He double checked the settings, and tapped 'Commit'. As an afterthought, he brought up the diagnostic menu, and saw that all the systems were green. Another tap and he checked the display on the card for the ETA to the next waypoint – two minutes.

Working as quickly as he could without betraying his haste, Mathews locked the tablet, and slipped it back into the backpack, using what appeared to be another look at the book to hold the backpack in place. Once he had the tablet tucked in, he moved the coffee pot, cup, and book to pack away the map, and then put the book back in the pack, before finishing his office.

Mathews rose, checked to be sure he had not left anything behind, and tucked a five euro note under the coffee pot as payment. Satisfied that he had done all he could for the moment, he shouldered the backpack and made his way south across Highway 10, never once looking in the direction of Abbud's store.

Abbud was still talking about his son when Al-Amriki caught a flicker of movement out the window. The westerner had been studying a map at Rashad's café, and as far as Al-Amriki could tell, paid no attention to Abbud's, apparently intent upon his work.

Moreover, Al-Amriki had not seen any other signs of other westerners on the street, and no one had joined the man at the café. Al-Amriki knew a great deal about the Americans and their methods. He thought it very unlikely that they or their British allies would send a single man, especially someone who was so obviously not a Jordanian, to hunt him, so he did his best to curb his initial urge towards paranoia.

Still, it would be wise to be cautious. Al-Amriki politely interrupted Abbud's latest tale of his son's academic achievements and thanked him for the coffee before making an excuse about having more errands to run. He paid Abbud for his purchase in euros, tucked away the small package of replacement USB memory sticks in his Thawb, and left Abbud's little store, doing his best not to show too much haste.

Rather than setting off across Highway 10 immediately, Al-Amriki just stood still, looking slowly up and down the roadway. There were one or two men walking east, and Al-Amriki recognized them as locals, remembering seeing them both with their wives and children on various walks in his time there.

An old white Toyota pickup drove past him on the river of asphalt, speeding west, Iraq far in its wake. He looked at the driver and immediately dismissed him – another Jordanian or perhaps Iraqi, intent on getting back to Amman or Zaqr quickly for another load of fresh produce or rice, judging by the stenciling on the empty crates and brown sacks in the truck bed that whipped back and forth from the turbulence created by the pickup's cab.

Thinking quickly, Al-Amriki crossed Highway 10 and walked over to

Rashad's café, doing his best to remain casual. When he reached the outdoor seating area, he chose a table nearest to the building, sitting with his back to the exterior wall – if a threat materialized it would not be from behind him. When Rashad came to ask for his order, he chose coffee and a small plate of baklava, wanting something sweet with the strong coffee Rashad always brewed, and stopped him before he could walk away.

"While I was over at Abbud's I noticed you had a westerner here."

"Ah yes," Rashad replied. "He was very polite, but overpaid as all western-ers do. I shall give the extra money to the Imam as Zakat." Tipping was not exactly frowned upon in Arab society, but Rashad was old-fashioned and preferred to be paid only what he believed was a fair price for his services.

"Yes, they do believe the world revolves around money. It is a shame they do not understand the true nature of things. Did he say why he had come to Ar-Ruwayshid?"

"No," Rashad shook his head. "He was studying a map of the desert to the east of here, and the book he used had many pictures of some of the ruins in the area. I cannot read English well you know."

"Ah," Al-Amriki said, "It was in English?"

"Yes, perhaps he is an archeologist?" Rashad opined. "I'll be right back with your coffee and baklava.

Al-Amriki sat there, watching the highway and surrounding buildings and musing on the situation. There was no sign of anything untoward. He noticed a small group of three Jordanian men walking along the highway towards the café. They stopped about fifty yards away, talking animatedly amongst them-selves and he could just catch snatches of their conversation as their voices rose and fell. From what he could make out, they were discussing which school would be best for one of the men's daughters. One of the men was dead set against the girl going to university, and the other two were vehemently disagreeing with him and trying to get the conversation back to which school to choose.

There was no sign of the westerner, and Al-Amriki began to feel that he was being overly paranoid. If the Americans or their allies were running a count-er-terrorism operation in Jordan, he would know about it from the sources the Islamic State had in the Jordanian government and from another source he kept in independent contact with.

For now, Al-Amriki thought the best course of action would be to watch the street a little longer, looking for any sign of surveillance while he finished his coffee and baklava. He had loaded all the dead drops before heading to Abbud's shop, and while he needed to continue his planning work, it could wait another hour or so.

Two hours later, with only a few baklava crumbs remaining on his plate and the dregs of his third pot of strong coffee in the bottom of the pot, and he still had not seen anything even remotely suspicious. He also had not caught any sign of the westerner. Surely, the man would have peeked around a corner, walked past the café, or come up with some excuse to return to the area if he was under surveillance.

Finally reassured that the presence of the western man in Ar-Ruwayshid posed no significant threat, and with the heat of the day rising as midday approached, Al-Amriki rose, leaving exactly enough dinar for the bill, and began to head back to his safe house. He took his usual circuitous route and backtracked a few times as an extra precaution, but by the time he had reached the little safe house, he was completely confident that the westerner had nothing to do with him.

CHAPTER 7

Nearly a mile away in the house Obeidat had rented him, Mathews sat at the kitchen table, staring at the video feed from the Raven. The man he thought was Al-Amriki had just entered a small house at the western edge of Ar-Ruwayshid.

Tapping quickly, he halted the real-time recording of the Raven's video feed and saved the last three hours of it to the tablet. Doing so created a gap in the real-time video coverage, since the bandwidth of the wireless link to the Raven was limited, and it could not support a simultaneous download of the MPEG video file from the Raven's on-board flash memory and maintain the live video feed.

While the Raven communicated with the tablet, Mathews went into the bedroom where he had left the Raven's Pelican hard case on the floor at the foot of his bed. He opened it, retrieved a spare four-gigabyte USB memory stick from the small cache of eight snuggly stored in the last layer of foam in the bottom and repacked, then closed the case.

When he returned to the tablet, the download was only a few seconds from completion. The download progress bar reached the one hundred percent mark and the tablet dutifully reported 'Download Complete' via a little pop up window, which dismissed itself after three seconds. The Raven's command software automatically restarted the live video feed without any prompting, and Mathews watched the video window carefully.

Mathews did not see any movement around the little house, and he had to assume that FULLBACK was still inside. The download had not taken more than a couple of minutes, and while downloading the mission data from a drone normally happened after its return to base, Mathews did not want to wait, and he was unwilling to recall the Raven early. He might miss FULLBACK's movements at the house.

Trying to contain his excitement, Mathews blew out a breath and considered his next steps. He double-checked the video feed, ensuring that the drone was still recording. Satisfied, he tapped a few times on the tablet's display, making the live video feed window embedded in the command application pop out into its own standalone window. He wanted to watch it while he worked.

Tapping quickly, he minimized the rest of the command software, slipped the USB memory stick into one of the tablet's USB 4.0 slots, and began copying the video file to it. The USB 4.0 interface ran at nearly twenty gigabits per second, and the copy action took only seconds to complete.

As the tablet worked, Mathews knew that it was automatically encrypting the file it wrote to the memory stick. As a routine precaution, the experts at NSA had prepped the tablet for the mission by ensuring that the tablet's program, download, and storage directories were completely encrypted with a 2048-bit key burned into the chips of this tablet and just one other, expressly for these kinds of missions. Having studied the details as part of his orientation as a member of the Wraith unit, Mathews had a great deal of confidence in the security of the data stored on the tablet if it fell into non-U.S. hands, especially since he was on his own in a foreign country.

If someone stole the tablet or the USB stick, or he lost them during the mission, the contents of those directories would be unreadable without thousands of hours of brute force trial and error with a modern supercomputer, or Mathew's twenty-character password and thumbprint.

When the tablet finished copying the files to the USB stick, Mathews opened the original file and began to review the three hours of footage, fast forwarding through the first thirty-five minutes of video as the Raven worked its pre-programmed patrol, and then deviated at Mathews' direction while he was sitting outside the little café.

He ran it at normal speed once he saw that area of Highway 10 appear on screen, a diagonal slash through the frame because of the Raven's flightpath. Another few seconds and Abbud's little electronics store was in view, then the café. Mathews caught brief sight of a man he soon recognized as himself carrying a loaded backpack and walking south away from Highway 10 as the Raven began to orbit the area.

Mathews recalled thinking immediately after crossing the highway that he could only trust in luck so much to get a positive ID on FULLBACK and it was imperative he get to a secure location where he could remotely command the drone as quickly as possible. He had quickly walked south nearly one hundred yards, and then worked his way west through the alleys between the houses until he crossed the road that bisected the town into east and west and led to his Range Rover.

Once across and sure he was out of sight, he practically jogged north to the corner of Highway 10 to reach his waiting Range Rover, started it, cut a sharp U-turn, and headed straight back to the rental property. As a precaution, he parked the Range Rover behind the rented house to keep it out of sight of the casual observer or FULLBACK – just in case the man had started prowling the neighborhood after their chance encounter.

Returning his attention to the video, Mathews watched for an orbit or two, but saw no movement on the street. Fortunately, the zoom level of the Raven's camera was wide enough that he could see the street-facing portion or the front door of Abbud's store no matter where the Raven was in its orbit of the area.

At the start of the third orbit, Mathews' impatience got the better of him and he started to fast forward, first at one and a half times normal, then two. As the video juddered and jumped a little, the increased playback speed amplifying the normally small sway and circular motion of the orbit, Mathews saw movement near Abbud's store.

Leaning closer to the tablet's display in his excitement, Mathews tapped the playback controls to drop it back normal speed and then rewound so he could watch from the beginning.

After waiting a few moments outside the store, the man he thought was Al-Amriki crossed the road toward the café with a purposeful but measured stride, choosing a table near the building and keeping his back to the wall. The owner came out, and presumably took his new patron's order, but then Al-Amriki called him back just as he started to walk away. A change in order? No. The owner seemed to gesture once or twice toward the table Mathews had sat at.

Mathews' eyes narrowed. Al-Amriki was asking questions about him. The exchange between the two men did not last more than forty seconds, Mathews saw, rewinding and replaying the segment again and checking the time display. Mathews decided FULLBACK was being cautious.

A few minutes later, the owner returned with a pot and a small tray of something, placing them on the table. No extended conversation this time, he just put the food and drink down and left.

Mathews scrutinized the video closely. Al-Amriki seemed to be watching the street and surrounding area carefully as he ate and sipped. After nearly ten minutes, Mathews decided to speed up the video, but not too much. He ran it at twice-normal speed and watched carefully, sneaking glances at the live feed from time to time.

The owner returned twice more, and each time Mathews slowed the recording to normal speed and watched carefully. He could not see anything to arouse his suspicions. No long conversations, nothing untoward. The owner just brought two more pots of tea or coffee and left while Al-Amriki watched the street.

He was waiting to see if I came back. The realization hit him suddenly, and he quickly rewound the recording to the moment when Al-Amriki first sat down, noted the time, and sped forward until he rose to leave. Nearly three full hours.

Returning to the beginning again, he advanced the recording at triple speed and watched carefully. Al-Amriki never reached for a cell phone or spoke to anyone other than the owner. Mathews had to give FULLBACK credit, he had courage. A lesser man might have called in armed assistance or for extraction. The professional part of Mathews' mind found himself grudgingly admiring the terrorist SOB. It wouldn't stop him from grabbing or killing the bastard, but Al-Amriki had guts.

Mathews rolled the tape at normal speed again to watch Al-Amriki walk home, wanting to look for anything he may have missed. He could instantly see that FULLBACK was employing counter-surveillance techniques. The Tango took a circuitous route, doubled back three times, and crossed Highway 10 twice, once south to north, then north to south before he approached a very small and nondescript house on the western edge of Ar-Ruwayshid and entered. Mathews froze the image on the playback and grinned suddenly. Found you, you bastard.

Just as quickly his smile died. He needed to confirm the identification. He reversed the playback again, looking for a specific moment when the man he believed was Al-Amriki crossed the highway, leaving the café. The Raven had been just crossing the south edge of the highway, and Al-Amriki was striding purposefully across the road, starting his counter-surveillance routine. His head was up and he looked to the right for oncoming traffic. There!

Mathews froze the image. The look angle of the drone's camera and the direction Al-Amriki was looking gave Mathews the still he wanted. Using the tools embedded in the tablet's software, Mathews digitally zoomed in on Al-Amriki, getting as tight a shot of his face as possible before the resolution of the image began to break down.

Thinking back to the images of Al-Amriki he had studied with Colonel Simon before the mission began, he was nearly certain this was the man. The shape and angles of his nose, cheekbones, and forehead all seemed right. The beard made the positive identification more difficult, hence the need for confirmation.

Reaching for his iPhone, Mathews unlocked it, and accessed the photos application and pulling up the album entitled 'Travel'. He had to page through the sixty or so images of Rome and Istanbul the techs at Wraith Base had loaded until he found the image of the Mediterranean taken on the south coast of Italy.

Tapping the image to make it fill the phone's screen, he turned the phone ninety-degrees to 'landscape' orientation. The image dutifully rotated, and then he rested his right thumb on the fingerprint sensor. The special software built into the photos application by the Wraith Base geeks noted the image selected, read his thumbprint, then unlocked and read an encrypted section of the phone's memory. The still images of Al-Amriki Cain had provided with the intelligence briefing appeared on the phone's display.

Mathews held the phone next to the tablet's screen, flicking through the images on his phone and comparing them with the still image captured by the Raven's camera. Even with the beard, it was a match. Bingo. Mathews pressed the button on the phone to return the images to the iPhone's encrypted memory and got to work. His field ID of FULLBACK was a start, but nobody back in D.C. was going to approve a capture operation based on just that.

Tapping away on the tablet, Mathews zoomed in and out on the still image, taking several 'snaps' at different magnifications. With each 'snap', the software automatically saved the day, time, and geocoordinates for where Al-Amriki stood, storing them as embedded data within each high-resolution digital image.

When he had a dozen different images, he saved them all off onto the USB stick as a precaution, and then compressed all of them as a single GZIP file on the tablet. Next, he called up images of the little house Al-Amriki entered, taking both wide-angle and close-up views from the recorded feed from the Raven. Then he compressed those as well.

With the images ready to go, Mathews took both zipped files and encrypted them, then moved the files, innocuously named 'Photos1.enc' and 'Photos2.enc', into a special directory on the tablet, before activating the Bluetooth radio on the tablet with a couple of taps.

Snatching his iPhone off the desk again, he activated its Bluetooth radio. The tablet and iPhone automatically linked via the short-range Bluetooth radio and both encrypted files transferred to the phone automatically. He checked the signal meter on the phone to be sure he had a good cellular link, pulled up the texting application and started typing.

Hi Uncle Dave. I'm all settled in here now. Went shopping today for some additional SD memory cards for my camera – I never pack enough before I travel. Thought you might like to see some pictures of the town and the people I met. Came across a really nice guy today that was kind enough to show me his house – thought you might like to see it too. Take care and tell Aunt Emily that I could really use her help with my camera work. It's rough doing so much of the photography all by myself on these trips.

Cain was reading a DIA assessment of the Islamic State's latest activity when his computer played the red alert sound again. He rolled his charcoal colored Herman Miller Aeron chair a few inches to the right, centering himself on his computer monitors and read the message from Mathews. Holy Shit! The kid found him already?

Cain saw the two encrypted files accompanying the text and did not hesitate. He rose from his desk and headed to the rear of the watch center, passing the small kitchenette/break area on the left, and entered the small hallway that led into the executive office and support area.

He took an immediate right into his personal office, walking past the small mahogany conference table and moving to the matching mahogany and glass executive desk on the far side of the room.

Sitting behind the terminal that matched the one on the watch floor, Cain spun the Aeron chair one hundred and eighty degrees. He opened the lower section of the credenza that served as his printer stand, exposing an off-white colored two-drawer safe. Each drawer was fitted with a single black X-07 digital combination lock.

He spun the dial securing the lower drawer rapidly, watching the small LCD window on the top of the black dial as he entered the three numbers of the first combination, then the second. Once the window flashed the letters 'OP', he spun the dial multiple times to the right until he felt the heavy latches retract.

Cain twisted the handle and opened the drawer. The ruggedized tablet containing the matching encryption keys to Mathews' tablet lay in the drawer, in front of dozens of classified files in hanging file folders.

Cain retrieved the tablet and re-locked the drawer quickly, then retraced his steps to the watch floor desk. The message from Mathews still burned bright on the screen, and Cain wasted no time. He pulled forward a loose Ethernet cable laying behind his monitor and snapped the plastic connector into the vacant RJ-45 port on the tablet.

When the two NSA technical wizards had stopped by to install the extra Ethernet cable, load a custom designed piece of software, and drop off the tablet, they had assured Cain that the movement and decryption of the files would be automatic once his computer and the tablet recognized one another by their hard-coded MAC addresses.

Cain watched the tablet and saw the machine spawn multiple windows with images, which his more powerful desktop also began to spawn. Seating himself again, Cain used the mouse to sift through the images on his desktop's screen, selecting one then another until he had checked them all.

By pure coincidence, Cain chose the same close up image Mathews had used to positively identify Al-Amriki. Cain studied it carefully. A couple of more mouse clicks, and the dossier he built on Al-Amriki for Simon and Mathews was open. He spun the mouse wheel, rolling through the pages quickly to find the photos he had pulled from the DIA's database of known Islamic State senior operatives.

He looked back and forth between the two images, comparing lines, angles and the position of the features. Cain took his time, knowing that his assessment would be the first senior level endorsement of Mathews' identification, and that endorsement would put the wheels of the capture operation in motion. After nearly five minutes, he reached for the phone, punching speed dial three.

The call connected on the second ring. "Simon. Heard from Mathews?"

Simon's opening line told Cain his caller ID on the secure line was working. "Yep. Looks like he's found FULLBACK and his current safe house."

"Have you confirmed it?" Simon asked, understandably surprised.

Cain brought up his e-mail and started attaching some of the images. "Yeah, I think his ID is solid, I'm sending you some of the images now so you can see for yourself."

Nearly three thousand miles away, Simon rose from his couch and moved behind his desk. In the corner, Zeus raised his muzzle a few inches off the thick cushion of his dog bed and looked at his master alertly as he moved across the room. Simon caught sight of the Shepherd's attention and put his hand over the mouthpiece of the phone.

"It's OK boy, go back to sleep," Simon said to reassure the animal. Zeus did not heed his master's request immediately, watching Simon for a moment or two before putting his head back down on the dog bed, eyes watchful and his ears erect and attentive to Simon's movements.

Simon unlocked his computer and saw the e-mail from Cain already in his inbox. A few mouse clicks later, and he was satisfied too.

"That's FULLBACK alright," Simon agreed.

"Yep. I need to put a few things in motion here," Cain told him.

"Me too," Simon responded before hanging up.

Mathews sat back from the remains of his meal, glancing again at the tablet, the Raven's command software glowing on the display. The live video feed had automatically switched to night vision mode once the ambient light had dropped below the level programmed into the drone's software. The sun had set nearly two hours ago, and Mathews had taken the time to grab a meal of broiled salmon and vegetables while he watched the video feed. The greens and blacks of the night vision mode were bright and clear on the display, and the silenced Sig Sauer rested on the table next to the tablet.

Mathews checked the diagnostic panel for the charge level of the onboard batteries. The readout said forty-eight percent. When it reached five percent, the drone would automatically return to where he launched it this morning. In the meantime, the Raven would continue to orbit slowly near Al-Amriki's safe house.

Mathews' eyes moved over the tablet's display, scanning Al-Amriki's house repeatedly, looking for movement. As he did so, Mathews did nothing but imagine the different capture scenarios that might unfold, based on the terrain, the size of the structure, and the unknown of the exact interior floor plan.

Every time Mathews ran through a scenario, he inserted himself into the capture operation. As the capture team approached Al-Amriki, he always imagined Al-Amriki making the inevitable reach for a weapon, and Mathews putting two rounds into Al-Amriki's head or chest himself, for Sam.

Mathews shook his head at his fantasizing, and then rubbed his tired eyes. It had been an unexpectedly long day. Developing the information the capture team would need would take time, and doing it singlehandedly was going to be a challenge. He needed to get a few things organized.

Mathews looked at the tablet again to check the video for the umpteenth time and then set to work. He rose from his chair, tucking the silenced Sig Sauer into the small of his back again.

Leaving the dish and silverware behind, Mathews snatched the tablet off the table to keep an eye on the video feed, then headed into the bedroom. He propped the tablet on the end of the bed and opened the Raven's Penguin hard case again, removing the top two layers of protective foam. Mathews pried the two lithium polymer battery packs out of the two slots near the hinge side of the case, then repacked everything.

Tucking the battery packs under his arm, he grabbed the tablet and headed back out to the main room, turning left to walk through the kitchen and out the rear door. Mathews opened the rear lift gate of the Range Rover and opened the built-in storage compartment in the floor. The battery packs fit snugly in the compartment. He re-latched the compartment's door before closing the lift gate.

Four trips later, with the tablet in one hand and various supplies in the other, he had cached two liters of bottled water, four vacuum-sealed foil packs of tuna, and a couple of boxes of crackers in the Range Rover's glove compartment. The supplementary supplies would serve him well in the event that Al-Amriki left town, and Mathews wanted to be well prepared to follow him.

After locking the Range Rover and returning to the house, Mathews retreated to the bathroom, carrying the tablet. He propped the tablet on the small vanity, laid the pistol next to it, and stripped. Once he was naked, Mathews started the shower and got in, soaping up and rinsing off quickly before shaving and wrapping a towel around himself, all with one eye on the video feed, looking for any movement. He stepped out to dry off and, noticing all the fingerprints on the tablet's screen in the diffuse light, he took a moment to wipe the screen with the damp towel.

Mathews picked up the tablet and pistol and headed for the bedroom, dressing in a pair of chocolate-brown cargo pants and a tan t-shirt, leaving a pair of sturdy boots near the foot of the bed before moving to the kitchen.

Mathews checked the safety on the Sig and slipped the weapon into his rear waistband, then pulled a bottle of water from the fridge. Before he closed the fridge door, he made another mental note to throw away the untouched plate full of Mansaf still sitting on the lower shelf before it spoiled. He took his water to the table with the tablet and sat before taking a healthy swig of the water and returning to work.

He made another check on the Raven's systems, and noted the battery life was near forty percent. Tapping the battery life indicator caused it to flip over, showing the estimated time until the battery power ran out: seven hours and eighteen minutes. Mathews knew that sunrise would happen in six hours and twenty minutes, and he made a quick decision.

Thinking that it would be better to work under the cover of darkness, and assuming that Al-Amriki was a devout Muslim that would pray at the usual times, Mathews began tapping on the tablet's screen, altering the Raven's programming.

He altered the stored flight path, commanding the Raven to return to its launch point in five and a half hours, which was roughly the time of the pre-dawn prayer. That would give him a comfortable margin of ten minutes to swap out the nearly depleted battery packs in the drone's fuselage with the second, already charged set he had just stored in the rear of the Range Rover, giving the Raven a fresh twenty-four hours of endurance.

Mathews thought his plan was simple enough. Run the Range Rover out in the morning, meet the returning drone as it landed, swap the batteries, re-launch the drone, and bring the depleted batteries back to the house where he could charge them with the portable charge station in the base of the Pelican hard case. Al-Amriki should be praying at that time, and there would be less chance the man might slip away during the battery swap. Of course, if he was wrong and the man planned an early drive somewhere, he would lose him. It was a risk he would just have to take.

Once Mathews had specified the return time, he also made two other changes, then saved them into the Raven's onboard memory. The first change was the landing zone. He moved the waypoint fifty feet south of the position stored by the Raven when it first reached twenty-feet over the ground, to have plenty of room for the recovery.

The second change was more complex, and he had to enter nearly a dozen waypoints into the navigation software to implement it. The new waypoints ordered the Raven to assume a different flightpath to FULLBACK's safe house in the morning.

Once it arrived, the Raven would fly a new orbital path to monitor the house, the first orbit at an altitude two hundred feet lower than the observation orbits for the rest of the day. The lower orbital altitude during the first pass would give the Raven the best height for good close-up views of the house. Mathews' plan was to capture a series of still images from the video during that orbit, along with the full motion video to study and send back to Cain.

Mathews knew once Cain had the new images and video, he would forward it all to Simon. The colonel would ensure that the fresh intelligence would be passed on to whichever Wraith team pulled the mission for the capture operation.

Lastly, Mathews stored the high-altitude portion of the flight plan so he could recall and execute it quickly if he needed to get it back to surveilling the house with a few quick commands, then double-checked everything.

Once Mathews was satisfied with his work, he got up from the table with the tablet to retrieve a small notebook and pen from his backpack, which lay against the wall, just inside the master bedroom door. Returning to the table, he sat, using the stand built into the tablet's protective case to prop the tablet on a good angle for viewing. The notebook would be his written log of Al-Amriki's movements, and for the next day or two, the tablet's screen would be his entertainment. He lay the notebook and pen next to the tablet and leaned back, taking another pull on the water bottle, his eyes locked on the video feed while he thought over the next phase of his mission.

It would now take a day or two to start developing the required 'pattern of life' information that would support the development of a viable capture plan for Al-Amriki. While Simon and the Wraiths studied the images to familiarize themselves with the area and FULLBACK's hidey-hole, choosing ingress and egress points, if the house became the focus of the op, Mathews would watch his movements and actions live via the Raven's camera.

Mathews' observations via the Raven would let him develop a daily log of Al-Amriki's activities, looking for a place and time that he would be most vulnerable to capture, allowing him to recommend ways to tailor the capture operation to take advantage of those vulnerabilities.

Now that Mathews had discovered FULLBACK's location in Ar-Ruwayshid, he knew he would have to alter his daily activities to fit the target's daily schedule. Eating and sleeping would conform to FULLBACK's activities, with the added burden of needing to scan the video recorded at times when he could not monitor the feed.

Mathews understood from long experience as a Tier One operator that while he could work for three or four days without sleep, it would be better to get at least four or five hours a night to stay combat effective over the extended length of this assignment. He would also need to maintain his cover by spending some time in the field, and most importantly, be seen by the locals doing so—or at least appearing to do so.

Mathews grimaced at that thought, suddenly remembering that Abbud would expect him to stop in tomorrow to pay for and pick up the SD cards he had ordered. Mulling it over, he thought he could skip going to Abbud's little electronics store tomorrow, to give himself at least one day to observe FULLBACK.

Mathews needed to know how often FULLBACK left his house, and whom he met with and when. Although being able to watch Al-Amriki for a week or more would be best, the one day would help him determine if the target frequented Abbud's or the café, or showed any signs of looking for the westerner he ran into today. More broadly, knowing where FULLBACK went in the little town and how often would help Mathews avoid running into him until he wanted to, preferably with an armed team.

Mathews knew he could explain the day's delay to Abbud as finding himself consumed by his research out in the eastern desert, and wanting to ensure Abbud had enough time to ensure the memory cards arrived. From a social standpoint, Mathews thought that would work. Abbud would expect him to be a hard-working student, and since no Middle Easterner would want to be embarrassed by being unable to provide a promised service or goods, he should easily overlook the day's delay. It was a cultural norm that played in his favor in this instance.

One of the other items of the pattern of life portion of Mathew's mission was trying to discover how FULLBACK communicated with the Islamic

State leadership. So far, Mathews had not seen any antennas other than the eighteen-inch, dull gray colored television satellite dish mounted on his safe house.

Mathews suspected FULLBACK used a cell phone or computer to contact the Islamic State, and he could only hope that he might catch the target out in the open using the phone. He would not be able to intercept the call, but the call times and the cell phone type, if he could capture a clear image of it from a low altitude, might be useful intelligence to pass along to Cain and the CTS crowd.

Mathews was not sure they could do anything with that kind of information, since the signals intelligence experts at NSA kept their techniques and capabilities closely held secrets, even from the CTS, but he would pass the information along anyway, if he could develop it.

The better 'get' would be the computer he used, and the opportunity to grab that would present itself during the capture op. The computer should be loaded with details of contacts, on-going plans, and other information that would be useful to the intelligence community after a detailed forensic examination.

Lastly, and perhaps most importantly, Mathews needed to learn whom FULLBACK met with. FULLBACK's associates might be Islamic State agents or supporters, and they might not. He knew it would be his responsibility to watch every interaction carefully, doing his best to judge from a distance whether each person was an innocent civilian, a terrorist, or terrorist ally, something that would be very difficult to do from just watching a video feed off a drone.

Mathews knew that most people in the Department of Defense and intelligence community called the endless watching of drone video 'Predator Porn', mostly for the twenty seconds of footage that recorded the impact of a high explosive projectile striking a known terrorist or terrorist facility after the approval of a strike order.

In reality, the endless hours of monitoring surveillance video could be extremely mind numbing. For that reason, teams of two usually handled pattern of life surveillance, working in shifts and relieving one another every few hours, to reduce the chance of missing something vital.

For Wraith field operations, Cain's team at CTS and people like Emily Thompson usually executed that kind of monitoring. Ten months ago, she had joined Mathews' team as an intelligence observer during the latter stages of one of the most difficult assignments he had faced as a newly-minted team leader, and Mathews expected he was about to gain a new appreciation for her skills.

Mathew's iPhone chimed softly, and he saw the first portion of the text message from Cain in the alert appearing on the locked screen. He unlocked the phone and opened the text window to read the entire text.

Hey nephew. Saw the photos – they're great. Your Cousin Simon and I both think you've made the right friend out there. Hopefully, you can learn a lot from him during your studies. I'm trying to get Aunt Emily to look at the photos, but as usual, she's busy on the computer. I'll let you know when she sees them. Keep up the good work. Simon and I are proud of you.

Mathews smirked at the response, easily seeing through the subtext of the message. Cain and Simon agreed that he had found Al-Amriki, and they expected him to continue his monitoring while they tried to get a drone dedicated to the area to help him out. Now he just had to maintain his cover, monitor the video feed from the Raven and make note of anything that would meet the mission needs, and wait for Cain to contact him again. The next message should tell him exactly what kind of help he could expect to keep an eye on FULLBACK.

In his safe house, Al-Amriki settled himself at his planning desk, put the westerner out of his mind for the time being, and returned to work. The laptop sitting on the left side of the table was hardly the latest technology, but it handled the USB memory sticks without any trouble.

Al-Amriki slid the one from the last dead drop in first, choosing a special decryption program that looked for a file hidden on the drive. Al-Amriki did not know all the details about this particular method of hiding data on a drive, but the technology geek who explained it to him called it an alternate data stream in the Windows environment. A simple method for hiding a message more or less in plain sight, it used the empty space in the area of the hard drive reserved for the characters of the file name to store the data you wished to hide. Even using a command shell to have the computer list the files on the drive would result in nothing more than a list of the stored file names, but not the extra characters hidden 'within' the filename itself.

Al-Amriki's decryption program looked for the characters hidden in the alternate data streams in the files on the drive, all of which were innocuous image files of flowers, trees, etc. Once it had found them all, it concatenated the streams of characters and prompted Al-Amriki for his passphrase. Typing in the twenty-five-character-long passphrase was tedious but necessary. The software applied the decryption algorithm and seconds later the plain text of the message burned bright on the laptop's screen.

Al-Amriki scanned the text quickly, memorizing the information before using the touchpad to order the laptop's decryption program to wipe the decrypted message and eliminate the streams of characters hidden in the filenames on the USB stick.

Next, he composed a reply, detailing the current state of his planning efforts and the nature of the target, and reminding the recipient that he was still waiting for additional intelligence about the target and the surrounding area. Once the reply was complete, he encrypted the message using the same passphrase, and ordered the software to load the encrypted characters of the message into the alternate data streams of each of the files in sequence.

Swapping the more sophisticated piece of software for a simple PGP or Pretty Good Privacy program, he loaded up the other USB memory sticks one at a time, decrypting the files stored on them, noting with a smirk that these were not hidden on the memory sticks in any way, simply appearing as normal file listings.

Some of the decrypted files were images, mostly handheld still photos of the target and the surrounding area. The other files were close-ups of some of the perimeter guards and the utility connection points where they penetrated the six-foot exterior wall that encircled the compound. Interestingly, the natural gas connection was above ground, most likely allowing the local utility provider easy access to the shutoff, Al-Amriki thought. Electrical power seemed to be fed from a large transformer mounted on a concrete base, conveniently placed just inside the perimeter wall near the rear of the facility. That might make a good excuse to get past the guards, he thought. jihadis posing as workers for the local utility company and carrying the proper credentials should be able to get inside. Perhaps they could use a large van...

Al-Amriki made a note to remember his line of thought for later and moved on to processing the rest of the USB sticks. More photos. The latest issue of 'Dabiq', the newspaper of the Islamic State, which he set aside to enjoy later and, last, a message from Akil exhorting him to finish his planning quickly to give the jihad another victory for the glory of Allah and the Caliph.

Al-Amriki shook his head. It would take at least two more days to get the rest of the intelligence he needed and complete his planning. When he finished tonight's work, he would need to find an artful way to tell Akil that he was making progress and ask for his patience. Akil would hear from him very soon.

CHAPTER 8

"Colonel Momani," General Crane said, "thank you for taking our call so late in the day." Cain could hear the general clearly over the encrypted conference call. Not only did the encryption algorithm the STE-IV phone utilized ensure the call could never be decrypted, even on the slim chance it was intercepted, the STE-IV also eliminated all the normal background noise on the line, making the call sound like the participants were sitting three feet in front of him.

"It is my pleasure, General Crane," Momani responded amiably. "It is not often that the commanding general of the legendary 152nd Joint Special Operations Unit reaches out to the military attaché of my nation."

Cain shook his head wryly at the very diplomatic response. He was sitting behind the desk in his office on the CTS Ops Floor, the door shut. The little LCD window of the STE-IV said the call was secured at the SECRET level, the common level of all the participants, and Cain knew that was solely due to Colonel Momani's participation.

Under normal circumstances, with just Crane, Simon, and Cain on the conference call, the LCD window read TOP SECRET SCI, since they were all U.S. citizens with high-level SCI clearances and were using STE-IV phones located within heavily secured government facilities known as Sensitive Compartmented Information Facilities, or SCIFs.

Crane and Simon were sitting in their offices deep inside their base. Colonel Momani was likely sitting in his office at the Jordanian Embassy along International Drive in Washington D.C. A quick glance at the multi-time zone clock hung on the wall over the conference table told Cain it was just after 5 P.M. He would need to call his wife after they were done talking to Momani and tell her he would be very late tonight.

"Well, I appreciate you taking the call nonetheless," Crane replied, matching Momani in diplomatic courtesy. "I trust you are enjoying the early fall weather in our nation's capital?"

"It's much cooler than I am used to, but after nearly two years of duty here at the embassy, I've come to enjoy it," Momani replied. "How can the Hashemite Kingdom of Jordan assist the United States?"

The formal wording of the question marked the beginning of the 'business' part of the call. Time to get to it, Cain thought.

"Have you had a chance to review the formal request the Pentagon sent?" Crane inquired.

Cain heard a rustling of paper in the background, which he suspected was purely for show. Momani would not have taken this call without extensive prior consultations with his defense ministry.

"Yes, I have, general. I must say, the United States is making a very generous offer. In fact, I have already spoken to my Minister about it and he was very surprised to see it." Momani paused briefly and Cain nodded his head. They are going to go for it.

"Unfortunately, I must convey to you, with regret that my Minister will not permit you to fly any drones of any kind over the sovereign airspace of Jordan unless we are given full and complete access to the information developed from its sensors in real time."

Shit! Cain thought to himself. That is not going to happen. We are not telling them about FULLBACK in case the Islamic State has an agent embedded in the Jordanian military or intelligence services. There is no way we can let them look over our shoulder while we set up and conduct the capture operation either.

Cain heard the silence lengthen, and he knew Crane was probably swearing to himself. The ex-paratrooper had a mildly volatile temper. Cain was mildly surprised when Crane's voice came back on the line, its tone betraying none of his temper.

"I'm sorry to hear that, Colonel. I regret that my orders do not permit that level of sharing with a friendly government. I'm sure you understand that we don't generally provide that level of access to any nation, even our very close allies." Cain and the other Americans knew the 'very close allies' bit was a lie, since the 'Five Eyes' nations—the United States, Great Britain, Canada, Australia, and New Zealand—shared practically everything. Momani almost certainly knew it too, but said nothing, knowing that pressing the point with this audience would get him nowhere.

Instead, Momani took a few seconds before replying, likely steeling himself for what he had to say next. "I must apologize, General Crane, but the instructions I have from my government are that there can be no overflight or encroachment on sovereign Jordanian airspace without such access."

Cain recognized that the Jordanians wanted to leverage the request for overflight permission into a look at U.S. drone capabilities, and he was sure Crane and Simon saw it too. An old quote, paraphrased from something French General Charles de Gaulle once said came to mind, 'Nations have interests, not friends.' It expressed the simple, yet inviolate rule of international relations Cain learned about during his graduate studies years ago.

"Colonel," Crane began, his voice steady, not betraying one whit how badly he wanted the Jordanian's cooperation on this. "My government is not likely to approve your request, but I will pass it along the chain of command. In the meantime, if your government would see its way clear to approving us..."

Momani cut General Crane off politely. "I'm sorry, general. My orders were quite specific. We will not allow the forward basing of any kind of drone on Jordanian soil without direct access to the real-time data feeds from it. The other elements of the U.S. government's request are approved without any preconditions. We are looking forward to conducting the joint exercise."

Crane let the silence hand on the line for about twenty seconds, hoping to make Momani sweat a little bit. Cain suspected that as an intermediary for his government not beholden to Crane in any way, it was unlikely Momani was sweating at all.

"The U.S. government appreciates your government's willingness to work with us during the proposed joint exercises, Colonel Momani. Thank you." Crane told him, recognizing the need for a little give-and-take in the situation.

"You're welcome, sir," Momani replied, without any hint of discomfort in his tone.

"I will pass the refusal on the drone up through my chain of command. Perhaps contacts at the ministerial level can work out the drone request." Cain recognized the general's statement as an acknowledgment that the Jordanian colonel was not the man to argue with about the issue.

"That seems like a reasonable compromise, general, thank you," Momani replied, obviously appreciative of the general taking him off the hook. Even at a Colonel's rank, being the intermediary is not generally a comfortable experience when the two sides disagree.

After a few more pleasantries, Crane signed off with the Jordanian. The Americans remained on the secure conference call by prior arrangement. Momani hung up and the STE-IV's electronically noted the absence of the non-U.S. terminal. Once Cain and the others saw the STE-IV phones reset themselves to TOP SECRET SCI, they knew it was safe to talk candidly.

"Any chance the Pentagon will have more luck?" Simon asked.

"I doubt it," Crane answered. "We'll need to make do with what they've approved."

"That won't help Mathews in the short term," Cain observed acidly. The kid was going to be on his own for a while longer.

"No other options?" Crane asked hopefully.

Cain thought quickly. "I'll sit down with my senior staff and see if we can give you a couple, but for now, our original plan for persistent surveillance on FULLBACK is reduced to Mathews and the Raven drone."

"Shit," Simon said, summing up the situation succinctly.

"Roger that, Colonel. Mathews has proven himself before, and he'll need to do it again now." General Crane responded.

"Understood, sir." Simon responded, knowing that continuing to vent would not fix the problem the Jordanians unexpectedly handed them.

"Mr. Cain, please get your team together and give me some options."

"Will do, general," Cain replied.

"And let Mathews know the bad news." Crane added before dropping off the link.

Hey nephew. I really can't get your Aunt to take the time to look at the photos you sent. She'd like to make the time, but the neighbors just keep talking about what they will and won't allow on their property and they're chewing her ear about it. I'll let you know when she has a chance to look at them. In the meantime, you'll just have to suffer through – sometimes it's rough traveling the world. Be safe.

Cain stared at the lines of the text message, rereading it for the third time and feeling just as dissatisfied with its content as he was when he drafted it. Knowing he had no other choice, he clicked 'send' with his mouse, and the text was gone, confirming in black and white to a young naval officer that he had no viable assistance for much longer than the original plan called for.

Annoyed at the unexpected turn of events, given the Jordanian refusal to allow the use of a drone in their airspace, Cain rose from his desk on the operations floor and headed straight back to his office.

He breezed through the heavy wooden door and shut it before sitting at the head of the small glass and steel conference table just inside the door. As he sat, the innocuous chat among the two men and one woman at the table stopped immediately. Cain looked them over briefly as they looked back at him expectantly. Two of them were uniformed military members in battle dress uniform and one was an NSA civilian. In the background, the clear glass of his observation window showed him the usual calm of the CTS operations floor in the background.

On his right was Erik Armstrong, the CTS's lead analyst for the Islamic State. Armstrong had a Dell tablet computer in front of him, no doubt with all the latest reporting on Islamic State movement and activities. Cain had relied on him for much of the intelligence he used to build the operations plan to capture FULLBACK, and Armstrong had always demonstrated in-depth target knowledge and the quick mind that came with earning two master's degrees from Georgetown. A major in the Army recently selected to command a battalion once his promotion to Lieutenant Colonel took effect, Armstrong watched him calmly out of pale brown deep-set eyes under a strong brow, his skin as dark as coffee grounds.

Across from Cain sat Stu Griffon, one of NSA's technical wizards from its Secure Communications Directorate. As with many of the men and women of one of NSA's geekiest organizations, Griffon eschewed anything that even approached what the rest of the world might consider 'business casual'. Griffon got away with it because he was one of their best, holding not one but two doctorates from MIT, one in information technologies and one in system dynamics. For this meeting, Griffon wore his usual workday best. Faded blue jeans, his favorite sandals, blue socks since his feet tended to get cold in the air-conditioned workspaces, and a lightweight NSA-logoed white polo shirt that would never know the sensation of being tucked inside a pair of pants. At least he's color coordinated, Cain mused. Most of the serious geeks at NSA would never put in that much effort. Griffon looked expectantly at Cain from his wide-set eyes, his pale skin and blond air giving away his Scandinavian ancestry—and his complete lack of time spent outdoors.

Master Sergeant Thompson, sat on Cain's left, and he nodded at her. He had already discussed how he wanted this meeting to go with her before Armstrong and Griffon arrived.

"Thanks for joining me, everyone," Cain opened. "As I mentioned in the Outlook e-vite, I've got a problem I need your help with."

Major Armstrong spoke first. "Something go wrong with your operation against ISIS?"

Cain smiled slightly, appreciating the fact that the man could put two and two together.

"As I'm sure you're aware," Cain said, looking directly at Armstrong, "the operation we have underway is compartmented. Without going overboard on the detail, I'll give you the short version."

Cain met Thompson's eyes briefly. Only she and Cain knew that what he was about to say was only part of the story.

"What I'm about to reveal to you is protected under the GREEN DRAGON security compartment." Cain paused, locking eyes with both men to communicate the sensitivity of what they would be hearing, but betraying nothing about it not being the whole story. The GREEN DRAGON compartment, intended to facilitate the sharing of some information about special operations activities, allowed necessary technical experts to help out, but without knowing all the operational details protected within the CAPTIVE DRAGON special access program. Griffon and Armstrong were not cleared for CAPTIVE DRAGON.

"SOCOM has a series of operatives abroad, some of which are trying to gather intelligence on ISIS," Cain continued with a nod to Armstrong and his prior conclusion, allowing him to think he was on target without revealing FULLBACK. "For now, we're unable to provide on-site surveillance to help the operators out, but several of them are equipped with Raven III drones. We're looking for options."

Cain and Thompson locked eyes again, and Thompson held her tongue, knowing that, as his lead drone operator, Cain wanted her to evaluate their proposals, since putting a drone into Jordan was not on the table right now.

Griffon spoke first, "Are they equipped with standard comm gear?"

Cain nodded. "Yes, in a few instances a couple of the assets have the paired laptop setup."

"Cell phones?" Griffon asked next.

"Yes. They vary though. Android and Apple smartphones…"

"Ours?" Griffon inquired, wanting to know if they had the special enhancements built in.

"Yes." Cain confirmed.

"They've got plenty of bandwidth available, then. How about the assets without the paired laptops? How are they controlling the drones?"

Cain thought fast and shook his head. "Standard issue SOCOM laptops. We haven't been able to field all the paired ones we would like to. You know what the build cycle is and the procurement budget isn't fully funded yet, since the last Continuing Resolution on the budget only passed last month. It takes weeks for the money flow to actually start, and it hasn't trickled down to us yet."

Griffon nodded sympathetically. "I hear you. My department is stuck too. Latest estimate from the finance folks is another six weeks for our funding to show up."

"So where does that leave us?" Cain asked, steering the session back where it belonged.

"Like I said," Griffon began, "your assets have plenty of bandwidth, at least in terms of what the phones and the laptops can pump out. The real issue is moving the video and command signals through the local telecommunications infrastructure. Some countries just don't supply the bandwidth to their subscribers."

"So, if the bandwidth is available, our guys could just send the video home and let us control the RAVENs across their cell phones?" Thompson asked.

Griffon shifted a little in his seat and leaned forward. "Not quite. The phones and laptops don't have any software on them to allow the two-way transmission of data, video and command signals back and forth. And your people out in the boonies without access to local comm infrastructure are still stuck."

Cain took a deep breath and let it out to calm himself, and mentally forced himself not to lean forward in his chair as his mind raced to keep the conversation from veering out of the GREEN DRAGON level. "We'll talk to SOCOM about getting the teams located beyond the reach of the local infrastructure SATCOM gear for the MILSTAR satellites. Any way to upload that software you mentioned?"

Griffon spread his hands open in a 'you're not getting it yet' gesture. "Uploading it is the easy part. The hard part is that we don't have the software to upload."

"Clarify." Cain demanded, dreading the answer he thought he was about to get.

"It hasn't been written yet." Griffon said resignedly.

"So why are we having this conversation?" Cain asked hotly, leaning forward now, feeling his face get warm, and knowing the look of frustration was plainly evident on his face.

Griffon held his hands up in wait gesture, "Because we can write it, it will just take a week or two."

Cain blew out another breath of frustration, "OK, a week or two won't cut it. If I get you priority from the Director, can you have it ready in twenty-four hours? There are a couple of kids out there working some long hours in the field, and this would really take the load off them."

Griffon shook his head. "No way in hell," he said emphatically. Looking apologetically at both Thompson and Armstrong, the only two people wearing uniforms in the room, he continued. "You know my team and I will do every-thing we can to support troops in the field, but the work is too complex. We also need to test it. The best I could offer you is two, maybe three days. And that assumes you get the senior staff to sign off on me stopping every other project we're working."

"I'll call the Director right after this meeting. You'll get all the top cover you need." Cain assured him.

"Good luck with that," Griffon said, obviously unconvinced.

Cain ignored him. The Director of NSA held the CAPTIVE DRAGON clearance and never avoided a call from Cain.

"Major Armstrong," Cain said, moving the conversation on, "talk to me about the Islamic State. Have you seen any indicators that they might be aware of any of our assets in the field?"

Armstrong was taken aback by the question. "Absolutely not. I would have reported it immediately if there were. I wear the same uniform those men in the field do, Mr. Cain."

Cain held up his hand and looked right into the Major's eyes. "I'm not trying to imply you aren't being professional, Major. I'm asking because you are a professional, and as one, you do everything you can to confirm your facts before you speak up, to ensure you don't send everybody into 'Flapcon One' over something that turns out to be bogus."

Major Armstrong smiled at the Flapcon One reference. A pun on the still-used DEFCON system for military alerts, the insider term for sending senior managers and field personnel into a frenzy of activity over crappy intel or half thought out requests from mid-level staffers couched as 'something the general wants' was universally understood in intelligence circles. Cain's use of it reassured the Major more than anything else that Cain appreciated his professional skills and respected his judgment.

"What I need to know is, do you have anything that is something more than a hint of awareness on their part, but not confirmed activity – if that makes sense. I need your gut read on anything you are watching a little more closely than usual."

Armstrong nodded his understanding. "I read you, sir. I'm watching two streams of reporting, one from the NSA and one from the CIA that both discuss Islamic State awareness that they are being watched by the CIA, and other 'infidel security services', as they term them. Nothing in those reports indicates anything more specific."

Armstrong's tablet chimed softly and he took a moment to open a file and scan it quickly before continuing. Rather than chiding the man for allowing the tablet's chime to interrupt his meeting, Cain waited patiently. Whatever alert had popped up was likely germane to their conversation, or Armstrong would have ignored it.

After taking a few seconds to scan the lead paragraphs of the report, Armstrong continued. "A report that's just come in from USCENTCOM J2 shows no changes in their threat level for the next twenty-four hours, based on the assets they have in theater and their liaison relationship with the Iraqi intelligence services, such as they are."

Cain nodded, reassured for now. "Good. Please send anything you think I need to know along immediately, without waiting for confirmation, as we've discussed."

"Will do, Mr. Cain."

"Master Sergeant Thompson, do you have anything to add?"

Thompson shook her head, making her newly-bobbed blonde hair sway across her face. "Not really, Mr. Cain. Hopefully Mr. Griffon's people can get that software ready quickly, and you know the RAVEN drone's capabilities and limitations from the brief I gave you last year."

"OK. Thanks for your time, everyone. Gentlemen, if you'll excuse us, I have some personnel matters to go over with Sergeant Thompson. A couple of her subordinates want my endorsement for their next assignments."

Both men said their good-byes and left Cain's office, and Major Armstrong, knowing that military personnel matters are usually discussed in private, pulled the door to Cain's office shut behind them without being asked.

Once Cain saw both men appear with their security escort on the other side of the glass observation window as they walked toward the CTS watch center exit, he looked at Thompson.

"What do you think, Emily?" The need to remain professional in front of Armstrong and Griffon was absent now, and he could revert to his preferred custom of using Thompson's first name.

Thompson looked hopeful. "If you can get DIRNSA to light a fire under Griffon's tail, that software should really help Mathews. We can take the load off by monitoring the RAVEN video feed and controlling the aircraft. That should free him up for the tactical planning he needs to do, and allow him to maintain his cover. The most he would have to do is change the batteries out for us."

"Agreed," Cain said, his eyes half focused as he visualized a lone man in potentially hostile territory without backup from his office. "I'm going to ask DIRNSA to really lay into Griffon's division chief if he has to. I want that code in twenty-four hours, forty-eight at the most. Mathews has got to sleep sometime."

"David, I spent time in the field with him and Team Four. They are some tough guys." Thompson assured him. "During some of the downtime, every one of the Tier One operators, Rangers, SEALS, Pararescuemen, Force Recon marines told me stories about their initial and follow-up training. In every case, minimal sleep was the routine. To a man, every one of them had planned and executed operations on as little as three or four hours of sleep, sometimes less."

"You sure they weren't trying to impress a woman in their midst?" Cain asked, a hint of doubt in his voice. Thompson was married with a young son, but she surrendered very little in the looks department to most women. Cain could easily envision a group of physically fit young men telling an attractive woman, married or not, some 'tall tales' to score some points.

"There were plenty of other women with us on that deployment," Thompson explained, "mostly flight crew and support types, across both officer and enlisted ranks. I asked some of them the same thing out of earshot of the operators, and not one of them thought the guys were embellishing anything."

Cain was not entirely convinced, but it was tough to argue with the opinions of people like Thompson. "Glad to hear it," he said, "it's good to know Mathews can manage for a while."

Cain leaned back in his chair and let out a deep breath of frustration. "I'm still not comfortable with Mathews being out there alone for as long as this. We're always there when they need us."

"David," Thompson said, "I'm with you on that. I don't like it either. I know first-hand how much they rely on our support, and this sucks. At least Major Armstrong isn't seeing any indicators yet."

"That's one good thing at least, but ISIS is tough to track and monitor," Cain told her. "By their own admission, those little bastards learned a lot from TRAVELING JUDAS, and their communications security is too good to guarantee that we'll catch anything from a slip up in that area. Our best short-term hope is bagging FULLBACK."

TRAVELING JUDAS was the cover term the intelligence community hung on the man who stole hundreds of thousands of classified documents from NSA and fled to China and Russia. The breach in NSA's security had resulted in increased communications security by potential adversaries, criminals, and terrorists; diplomatic earthquakes, and the loss of incalculable man-hours and millions of dollars in source and technique development. Cain knew that TRAVELING JUDAS would pay a heavy penalty for his colossal ego and incredible ignorance one day, preferably with a lifetime stay in a federal prison in Colorado, but that was for another day. Uncle Sam had a long memory.

"I know you didn't want to say anything in front of the major and Griffon, so tell me what you held back," Cain instructed her.

Thompson thought a moment. "The biggest issue I see is that the RAVEN doesn't have any target designation capabilities. We won't be able to mark a target for tracking or a strike."

Cain had briefed her about Mathews' mission before Griffon and Armstrong had arrived, but she seemed to need a gentle reminder of the mission goal. "You know that a strike is completely out of the question. Mathews is surveilling the objective for a capture operation, not a strike. Besides, the RAVEN isn't capable of carrying any munitions."

"I know, David," she replied, unfazed by the reminder, "but my responsibility is drone support, and I'd prefer to have all the capabilities available. Mathews could run into ISIS foot soldiers or unexpected security at the capture location, and for now, the best we can do is sit back and drink coffee while it happens. If Griffon can get us the software we need, we might be able to watch it real-time on video. If we had a laser designator, we could..."

Cain clearly heard the frustration in her voice, and shared it, but cut her off. "Yep, we could, but that isn't going to be an option. Besides, we would need Presidential authorization for a strike inside Jordan, even if it were against ISIS operatives chasing the capture team." Cain saw she wanted to press the point, so he decided to change the subject. "You're going off shift in a little while, right?"

"Yes," she said brightly, smart enough to know that Cain did not want to discuss it further, and acquiescing to the subject change. "My husband and I are taking Jeff to the Baltimore aquarium tonight. He loves to see the fish."

Cain smiled. "That sounds nice. Get out of here for the night and have a nice time with your family. I've got a call to make."

Thompson stood up and headed for the office door. "Goodnight, David." She closed the door behind her.

Cain sat behind his office desk and reached for the secure phone, punching the speed dial.

"General Holland."

Cain liked Holland. A career intelligence officer in his late forties, Holland was also a serious iron-pumper with silver in his short dark hair, whose fast rise to four-star general was an anomaly in a service that flew planes. Fortunately, SECDEF and the current Chief of Staff of the Air Force were savvy enough to understand the need for senior officers steeped in intelligence operations as much as flight operations. He was an ideal fit for the position of Director of the NSA, a post he had occupied for nearly three years now.

"Sir, this is David Cain."

"What's going on?" Holland knew that Cain never called his direct line for small talk.

"I just met with Stu Griffon and Major Armstrong about our options for the FULLBACK surveillance," Cain informed him. "Stu is going to need some top cover. I need the software he's proposing put on a fast track."

"Give me the short version – what's the software going to do for you?"

"Allow us to communicate directly with the operator's RAVEN drone, and take a live feed from it through the cell phone and tablet PC he has in the field."

"Without the dedicated comm gear you usually use?"

"Affirm. The operator is completely alone out there without us, and if you think back to my briefing on FULLBACK, our operator is in eastern Jordan and he could not haul into country the usual VSAT set-up we use. It would have been too bulky to bring in and might have blown his cover as a graduate student. If we can take the monitoring off his plate, we can lighten his load a bit."

"I hear you, David. I'll call the CIO and his division head and tell them he's working a priority project for me. Hang on a second."
Cain did not hear anything for nearly a minute.

"OK, I just queried the available set of cover terms for projects I set in motion. We'll use WINDOWPANE for this one. I'll have my chief of staff flag it out to the senior staff immediately. Call Dr. Griffon and give him a heads up. His division chief should call a couple of minutes after you hang up with him."

Cain recognized that Holland was pulling out all the stops on this one. Allocating a DIRNSA assigned cover term to the project guaranteed immediate, top priority action and funding.

"Will do, sir. Any luck on the FISA warrant for FULLBACK's communications?"

FISA, the Foreign Intelligence Surveillance Act, was the law that constrained NSA's SIGINT operations, specifically as they related to U.S. citizens. Since FULLBACK was a known U.S. citizen, any attempt to intercept his communications, even though he was a known senior planner for a terrorist organization, required that the special court set up by Congress issue a warrant as required under the 4th Amendment of the Constitution.

"Yes. The FISA Court signed off on the warrant two days ago."

"Any luck yet?"

"David, you are not part of the SIGINT production chain..." Holland began.

Cain cut him off politely. "Sir, I'm not interested in how you're getting it. I just want to know if you've had any luck yet."

"David," Holland said, a mild admonishment in his tone, "we've covered this ground. I know it's frustrating, but I will not cover the details of how we discover or gain access to a target's communications."

"Yes, sir. You know how frustrating this is for me."

Holland let out an exasperated breath of his own. "It's frustrating for all of us. Sensitive sources and methods information is far too perishable, and I will not discuss them with you, so stop asking, Mr. Cain."

Properly chastened, Cain surrendered the point, but not his concerns. "I understand sir, but right now I'm worried about one man in the field, completely on his own."

Holland heard the contrition in Cain's voice and respected his point. "David, so am I, but I also have to balance the responsibilities I have as DIRNSA to ensure that we conduct an effective foreign intelligence mission in a way that continues to protect our constitutional values, and I will not step outside the confines of what the lawyers tell me is legal under FISA. None of my predecessors did. Bottom line: your operator will just have to wait a few days and hope that, at least from my end, we get lucky.

"Yes, sir." Cain acknowledged.

"I'm sure he can manage," Holland assured him. "David, you will get what we can get you, when and if we can find it."

"I understand sir. I appreciate you giving Doctor Griffon the top cover he needs."

"Anytime, David. Don't hesitate to call me if you need anything else. Keep me in the loop on the capture op. This guy has been helping terrorists kill his fellow citizens and I want him back here to stand trial, after the joint interrogation team gets finished with him. Out here."

Cain hung up after Holland's sign off, but sat in his chair mulling over the conversation. He could not fault Holland for wanting to ensure that they did everything under the law. Moreover, when the law changed over time as technology advanced, NSA complied with it. NSA had always operated that way, in spite of the allegations that had appeared in the media after the TRAVELING JUDAS leaks, and there was certainly no reason to change that now.

In fact, Cain had always taken a great deal of professional pride in the fact that, within an employee population that exceeded one hundred thousand globally, there had only been less than half dozen malcontents who claimed NSA was doing something illegal. People whose half-baked theories, lack of understanding of existing controls and processes, and personal agendas played right into the hands of opportunistic journalists and ACLU lawyers who see government conspiracies at every turn.

Cain's assessment, based on his twenty years on the front lines of intelligence production, was simple and straightforward. If the NSA or any other element of the intelligence community were breaking laws and violating Constitutional rights in an intentional, systematic, and pervasive manner, there would be many more men and women walking out the door and talking to Congress and the media than just one publicity seeking egoist and his band of ill-informed supporters.

Cain knew that he could rely on the NSA's professionals. If they could develop anything from FULLBACK's communications, he would receive the reporting. Until then, he would just have to make do with what they already knew and count on Major Armstrong's updates to keep him situationally aware. In Cain's opinion, waiting and uncertainty were the hardest things to endure in his profession.

Cain adjusted his position in the chair behind his desk and reached for the phone again. It was time to tell Griffon about project WINDOWPANE.

CHAPTER 9

Mathews walked back into the safe house, the Range Rover once again parked safely off the street in the rear, a nearly depleted battery pack from the RAVEN III in his left hand, the live video feed from the RAVEN up on the tablet in his right.

Once he had the battery connected to the portable charger in the bedroom, Mathews ambled over to the kitchen, filled a small pan with water from the tap and set it on the stove to boil. Next, he tore off the top of a small packet and filled a white cereal bowl with the pre-packaged oats. Last, Mathews used a stick of butter to lightly coat the interior of a ten-inch spun aluminum skillet, and set it on the electric grate of the tiny stove alongside the small pan full of water.

The water in the pan would be enough for the bowl of oatmeal and two cups of coffee, which would go nicely with the two eggs he would scramble once the skillet warmed up. Mathews really wished he had some grated cheddar for the eggs, but he had already been lucky enough to score the fresh eggs from Youssef during his brief trip into the center of town yesterday. He had also managed to get the SD memory cards from Abbud and, as expected, the man showed no hint of concern over 'Mr. Forrestal's' delay, and even refused to allow Mathews to pay him five percent more for his trouble. "A thousand times no," Abbud had said.

Mathews had really wanted to ask Youssef to deliver groceries directly to the safe house every other day, but did not want to take the risk that FULLBACK might leverage the man for information, perhaps threatening his family in the process.

Instead, he had pre-paid Youssef for a regular supply of food from Amman or Zarqa, whichever was easiest, for the next two weeks. As much as he wanted to indulge a bit, he kept the list of groceries short and asked Youssef to buy cheaper items, in keeping with his cover as a graduate student working on a limited budget from the university that sponsored his trip.

For now, he had secured a steady supply of a half dozen eggs; evaporated milk, which he could easily cut with water to extend his supply; a couple of foil-sealed pouches of salmon and tuna; fresh vegetables; eight liters of bottled water; and, as a small treat, three or four bags of chocolate M&Ms; all to be picked up every other day. Youssef was so satisfied with the extra business, he said he would include a half a dozen of his wife's home baked pita bread without charge.

The only downside was going to Youssef's store to pick up the parcel every two days, but Mathews thought he finally had enough of a handle on FULLBACK's routine that he could do it without running into the man again unexpectedly.

Moreover, he would vary his route to and from Youssef's and use the drone to check the area around Youssef's for a few minutes before he left for the store. Mathews felt he could risk leaving FULLBACK's location uncovered for five minutes without untoward consequences, and he could always wave off the grocery run if something developed.

Mathews cracked the eggs over the skillet and turned down the heat under the pot to keep the water boiling steadily for the next few minutes. He was using the tap water this morning to help conserve his bottled supply, and wanted to make sure the water was properly purified before using it for his breakfast.

As the eggs began to firm up, Mathews started to stir them into a fluffy mass while sneaking occasional glances at the tablet propped on the counter. Still no sign of movement at FULLBACK's location, but it was still early.

After plating his eggs and mixing the hot water with his oatmeal and a teaspoon and a half of instant coffee, he moved to the small table and settled himself, the tablet propped in clear view and the small notebook he was using to track FULLBACK's daily activities at hand.

Once he had finished his meal, Mathews left his dishes in the sink, made another cup of coffee with the remaining hot water, and returned to the table. Sipping his coffee slowly, he concentrated on his notes from the last two days, keeping one eye on the ruggedized tablet's display at all times.

Ever since he received the last note from Cain telling him that CTS would not be able to run the full-time surveillance on FULLBACK as originally planned, Mathews did everything he could to keep track of his target for the last forty-eight hours.

Mathews had adjusted his day to match FULLBACK's as best he could. The target never moved beyond the confines of his house or its immediate vicinity beyond either getting some fresh air right outside his door, or taking twice daily walks through the town, apparently as some form of exercise. He had not made a trip to Youssef's grocery store, and didn't appeared to have a car, either. Mathews knew he would need some kind of foodstuffs at some point, and resolved to keep an eye out for it – it might prove to be the opportunity they needed.

Looking at his notes again, Mathews began crosschecking some of the entries, looking for patterns he may have missed and highlighting a few items. He was about to start making some summary notes when his eyes caught movement on the tablet's screen. He pulled the device closer.

The RAVEN was back on station, slowly orbiting FULLBACK's safe house, flying the preprogrammed set of way points that kept it high enough and far enough away from the safe house to limit the chance of visual or audio detection.

FULLBACK was on the move again. Mathews observed him carefully as the target stepped out of his safe house and stopped to look around. Mathews had seen this before. He checked the time – nearly 1000 hours. He made a quick note and checked the last two days of notes. Al-Amriki was consistent in his departure times. On Day 1, it was 0952. Yesterday it was 0955 hours. Today it was 0957. If he remained consistent, FULLBACK would now take a lap around town, stopping at certain points along the way. The first should be the small makeshift café across from Abbud's store.

What concerned Mathews was the reason behind FULLBACK's obvious scanning of the area around his home before leaving. The easy explanation was that he was looking for anything or anyone out of place, but Mathews wanted to know exactly what he looked for. He tapped on the tablet's screen a few times, ordering the Raven to move toward the next orbit point.

He had reprogrammed the RAVEN's onboard nav system last night using FULLBACK's last two morning walks to preselect the orbit points, hoping to keep the Raven in an optimal observation position for each of FULLBACK's expected stops.

Mathews watched as FULLBACK walked off at a good pace, his pale-brown Thawb flapping from his movement. From what Mathews could see, he was heading out on the same route he usually walked, most of which was along roadways that inevitably had some members of the Ar-Ruwayshid community along them.

About ten minutes later, FULLBACK entered the little café. Mathews checked his notes. He should be in there for fifteen or twenty minutes. Unfortunately, he could not see through the walls to see exactly what FULLBACK was doing in there, but a morning coffee break from whatever planning work he was up to for the Islamic State seemed reasonable. Ten o'clock was coffee break time after all, wasn't it?

Mathews took the opportunity to get a bottle of water from the fridge and wash the dishes, the tablet propped in its usual place on the counter where he could see it. By the time he finished drying the dishes and returned to the table, FULLBACK was on the move again.

Mathews checked his notes. The bench should be next. Mathews tapped on the tablet, and the RAVEN shifted its orbit path again. Mathews watched carefully, tapping again to manually zoom the RAVEN's camera in even closer to FULLBACK. The bench was the only outdoor stop on FULLBACK's route, and Mathews wanted more closeup photos of his target.

FULLBACK approached the bench at the bus stop along Highway 10, and sat down before looking around, up and down the ribbon of asphalt that bisected the town. Mathews kept watching, wondering what went through FULLBACK's mind on these walks. Probably just routine counter-surveillance techniques, Mathews mused.

What was that? FULLBACK had just taken a closed fist out of his Thawb, and reached under the bench. When he pulled his hand out, it was open and appeared empty. A few seconds later, FULLBACK stood and headed off to his next stop on his morning route. Mathews checked his notes quickly. FULLBACK's next stop was on the other side of town and it usually took him fifteen minutes to get there on foot.

Mathews grabbed the tablet and began tapping in commands as quickly as he could. The first ordered the RAVEN to dump the last five minutes of video, and the live feed cut off immediately. The next ensured the RAVEN was still recording the live feed in the background. The download took nearly two minutes, and as soon as the video was in the tablet, he replayed it after moving the live feed into a small window.

There! Mathews rolled the video back several seconds, played it at a slower speed, and leaned in towards the display to watch more carefully. FULLBACK reached into his Thawb with an empty hand, and when he pulled it out again it was a closed fist. He reached under the bench, and in less than two seconds pulled it out again, open and empty.

Mathews leaned back, the image frozen on the screen of FULLBACK's empty hand. Mathews face split into a huge grin. He's loading dead drops! The tradecraft was very old school, but obviously worked for the Islamic State. Mathews jotted some notes in the Day 3 section of his notebook, and made a quick note to check the video from the last two days for further confirmation before he went back to watching the live feed, energized by his new discovery.

FULLBACK was still walking east, heading for his next stop on the eastern edge of the town, greeting the men he passed with a raised hand and likely a pleasant, 'Assalam Alaikum' as he passed. Mathews reasoned that each stop was a drop location, and added that to his notes as well. If the pattern holds, FULLBACK would make two more stops on the return trip, and then be inside until 3 P.M. or so when it was time for FULLBACK's regular afternoon walk.

Mathews swiped at the small iPad with his finger, turning the page of the latest Jack Reacher novel when he noticed movement on the tablet's screen again. FULLBACK was heading out on his afternoon walk. His afternoon trips usually skipped the café and took him straight for the bench. He put the novel aside and headed for the fridge, pulling an orange from the crisper drawer and snatching some paper towels off the counter before returning to the table.

He sat and began peeling the orange after noting FULLBACK's departure time in the notebook. Mathews munched on the juicy orange sections with relish as FULLBACK made good time heading for the bench. The last two days had been mostly boring observation and note taking, but now he had discovered something important about his target and his focus had gone from semi-detached interest in expectation of a long surveillance effort, to a laser-like focus on his objective's actions.

Mathews had taken the rest of the morning to adjust the RAVEN's flight path for FULLBACK's expected afternoon route, making sure to have the drone's loiter point far enough south of the bench to ensure a good viewing angle with the afternoon sun.

FULLBACK reached the bench and sat, and Mathews leaned in again, studying the video feed carefully. Again, FULLBACK studied the surrounding area and traffic coming and going on Highway 10. Once Mathews saw FULLBACK start to look around, he ignored the target's face and focused on his hands. There! FULLBACK put his right hand under the bench, just for a moment, and then withdrew it, his fist closed, before quickly putting his hand in his Thawb again.

Mathews knew from his own special operations training that loading and unloading a dead drop in the open like this was particularly risky, but he could easily see why Al-Amriki did it. No one in this little town in eastern Jordan was likely to be watching for this kind of thing, and moreover, with the acres of bare ground surrounding the town proper, the bench at the bus stop was a handy drop point. Any number of people would go there during the day, and since it was a fixture, the locals would ignore what was hiding in plain sight.

Mathews grasped the water bottle next to the tablet and saluted the screen with it. "Nicely done, you son-of-a-bitch." He took a healthy slug of water as FULLBACK headed off to the east side of town again. The afternoon routine included three more stops, all indoors. After his last indoor stop, FULLBACK headed to Youssef's store. Ten minutes later, he left the small grocery holding a couple of bags undoubtedly loaded with food.

Mathews understood that zooming the RAVEN's camera in on the bags would not help him learn anything – the lack of sufficient camera resolution at the drone's current altitude alone precluded that, even if the bags were open, and ordering the drone to descend would raise the possibility of FULLBACK hearing the RAVEN's engine. With nothing else to do, Mathews just watched Al-Amriki carefully as he returned home.

After a quick trip to relieve himself, Mathews returned to the table to scribble some notes about FULLBACK's afternoon stroll and consider the situation.

The dead drops were worth reporting, but he still could not come up with an oblique reference to them in a text to his 'Uncle David', so he tabled that for now. Instead, he brought up an electronic map of the area, using his notes to trace out the route FULLBACK took in the mornings and afternoons, looking over the area, and thinking back to FULLBACK's actions on the video feed over the last three days.

It was time to try and figure out a way to capture Al-Amriki and

Mathews set his mind to it. A grab on the street in broad daylight was out of the question. FULLBACK's walking route was never more than two minutes away from Highway 10, and there were usually civilians out and about all throughout the area during the day. Even setting up a quiet takedown behind a building was not going to work. One shouted word on FULLBACK's part or, worse, a civilian stumbling into them in the middle of it, and the whole operation would go sideways in seconds. Moreover, getting a capture team in close proximity in a town like this where the locals would spot anything out of the ordinary would kill the operation before it began.

Grabbing him inside Youssef's was a possibility, but Mathews discarded it immediately, unwilling to put the innocent store owner at risk. The simplest solution, based on what Mathews had witnessed so far, was to focus on the house. FULLBACK spent nearly twenty hours a day in that little house, and a night raid on the house would reduce the potential for civilian interference and offer a contained area for the takedown to occur out of sight.

Mathews rechecked his notes. FULLBACK never left the house prior to 9 A.M. and, based on when the lights went out, he seemed to crash around 11 P.M. The darkness, a stealthy approach, coupled with a very small team that looked like part of the local scenery should give them the edge during the capture op. Give FULLBACK an hour or two to be asleep, and a stealth entry, and it would all be over in seconds.

A small part of Mathews' mind whispered this is your chance. A small very small team virtually guaranteed he would lead the entry, and if Al-Amriki even glanced in the direction of a weapon, he would get two rounds center-mass from his silenced Sig. Maybe Sam would rest more peacefully then.

Having settled on a course of action, Mathews started drawing up a more detailed operation plan, or OPLAN, using stills of FULLBACK's safe house from the video, then the Snagit screen capture software on the tablet to annotate the stills, turning them into graphics depicting the operational concept.

Mathews used his finger to mark the infiltration route on the tablet's touchscreen, being sure to keep the capture team off the street as much as possible, and then laid out the exfiltration route. The pickup point for FULLBACK was the only sticking point. Walking the man bound and gagged onto an international flight was not really an option and, judging from Cain's last text, the Jordanians were not cooperating as planned.

With any luck, submitting his plan would get the wheels moving back in the States. Mathews photographed everything, along with a hand written operational plan, then encrypted and compressed the images, attaching them to his latest text message, and hit send.

Hey Uncle Dave. I've got a good plan for the days ahead, but I could really use Aunt Emily's help looking over some of the videos I've taken. Is she done arguing with the neighbors yet? I know it can take a while to get them to agree to anything. The work is hard, but I'm managing my days without any trouble. The locals are really nice folks, but it sure would be nice to have someone from the university to talk to about my findings. Could you get Uncle Simon to look at the diagrams and plans of the ruins I drew up? I'd love to get his input on my progress since he's studied these sites with you before. Oh, and ask him what he thinks of my travel plans for coming home. Hope things are well with you all.

At his ops floor desk in CTS, Cain reread the text message while the paired tablet did the decryption of the compressed attachments. As soon as the attachments were decrypted, he moved them to his desktop machine and opened them.

After a quick look to verify that the files were not corrupted as well as the scan of the plan Mathews had sent along, Cain began attaching them to an e-mail with the subject line 'FULLBACK Ops'. He added two recipients in the 'To:' line before verifying that the encryption option was selected for that e-mail, then swore silently to himself.

In his haste, he had not classified the e-mail properly. Leaving a formal classification banner off an e-mail did not mean that the information contained in it was unclassified, as a former Secretary of State once found out the hard way during an FBI investigation, but proper procedure dictated that every classified document including e-mails be properly marked. Quickly typing in the required 'CLASSIFICATION: TOP SECRET//CAPTIVE DRAGON' banner at the very top of the e-mail only took a few seconds, and he clicked the send button in Outlook.

Snatching the Gray Phone next to his computer keyboard off its cradle, he punched in an internal extension.

"Yes, David?" Thompson's voice betrayed her expectation of his call.

"How did you know?" Cain asked as he peeked around his paired Dell computer monitors from his elevated desk position toward the drone desk to see

Thompson looking back over her shoulder at him with a satisfied grin on her face and the phone to her ear.

"I heard the red alert sound. You might want to turn it down a little more."

Cain shook his head wryly. "I'll do that. Just shot you an e-mail. Look at the images from Mathews' RAVEN and see if you can enhance them at all. Don't sweat it if you need to remove his annotations to do it, I've got copies of the originals on my machine."

"Will do," Thompson said, turning back to her multi-display console and beginning to manipulate the mouse with her free hand. "What's the timeline on this?"

"Inside an hour or so would be great, and for now, you only talk to me about this."

"OK. I'll get back to you."

Cain hung up and dialed a second number, and as the call started to go through, he began typing another e-mail.

"Hey David."

"What do you think?"

"I think the kid is batting a thousand so far. Gotta love the imagery he's gathered, and I'm still reading his operational plan, but so far, so good. I'm not letting him do it alone, though."

"Did he ask for that?" Cain asked, surprised that Mathews would do so. Tier One operators were not spies, and never pulled a 'James Bond' in their line of work – they knew better.

"Not directly, but his OPLAN is written for a small team, and it seems to me based on the language that he's implying that it could be done solo."

"I'm shooting you his last text to me," Cain said as he hit send again. "He's itching to know if the Jordanians are playing ball. Are you willing to let the op play out the way he's described it?" Cain inquired.

Simon didn't mince words given how long he and Cain had worked together. "Fuck no. I am not letting one of my kids go into any capture mission solo. Doing a solo surveillance is pushing it, as far as I'm concerned. Anything beyond that gets done under the usual protocols. Fortunately, we're prepared for that."

In the background, Cain could hear the electronic 'ping' which meant his latest e-mail had just hit Simon's computer. Cain gave him a few seconds to digest it and respond.

"Unfortunately," Simon continued, "the Jordanians are still unwilling to allow a drone in country. How are things on your end?"

"Better news here. The NSA wizards are testing the code now. I should be able to send it out to him by the end of the day."

"Great news, David, thanks. I'll feel better if your team can take over the ISR on this one."

"That's the plan." Cain assured him. Intelligence, surveillance, and reconnaissance was CTS's job, and he wanted his people doing all they could for Mathews. "I've got Thompson working the image enhancement on the stills he sent in. We'll see if we can learn anything more from it, but I think we'll just end up with some really clear shots of the objective location."

"Roger that." Simon concurred.

"What's next, then?" Cain asked.

"I need to talk to Crane. Back to you in an hour or so."

"Out here," Cain said, hanging up.

"Out here," Simon replied, resting his thumb on the hook for a second before punching a speed dial button. While he waited for the call to connect, he glanced around his computer monitor to check on Zeus, who was happily gnawing on a huge chicken-flavored Nylabone on his bed. Seeing Simon's look, he dropped the bone and looked at his master, nose twitching as he sniffed in the direction of Simon's desk. Clearly, the big Shepherd knew something was afoot.

Thirty seconds of conversation with Crane's executive officer later, and Simon rose from behind his desk and headed out the door, walking the thirty steps across the executive suite to General Crane's office, Zeus hot on his heels at the sudden movement.

Simon tapped on the open door and walked in without pause. Crane's exec had told him the general was free.

"Take a seat, Aaron. What do you have for me?" Crane still wore the buzz-cut he cultivated before attending special forces school twenty-eight years earlier, his camouflage battle dress uniform adorned with only a master parachutist badge and the subdued, two-star rank insignia. The buzz-cut did not hide the fact that his hair was mostly silver now, but his daily habit of falling out with one of the Wraith Teams for their morning physical training sessions kept him fit and helped him get to know the young men he commanded. Crane was not what anyone would call an 'armchair general'.

"Mathews just sent in his proposed OPLAN for capturing objective FULLBACK."

"What do you think?"

"Overall, his plan is simple, straightforward, and sound."

"But..." Crane prompted Simon. There was always a 'but'.

"He recommends minimal personnel for the capture, and the way he wrote it up, it sounds like he'd like to run it solo."

"Absolutely not." Crane's voice was flat and broke no argument.

"My feeling exactly, sir. We'll go with Option JULIETT for the event. The asset we need is already in country and can be in place in less than eight hours. The rest of Operation RAILROAD will be set up in twenty-four hours or so. Any movement on the Jordanian's part to approve the UAV component?"

Crane frowned. "I talked to SECDEF yesterday. The Jordanians are drawing a hard line on it. Polite, but firm."

Simon nodded. "We might be able to mitigate that a little, but without the long-term dwell time we usually get from a GLOBAL HAWK." Both men knew the RQ-4 could remain on station for more than thirty-six hours watching adversary movements and actions. Unfortunately, with the Jordanian refusal to allow one in their territory, that option was out the window.

"Cain and the geeks at NSA find a way?" Crane asked.

"Looks like it. I talked to him a few minutes ago, and he said they are testing the software now. If it works, Cain can get him the new software by CoB."

"Nice," Crane observed. "If they get it to our man on time and it's effective, I'll be sure to call Holland and SECDEF and make sure the right 'attaboy's get on their records."

"We're going to need approval for this." Simon reminded his general.

"Right," Crane acknowledged as he reached for the red phone on his desk. The red-colored phone was the only one of its type on the entire base. Normally installed only in the offices of theater commanders, commanders of major commands, and cabinet level officials, the mere existence of the phone in Crane's office spoke volumes about the uniqueness of the 152nd Joint Special Missions Unit.

Crane lifted the receiver and punched a speed dial button. While the general could put the surveillance operation against FULLBACK in motion at his level in coordination with Cain and Holland, the actual capture operation needed approval from higher up in the chain of command.

"Yes." The male voice on the other end of the phone did not identify himself. If you called his direct line on this particular phone, you already knew whom you were calling.

"Mr. Secretary, Crane here."

"Hello General Crane. What can I do for you?" Crane smiled tightly; appreciating the fact that the Secretary of Defense always asked his Generals what he could do for them. As far as Crane was concerned, asking that question was the mark of a political appointee who actually understood his job, a rare commodity in any presidential administration.

"Mr. Secretary, do you recall the briefing package I sent you a few days back on the objective we've codenamed 'FULLBACK'?"

"Vaguely, general. You know I see quite a few briefings in the course of a day. Give me the short version to refresh my memory."

Crane did so, recapping the mission, Mathews' current location, what they had learned about Al-Amriki, and his value as an intelligence source if they could interrogate him, along with the current situation. Crane purposefully did not name Mathews or provide his background in order to avoid unduly prejudicing SECDEF's decision-making by putting a single face on the operation.

"OK, general. I'm synched up with you now. I take it you need approval to execute the capture?"

"Yes, sir." Crane confirmed. "We sent you the review and approval package two days ago." The review and approval package, known informally by the staffers as a RAP, provided the outline of the operation in more detail, along with the required legal and other opinions in coordination with all the relevant elements of the joint staff and the intelligence community. In this case, given that it was a Wraith operation, the coordination was limited to the CIA, DIA, and NSA senior staffers and liaisons cleared for the CAPTIVE DRAGON compartment, along with Cain at CTS.

Crane could hear movement in the background. "Got it," said SECDEF. "I remember it now. I spoke to the President about this yesterday during our weekly conference call. The president understands the nature of this man's threat to U.S. and allied national security, and the risks inherent in asking the

Jordanians to capture and extradite him."

Here it comes, Crane thought to himself. Do we get a green light or do we bring the Mathews kid home and hope the Jordanians don't fuck it up?

"The president," SECDEF continued, "agrees that asking the Jordanians for help might compromise the operation, given the concerns in the intel package about Islamic State infiltration of the Jordanian military and intelligence services."

Crane let out a breath. They were go mission.

"However," SECDEF added, causing Crane's prediction to fade as quickly as it had come. "I need your assurance you will be able to get FULLBACK out of Jordan cleanly. It's going to be bad enough that the President will need to call the King personally to apologize for intruding on Jordanian sovereignty on this one. That would become very complicated if your team is caught by the Jordanian authorities, and unforgivable if a firefight starts in the confusion if things go sideways."

Crane had to give the Secretary his due. He spoke using a uniformed person's lexicon, and summarized the situation very nicely. "Yes, sir, I think we can get FULLBACK out quietly. The timing is delicate, but I believe it's doable."

"Convince me." SECDEF ordered.

Crane ran through the extraction plan and waited.

"The Boss is going to want to throw the King a bone or two to convince him why we didn't trust his government with this," SECDEF said, "but he told me that he would order the CIA to share at the ministerial level what they know about the infiltration of the Jordanian government by ISIS." Crane could hear the secretary take a deep, contemplative breath. "The president believes giving the King the names of a couple of Islamic State moles should calm the waters nicely," he mused aloud. "The mission is approved, general. I'll inform the president and send you written confirmation before I head home later tonight."

Crane looked at the clock. It was already 6 P.M. on the east coast. SECDEF sounded like he would be there for a couple more hours at least. "Thank you, sir. I'll keep you informed."

"You'd better," the SECDEF admonished good-naturedly, but the serious undercurrent in his words got through before the call disconnected.

Simon sat still, quietly scratching Zeus behind the ears while he waited. He'd gotten the gist of the call from Crane's side of the conversation, but the chain-of-command needed to be followed. "Sir?" he asked expectantly.

"Green light, colonel," Crane said, his voice and manner slipping back into Green Beret mode. "Bring FULLBACK home to atone for his sins."

"Roger that." Simon told him, rising from his seat, and heading back to his office, Zeus trailing along at his side.

Once through the office door, Simon used a hand gesture to tell Zeus to lay on his bed, and the jet-black Shepherd settled himself instantly, watching his master intently. The tension in the dog's muscular frame as Simon put a call through mirroring the surge of adrenaline in Simon's bloodstream. It was moments like this when Simon was certain Zeus understood the sense of mission the humans he worked with felt.

"Cain."

"Hey David. We're go mission on FULLBACK. I'll have a message for you to relay to Mathews in an hour or so. Make sure he gets that new software ASAP. I want you watching his back on this."

"Will do. I'll send him what we're calling the WINDOWPANE package, and keep an eye out for your e-mail."

"Thanks, out here." Simon disconnected the call, and immediately dialed another. This one took several seconds to connect, passing through several telephone switches on the secure phone network before exiting a special relay into the international public network, and making its way to the Middle East at the speed of light.

"Yes?" the voice was deep and male, but did not identify itself.

"RAILROAD is a go. Option JULIETT." Simon looked at the clock on the wall, using the minutes after the hour to determine the simple voice confirmation code all Wraith team members were trained to expect, especially over an open line. "Confirmation Zulu Tango Four Five."

"Copy RAILROAD is go mission, option JULIETT in effect. Will relay," the deep voice said in reply.

"Out here." Simon told the voice, hanging up.

CHAPTER 10

Hi favorite nephew. Your Aunt Emily looked at your photos – she thinks you've got a good eye for photography and likes them alot. Uncle Simon went over your travel plans and approves of your route, but he thinks it would be best if you had someone from the university travel with you – you'll need an extra hand with your luggage on the return trip (you remember what happened with Juliet, right?). I'm attaching a new app you should try out – I think you'll like it a lot. It's great for photo sharing – Emily loves it. Keep me in the loop on your plans.

Mathews' day was off to a good start. He had received Cain's text and some attached files late last night, but elected to hold off looking at the files until the morning so he could get some sleep, banking the rest in anticipation of a busy day of watching FULLBACK and maintaining his cover.

The alarm on his iPhone woke him at 7 A.M., and he took the time to check the video from the overnight hours by fast forwarding through the down-loaded file before getting out of bed. Seeing nothing, Mathews rose, donning a pair of lightweight and airy swim trunks to work out for an hour, doing pushups, sit-ups, and some additional core work before showering, all with the tablet's live video feed where he could see it.

Still damp from the shower, Mathews made and ate a breakfast of scram-bled eggs and toasted pita bread before settling himself at the table with the tablet, his iPhone, and a second cup of coffee. Moving the files on the iPhone to the tab-let took a few minutes, and then the decryption process had to run to completion. Once the tablet had finished running the algorithm, along with an executable file, he found a cover note from Cain in the directory.

Mathews, use the instructions below to install the executable file on your tablet. Be sure your Bluetooth headset is paired with your iPhone and turned on before you start the installation process. We've found a way to give you some help from here.

Mathews checked the more detailed installation instructions and followed them, tapping away as needed on the ruggedized tablet's screen. A few minutes later, the install was complete, but he did not see any changes to the RAVEN's command interface, or new icons on the Windows desktop. Then, without warning, a pop-up window appeared on the tablet: 'Restart RAVEN Command Interface?'

A brief surge of panic gripped him, and he thought back to the two days of training on the RAVEN and its command software. If the drone lost communication with the tablet, it should stay on its programmed flightpath until the laptop re-established the connection. Mathews checked the instructions again. Finding no mention of the restart pop-up, he elected to risk it, trusting in the engineers back in the States to have done their jobs properly.

Acknowledging the pop-up, he let the command software reboot while he checked his earpiece, making sure it was powered on, and hooked it over his ear, immediately forgetting about it. Nearly two minutes later, the command interface was back, and the first thing Mathews did was check the RAVEN's systems status. Everything seemed nominal, and the live video feed came up a short time later, still focused on FULLBACK's house. Relieved, Mathews let out breath and double-checked the RAVEN's systems for anomalies.

Unexpectedly, Mathews heard a short beep in his right ear. What the... Mathews checked his iPhone and saw that the Bluetooth link was still active. Not sure what good that was going to be. It was after 9 A.M. now, and FULLBACK would be making his morning rounds in less than an hour.

Without warning, he heard a male voice in his ear, and nearly jumped out of his chair. "Wraith Four Six, this is Charlie One."

Mathews recognized Cain's voice immediately. Collecting himself, he responded, self-consciously and a little foolishly looking around the empty room out of reflex to be sure no one else was listening.

"Charlie One, Whiskey Four Six. Read you five by five."

"Good," Cain replied. "We can ease off the radio procedure for the moment. Like the new toy?"

Mathews' first concern was an obvious one. "Are we secure here?"

"Yes," Cain assured him. "According to the NSA comm guys who set this up, the only unsecure part of the link is the Bluetooth tie from the headset to your iPhone. That part of the connection is low power and it's very unlikely anyone where you are will be trying to hijack or intercept your Bluetooth link. We're considering it a SECRET level link for limited operational purposes only."

"Sounds good to me," Mathews told him. "I like the idea of a friendly voice in my ear."

"Well," Cain told him, a hint of mischief in his voice, "it gets better."

"Oh?"

"The software you loaded also allows us to remotely command the RAVEN for you, and get a real-time feed from the video camera."

"That is very cool." Mathews told him. As usual, he was impressed by the level of support he received from NSA and the CTS. They were always a 'mission first' bunch.

"Yep," Cain agreed. "Your days of babysitting the drone surveillance on FULLBACK are over."

"Still need to change the batteries for you though." Mathews told him, recognizing that he still had some caretaker duties to perform for the little drone.

"Yes. We'll coordinate the times with you. Oh, and you'll need to be very sure your phone and Bluetooth receiver are set up and fully charged at all times so we can keep the data and voice links active. Also, the tablet and iPhone can never be further apart than the Bluetooth specification allows."

Not being fully versed in geek-speak, Mathews had to ask. "How far is that?"

"About thirty feet," Cain answered, expecting the question. "I'll give you the short version so you know exactly what we've just done."

"OK, shoot." Mathews told him.

"The software you installed on the tablet also installed a small application on your iPhone via the Bluetooth link. The software on the tablet is encrypting and routing the RAVEN's video feed and command signals to your phone. Your phone is relaying the data across the Internet via the Jordanian public access Wi-fi network. We're pulling it in from the internet using some wizardry I won't get into, and it arrives back here at CTS, where we decrypt it and route it to our drone desk. Master Sergeant Thompson is looking at the live feed from the RAVEN now, and can remote control the drone the same way you can via the tablet."

"Very nice," Mathews observed. He felt better knowing Thompson had his back, and checking his watch, he could see from the local time that both of them had come in around 3 A.M. east coast time to be ready when he installed the new software.

"The application," Cain continued, "installed on your phone also sets up a separate encrypted channel to enable this voice link."

"That's great." Mathews told him appreciatively, and then moved on to a more urgent matter. "So where are we at with the Jordanians?"

"Not very far," Cain told him, his voice falling flat. "They absolutely refuse to allow overflight for a GLOBAL HAWK, which is why we came up with the new software."

"What about the extraction?"

"The assets are in place now. When you are ready to do the grab, they'll be synched up and waiting at the exfiltration point."

"Good." Mathews was pleased something had gone to plan, at least. "Do you have orders for me?"

"Not yet. Simon has some help coming your way. Until that gets there, you're to sit tight and we'll share the load on target surveillance."

"Sounds good," Mathews told him, and then added, "What do we do for a comm schedule? I'm assuming you don't want me running around with this thing in my ear twenty-four/seven, listening every time I have to hit the head."

Back in CTS, Cain smiled. "Right. We've been thinking a top of the hour comm check, and based on FULLBACK's movement patterns, we'll sign off for the night at 20:00 local your time, and then have a 'wake-up' check in at 0700 local time. Sound good?"

Mathews thought that over. As usual Cain and his people were all over it. "I think that will work. What about a duress code?"

Cain raised his eyebrows at that, "Good idea. What will work for you?"

"How about I say something about the weather if I'm compromised?"

"I like it," Cain responded, "Simple and innocuous. Hold one."

Mathews waited, wondering what caught Cain's attention. After a minute, he was back.

"Looks like your target is on his morning rounds. We'll cover him for the morning trip."

"Thanks," Mathews told him. "In fact, why don't we test this new thing out a bit? You track him around town, and I'll make a trip out to the eastern desert and the store in town for groceries. You can help me avoid him, and we can verify that this new software and the comms won't crap out anywhere in the local area."

"Good idea," Can responded. "Let us know when you're ready to head out. Remember, with only one camera, you'll need to call out your movements to us."

"Will do. Is Charlie Four on the link?" Mathews used Thompson's radio call sign out of habit.

"She will be by the time you're ready for your trip out on the town."

Thompson's soft voice came through the Bluetooth link clearly. "OK, FULLBACK just left the bench and headed east. Looks like he serviced the dead drop too."

"Copy," Mathews said quietly, continuing to amble his way towards Highway 10.

Mathews had a sudden idea as he was leaving the rented house, which he communicated to Cain for approval. Cain coordinated quickly with Simon and both men concurred, but the window for action was going to be relatively slim.

"Where is he?" Mathews asked sotto voce. He had changed into a brown Thawb, and wrapped a white and brown keffiyeh around his head to cover his face, his backpack already secured over both shoulders. As long as no one tried to engage him in conversation, he should be just part of the background to the locals.

"Heading away from the bench at a good pace. Doesn't look like he's checking his back trail," Thompson said from her desk in CTS, eyes glued to the RAVEN's video feed.

"Coming up on the highway." Mathews told Thompson.

"Be sure to look both ways." Thompson admonished him in a motherly tone, in spite of the seriousness of what they were about to do.

"Yes, Mom." Mathews said in the tone of an annoyed teenager as he passed the last house on the corner and looked to the right. In the distance, he could see the retreating figure of FULLBACK, his white Thawb flapping around his legs. Walking briskly without trying to be too obvious, Mathews crossed to the north side of Highway 10, and turned his back on FULLBACK, walking west to cross the forty yards to the waiting bus stop.

"I see you," Thompson chimed in. "No one appears to be heading toward the bus stop. I'll call out if someone starts walking toward the stop. You'll be in sight for another couple of minutes."

"Copy," Mathews answered tersely. The adrenaline was flowing through his veins now, and he kept flicking his eyes back and forth, scanning the roadsides and looking for oncoming traffic. Their biggest concern now was the sudden appearance of a bus, especially since they did not have a solid feel for the schedule.

To guard against that unknown, both Mathews and Thompson were staying alert and aware. Mathews would watch the highway for a bus and the surrounding area for anyone taking an interest in him. Thompson's task was to keep her eyes on FULLBACK and the immediate area around the bus stop for as long as she could, given that the RAVEN would have to move east to maintain coverage of FULLBACK in a few minutes.

Mathews sat on the bench heavily, sliding the straps of the pack off his shoulders as he did so, and letting it rest between his feet on the bare dirt. Shifting only his eyes, he glanced around.

"Here we go," Mathews whispered, doing his best to move his lips as little as possible.

"Copy," Thompson said in his ear, "I can stick with you for another thirty seconds before the RAVEN has to move east."

Mathews leaned forward and unzipped the top of the pack, using the move to slip his hand under the bench and feel around as carefully as he could. There. He felt the object beneath the bench and closed his eyes briefly; trying to envision the size and shape of what he was touching. Bending down and looking under the bench was not an option.

It felt like a small rectangle, open at the end facing the highway, about half the width of a cigarette pack. In the center, there was a finger-sized cut-out, and he could feel a thin, roughly rectangular shape move when he pressed up on it. Intuitively grasping the container's design, he pushed up with his finger, and used the traction created to withdraw the object. Clenching his fist around it, he pulled his hand from beneath the bench and put it into his open pack to shield his hand and the object from casual observation.

Opening his hand, Mathews instantly recognized it as a USB thumb drive, similar to one of the ones he had bought from Abbud.

"I've got a thumb drive," he reported back to Thompson.

Cain came on the line. "Wait one. I'm going to have a quick chat with the CIA liaison here.

Mathews looked casually around. There were a few cars heading toward him. Two from the west and one from the east, but neither appeared to be a threat, speeding by him at the customary break-neck speed everyone drove on the highway. The closest pedestrians in the area were thirty yards away and paying him no attention at all.

"FULLBACK is still moving east," Thompson reported. "Looks like another half mile before he hits his usual turnaround point."

Mathews did not acknowledge, waiting for Cain to come back on the line.

"Whiskey Four Six. We run the risk of wiping the USB stick if you plug it into the tablet and it's rigged electronically."

"Copy," Mathews said. "Will it damage the tablet?"

"Not likely," Cain replied, "but it would potentially tip our hand. The recipient will report to FULLBACK somehow and ..." Cain trailed off for a few seconds, and then Mathews heard, "Wait one."

Again? Thought Mathews. My ass is hanging out here. The minutes ticked by.

"FULLBACK is still moving towards his usual turn back point." Thompson called out.

Mathews kept up his visual scan while he waited. The tension and uncertainty began to gnaw at him. He was free to walk away if he felt he was in danger of discovery, but he was not going to miss this opportunity if he could avoid it.

"Mathews," Cain came back on the link, "I've spoken to Major Armstrong, our expert on the Islamic State. Based on the reporting he's seen, he thinks the contents of the drive will be encrypted. We have no idea if NSA will be able to break the encryption, but it won't hurt to give them the file."

Thompson chimed in. "FULLBACK is at the turnaround. You've got less than ten minutes."

"Copy," Mathews called in.

Throwing caution to the wind, Mathews popped the protective cover off the USB stick and inserted it into an open port on the tablet, then pulled the tablet partially out of the bag. The file manager was already open, and he could see that the tablet had recognized the USB stick and loaded the driver to read it. He tapped a few times, and saw a short list of files on the newly mounted drive.

Tapping quickly, he began copying the files off the USB stick. Once the tablet showed the copy operation in progress, he spoke. "Making the copy now. How long on FULLBACK?"

"Seven minutes, best guess. He seems to have hit his stride." Thompson responded instantly.

Mathews looked left and saw nothing. Highway 10 curved very gently toward the south as it approached the eastern edge of Ar-Ruwayshid, and hindered FULLBACK's direct line of sight to the bench. That would change in a minute or two. If FULLBACK saw someone sitting at the bench he used as a drop point, he might choose to investigate, and Mathews knew FULLBACK would put it together the moment he saw blue eyes behind the keffiyeh.

Mathews checked the tablet's display again. The copy was eighty-percent complete. Another glance down the road. Ninety percent.

"How long until he hits the bend?" Mathews asked.

"Maybe a minute," Thompson told him.

One hundred percent. Mathews pulled the USB stick out of the tablet, recapped it, and slid it back into the holder under the bench. Once it was secured, he checked the traffic as he rose, re-zipping the backpack and slipping it over his shoulders. A white Mitsubishi cargo van speed past him heading west, the smell of oily exhaust in its wake, and he immediately crossed the road behind it.

"He's at the bend." Thompson called out. "I see you crossing the highway."

Mathews hustled, lengthening his stride to cross the eastbound lane of the highway and move down the street to avoid drawing attention to himself by jogging.

"Clear," he announced over the link.

"FULLBACK is now clear of the bend. Whiskey Four-Six, turn right at the third house down, head down the side street about ten yards and wait. The area is clear of civilians."

Mathews did not answer her and followed instructions, relying on Thompson to be his eyes, and trusting her judgement completely.

"He's passing the bench now," Thompson reported. "He didn't even pause. Looks like he didn't see you."

"Copy." Mathews responded, and then let out the breath he had not realized he was holding. Now he could circle back to the safe house, and drive out into the eastern desert a mile or so to run the comms tests, and he was pretty sure it would be the easier part of this little trip into the field.

The tablet sat on the table, its display clearly showing the video feed from the RAVEN, now locked on FULLBACK's house. Mathews transferred the file he stole off the USB memory stick at the drop as soon as he returned from his brief drive in the eastern desert, then signed off from the encrypted link before making some lunch.

The comm link had held up surprisingly well until he was about twenty-two miles out of town, which is what Cain's people predicted based on the standard characteristics of a cellular signal. At that distance, the voice connection had gotten very choppy and distorted, and he turned around. A hundred yards or so closer to the town, and the voice link was clear as a bell.

Mathews was not due to check in again for another twenty minutes, and he let his eyes wander over the remains of his lunch, trying to decide if he should have an orange after the tuna sandwich he'd made with the fresh pita bread.

The knock on the safe house's front door shattered the stillness, causing him to freeze for a second before years of training took over. Mathews snatched the silenced Sig off the table and rose from the chair in one smooth motion. He moved to the left side of the door, extending his arm to allow the pistol's muzzle to point at the center of the door, adrenaline surging through his veins.

Briefly considering his options, and realizing he had little choice, he spoke aloud to the door. "Who is it?"

"Beware Djinns bearing gifts," a familiar male voice with a Midwestern accent responded.

Mathews lowered the silenced weapon, then unlocked and opened the door.

Senior Master Sergeant Robert Simms stood there, a wide grin on his face, straight white teeth shining from his perpetually tanned face framed with light brown hair that was shaggier than Mathews. He wore jeans and a loose lightweight tan canvas shirt, a pair of brown work boots, and carried a leather and oiled canvas duffle bag.

"You need a haircut," Mathews told him good naturedly, reaching out to shake the older man's hand. Simms was Mathews' Team Four NCOIC, normally responsible for the training and discipline of the enlisted men on the team when they were in garrison, and one of his element leaders when the twelve-man unit needed to be broken into smaller fire teams in the field.

Simms ignored the question with a tilt of his head and a 'You're kidding me, right?' look on his face as he ran his right hand through his shaggy locks. As much as Mathews liked the clean-cut military haircut that went with the uniform, Simms would rather wear his hair long, and used any mission in the field as an excuse to avoid the base barber for as long as possible. He may have been in the military, but being a Tier One operator had given him a chance to express his independent mindedness without any serious disciplinary blowback.

Mathews motioned Simms into the little house, grateful for the company of a brother in arms, closing and locking the door behind him again. "Just you?" Mathews asked.

"Yep. I'm option JULIETT," Simms said with a grin once Mathews locked the door again. "Simon didn't think you'd need more given your OPLAN. It would take another week or so to bring more of the team in country, and that just isn't practical."

Mathews nodded. Option JULIETT in the original mission plan covered the deployment of additional team members for the capture and extraction operation, codenamed RAILROAD. The number of team members was a scalable value, and given the OPLAN he submitted, he was glad Simon agreed with his call.

"How the hell did you get here so fast?" Mathews asked, a little perplexed at Simms' sudden appearance.

"I've been in country for nearly three days," Simms told him, dropping the duffle on the floor inside the door. "Simon sent me out right behind you, using a similar cover, graduate student in Middle Eastern studies. I've been enjoying the comforts of the Hilton Hotel in Amman for the last couple of days, walking around and playing tourist. Simon wanted at least one of us within driving distance to back you."

"Nice of him to share that he was putting you in the game early," Mathews groused half-heartedly.

Simms smiled. "You know the drill. Compartmentalization can be a good thing. I even brought some additional gear and a rusted out little piece of shit Toyota. Where are we at with FULLBACK?"

"They hooked me up with a Range Rover," Mathews said over his shoulder as he headed to the fridge to grab a couple of cold bottles of water. His operator's ego would not allow him to let the older man to go unneeded.

"Nice," Simms said sarcastically. "Figures they would give an officer the better ride."

Mathews motioned Simms to sit at the table as he exited the kitchen, then filled him in while they sipped the icy water from the bottles.

"So, you think we can grab him at his place?" Simms asked ten minutes later.

"Yes," Mathews confirmed. "He's housebound for the bulk of the day except for his two daily walks. Unless he's pulling a 'Bond villain' on us and there is an elevator down to his secret base beneath the house with dozens of guards, grabbing him should be a snap."

Simms studied the video feed of the house, turning his CO's plan over in his head. "No sign of any kind of guard or protective team?"

"None. Certainly no one is trailing him on his little walks." Mathews confirmed.

"Seems odd." Simms observed critically. "This guy is a senior operations planner for the Islamic State, and nobody is protecting him. He's a gold mine for us – they should be protecting him with a full team," Simms opined.

"Roger that," Mathews couldn't help but concur with the most experienced NCO on his team. For military personnel, security meant barriers, thick walls, many automatic weapons, lots of manpower, and clear fields of fire. Air support too, if you could swing it.

"I think they are trying to do this low-key, hoping to keep his location a complete secret by avoiding a very visible security team, convoys that might indicate a VIP passenger, etc.," Mathews countered. "I think that's one of the reasons they stashed him out here."

Nodding sagely, Simms asked, "So when do you want to do it?"

"According to Cain, the op is green lit, and now that you're here, I don't see any reason why we shouldn't grab him tonight," Mathews told him.

"That's a little bit cowboy, don't you think?" Simms asked, surprised that Mathews would suggest the grab less than thirty minutes after he arrived.

Questions like that were one of the reasons why Mathews trusted Simms completely. The man was not shy about questioning his team lead's orders if he thought they might be ill conceived. Moreover, he was forcing his officer to explain the reasoning behind the decision.

"Not really," Mathews responded, "I think we've got good conditions here. The objective is isolated at a known time and in a known location. With the extra gear you've brought, the two of us should be able to handle the grab and the transport to the exfil point, with a minimum of risk." And if I'm lucky, the little bastard reaches for a gun, then we just stuff his body in a box in the cargo compartment.

Simms leaned back and took a couple of long swallows from the nearly empty one-liter bottle, eyes on the tablet's display. Mathews let him think.

"Alright," Simms said after a couple of minutes, "let's run through this again."

Al-Amriki rubbed his eyes. The laptop's clock told him it was nearly eleven. He did some mental arithmetic. Not counting his two walks and a couple of breaks for meals, he had been working to finalize his plan for nearly twelve hours.

He slid the small yellow notepad he used to the left, centering it in front of him, and turned back six pages to where his final set of operational notes began. Working slowly, he scanned them, turning pages and rechecking everything.

Logistics – the jihadis would travel by plane mostly. The Islamic State had captured a Syrian passport machine eight months ago, and generating completely valid passports was no longer a problem. He had even selected one of the smaller safe houses the Caliphate maintained to serve as the jihadis' base for this operation. Al-Amriki scratched a note to request that the Caliph's head of intelligence acquire a few more properties to use for future operations.

Weapons – normally they would be difficult to get, but for this target, their brothers-in-arms in Yemen had sent three crates of AK-105 assault rifles and nearly two thousand rounds of ammunition via truck to a warehouse near the target. The jihadis assigned to this target could easily use the warehouse to check weapons and as a secure rally point for later.

The assault – two jihadis would steal a utility truck and be the spearhead for the attack, eliminating the guards at the entrance and opening the way for their brothers dressed in business casual attire, who would rush into the facility, cutting the power and killing as many of the infidels as possible.

Retreat and regroup – once the infidels were dead, the jihadis would set fire to the buildings and leave the site in the ensuing confusion, leaving their weapons behind. As the first responders and police arrived, they would be more interested in evacuating the unarmed 'civilians' than containing the site. The jihadis would regroup at the warehouse, arming themselves for phase two – the assault at the hospitals caring for any survivors or injured first responders from the attack site.

The men chosen would all expect martyrdom at that point, holding the emergency rooms and fighting off the police and other law enforcement or military forces. Al-Amriki scribbled another note – a strict order that the doctors and nurses were to be released unharmed. Their terror-stricken faces appearing on live news feeds around the globe would inspire countless jihadis and demoralize the infidels watching.

Al-Amriki put the notes aside, resolving to write the entire plan up tomorrow, encrypting it and loading it into the dead drop, as well as requesting another face-to-face meeting with Akil. Akil would need to sign off on the operation and ensure the fighters chosen for this operation were properly indoctrinated, trained, and prepared for the martyrdom that awaited them.

Rubbing his eyes again, Al-Amriki shutdown the laptop, closing the screen with a solid click. It was time to sleep. Maybe some music to relax before I crash, he mused.

Mathews checked the luminous dial of his G-Shock watch. The glowing green hands told him it was ten minutes after midnight. He and Simms had spent the rest of the afternoon checking their equipment and rehearsing the plan, and both men had grabbed a couple hours of rest after dinner while CTS monitored the RAVEN's video feed.

After waking, Mathews and Simms covered the plan again, assuring themselves they knew exactly what actions they would take from the moment they stepped outside of the small safe house and drove over to FULLBACK's location. Then it was time to get ready.

Both men had donned lightweight black t-shirts, black cargo pants, and boots, before strapping their suppressed .40 caliber Sig Sauers to their thighs. They also wore the special lightweight body armor Wraith operators usually wore for assault missions.

The armor had two very thin layers of Kevlar containing a one-quarter-inch thick inner layer of magnetorheological fluid. Fiber optic sensors were embedded in the Kevlar layers, creating a pathway for signals to a special micro-processor that detected penetrations of the vest by bullets or knife thrusts.

Powered by a tiny lithium ion battery pack, the microprocessor would detect the penetration, then send a small electric current to the magnetorheolog-ical fluid at the point of entry, causing it to harden to the density of thick steel in less than a hundredth of a microsecond. While the armor did not make the operator wearing it superhuman, it could withstand impacts of rounds up to .50 caliber, although the high velocity of a .40 caliber or higher round striking the vest would cause an operator to stagger back a pace. Its only weakness was that multiple rounds hitting the exact same impact point, plus or minus a half inch, would get through. On the upside, the fluid and Kevlar combination made the vests very thin, lightweight, and nearly invisible if you chose the proper clothing, making them ideal for this kind of covert work.

Over the body armor, both men donned the ubiquitous Thawb to hide the gear, both in dark chocolate brown. Both garments had long slits cut along the right thigh to allow the commandos unimpeded access to their sidearms. They also carried Tasers as non-lethal options, and Mathews had a small black auto-injector filled with a fast-acting combination of barbiturates that would make FULLBACK easier to handle without causing medical problems for their target.

The lights had been off inside the little safe house for about thirty min-utes to let their eyes adjust to the darkness outside. As a precaution, Simms had been sneaking peeks out the window every few minutes to assure himself that the area around the house was clear, since they were unable to rely on the RAVEN's video camera, still focused on FULLBACK's location. Both men also had their Bluetooth headsets in their ears, and dark brown keffiyehs wrapped around their faces to hide their features and the Bluetooth headsets.

Mathews was already sweating a little from the extra gear and clothing, and he was sure Simms was too, but neither man complained. Their training and combat experience made them used to this kind of discomfort, and they simply ignored it as unimportant. They could shower later.

"Charlie Four, we're good to go," Mathews said over the open link. Simms could hear it as well, since Cain had sent him a text with the special attach-ment earlier in the evening after Mathews had reported his arrival.

"Copy Whiskey Four Six," came the sound of Cain's voice. "This is Charlie One. We have confirmation of execute authority. Whiskey Six Actual is monitoring."

Mathews understood Cain's reference to Whiskey Six Actual to mean that General Crane, and very likely Colonel Simon, were listening in on the encrypted comm link, relayed from CTS out to them at Wraith Base. Tactical control of the mission was now in his hands.

"Charlie Four, this is Whiskey Four Six, confirm target location." Mathews had put the tablet in the backpack, which was now sitting on the floor near the door. Simms would grab it on their way out.

"Whiskey Four Six, this is Charlie Four," Thompson's voice said in his ear, "Lights went out at the target location forty minutes ago. All quiet on site, no civilians present on the street within three blocks of the objective. Everything looks good from here."

"Copy that," Mathews told her. They would still need to drive the Range Rover to a spot near FULLBACK's house, the decision to use it rather than the Toyota Simms brought from Amman dictated by the large cargo area in the rear and that its motor ran smoothly and more quietly than the Toyota's. The tarp Simms had brought along was now sitting in the back of the Range Rover. It would cover up Al-Amriki nicely until they got him to the exfil location.

Mathews looked at Simms, and locked eyes with him, asking his NCOIC a silent question. Simms nodded once slowly.

"Charlie Four, Whiskey Team is moving. ETA to the insertion point, five minutes."

"Copy," Cain responded, "Railroad has the word. They'll move once you have the objective."

In CTS, Cain stood near his desk on the operations floor. It was not quite seven at night, 2355 Zulu, but the floor was fully manned, each of the on-duty liaisons aware that a capture operation was in play, but not the specifics yet.

Everyone was wearing their headsets, allowing them to communicate amongst themselves on the CTS internal loop as well as monitor the radio traffic from the op. Emily had even put the RAVEN's video feed up on the center main monitor. Cain ordered the entry and exit doors to CTS electronically locked an hour ago to prevent unexpected interruptions. Even the president could not walk in without Cain's approval until the operation was over.

Cain made a quick note of the time and keyed his microphone to address the watch standers on the internal loop directly. His voice was all business, but he could not keep the excited edge out of his voice as another mission to protect his country got underway.

"Ladies and gentlemen, as you are generally aware, there is a capture operation in motion. The capture team of two Wraith Team members has just departed for their infiltration point. Please notify your agencies of the operation in progress and have them report any intelligence that may affect this operation. The objective is one Omar Abdur Razzaq, referred to by the Islamic State as Al-Amriki, aka The American, codename FULLBACK."

CHAPTER 11

Mark Walker was working late again. As the Chief of the CIA's National Clandestine Service, formerly known as the Directorate of Operations, Walker almost never worked a 'normal' schedule. When the former director asked that he accept the promotion to this job, she had warned him, based on her own experience in the position, that normal days would be a thing of his past. She had even told him to say goodbye to his family on the day he reaffirmed his oath during the promotion ceremony.

She was right. If it was not a briefing on the latest crop of field operatives graduating from 'The Farm', it was a pile of source evaluations, usually about sources that had turned out to be disingenuous or outright liars hoping to score a quick buck from an American government always hungry for information about a wide variety of subjects. Mix all that in with the routine set of policy, planning, and budget meetings that happened daily at his level, and he considered himself lucky to get home before 10 P.M. six nights a week. Sunday mornings he normally spent with his family, but he inevitably ended up on the secure phone in his private study at some point in the afternoon, if not having his security detail drive him in to Langley, so he could catch up on some work while the Monday through Friday workforce was home with their families.

Days usually started at 7 A.M. with his usual intake of coffee. A big Texas Longhorn banner hung on the wall above the credenza his personal Keurig coffeemaker sat on. Taking his reading glasses off to rub his tired green eyes and let his mind drift from work for a few moments, he found himself wondering, who keeps restocking the Dunkin Doughnuts coffee pods for the Keurig? It was probably Stephanie, his assistant, who was fortunate enough to have a more normal schedule, and was kind enough to realize that he did not. Walker grinned lopsidedly, that and they fact that she would not let a fellow Longhorn fan go without the coffee he liked. He resolved to ask his wife to get her something nice for Christmas as a thank you. Thinking of his wife made him glance at the photo on the corner of his desk.

Why she ever fell for him was still a mystery in some ways. Taken in Hawaii during their last vacation, the photo showed a slim blonde-haired woman on the arm of a bald, bespectacled, middle-aged man whose head was beet red from too much sun and not enough sunscreen. Sharon's girl-next-door good looks, dazzling smile, and perpetually curly hair looked so out of place next to him. Grateful for every day he had with her, he shook his head at how things worked out in life, and thought back over his workday.

A staff meeting with the Director, which as usual ran a half hour over schedule while they discussed Congress's latest request for information: the Senate intelligence committee was still looking for documents related to the last upgrade to the agency's aging IT infrastructure, now that they knew the contractor had overcharged the government by nearly ten million dollars. Once the director's staff meeting was over, he chaired his own staff meeting, managing the CIA's hundreds of case officers and Chiefs of Station, and taking the opportunity to pass on to his division heads relevant items from the director's meeting before heading off to grab some lunch in the huge food court.

Of all the vendors in the food court, he preferred the pizza from Sbarro, but settled for the on-site chef's salad and soup combination instead, doing what he could to cooperate with his doctor who had been pestering him about his twenty-pound weight gain since he took the new job. It was bad enough he had gone bald by forty-five, but being fitted for new suits because of the weight gain was just not possible with his schedule now, especially since Morty Sill's in Georgetown was only open from 9 to 6 on weekdays.

As usual, he ate at his desk while he caught up with his e-mail on the secure system, reading and responding to nearly sixty-five e-mails in an hour, a new record that still left him with three-hundred unread e-mails in his queue, which occasioned a frown before he hit the men's room to relieve himself and wash up.

The afternoon was full of one briefing after another about various human intelligence operations his subordinates were monitoring. Each division or branch chief came in to his office in rotation, briefed him for five or ten minutes, answered his questions, and left, in a stream that continued until 5 P.M., finally leaving him some free time to do some actual work.

After a quick run down to the Food Court to give in to his pizza urge with a couple of slices of pepperoni to balance out the salad from lunch, he got back to work. In short order, he reviewed and edited an analysis for the National Intelligence Estimate on worldwide proliferation of weapons of mass destruction due next week. Next up, Walker read through his division's documentation on the IT contractor's work before e-mailing it to the director, her chief of staff, and the congressional liaison office, and started working on the proposed budget for the next fiscal year. The e-mail queue was up above four hundred now, and he was hoping to put a dent in it once he was done with the budget documents.

Walker was just turning the last page on the GAO's analysis of the proposed intelligence community budget for the next year when the phone rang. Shit. Walker thought, glancing at the clock. His phone ringing at 7 P.M. cannot be a good thing.

"Walker."

"Sir, this is Sandra O'Toole on the watch." The woman's voice was soft and pleasant with no hint of panic or urgency in it, Walker noted. Maybe this was not quite as bad as he initially thought. The career professionals staffing the CIA Watch Center were not normally given to panic, unless something truly catastrophic was in motion.

"What can I do for you, Miss O'Toole?" Walker inquired. He thought she sounded young enough to be a 'Miss'.

"I'm sorry to disturb you, sir, but the status board said you hadn't left for the night and you are on the required coordination list for terrorist capture/kill operations by the DOD. We were just informed by our CTS liaison that there is an Op in progress now."

Walker frowned. There was nothing in the daily brief about that. Like everyone else in the business of hunting terrorists, Walker knew it was standard practice to pre-coordinate those kinds of operations. One of his people or the DOD's might have dropped the ball on the coordination. Walker resolved to call CTS and General Crane in the morning and ask them to pass the word on their ends, and I'll mention it in my staff meeting tomorrow.

"Sounds good to me," Walker told O'Toole. No need to share with her his coordination concerns. It was not her issue to deal with. "Colonel Simon's

Wraith Team operators are some of the best we have. Who's the target?"

"Codename FULLBACK, real name Omar Abdur Razzaq, referred to by the Islamic State as Al-Amriki."

Walker's hand gripped the phone so hard he was surprised he did not crack the case. "I'm sorry, Miss O'Toole, I was reaching for a pen, would you repeat that identification?" Walker made no move to get a pen. In fact, the adrenaline running through his system had his mind in overdrive.

"Sure, sir," O'Toole responded, "Codename FULLBACK, real name Omar Abdur Razzaq, referred to by the Islamic State as Al-Amriki. Do you need me to spell the Arabic names for you sir?"

Walker's hand was starting to cramp. "No, thank you," he responded in a calm voice. "Thanks for passing that on. You said the Op is in play now?"

"Yes, sir." O'Toole answered, "The capture team is heading for their jump-off point. In fact, they should be there now."

Walker swore to himself. "Thank you, Miss O'Toole." He hung up without waiting for her reply, his mind racing. He literally had seconds to act.

He picked up the handset for the red phone on his desk and punched a speed dial button. The call was answered immediately.

"6657, Major..."

Walker cut him off. "This is Mark Walker, Chief of the National Clandestine Service at CIA. I need to speak to General Crane immediately."

"Sir, the General..."

"Listen son! I know exactly what he's doing. He's monitoring a capture Op that's already in motion. I need to speak to the General! Get him on this fucking phone now!"

"Wait one," the unnamed major answered in an unruffled tone, finally acceding to the urgency in Walker's voice, but too experienced to get his feathers ruffled by a senior civil servant not in his direct chain of command.

Walker looked at the clock on the wall. Nearly a minute had passed. Walker knew that it had already taken minutes for the liaison at CTS to call the CIA watch center, the watch center to call him, and now for him to call the general, the capture team was probably already moving toward their objective. It may already be too late.

"Whiskey Four-Six, in position at the insertion point." Mathews said as he killed the Range Rover's engine. He had left the headlights off for the last three blocks after Thompson had confirmed that there were no civilians in the area. Two blocks away he turned hard left onto the dirt track that bisected the tract of houses that ran north-south along the very western edge of Ar-Ruwayshid.

The space between the sparse grouping of houses at the edge of town was nearly sixty feet, and Mathews held his speed to less than five miles an hour, hoping that distance and the relatively quiet Range Rover engine would not cause the neighbors on either side to look out their windows.

Nearly three hundred yards away from the houses, Mathews turned one hundred and twenty degrees to the right and drove back toward the town, angling toward a single house, set back nearly fifty yards from the north-south road. As they approached, Simms leaned forward to reach between his feet and donned what looked like a black motorcycle helmet. With the keffiyeh on, it was a snug fit, but both men had agreed that wearing the cloth head cover was much less suspicious than wearing the helmets inside a car during the ride across town if someone were to see them.

Part of their normal assault kit, the helmet provided ballistic protection, with its impregnated Kevlar weave for his head and neck, and a set of adaptive, full field of view night vision optics. Under normal circumstances, CTS could push them targeting cues based on data from orbiting drones or other assets, enabling the helmets to show them an augmented reality view of the world, projected onto the inner ballistic plastic face shield. Unfortunately, the RAVEN had not been built with that ability, and the rest of the high-tech gear they for that was back in the States.

For this mission, the helmets would be running only off the thin lithium-polymer backup batteries mounted deep within the thick Kevlar walls of the helmet's rim – which would give them about forty-five minutes of use for the night vision systems. Simms touched an inset button on the right side of the helmet under the rim, and studied FULLBACK's safe house and the surrounding area.

"No sign of movement," Simms said quietly. Neither of the men had their seatbelts on, and Simms's right hand rested on the handgrip of his holstered Sig Sauer.

"Area remains clear," Thompson called out over the link. "No sign of movement at the target."

Mathews donned his helmet and activated it, the green and black light amplification mode showed him the rear of FULLBACK's house complete-ly. "Confirmed, no sign of movement." Mathews announced over the link. "Executing."

As soon as the word was out of his mouth, Mathews and Simms opened the Range Rover's doors and exited the vehicle, leaving the doors open. Both men drew their matte-black sidearms in smooth motions, held them in two-handed grips for improved stability, flicked off the safeties, and began to walk toward the rear of Al-Amriki's refuge.

Mathews watched the house carefully as he and Simms closed the gap. This is it, you bastard. Please make a move for a weapon rather than surrender-ing. Mathews gripped his weapon a little tighter and continued walking. He and Simms both swept their heads back and forth across the objective house and surrounding area, checking for any signs of innocent civilians or movement. Mathews could feel the sweat on his forehead drenching the keffiyeh's cotton cloth under the helmet, the soft crunch of his footfalls the only sound in the still night air even with Simms less than eight feet from him.

The distance they had to cover was less than fifty feet, and thirty seconds later, they were stacked on the rear door, Simms in the lead position, Mathews covering him. Moonrise was in twenty minutes – they had plenty of time.

In CTS, Cain was staring intently at the main display on the far wall. Thompson had commanded the drone to increase its altitude a few hundred feet, and orbit in a tight circle around the house like a buzzard circling an antelope about to be attacked by wolves, knowing it would feast soon.

Like Mathews and Simms, Cain watched the house for any sign of move-ment, but had the added advantage of being able to use the RAVEN's vantage point to scan the area around it as well. No civilians, no sign of lights or vehicles. It was nice and quiet. This was going to be a textbook takedown. He was about to reach for the button to key his microphone and give the extraction team a final 'all clear' when his secure phone started ringing.

He grabbed the receiver and put his eyes back on the display. One of the men was defeating the lock on the door now.

"Cain," he said tersely. What he heard made his eyes go wide as he saw both com-mandos enter the house, weapons up and looking for targets.

Mathews reached in front of Simms and made a motion like turning a key in a lock. Simms gave him a thumb up and tried the doorknob. Two gentle turns later, one clockwise, and one counter-clockwise told him it was locked. He extracted a pair of lock picks from his pocket and worked the lock. Simms could tell by feel it was a simple four-pin device, and in seconds, he had defeated it with an audible 'click'.

Mathews and Simms both winced at the sound which, with the adrenaline coursing through their veins, seemed louder than it actually was, and Simms put the picks away, drawing his sidearm again. Mathews blew out a soft breath to calm himself, and laid a hand on Simms shoulder, pressing down and forward slightly.

Simms turned the knob with his left hand and swung the door open. The brief squeak of one of the hinges made both men grimace, but they were committed now. Simms entered the house, weapon up and searching for targets, Mathews hot on his heels. Simms moved left into the kitchen and then forward toward the front living area, Mathews half a pace behind him.

Once in the living room, Mathews turned right, carrying out the entry plan he and Simms had discussed, assuming the floorplan of the little house might be similar to Mathews' own rental, based on the roof design and dimensions. He saw a small table near the corner, strewn with papers, what looked like maps, and the thin shape of a laptop computer – all would be good candidates for exploitation if they could grab them after they had dealt with FULLBACK.

Mathews hugged the corner wall separating the kitchen from the rest of the house, covering the short hallway and seeing a faint light in his night vision gear coming from what should be the master bedroom at the far end.

Simms moved in on his left, entering the hallway and stepping in through the first open door on the left side, emerging a few seconds later after determining the second bedroom was devoid of threats.

Mathews moved down the hallway, intentionally crossing Simms' line of fire to hug the left wall in a pre-arranged pattern to get an angle on the bathroom on the right. Simms lowered his weapon's muzzle briefly to avoid sweeping Mathews' body, bringing it back up again to cover the right side of the hall, now a pace behind Mathews.

As soon as Mathews could see into the tiny bathroom and be sure no one was in it, he shifted his aim left, now a yard away from the open door to the master bedroom, the faint glow brighter now.

Al-Amriki sat in bed, the lights out, listening to a radio station across the Internet, the live broadcast from the early evening show out of Chicago reminding him of his parents and the long and somewhat twisted path that ended up with him so far away in Jordan. As usual, he only had one ear bud from the iPhone in his right ear, the other hanging loosely from its thin white cable.

Al-Amriki tried unsuccessfully to stifle a yawn and glanced at the clock. He was usually asleep by now, but he had wanted to jot down some new thoughts about the next operation before he slept. These kinds of intensive planning sessions always challenged him mentally, taxing his concentration, especially as the day wore on and night fell.

What was that? Al-Amriki quickly turned off the radio station with a tap, the glow from the iPhone's screen still casting a soft light out into the room. He pulled the earbud from his right ear and turned his head, opening his mouth a little. He thought he had heard a distinct metallic sound from the inside the house.

Without warning, he heard another noise that sent a surge of adrenaline coursing through his veins, and his heart began to pound. Someone had just opened the back door. The brief squeak of the un-oiled hinge was distinctive. In one fluid motion, he slid from under the sheets, withdrawing the Caracal C .40 S&W pistol from under the pillow, leaving the still-active iPhone laying on the sheets, its bright glow projected up onto the bare ceiling. He took one long step and dropped to one knee in the corner away from the bed, the pistol pointed at the open doorway.

Footsteps in the hallway. He could hear them coming now. Softly, silently, but the faint footfalls, and several millennia of human evolution, told him instinctively that there were other people nearby in the dark. The light from the still active iPhone was just enough to see the outline of the bedroom door, and he used his thumb to flick the safety upward on the pistol's frame.

Mathews heard a metallic click from inside the bedroom and stopped dead in the hallway, holding up his left fist while his right hand kept the Sig pointed at the open doorway. He easily recognized the sound: a pistol's safety disengaging. Shit. Maybe we should have brought flashbangs. The next few seconds seemed to last minutes as the adrenaline rush in his bloodstream caused his perception of time to distort. They were compromised.

The frustration of the moment caused the image of Sam's dead body to rise unbidden from his memory. The clarity of Sam's misshapen head, deformed from the high-velocity impact of the round, was surreal and overwhelmed Mathews' reason and duty. His soul screamed for revenge.

Mathews decided in that moment to disobey his orders and deal with this terrorist once and for all. They will not win again. Not after what happened to Sam. This one will die as payback for what happened to Sam. He doesn't need to be interrogated, just killed. Sam would rest easier. Kill the fucker.

Mathews knelt to reduce his exposure, hoping the target was aiming high. It would give him a vital half-second or so of time to shoot first after he rounded the corner to take aim.

As he started to lean forward toward the doorframe, he heard Simms's voice on the link. "Boss?"

Simms's wanted to know the play before Mathews acted, but the single question also served to derail Mathews' murderous intent.

Simms, standing just a few feet behind him, had just reminded him with one word of his ultimate duty to bring his team home alive. Mathews chided himself for forgetting that Simms was there even for a few seconds. It was a cardinal sin among special operators to think of yourself first. Your country, unit, team, and self, in that order. It was a way of life, and he could not violate that code of conduct.

Mathews breathed in slowly and deeply, then let out a slow, measured breath through his mouth to help regain his control, mentally pushing the image of Sam's dead body back into the recesses of his mind as best he could. After a moment, he said quietly, "I'm good," to reassure Simms. "Taking a quick look. Cover me."

Putting his left hand up and motioning forward, Mathews prepared to peek around the corner, using the wall as cover and hoping the brief exposure would show him a man cowering in fear, but prepared to backpedal if fired on, or shoot if the target rushed him. Simms kept his distance to cover Mathews, but stayed within arm's reach in case he had to drag Mathews clear.

Suddenly, Mathews heard Cain's voice in his ear, the tone measured but urgent.

"Whiskey Team, this is Charlie One! Abort! Abort immediately."

What the fuck? This could not get any more complicated. "Confirm."

Mathews whispered, "We're outside the door. Probably compromised."

In CTS, Cain said into the phone at his ear without keying the radio microphone, "They are standing outside the door. Mathews says they may be compromised." Every member of the watch team was on his or her feet, staring alternately at the main video display showing the house and its open back door and Cain. Every one of them had heard Cain's radio call and Mathews' response. Cain stood rooted his watch floor desk, headset half on his head, the handset of the red phone against his left ear.

Cain listened for a few seconds and keyed the mic. "Whiskey Four Six, listen carefully, this is an order."

Mathews could not believe what he was hearing. 'Complicated' did not quite cover this situation anymore. "Say again, Charlie One," he whispered in reply, his eyes locked on the open doorframe in the wall. If Al-Amriki charged them, Mathews would have no recourse but to shoot him until his Sig locked open on an empty magazine.

Mathews heard Cain repeat the instructions and stood there, mouth agape under the helmet, anger rising again to mix with confusion and the adrenaline rush of a combat operation. *I can't believe what he just ordered me to do.*

Holding the kneeling position, he spoke aloud, the words ringing in the helmet.

"Grand Mufti Akbar sends you greetings from the west."

Inside the room, Al-Amriki nearly dropped the Caracal C .40 S&W in shock. Not only did the man outside his door just give away his kneeling position behind the wall, his words had shattered Al-Amriki's brain. It's not possible. In English he said, "Repeat that."

The man outside his door spoke again, "Grand Mufti Akbar sends you greetings from the west."

Al-Amriki tried unsuccessfully to put the shattered pieces of his mind back together, and after a few seconds found his voice again, saying the only thing he could think of, the Caracal C now trembling in his hand.

"Either come forward and speak to me as a man, or leave my home!"

Outside the door, Mathews stood and backed away until he felt Simms' hand on his shoulder. Both men turned on their heel and left the house, closing the rear door behind them.

This time they did not walk, but jogged back to the Range Rover, doffing their helmets as soon as they were onboard. Mathews started the Range Rover's big V-8 and backed away from the house slowly, retracing their path as quickly as he could without waking anyone in the nearby houses. Once they were back on the north-south road, Mathews turned the Range Rover's lights on and turned onto Highway 10.

"Now what?" Mathews asked acidly across the still open link. Fuck radio procedure.

"Return to your safe house now," Cain's voice said in their ears. "We're pulling the drone off station and sending it to the usual landing site for a battery change. After it lands, and you've swapped out the batteries, you two are to clean-up and drive to the U.S. Embassy in Amman. They'll be waiting for you."

Mathews was fuming. "What the fuck happened, Charlie One?"

"Not now," Cain told him. "This link isn't secure enough for explanations. Get to Amman. Crane's orders."

"Shit." Mathews said aloud, not caring that everyone on the link heard it. "Copy that."

By the time Mathews and Simms reached the safe house, picked up the charged battery pack for the Raven, and drove to the RAVEN's secluded recovery point outside of town, the little drone was already waiting for them.

Five minutes later, the drone had fresh batteries and they launched it. Forty-five minutes after that, the men had showered and changed, brewed strong coffee for the trip, and were in the Range Rover on their way to Amman at seventy-miles per hour.

Cain sat at his desk in on the watch floor, monitoring the Raven's video feed. The Range Rover with Mathews and Simms aboard was just leaving the field of view of the RAVEN's camera, heading west on Highway 10 toward Amman.

Cain leaned to the right to look over at Thompson sitting at the drone desk. She was already looking back at him, expecting the order. "Emily, back on FULLBACK's safe house, please."

"Roger that," Thompson replied. A few seconds later, and the drone's camera slewed back to their primary target. Mathews had left the tablet and his iPhone at the safe house to facilitate CTS' communication with the RAVEN. To ensure their comms would be uninterrupted, Mathews had left both plugged in to power outlets to keep the batteries from being depleted.

Cain sat still for a minute, considering the events of the last hour or so, and blew out an exasperated breath before reaching for the secure phone again.

"They are on the way to Amman."

"Good," Crane told him, the angry tone in his voice still not completely absent.

"So, what did you do?" Cain asked.

"I called the Chairman as soon as Mathews and Simms were clear of the target house."

"What did he say?"

"Off the record, he was pretty pissed. He told me he would be contacting the SECDEF and getting his support for a meeting with the president when the White House called him. I haven't heard from him since."

"You know what we stepped in, don't you?" Cain asked.

"Yes, I know," Crane assured him. "The question is, what are we going to do about it, and why didn't we know beforehand?"

"Our friends at the CIA have been playing things too close to the vest," Cain said resignedly, knowing full well that the CIA's perspective on what was referred to as 'equities' in bureaucratic parlance was not unique to that agency alone.

No matter how much the leader of an agency or the director of national intelligence might preach and enshrine in policy the principles of collaboration and cooperation, long term professionals often viewed their specific intelligence operation or activity as the most important thing in the world, and their province alone. In Cain's view, it was an attitude that quickly led to losing sight of the fact that their operation was always a part of a larger mosaic in the national intelligence strategy or ongoing military operations.

"What are you doing on your end?" Crane inquired.

"I've rechecked my e-mail and the pre-coordination actions on our end," Cain told him. "We have a sign off from the head of CIA's counter-terror division, along with all the other agencies that were part of the planning cycle. I'll need you to join the conference call with General Holland in about thirty minutes."

Since CTS was actually located inside NSA's secure campus, SECDEF had designated the Director of the NSA as the host installation commander, rather than the garrison commander of Fort George G. Meade. As such, Holland was both caretaker and de facto advocate for the CTS mission. Cain knew without reservation that both generals would back him to the hilt, so long as CTS had done its job properly, and Cain knew he could prove that with the e-mail chains, the documented intelligence and, most importantly, the CIA's concurrence for the operation against FULLBACK.

As much as he detested it, this bureaucratic exercise had to be accomplished, even with two Tier One operators still out in the field. For now, Mathews and Simms were both safe and heading for the U.S. Embassy, and that meant Cain could afford the luxury of making sure his organization did not take a hit for initiating and executing this op with the Wraiths.

"Make sure I get a few minutes with Terry Holland before the call," Crane said. "I want to be in sync with him so we can back you and get to the ground truth on this with Walker over at the CIA."

Al-Amriki looked at the iPhone's luminous screen again. It would be dawn in an hour. He sat still on the bed, still holding the Caracal C .40 S&W loosely with one hand, spending long minutes staring at the bedroom door and stealing occasional glances at the iPhone.

He kept going over and over it in his mind. The squeak of the hinge on the rear door. The sound and feel of the footfalls in the hallway. Crouching in the dark, his hands wrapped around the grip of the Caracal C .40 S&W, a slight tremor in the sight picture from the adrenaline, not knowing what was coming through the door – death or capture.

An American kill or capture team had come for him. That was clear from the fluent English he heard the man outside his door speak. The question now was what should he do about it?

Reach out to his colleagues in the Islamic State? No. They would undoubtedly send a small assault force to extract him and spirit him away into territory they controlled inside eastern Syria or northern Iraq. He would not be able to continue his planning there. His contacts and resources had all been centered on this small town and moving them would take time.

If he failed to report the attempted capture, and the leadership of the Islamic State was watching him, they might question his loyalty. Perhaps it would be better to report it?

Al-Amriki dismissed that thought as ill considered. He had taken his regular walks in town looking for surveillance teams and seen nothing. No. Wait. He had seen something. The young westerner a few days ago.

Although he had not seen the man again, he might be one of the men who had come for him in the night. He had barely heard him speak in Abdul's little store, and could not be certain that it was the young westerner's voice. In any case, as he replayed the moment, the voice was slightly muffled, as if speaking through a wall, which made no sense at all.

As Al-Amriki replayed the memory again. The unexpected and shocking words the unknown American said echoed again in his mind, causing his thoughts to continue to race, even as the sky lightened, and the sun rose to begin its steady arc across a clear blue sky. "Grand Mufti Akbar sends you greetings from the west."

CHAPTER 12

"There it is," remarked Mathews as they rounded the corner, turning from Queen Zein Al-Sharaf Boulevard onto Al Umaweyeen road. It was Mathews' first look at the U.S. Embassy in Amman, and he was impressed by the size of the facility, in spite of the overview he was given as part of his mission brief.

The nearly three-hundred-yard-long and two-hundred-and-fifty-yard-wide compound housing the embassy building was surrounded by a twelve-foot-high concrete wall because of the inherent security concerns of life in the Middle East for Americans. The compound also housed the U.S. ambassador's residence, a small apartment block for the sixty or so state department employees assigned there for two-year tours of duty, an armory and bachelor quarters for the Marine security detachment, two sets of tennis courts, and an Olympic-sized pool.

Married state department employees or those with families could live in nice though modest apartments or villas in Amman proper. The vast majority however, chose to work in Amman unaccompanied by their families, given the regular spate of protests and other demonstrations held just outside the embassy's high concrete walls whenever U.S. foreign policy in the Middle East ran counter to what many in the region felt was appropriate.

The entire edifice, made of reinforced steel and concrete looked very delicate. The pleasing outer shell of sandstone plates decorated with a simple yet elegant red trim belied the solid structure beneath, and its imposing height was the physical presence of American interests and its military partnership with Jordan. The huge eight-foot-long and five-foot-high American flag flew proudly from the central aluminum flag pole before the embassy building itself, flapping gently in a 10-knot wind. Mathews' spirits brightened a little when he saw it.

"Where is your girlfriend meeting us?" Mathews asked Simms.

Simms frowned at the reference, since he knew that Mathews was well aware of his track record with women, and the two resultant divorces. An hour ago, Simms had taken a call on his iPhone 6s from a woman who identified herself as Sally who, by way of identification, informed him she was in charge of getting the rental cars for tourists in Jordan. Both men knew from their mission briefings with Simon she was the CIA's lead undercover agent in Jordan, known formally as the Chief of Station.

"She isn't," Simms told him. "She said your Uncle Simon sent a driver and a car to pick us up at the Abdoun Mall to the southeast. Go straight through the traffic circle. The Mall will be on the left."

"Copy that," Mathews responded, fatigue and remaining anger from last night's aborted operation rising to the surface again. He needed answers from somebody inside that embassy.

"She also said Abdoun and the surrounding area is one of the most afflu-ent in Jordan, so drive 'wealthy'."

"Right," Mathews said, his mood not improved by Sally's poor attempt at humor. Their Range Rover was hardly showroom new, and after the round trip out to Ar-Ruwayshid and back, was covered in dust and fly spattered.

"Once you see the Mall, take your first left. She said we'll see the signs for the underground car park. It's only two levels. Head for the lowest. We're looking for a black Merc. An S550 with embassy plates."

"What about video surveillance?" Mathews asked with some urgency in his voice. It would not do to break field craft now and blow their cover.

"None, according to Sally. Crime in this part of Jordan is practically non-existent, and the Pakistani watchmen that keep an eye on the underground garage make hourly passes on golf carts."

Mathews wove the Range Rover through the circular roundabout and identified the Abdoun Mall immediately. The curved L-shaped building sheathed in white limestone occupied the entire block with its distinctive white ceramic and glass dome over what he presumed was the food court. It rose nearly six stories.

Taking the first left past the Mall, Mathews scanned the left side of the road for the underground car park entrance and saw the blue sign with the white 'P' almost immediately. The electronic sign over the entrance told him the first level of the underground lot held nearly sixty cars, but the second, lower level held only forty.

"Eyes open," Mathews said aloud, but Simms was already scanning the lot as Mathews guided the Range Rover through the descending spiral of concrete support columns and marked parking spaces.

On the lower level, Mathews spotted the black Mercedes instantly. The brand new S550 was polished to a mirror finish, and its windows were heavily tinted. Parked near the middle of the first row of parking slots, well away from the elevator and stairs that led upward to the ground floor of the mall, it sat silently.

"I see vapor from the twin exhausts," Simms reported. The driver obviously had the motor running.

"Is there a recognition code?" Mathews asked.

"The front wheels should be turned away from the mall if it's clear." Simms answered.

Mathews pointed the Range Rover toward the gleaming glass and aluminum doors of the entrance, choosing the outermost lane to give Simms a chance to eyeball the Mercedes as they passed.

"Looks good, Boss." Simms reported. "Park next to him. The driver should step out and look in the trunk. Young kid, obviously American."

Mathews eased the Range Rover into the slot to the right of the Mercedes, blocking its direct line sight from the mall's elevator core, but prepared to slam the rugged four-by-four into reverse the instant something seemed amiss.

The driver's door to the Mercedes opened, and a young man no more than twenty-five years old stepped out, wearing a white shirt, black tie and coat, and the ubiquitous billed cap of a chauffeur.

"Doesn't he just scream 'Marine'?" Mathews observed. 'Uncle Simon's driver' indeed. The kid's erect military posture, broad shoulders, and stubble of a crew-cut marked him as one of the marines from the embassy's security contingent.

The kid closed the trunk and headed back to the driver's side as Mathews killed the Range Rover's engine and opened the door.

"Rear doors are unlocked," the kid said over the roofline of the Mercedes before slipping behind the wheel again.

Mathews gave the underground garage's interior another quick scan and, seeing no sign of the watchmen Simms had mentioned, slid into the rear seat of the Mercedes, moving behind the driver to make room for Simms.

Simms exited the Range Rover, crossed behind it to the Mercedes and jumped in without so much as a backwards glance, settling himself in the right rear seat. Mathews locked the Range Rover with the remote as the kid backed the Mercedes out of the slot.

"Which one of you is Mathews?" the Marine driver asked.

"I am," Mathews responded.

"Nice to meet you, Lieutenant Commander. I'm Lance Corporal Al Shew. The car belongs to the embassy. Our tech guys sweep it twice a week for bugs. You're safe to talk in here. My orders are to take you to Sally. Sound good?"

Reassured, Mathews finally relaxed a little. "That sounds very good, Corporal Shew."

Mathews had expected trouble trying to get into the Embassy, but Corporal Shew was well prepared. The Jordanians had only a few men on duty at the main entrance, and Shew told Mathews and Simms to sit quietly and say nothing.

A quick wave at the two Jordanian army NCOs at the main gate, and Shew guided the big Mercedes sedan through the opening in the twelve-foot high security wall and its thick steel doors. Inside the steel doors, four Marines in camouflage utilities, armed with pistols and assault rifles stood post. Two of them carried 5.56mm M4 carbines, the other two, 5.56mm M27 infantry automatic rifles.

Based on his background briefing, Mathews knew that the Jordanians took security at the American Embassy seriously, given the number of regular protests, and he was surprised at how easily they passed through the outer layer of security.

"I expected a stricter security perimeter," Mathews observed aloud.

"I make regular trips in the car picking up people from the airport and shuttling embassy officials, visiting VIPs from various companies, etc." Shew replied over his shoulder. "Unless there is an active protest, the Jordanian army is pretty laissez-faire about the perimeter."

The marines were less casual, and one waved at Shew to stop the car. Shew waved and stepped on the brake, touching the armrest control to lower the window.

"Hey Al," the young marine said, glancing in the rear of the Mercedes. "New friends?" he said, raising the muzzle of the M4 slightly.

"Yeah, it's no sweat, Mike. Sally asked them to come in for a visit. They're both active duty."

The young marine nodded once. "Proceed."

Shew drove the Mercedes the rest of the way through the embassy entrance and turned right, guiding the car around the vast expanse of the embassy building and turning left to pass between the embassy on the left and the ambassador's residence on the right. Mathews let out a slow breath, finally able to relax a little now that he was in territory of the United States again.

Shew positioned the Mercedes directly beneath the natural canopy formed by a small grove of trees planted to form a natural tunnel between the ambassador's residence and the embassy, and parked.

Mathews and Simms exited from the car and Shew led them toward the embassy, but turned left before entering the building, heading directly to a narrow concrete stairwell set up against the exterior wall.

Shew trotted down the concrete steps, Mathews and Simms right behind him. The steps ended in a landing sheltered from direct observation by the patio overhead, and a heavily reinforced steel door set into the embassy's basement wall. Shew knocked twice, and the door opened immediately.

Mathews' eyes widened. The woman standing behind the door was strikingly beautiful. Tall and generously proportioned, she had angular Mediterranean features, with black hair that fell like an inky river down her back.

"I'm Sally." Her voice was pleasantly modulated, but with a husky edge.

"Hello," Mathews said, suddenly feeling like he was back in high school working up the courage to ask a girl out for the first time.

"Thank you, Corporal," Sally said to Shew, obviously dismissing him. Addressing Mathews and Simms, she said, "Follow me," before heading off down a well-lit corridor leading deep into the embassy. Sally was wearing a light dress in dark blue silk that, while modestly cut, could not hide the hourglass shape of her figure or the sway of her hips while she walked. The matching shoes were good quality but flats instead of heels, which Mathews thought slightly odd until he remembered what organization employed her. Heels were not conducive to running from or evading the local security forces on foot.

Mathews and Simms exchanged one masculine look of mutual understanding, and then followed her wordlessly as Shew shut the door behind them. Sally led them through the basement level of the embassy, a maze of corridors that Mathews assumed was just the first level of the embassy basement, until she reached another heavy steel door, tapping in a six-digit code on the number pad next to it to release the electronic lock.

Sally waved the two men through the door and shut it behind them. Mathews scanned the room quickly, noting the thick carpet on the floor and soundproofing on the walls, the tall, five-drawer steel-gray safe in the far corner, the simple conference table and chairs that dominated the center of the room, and the next-generation video teleconferencing equipment facing the table in the brightly lit room.

Sally indicated the chairs facing the video equipment. "Please sit, gentlemen."

Mathews and Simms took their seats, eyes on Sally.

"Thanks for all your help, by the way," Mathews told her.

"Think nothing of it," Sally said as she sealed the door.

"You're attending a VTC that will start in about five minutes," Sally informed them.

"Forgive me," Mathews said, "but I have to ask. You're the station chief, right?"

"Yes," Sally nodded.

"How does a woman with your looks stay undercover in Jordanian society? I've heard the men here tend to be less than polite to women in public settings." Mathews asked unabashedly.

Sally smiled ruefully, "It's not that difficult, actually. Men in general tend to see only my face and figure, and they generally aren't smart enough to think I might have a brain to match. In Jordan, that's amplified quite a bit due to the local culture as you mentioned, with the exception of some of the more educated members of the government and universities."

"Yes," Mathews pressed on, undeterred, "I can see how that would work, but still, you must get more attention than you would prefer."

Sally gave him a blindingly bright smile, "No more so than I did working my way through Yale. Jordanian men are like frat boys, but without the beer. In this culture, as a woman, if you protest loudly enough when the men cross the line in public, they immediately apologize and withdraw. Moreover, other men and women in the area are immediately drawn toward a woman who is obviously warning off a man who is being too forward – another cultural imperative on their part. That's a nicer part of their culture in my estimation. Back in Connecticut, if a guy had a few too many beers for a polite or even a loud 'No' to have the proper impact, I usually ended up practicing some Aikido techniques on him before anyone else thought to come to my aid."

Mathews smiled. Yale educated and trained in Aikido? No wonder this woman was a station chief for the CIA. "I'd imagine word got around fast that the fellas should remember to be polite to you when asking for a date."

Sally headed for the door, "Yes, but that stopped being a problem after a while; once word got around." She opened the door to leave, and then looked back over her shoulder at them, "I only wanted to date women." The door shut behind her with a solid metallic click.

Mathews and Simms shared a 'Holy Shit' look and started chuckling. 'Sally' was a piece of work.

"Well that trashes some obvious fantasies," Mathews opined aloud. He could hear the VTC starting to chime as the secure links activated. "I wouldn't be surprised if she's the next CIA Director."

"Based on what she's done for us so far, she sure as hell seems competent enough," Simms agreed, tactfully ignoring his officer's other comment, "but does she have the right political contacts?"

"An excellent question," Mathews answered, knowing that nomination to be the director of the CIA was more a political reward than something offered to a career CIA officer, with one or two exceptions.

As the VTC monitor began to display the connection dialog, Mathews turned his attention to it. In seconds, the monitor displayed three locations. The first appeared to be Cain's office in CTS – he recognized the cabinet sitting behind Cain's desk. His assessment was confirmed when Cain himself stepped into view, sitting down heavily in the chair behind his desk. Cain looked tired and grim, and Mathews suspected Cain was as pissed as he was about how badly this mission had turned out and probably had not gotten a lot of sleep, since it was nearly 4 A.M. on the east coast.

The second was Wraith base, Simon and General Crane looked similarly annoyed and weary in his opinion – and it was two hours earlier in the Mountain Time zone. Both men were seated in one of the conference rooms on level seven, judging by the décor.

The last location he did not recognize, but he assumed that the bald, slightly overweight man seated in the small conference room with the oak conference table on camera was CIA, since the CIA's seal hung on the wall behind him.

"Good morning, Mathews," General Crane said over the secure link.

"Good morning, sir," Mathews responded, not bothering to keep the frustration from his voice.

"How are you holding up?" Colonel Simon asked.

Mathews resisted the urge to swear during his reply. "Better once someone explains to me what happened."

"I'm looking forward to hearing that too." Cain added from Fort Meade. Both he and Crane had decided during their conversation with General Holland that the CIA needed to come clean about exactly why Mathews and Simms were called off.

Silence reigned on the link for nearly ten seconds while they waited.

"Mr. Walker, that was your cue," General Crane said with barely restrained hostility.

The bald man at CIA rubbed his eyes and let out an exasperated breath before speaking. "For the benefit of the two men at the Embassy, my name is Mark Walker, and I am the head of the National Clandestine Service of the CIA."

Walker opened a file folder on the conference table before him and continued. "Gentlemen, what I am about to tell you is classified as a special access program. Not thirty minutes ago, I received written approval from the Director of the CIA to allow you access to the program we call CONSTANT ALCHEMY."

Mathews shared a 'Here it comes' look with Simms.

"Within that program, you are also being accessed to the sub compartment called SILVERSMITH. SILVERSMITH is our long-term effort to place a CIA operative close to the leadership of the Islamic State. You know our SILVERSMITH as FULLBACK. You were outside his bedroom door last night."

Mathews looked at the monitor incredulously, composure shattering. "Son-of-a-bitch! Are you telling me we conducted this Op against a deep cover CIA asset? What the fuck are you people doing back there in D.C.?"

While Mathews was mad, it did not come close to how pissed off Cain was. Cain actually leaned toward the camera on his desk, raising his voice to the point where he was sure the team on the CTS watch floor could hear it through the solid walls and closed door of his office.

"Mark! Why in the hell didn't this come out in the coordination for this mission? We vetted this through your people and they didn't say a damned thing!"

Crane was trying to talk at the same time Cain was, his face red and the angry tone making it through the link intermingled with Cain's words. Walker held his hands up in a plea of surrender.

"Whoa! Guys! Stop! Yes! We screwed up the coordination on this one, and we'll figure out why later. The short answer is we played this one very close to the vest internal to the Agency, and the people we have coordinating with CTS aren't read into CONSTANT ALCHEMY. We will work internally to fix it. For now, we need to figure out what to do next."

Cain leaned back from the camera at his end, the frustration still visible on his face. Crane's face was less red, but anger still burned hot in his blood.

"What we do next is simple, Mr. Walker," General Crane said in his command voice, "ROGUE SENTINEL is terminated immediately. My operators are coming back home on the first plane out of Amman we can get them on. Your director will also be getting a call from the Chairman and SECDEF. Putting soldier's lives in danger unnecessarily tends to piss them off too."

Mathews was all for that. This mission was a total wash at this point. It had gone about as badly as it could have. As he continued to think it through, Mathews realized, I damn near killed a deep cover operative for the CIA because I wanted to balance the scales for Sam's death.

The revelation shook him more than his realization inside FULLBACK's safehouse. His grief and anger over Sam's death had impacted him so much that he had almost ended an innocent life. Worse, he had almost killed one of his fellow citizens serving his country and putting his life at tremendous risk to defeat the Islamic State. If he had killed Al-Amriki, Mathews knew he would be guilty of murder. He closed his eyes and hung his head for a moment as he finally understood what Kristen was trying to tell him. Oh god. The best thing to do was get out of Dodge now. I need to hold Kristen right now and ask her to forgive me for being an idiot.

Cain's angry voice pulled him back to the here and now. "Sounds good to me," Cain said sarcastically. "You screwed this up massively, Mark."

Walker shook his head adamantly. "No, we didn't. We protected our operative the same way you would protect one of your sources, David."

"Yes, Mark, I would have protected my source," Cain responded, "but I would have done the proper coordination to keep the whole thing on the rails and not put people's lives at risk. How badly is your asset exposed on this?"

"In my estimation, SILVERSMITH's cover is still secure, since your operators were not seen or discovered by anyone else." Walker answered. "We do have a bigger problem."

"What problem?" General Crane demanded.

"SILVERSMITH has been planning a major operation for the Islamic State. As part of the planning he's got to meet with their director of operations. A man named Akil." Walker hesitated before continuing.

Cain jumped in before Walker could continue. "Oh, yes! I'd almost forgotten what put him on our radar to start with! Your asset has been planning operations for terrorists. Like the one in Dubai? How many innocent people died in that one?"

Even with the camera at Walker's end not close-up on Walker's face, Mathews could see it turning beet red in anger. "That is none of your concern, David."

"Try again, Mark," Cain said, his voice flat and deadly serious. "If your asset is planning operations that have resulted in the deaths of innocent civilians at the hands of terrorists, you and your agency are in deep shit. Talk to me, Mark. Right now."

Mathews glanced at Simms. Simms locked eyes with him and the two men communicated silently. People at their level almost never saw seniors get in each other's faces.

Walker spread both hands apart on the conference room table and looked at the camera. "Yes, SILVERSMITH has been planning operations for the Islamic State. Once the leadership approves those operations, he gets us a copy of the plan. We launder the information internally and you see it as threat warnings from the source known as GOLDPLATED. As for the attack in Dubai, the details were passed on to State and the FBI. They have good contacts with the cops out there. What we heard back was that the Emir's people got the message, but did not believe the threat was credible."

Cain had seen some of the GOLDPLATED reporting, and it was excellent, but it was not feeding the bulldog as far as CIA and SILVERSMITH's actions were concerned. "That's a start. I'm still waiting for the part of this conversation where you say Congress and the president knows about SILVERSMITH and what he's been doing," Cain said flatly.

Walker started to look annoyed. "David, I don't work for you, you do not give me—"

Cain cut him off. "That's right, Mark. You don't work for me, but I know the oversight laws as well as you do. If you don't tell me, when I report up the chain to DIRNSA in writing about why ROGUE SENTINEL was scrapped, I will describe the minutes of this teleconference. If I don't include in that report a statement that Congress is aware of CONSTANT ALCHEMY and SILVERSMITH and what he is doing, I promise you DIRNSA and I will head to the Hill and speak to the chair and ranking members of the HPSCI and SSCI before noon tomorrow."

"And the SECDEF and Chairman will meet with the president, as soon as they can get on his calendar," General Crane added forcefully.

Mathews did not know much about intelligence, but he knew the House Permanent Select Committee on Intelligence and the Senate Select Committee on Intelligence were never shy about jumping on the CIA or any other intelligence agency if they even suspected something improper or illegal. Mathews had always thought Cain was a straight shooter, but seeing him threaten a senior leader at the CIA just confirmed it, and Crane's threat to send the SECDEF to see the president doubled down on the threat.

The silence on the secure link stretched as Walker got even redder. "The Director and I have a meeting with the committees in the morning to brief them in," he paused for a few seconds, reluctant to add, "after we've seen the president."

Cain nodded. "Good. Then once the DIRNSA's report goes to the Director of National Intelligence and he forwards it on to the committees, it should dovetail nicely with what you've already told them."

The look on Walker's face told everyone on the link he was not happy that Cain's report would be filed anyway, and that the obvious implication was that Walker had damn well better talk to the two committees on his own, before Cain's report forced him to. "If we can move on now, Mr. Cain..."

"Please, Mr. Walker," Cain said, extending the prod, not happy that a senior CIA officer who should know better was playing fast and loose with the oversight rules. "I'm looking forward to hearing how the CIA will support getting

General Crane's men home safely."

"So am I," Crane chimed in, the tone of his voice clearly supporting Cain's position on more than just the retrieval of Mathews and Simms from Jordan.

In spite of Cain's tail-twisting and threat to go to Congress with what might be an operation the intelligence committees were not fully informed about, Walker suddenly assumed the air of a poker player holding a royal flush, ready to go all in. "Actually, we were hoping they would stay in country, with a slightly modified mission goal."

"Exactly what mission goal?" Crane inquired acidly.

"Helping SILVERSMITH kill some of the Islamic State's top brass," Walker said with a grin.

Simms leaned forward to stab the button to mute the microphone on their end. "Check out the balls on this guy. He may be about to go in front of the president and Congress to explain a potentially rogue operation, and he asks us to help his field agent out."

"Brass ones for sure," Mathews agreed. "Let's see how it plays out. In the end, I'm the commander in the field, and if I think it's too dangerous, I'll veto it. I'm not risking your life more than I already have."

Mathews put his attention back on the link, but no one was saying anything. Stunned silence was his best guess. He saw Cain lean toward the camera again to speak, but General Crane started speaking first.

"You sneaky bastard."

Walker nodded. "In spite of what you or Mr. Cain might think in terms of how we've run CONSTANT ALCHEMY, our asset is well placed inside the Islamic State and we might not get another opportunity like this."

Mathews unmuted the microphone. "What opportunity?" Mathews asked.

"SILVERSMITH's last report told us he was nearly ready to set up a final meeting with Akil, the director of operations for the Islamic State himself. He has to get final approval for his latest plan – an all-out assault on the U.S. embassy in Qatar – VBIEDs, suicide bombers, three assault teams, the works. If it plays out, there will be a lot of dead Americans and Qataris in the embassy compound."

Walker folded his arms and leaned forward on the conference table, his body language unconsciously demonstrating the satisfaction he was feeling in how this discussion was playing out. "The last few times SILVERSMITH has met with Akil, he's always brought along another senior leader in ISIS. The first time it was the so-called Caliph's prime deputy, and last time it was a senior commander for operations in Iraq. SILVER SMITH has been moving up in the organization rapidly. He's just been made 'Senior Engineer of the jihad' and might even make director of operations one day, opening up the possibility of killing every senior leader of the Islamic State. In any event, when he meets with Akil again, it presents an opportunity to eliminate him."

Killing Akil would be a major intelligence, operational, and political coup, Mathews knew, but they needed a good plan to eliminate the Tangos SILVERSMITH met with and still keep his cover intact. "I presume that since SILVERSMITH is your source on this, the intel is solid, but how do we kill them and keep your agent's cover?" Mathews asked.

Walker replied without giving it a second thought. "You kill them, and anyone else at the meeting site except SILVERSMITH. Since he's the only one who will get out, he can make up whatever story he wants to keep the ISIS leadership happy. We can even work out a scenario where you shoot him in a non-vital part of the body to help him sell it."

Before Mathews could answer, Crane piped up. "First of all, my men killing the Islamic State leaders is not a problem, so long as the president and SECDEF authorize it, not the CIA. You are not in their chain-of-command, Mr. Walker. They will also eliminate anyone who is a direct threat to their safety or SILVER SMITH's, assuming we even get to the point where I recommend authorizing their participation to SECDEF. You want them killed outside of those parameters, call in your own black bag boys and girls, or have the Air Force hit the place with one of their drones or bombers. The rules of engagement my men work under will not change without a presidential order."

"Grabbing them," Cain added from CTS, "is a better option. You could interrogate them for months and not learn everything they know."

Walker shook his head in frustration. "You know as well as I do that capturing them is problematic. You have to get them out of the country, and neither Syria nor Jordan is going to let you just waltz out of the country with one or more of ISIS's leaders. Killing them simplifies things, and if need be, I'll get the president to put it in writing for you."

"We'll wait for the official word from SECDEF," Crane responded.

Walker glanced up at something above the camera. "Look, I need to get off the link and grab a quick shower. I'm due in the director's office in forty minutes. She and I need to huddle before we head for the morning intelligence briefing with the president."

"Were you originally on the hook for that today?" Cain asked pointedly, nearly certain what the answer was.

"No," Walker said, chagrined. "The usual briefing officer will be with us, but the original agenda will be supplemented with an introduction to CONSTANT ALCHEMY and our recommendation to let SILVER SMITH set these guys up for your Wraiths to kill them."

"I still think—" Cain started.

Walker cut him off. "That's not your call, Mr. Cain." Cain started to protest, but Walker waved him off. "It's not really mine either, David," he continued, extending a professional olive branch. "I'll just be making the recommendation. The ultimate decision will be made by the president on the advice of his national security advisor and anyone else he asks for an opinion."

Cain let it go. Walker was right. His concern in the end was ultimately supporting Mathews and Simms if they were given the mission. He would still file his written report, and be damned sure General Holland knew what his recommendation was.

"We'll catch up with you later, then," Crane said, giving Walker a chance to sign off.

"Out here," Walker intoned, pressing a button on the terminal in front of him just before his video feed vanished from the encrypted video link.

Mathews piped up, by default directing his question to Crane. "Now what do we do, sir?"

"Let's expect that we will need to plan for an op against the Islamic State leadership, using SILVERSMITH's intelligence."

"Any chance you can get the rest of my team into the country in time?" Mathews inquired.

Crane looked at Simon. "Well?"

Simon shook his head. "No, sir. Given the short timeline, I don't think so, but I'll get the deployment kits started for the remaining members of Mathews' team. It will take time. We don't have enough available cover identities for all of them. They'll need to be generated, and to keep their covers, we'll need to slip them in on commercial flights. All of that will take time. I figure four days at the earliest."

Mathews knew four days might not be fast enough. "There are still a lot of unknowns here. We need to coordinate directly with Walker and SILVERSMITH and get more information."

"That's my job," Cain said. "I'll keep in touch with Walker and Colonel Simon and start building the intel package for this so you can start planning. If we can get you in touch with SILVERSMITH in a way that won't compromise him, we will."

"Can you get any other assets in the area to help them?" Crane asked.

"Not unless the Jordanians approve them, or the president approves us violating Jordanian national sovereignty," Cain told him.

"We'll get back to you on that. I think it's time we had another conversation with our friend the Jordanian military attaché," Crane stated grimly.

"Then what are our orders in the meantime?" Mathews asked.

Colonel Simon spoke up. "Talk to Master Gunnery Sergeant Tobin, and tell him you need the other care package I sent for you two. Pick it up, then get back to the safe house in Ar-Ruwayshid. I want you closer to SILVERSMITH, rather than farther away. If he yells for help, I want you there in minutes."

"Copy that, sir," Mathews responded.

"We'll be in touch," Cain promised.

"Same here," said Simon.

Mathews was going to take a chance and ask Simon to tell Kristen he said hello, but both video feeds from CTS and Wraith Base cut off. Damn.

Mathews and Simms found Corporal Shew waiting by the car outside the embassy, and he promised to load their 'care package' into the trunk of the Merc. He had even arranged for Mathew and Simms to use a vacant apartment in the housing block to refresh themselves.

While they were using the facilities, Corporal Shew grabbed them some breakfast sandwiches and two thermoses of hot coffee from the embassy canteen after loading up the care package.

Returning to the black Mercedes to find Mathews and Simms waiting near the rear doors, Shew asked, "You need to head back to the mall?" He handed over the food and thermoses.

"That's right, Corporal Shew," Mathews answered him, "thanks for shuttling us around."

"Any time, sir," Shew responded, "It's easy duty, and I'm sure it's helping the two of you out."

Mathews' estimation of the Shew rose a couple of notches. The young marine seemed to be able to grasp the situation without being told old the specifics. He would go far in the Corps.

Mathews and Simms ate the sandwiches with gusto during the short ride back to the mall, saving the coffee for after they were back on the road. After reaching the still-deserted lower level of the parking garage under the mall, Shew popped the trunk.

Mathews exited the Merc and boarded the Range Rover, firing up the engine and scanning the garage for other people, while Shew and Simms to transferred their care package from the Merc's trunk into the cargo area of the Range Rover.

Simms shook the kid's hand, thanking him again, and climbed in the passenger seat of the Range Rover while Shew shut the Mercedes' trunk and headed toward the mall for some 'cover shopping', as he termed it.

By the time Shew was twenty steps away, Mathews had the Range Rover headed back up the ramp onto the streets of Amman. Fifty minutes later, as Mathews turned off Highway 40 north of Zarqa onto Highway 10 heading northeast, Simms quipped, "Know the way home from here?"

"Funny," Mathews responded flatly, extending his right foot to bring the Range Rover up to 110 kilometers an hour on the only highway in this part of Jordan. Ar-Ruwayshid was a little more than an hour away.

CHAPTER 13

Al-Amriki was back at his planning table, staring at the plans and his notes for the embassy operation without really seeing them, absentmindedly caressing the Mont Blanc pen his mother had given him – his only touchstone to his real identity and allegiance.

The laptop sat idle on his left, his Islamic State provided iPhone X next to it. The day had dawned bright and clear, with the sun's heat warming the chilled desert air to a comfortable eighty degrees amid a breeze from the west. His morning walk through town to service the dead drops was complete, and he had intended to return to work to go over the planning for the attack on the embassy, but his mind kept drifting.

Why didn't Langley warn me about the capture team? Better yet, why didn't they make sure the mission was called off before they got that close to me? His mind kept going over the events of last night, replaying them, turning it over in his mind, hoping to get a better handle on what had happened and why.

He had been under deep cover for six years now, and his identity as 'Al-Amriki' had overwhelmed the name his parents gave him. His parents had raised him as a devout Muslim, but allowed him to experience all that America had to offer in early twenty-first century Chicago: baseball games, popped corn, freshly baked salted pretzels, movies, and so many friends of different faiths and colors.

He had learned the value of tolerance and respect for others from his parents, his childhood friends on the playground, and his formal education, and he held onto that belief as he matured. He was in middle school when al-Qaeda hijacked the planes on 9/11, and watched the live news coverage that morning in his second period science class as first one and then a second tower of the World

Trade Center collapsed. Omar remembered the shock he felt that people claiming to share his faith would do such evil.

His high school years passed quickly, with friends and family proud of his grades and his embrace of baseball, the strength of his faith – all achievable because of the promise of America and the acceptance he felt from those close to him.

During his junior year in college, destiny approached him in O'Doul's Bar & Grill in the guise of an attractive Pakistani girl named Padme with intense eyes, a flawless complexion, and a very well-rounded figure. She had noticed his choice of beverage: a Perrier with lemon, the bottle sitting next to the Tom Collins glass the waitress served it in. He noticed the depth in her brown eyes and told her without hesitation that it was against his religion to drink, and she sat down without asking, telling him it was against hers as well.

They closed the bar together and, while standing close to her in the frosty early morning hours hoping for a clue in her body language that she might want to be kissed goodnight, she told him to his romantic disappointment that she was a recruiter for the Central Intelligence Agency. Surprised and intrigued, he chose to undergo the application process.

His background check and formal training lasted through his senior year, as did his intense affair with Padme, after a second, not-so-chance encounter in O'Doul's after his time at the Farm. Their affair lasted a wonderful five months, before they had to bow to the inevitable. They took a two-week-long 'I'll miss you' road trip before he bid Padme a fond farewell after graduation, forced to cut off all communication with her before heading out on his first undercover assignment in Belgium. He had been on the CIA's payroll for nearly two years when he landed in Brussels.

Omar rose from his planning table and went to the kitchen to brew some coffee. It was early afternoon now, and the events of the last twenty-four hours were a major glitch in his mission. Bringing the hot cup of coffee back to the table, Omar considered the gains so far and found them insufficient.

He still needed to draw out the senior leadership of the Islamic State in a way that would enable the decapitation strike. Finding a way to do that was proving problematic. Their security precautions for his face-to-face meetings were very tight, his electronics were always confiscated, and he was never left alone with any of them. Bringing a weapon was out of the question, of course.

Omar shook his head and sipped his coffee, thinking. Two hours later, he was still turning it over in his head, searching for some scenario that would enable him to decapitate the leadership of the Islamic State and hopefully get out alive. As his focus came back, staring into the now-empty coffee cup, he began to accept the inescapable facts of the situation as it stood.

Every time he examined the problem, he kept coming back to the same conclusion. He needed some luck, and some outside help from the agency. The luck he would have to keep his eyes open for. The help would need to be agile, available on a moment's notice, and possibly technical, given the need to track the leaders in such a way that a military drone strike would hit the right targets.

Without warning, the iPhone X rang, the 'Radar' ringtone rising and fading in volume a distinctive message in and of itself. The sound made him start, and he stared at the phone without answering it. The caller ID read 'Unknown'. After a few seconds, it stopped, and still he waited. Twenty seconds later, the phone chimed, and the screen said 'Voicemail'.

Omar laid the pen carefully on the table, picked up the phone and tapped. As usual, the female voice on the voicemail sounded middle-aged, and was pleading. "Abed! Why don't you call your mother more often? It's been three days! I am at your Aunt's house. Call me! She has a niece your age that might make a good wife for you."

The phone clicked off and Omar smiled. One day he would have to ask somebody at Langley to tell him who she was. More importantly, the message meant he had somewhere to be.

Twenty minutes later, he was on the east side of Ar-Ruwayshid, standing before one of the many non-descript houses about sixty yards south of Highway 10, the third to the last north-south row of homes at the edge of the small town.

The sun shone brightly, well past its noon apex, and Omar could taste the desert on the warm breeze blowing between the buildings. He looked around carefully and, as usual, there was no foot traffic in sight.

The house was the first step in his emergency escape plan, and his survival cache. A change of clothes, two fresh passports with matching credit cards, $2,000 in cash split evenly between euros and dollars, and two completely clean burner phones awaited him, hidden inside one of the kitchen walls. One of the burner phones should hold a message from his controller that would clear up what happened last night. If not, he could call his controller in complete safety, without fear of being overheard by the Islamic State.

Confident after his visual inspection of the area that he was unobserved, he unlocked the door and strode in, automatically shutting the door behind him.

"Good afternoon," said a male voice whose unexpected words chilled him to the bone in the warm, dry air of the house's interior.

Omar froze at the unexpected sight of two armed men standing in the living room of the small safe house he thought that only his case officer knew about. One was older, late thirties and tall, with dark hair. The other man was younger and closer to his own height, late twenties, with sandy hair and blue eyes. Both men were obviously in good shape, but where the tall one was wiry, the shorter one had the broad shoulders and strength of an NFL running back. They were armed, and the wicked-looking suppressors screwed to the muzzles of their automatic pistols were pointing right at him.

The younger, shorter man spoke again. "We bring greetings from Grand Mufti Akbar."

Omar's heart was racing, but it began to slow as the man's words got past the sudden panic in his mind. He kept his hands in the open as he answered.

"His battle plans were always useful during the dark times."

Both men lowered their weapons. "I'm Mathews; this is Simms."

"SOCOM?" Omar asked, his heart still pounding hard enough in his chest that he could feel it.

"We're Special Forces, but we don't answer to SOCOM or your parent agency," Mathews told him, unscrewing the suppressor from his Sig Sauer P226. Simms did the same, slipping the six-inch long suppressor into a pocket before walking over to shake Omar's hand.

"Nice to meet you, SILVERSMITH." Simms said with a huge grin.

Omar's eyes grew wide with disbelief as Mathews came over to shake his hand as well. "How the hell do you know that codename?"

"Our mission was to come to Jordan and capture a high level Islamic State operations planner. When we damn near did, CIA finally owned up to you being their asset and called us off. Simms and I just got back from the embassy in Amman where we were briefed into CONSTANT ALCHEMY and your identity." Mathews wasn't about to tell Omar how close he came to having an impromptu shoot out with the two commandos last night.

Omar had to sit down. He walked into the living room and dropped heavily on the couch. As he did so, a small cloud of dust rose from the cushions and wafted through the beams of filtered sunlight sneaking past the closed curtains. Keeping the safe house clean was not something he spent time doing.

"You really should stop by and dust once in a while," Simms observed dryly, before settling himself opposite Omar on the arm of one of the easy chairs in the room.

Omar looked up, still taking in the unexpected exposure of what, until now, had been an airtight cover. "Alright fellas. My life is on the line here. Take it from the top. Exactly who are you and what are you doing here?"

Mathews spent the next few minutes filling Omar in on Operation ROGUE SENTINEL.

"Why the hell didn't Langley call you guys off before you left the States?" Omar asked when Mathews was finished.

"Based on what we heard during the VTC," Simms told him, "your director and the head of the national clandestine service were pulling out all the stops to maintain your cover back in D.C. Even the senior and mid-level operations and analytic types weren't aware of your operation. It took a director-level authorization to read us and our senior leadership in once our Op was shit-canned last night in your house."

"It looks like the coordination on our Op was handled at a low enough level at Langley that it was cleared by someone not on the 'need-to-know' list," Mathews added.

"So here we are," Simms finished.

"Am I secure?" Omar asked, only half expecting an answer.

Mathews handled that one. "From where we stand, you should be fine. The only people in Jordan that know you are a deep cover agent for the CIA are the three of us. Back in the States, outside of your director and the head of the clandestine service, only our commanding officer, our director of operations, and the head of the unit at the NSA that provides us real-time support during field Ops know."

"That's a shit load more people than knew before yesterday," Omar observed acidly.

"Hey!" Mathews admonished him, "Every one of those people are senior officers with long service records in the special operations or intelligence fields – all of whom I've trusted my life with for the last few years. I don't think they are going to be calling the ISIS leadership and burning you."

Omar was not convinced. "I hear you, but it's my ass out here."

"It's ours too, now," Simms told him.

A puzzled look came over Omar's face. "What?"

"Our mission was changed a couple of hours ago. At the direction of the SECDEF, we are to assist you in your mission if at all possible."

Omar blinked. Looks like his request for help had been fulfilled before he could make it. He was still uncomfortable with his cover identity being known outside of the CIA, and it must have showed because Simms looked at him closely, then settled himself in the easy chair, ignoring the small dust cloud that rose from it.

"Look..." Simms trailed off, not sure which name he might prefer being called.

"Omar, please," said the man who assumed the identity of Al-Amriki, senior engineer for the Islamic State.

Simms nodded, and looked at Mathews who also nodded in assent. It was get to know you time.

"Look Omar," Simms started again, "Mathews and I are dyed in the wool military. He's a SEAL, and I'm an Air Force combat controller. We've both been in the SOCOM community for years, and we understand what it's like to be out there at risk on a mission. You already know how we got here, why don't you tell us how you ended up here? We're going to be working together now, and as much as you need to trust us, Mathews and I need to be able to trust you. All our lives are on the line now."

Omar considered the older man's words and looked from Simms to Mathews. Being undercover had been everything his training had predicted, and here was a chance to feel like he belonged again. His instincts had served him well in the past, and his instincts told him he could trust these two men now.

"Do you remember your swearing in?" Omar asked.

"Of course," said Mathews as Simms nodded in agreement.

"Me too," Omar told them, the words of the oath coming easily. "I, Omar Abdur Razzaq, do solemnly swear that I will support and defend the Constitution of the United States against all enemies, foreign and domestic; that I will bear true faith and allegiance to the same; that I take this obligation freely, without any mental reservation or purpose of evasion; and that I will well and faithfully discharge the duties of the office on which I am about to enter. So help me Allah."

If Mathews and Simms took exception to the 'Allah' at the end of the oath, Omar could not detect it.

"I added the 'Allah' to the end of it almost without thinking," Omar told them. "I asked the officer swearing me in if I needed to repeat it – he told me 'no'..." Omar's voice cracked a little as he finished. "...there was no reason why I should; you could say God whatever way you wanted to in America."

Mathews looked at the floor and wiped at one eye. Simms just nodded and took a deep breath.

"After college," Omar continued after swallowing hard, "they sent me to Brussels to infiltrate a Mosque known for the radical attitudes of some of the members. It took five months."

"How bad was the radicalization?" Mathews asked.

"Three people out of two hundred moderates who practiced their faith peacefully, and taught their children the same." Omar told him.

"It took them a while to approach me, and they did it in broad daylight, nowhere near the Mosque. I started meeting with them regularly and the discussion shifted towards American policy in the Middle East. That led to the 'crusader' occupations of Afghanistan and Iraq, the role of the cherished martyrs in winning the war against Islam, and the need for all proper Muslims to join the fight."

"Typical radicalization propaganda." Simms noted.

"It was," Omar told him. "I continued to ease myself into their confidence by appearing susceptible to their approach, and then started expressing more interest in the jihad as they showed me Islamic State produced propaganda videos and gave me copies of DÇbiq, the Islamic State's magazine, to read."

"They have a magazine?" Mathews was surprised.

Omar nodded, "Yes, their propaganda machine is well oiled."

"Then what?" Simms prompted him.

"Eventually," Omar continued, "I told them I wanted to fight in the jihad and revealed to them that I was an American citizen."

"And they didn't kill you where you stood?" Simms asked wide-eyed.

Omar shook his head. "No, I played my citizenship as a personal failing that I expected they would use to reject me. I hoped that all the groundwork I'd laid with them as a practicing Muslim, which I am, coupled with my personal heritage and my interest in their cause would mitigate the risk."

"What is your ancestry?" Mathews asked, curiosity getting the better of him in the midst of Omar's tale.

"My parents are Palestinian" Omar responded. "They immigrated to America before the First Intifada. When they settled in Chicago's Little Palestine, my father resumed his medical practice, and when I was born, they sent me to school, eventually to university. I studied chemistry and metallurgy."

"So, you're a citizen by birth?" Simms inquired.

"Yes," Omar smiled. "I grew up watching the Cubs. Unfortunately, I was in Iraq spending my time teaching jihadis to make bombs in Erbil when they won the series."

"Bombs?" Mathews asked, a hard edge to his voice.

Omar nodded. "Yes, the intent was to screw up the manufacturing and cause either fizzles or premature detonation to kill the other bomb makers."

"That sounds pretty risky," Simms observed. "They could have caught you."

"It's tough to catch someone screwing up the formula when the lab blows up destroying the evidence or the bomb makers die when planting them." Omar said flatly.

"Go on," Mathews prompted.

"The recruiters in Brussels passed me on to a low-level training cell in Adana, Turkey, using their contacts to get me admitted to Cukurova University. During the day I'd work on my master's degree. At night, I'd attend training classes in the techniques and tactics of the jihad, Islamic State style." Omar's tone spoke volumes about the quality of the training, but he added sarcastically, "My instructors at the Farm would not have been impressed."

Omar paused as the two commandos smiled at his assessment, then asked, "Do either of you have a bottle of water?"

Mathews nodded, "Sure," and reached into the pack he left on the floor and tossed Omar a bottle.

After taking a long pull on it, Omar continued. "Since my university courses included chemistry courses, I started pointing out the mistakes I was seeing in jihadi night school during their suicide vest building tutorials. That brought me to the attention of one of their senior bomb makers, normally referred to as an 'engineer', who eventually dissuaded me from becoming a Martyr."

"I'd imagine that wasn't too difficult," Simms opined with a smile.

Omar smiled back at him, the banter between fellow Americans feeling good after so long. "Not at all. Two weeks after I completed the graduate program at Cukurova University, I had an Islamic State provided Syrian passport and plane tickets to Damascus. From there I made my way to Baghdad, then Erbil, where I started out as an apprentice bombmaker and my cover was pretty much set. As long as I had a good explanation for why the bombs didn't work or pre-maturely detonated, and assembly error usually covered that, I was able to work my way up the ranks to being an operational planner."

"And then?" Mathews asked, fully engaged in Omar's story.

"I planned an operation to capture an oil storage depot outside of Mosul, and thanks to my handler cueing the Iraqi's to be somewhere else, it went down without a hitch. That brought me to the attention of Akil, and a few weeks later, as the coalition offensive in northern Iraq began, he had me move here for safety while I continued my work."

"Wow." Mathews said appreciatively, "I'm impressed."

"Me too." Concurred Simms.

Mathews crossed the living room floor towards Omar, his hand extended in genuine admiration. Omar was as courageous as any Tier One operator he had ever worked with, and he did it alone, without the kind of military force Mathews was accustomed to. In fact, it made his few days undercover in Jordan seem like a short vacation in the desert.

"I'm Shane Mathews," Mathews told him, the formality of the introduction sealing his friendship with the man. "Nice to be working with you."

Omar grasped Mathews hand firmly, "Omar Razzaq. Nice to be working with you too."

Mathews released Omar's hand and turned to complete the introductions. "My team NCOIC, Bob Simms."

Simms shook Omar's hand as well. "I think it's time we sit down and pool our knowledge, and see if we can come up with a plan."

"Sounds like a good idea," Mathews responded, looking at Omar. "Just one question first."

"Shoot," Omar told him.

"Grand Mufti Akbar," Mathews said with an arched eyebrow, "is he who

I think he is?"

Omar smiled broadly. These two were fast becoming men he knew he could trust. "Probably. I'm a big fan of Lucas' old movies, and his strategies always helped the Rebels win against the Empire."

Mathews shook his head with a smile. It was time for three Americans to come up with a plan to deal with the senior leaders of a real enemy.

CHAPTER 14

Mathews held one of Omar's burner phones to his ear after dialing the number from memory. Their planning discussion had moved to the kitchen, since it had the only counterspace in the house. Omar and Simms were still talking quietly, going over the last two hours of planning again, making sure the three of them had not missed anything. The call connected after only two rings.

"6644."

"Hi Uncle Dave." Mathews said lightly, glad to hear Cain's voice again.

"Nephew! I really didn't expect you to call me at work." Cain's voice was clear and distinct, but the surprise and concern in his voice was unmistakable.

"It's no trouble. I borrowed a phone from a new friend of mine."

"Really..." Cain said, trailing off. Suddenly, Mathews heard an electronic squeal in his ear, and held the phone a few inches away from his head. When the squeal went away, he put the phone back to his ear.

"Can you hear me now?" Mathews asked, referencing the old commercial.

"Five by five," Cain answered, ignoring the attempt at humor, "and we're secure now, up to TS/SCI."

"Nice. I didn't know the burners our friend has were equipped with the right encryption," Mathews said.

"They were provided to him by the CIA's branch of technical services, who worked with the NSA."

"Ah, that explains it."

"Are you and Simms getting along with Omar?"

Mathews looked back toward the kitchen. Simms was gesturing at something on the ruggedized tablet's screen.

"Famously. We think we have a plan."

"I'm listening." Cain told him.

"Good, because we are going to need a few things." Mathew said before elaborating further.

"So how long have you two been working together?" Omar asked.

"Mathews and I have been with the Wraiths for nearly three years."

"The Wraiths?"

"The informal name for our unit," Simms told him with a sly smile.

"Have you guys done a lot of these kinds of jobs?"

"Helping out the CIA? No. It's our first time. Mostly we run our ops with a lot of cooperation from the host nation government, all on the down-low, of course. Strictly off the books, but all within well-established rules of engagement. We've worked with some of the best special operators in the world, Israelis, Saudis, Aussies, even the Russians once." After a moment's thought, he added, "We even get air support when we need it, most of the time."

"It must be nice," Omar said, envious of the older man's support infrastructure. "My nearest help is the station chief in Amman, and to get to her I need to use a couple of pass phrases, since we've never met."

"If you get the chance," Simms told him with a knowing look, "use the pass phrases. She's hot."

"Really?" Omar asked with an arched eyebrow.

"Yeah," Simms said, readying the other shoe, "but don't ask her out." Simms' reward was the puzzled expression on Omar's face.

Mathews ended the call to Cain and dialed another number from memory quickly.

"Yes?" the woman's voice was soft and pleasant, and he had forgotten how much he missed hearing it.

"Hi honey."

"Oh my god. Should you be calling me now?"

"Probably not. I can't stay on the line for long, but I wanted you to know I miss you."

The pause on the other end of the line only lasted two seconds, but it seemed like minutes before Kristen answered him. "I miss you too."

"I want to have a long talk with you when I get home."

"I'll be waiting," Kristen told him, "please be careful."

Reassured, he said, "I will. I have to go now. Love you."

"Love you too."

Reluctantly, he hung up and headed into the kitchen. Simms and Omar looked at him expectantly.

"I told them what we need."

"And..." Simms prompted him.

"Cain said he would do everything he could. He's probably talking to Simon and Crane now."

"If you have to..." Omar started to ask, but Mathews cut him off.

"If we have to, we'll go to Plan B and do it ourselves." Mathews saw the less than confident look on Omar's face. "Are you OK with that? If you think the risk is unacceptable, we'll wave off."

Simms took a long look at Omar too. He was taking too long to answer. "Omar, this is how we do this. You are on our team now, and team members look out for one another. We've got your back from now on. You're not alone anymore."

Omar looked up; shifting his gaze from Mathews to Simms and back again, and recognized the commitment they just made to him – a man they had known for less than a few hours. Although he was obviously of Middle Eastern extraction, they had not asked if he was a Muslim. They just accepted him as another American on a mission to defend their nation. Belatedly, he realized one of the unspoken benefits of his work with the CIA. Working with fellow Americans like these two.

Omar nodded. "I can handle the risk, even if we go with Plan B."

"Good," Mathews nodded. The burner phone he was holding started ringing.

"Yeah," Mathews said into the device, then held it away from his head while the phone on Cain's desk secured the link. He listened for a few minutes before speaking.

"Got it. We'll keep you in the loop."

Mathews disconnected the call and addressed Omar and Simms.

"We're going with Plan B."

To Omar he said, "Go make your call."

Omar sat at the planning table in his safe house, the plans for the attack on the embassy in Qatar laid before him and his ISIS-provided iPhone X in his hand. He, Mathews, and Simms had discussed how this conversation should go, but given how Akil had handled the security for their meetings, there really was only one way to do this. Nonetheless, he sat pondering the danger involved, his courage bolstered by the presence of both commandos. They were back in their safe house, getting some rest after the last 24 hours and waiting for word from him.

Omar glanced at the silent iPhone's blank, dark screen. He had sent the initial encrypted text message nearly two hours ago, and he was still waiting for a response. To pass the time, he tried to play the forthcoming conversation with Akil out in his head, going over it again and again, imagining the flow of the words and the best way to get Akil to agree to meet at a place of his choosing. The iPhone chimed, and Omar tapped quickly to answer it.

"Sahib?"

"You are ready?"

"Yes, I would like to meet..." Omar began, before Akil's voice over rode him.

"Two days from now. Follow the same path as our last meeting."

"Sahib, no. I do not think that would be possible." Omar said.

"Why not?" Akil said, suspicion mixed with curiosity in his voice. "Why is meeting me now a problem, when you have done so many times before?"

"Yes, Sahib, I have, but on the return trip from our last meeting, one of the immigration officers warned me that stricter security precautions were being implemented the following morning. They were to continue for the next two weeks. All passports will be electronically checked, all baggage and cars searched."

"Why?" Akil demanded.

"The United Nations recently condemned the Iraqi and Syrian governments for permitting the movement of young jihadis and jihadi brides into those countries, and they demanded better border controls. The Syrians will be running more thorough checks as a result, increasing the chance that I will be discovered."

"Why would this immigration officer give you this kind of information?" Akil demanded, his suspicions aroused.

Omar took a deep breath and beseeched Allah silently for His aid. "As 'Dr. Hafiz', he believes I travel across the border regularly from Jordan to work with the WHO. My passage through the checkpoints is a matter of routine and they merely stamp my Syrian passport. He wanted to warn me, as a medical man, that I might be delayed for a long period of time if I needed to cross back into Syria during the period when the border controls are tightened."

"I see," Akil said, his tone of suspicion moderating as he pondered a way around this complication.

"What concerns me, Sahib, is that now they will run my passport through their database, and they will undoubtedly determine that the government did not issue it. I will be arrested immediately."

Akil began to speak, but Omar cut him off, adding quickly, "Moreover, I had intended to bring all my notes and the source material for the operation. I know you would prefer to see everything I've been basing my decisions and planning on. It would surely be discovered if the Syrians are thorough in searching my belongings at the border."

Omar heard Akil let out an exasperated breath over the line. "I appreciate your concern. Perhaps we will have to wait until the border controls return to normal before we speak face-to-face again."

It was moments like these that Omar was grateful to his instructors at The Farm. Give the target a set of overwhelming problems, then show him your way out of them.

"I may have an alternative, Sahib, if you are willing."

"What do you suggest?" Akil asked.

"The open desert between the western borders of the Caliphate and eastern Jordan are not well patrolled or guarded. I have seen the vehicles you use when we have met. They could easily navigate the border region and bring you here to Jordan. We could meet in safety at the old desert fortress by the lake, northwest of this town. My vehicle is not capable of a trip through the desert, and you would not have to concern yourself with Syrian border controls. Would that be convenient for you, Sahib?"

"Wait a moment."

Omar held the line and waited. It took nearly ten minutes by his watch before Akil came back on the line. "I have consulted with my security chief and directed him to make preparations. My guard force will easily protect me from any unbelievers or lone patrols from the Syrian army. As you know, the borders of the Caliphate are quite close to the Jordanian border in that area, but you must understand that I will not tolerate having my time wasted. You are sure you are ready?"

"Yes, Sahib." Omar said, fully in character again and adding a slight tremble to his voice to convey nervousness.

"Good. I have other pressing business for the Caliph, but I will make time to meet you. Be at the old fortress at 9 P.M. tomorrow night."

"I apologize for inconveniencing you," Omar said, hoping to add the attitude of a properly regretful subordinate to the conversation. "I will be there at 9 P.M., Sahib. I will bring fresh water and fruit for your guard force, Sahib."

"That is not necessary," Akil told him, refusing the offer of hospitality as was custom, just as it was proper for Omar to offer, and gently insist as he now would.

"It is my obligation, Sahib. You and your men will have traveled far by the time you reach me."

"Nusrat will bring the usual compliment of eight men," Akil told him, adding with a hint of menace in his voice, "See to it that you are on time."

"Yes, Sahib," Omar responded to the disconnected phone line.

Omar tossed the phone onto the planning table, a wide smile on his face, more than satisfied with the outcome of his conversation with Akil. In a little more than a day, he would accomplish a major element of his mission to cripple the Islamic State leadership.

Akil put the iPhone he used to contact Al-Amriki back in the lower left-hand drawer of his desk, slid the drawer shut, and locked it. The desk was a beautifully carved piece of Lebanese Cedar from Saddam Hussein's palace in Tikrit. It occupied the central location in his office, which he had tastefully decorated in light brown and green. Located near the rear of the spacious two-story house in an upscale neighborhood in Homs, Syria, the office looked out onto the walled garden and small swimming pool he shared with his latest mistress.

His house was located in Syria for the same reason Osama Bin Laden has his house in an affluent neighborhood in Pakistan. Akil was a leader, and no longer dirtied his hands by actually fighting the jihad. He had, after all, earned his position of leadership, and deserved its spoils.

The house was bought through a real estate broker, the money wired from a bank in Sevastopol, owned by a Russian oil company, Energeia Limited, one of many companies that bought a great deal of smuggled crude from the Islamic State.

His neighbors, and the mistress, a thirty-year-old brunette still harboring the dream of movie stardom, merely thought him a wealthy businessman with a capable and well equipped personal security detail. Such trappings were not unusual in Homs, a city close to the lands held by the Caliphate of the Islamic State, and touched by the fighting the civil war had brought to Syria a few years ago.

Moreover, his immediate neighbors found his armed security guards a blessing, because whenever he or the mistress were in residence, at least one imposing black Land Rover Defender and four armed men were plainly visible on the grounds and the somewhat longer than normal drive. Their mere presence caused beggars and would-be thieves to consider other neighborhoods more attractive targets, and helped keep the neighborhood tranquil.

Akil took a moment to savor his senior position in the Islamic State and the comforts it now afforded him, and rotated his chair right to caress the top of the desk. He had coveted the massive two-meter-long desk ever since he had been called into Hussein's presence to report on the disposition of the bodies of the last two young women unfortunate enough to capture the attention of Uday Hussein's violent libido one night in 2003, just prior to the American invasion.

Uday had always been volatile, especially after the 1996 assassination attempt left him initially paralyzed, then with a permanent limp, along with lingering sexual performance problems that no one, not even his father, ever discussed aloud. Uday's outbursts and violent mood swings were legendary within the Iraqi Republican Guard, and after Uday shot three members of his bodyguard detail, Saddam himself assigned Akil and five other men to replace them.

Their instructions, issued by Saddam from behind this very desk, were to protect Uday, keep his playboy appetites sated, dispose of any bodies that might result and, once Uday had been removed as Saddam's direct heir, defend themselves as needed should he try to kill them.

To ensure his survival, Akil directed that the six of them on the detail always worked in pairs when dealing with Uday, especially if he was drunk, which was practically every night. Akil shook his head at the memory. Uday claimed to be a Muslim, but the number of times he hosted drunken parties came close to equaling the number of days in the year, and Uday always made passes at women, mostly married ones.

When he was unsuccessful, on a good night, he might only produce an AK and fire rounds over his guest's heads. On a bad night, some of the guests, particularly any man who might have attempted to defend one of the women Uday desired, would be shot, and the woman forced to comply. Her body would often end up on the bed or floor the next morning in a bloody mass of torn flesh and protruding organs – particularly if he had experienced any kind of dysfunction, or if the woman was not sufficiently 'appreciative' of his attention.

Fortunately, Akil was reassigned by Saddam a few weeks before Uday and his brother Qusay were trapped like rats in a villa in Mosul by the American occupiers. The three-hour firefight that ensued at least proved Uday and Qusay were men enough to die fighting, but in the end, the infidels had more men and material, and while Saddam's sons acted bravely, the outcome was never in doubt.

"Sahib?"

The question brought Akil back to the present, and he found Nusrat, the head of his security detail, standing at the door to his office.

"Yes?"

"I have put the usual security precautions in place for your trip. Would you care to see the meeting site?"

Akil nodded, pleased as usual at Nusrat's efficiency. Nusrat entered the office and came around the desk, his average height and looks disguising his extensive training and ten years of experience in Syrian intelligence before joining the Caliphate. As was his usual practice for when he was not heading out into the field, Nusrat wore a conservative dark suit coat and trousers with a plain white shirt, unbuttoned at the collar.

Standing beside Akil, Nusrat laid out four images, still hot from the color printer. "I've done some research, Sahib. The old fortress, known as Qasr Burqu, sits near a lake and dates from the time of the Romans. They built it to protect the seasonal lake that provides one of the sole sources of water in the area, eventually constructing a dam in the third century to ensure a water supply for the constant flow of caravans from Arabia to Syria."

Nusrat drew one of the close-up images of the collapsed fortress nearer to Akil to highlight his words before continuing. "During the years of the Byzantine empire, it was a monastery, before being restored by the Umayyads around 700 A.D. as a fortress. It's been abandoned for many years, but tourists interested in desert adventuring used to camp near the lake or the ruins. Since the outbreak of the Syrian civil war and the subsequent control of much of eastern Syria by the Caliphate, few venture out on such trips anymore. Even the Bedouin in the area moved south and east, seeking the protection of the less contested areas in the desert."

Akil could clearly see the fortress's state of disrepair. Only one of the towers remained standing, and even it had partially collapsed. The rest of the structure was not more than a roughly arranged pile of stones in the outline of the fortress walls and interior.

"It looks like the crossroad paths are deeply etched into the surrounding area," Akil commented as he examined the image.

"Yes, Sahib. That will make ingress and egress simple with our vehicles. I see no reason to augment the security team. We can use our local jihadis to secure our border crossing behind us until we return. Coupled with our other security precautions, I am confident we can protect you."

Akil nodded, appreciating Nusrat's abilities. "I will have Ghalib join us. It is important that his faith in Al-Amriki's skill continues to grow. They will be working together on an important project for the jihad in Iraq in the near future."

Nusrat considered that. "With your permission, then, I will ensure we have weapons for him as well. He is a proven fighter and will give me another skilled hand for your security, if needed."

Akil nodded again. "I trust Ghalib completely. Ensure he has the best from your armory."

"Yes, Sahib. I will continue our security precautions and update you as needed."

"Thank you, Nusrat," Akil said sincerely as a dismissal, making a mental note to increase Nusrat's pay. "You've done well."

Omar headed out on his evening dead-drop servicing route late because of the phone call to Akil. The sun was low on the horizon and warmed his back as he headed east on the pre-planned route. Walking briskly from the first dead drop at the café towards the drop at the bus stop, he had to force himself not to look up.

Mathews had told him about the small RAVEN drone that was constantly flying over the town and, not having much direct experience with drones in general, was surprised that it did not make more noise as it completed its appointed rounds.

Mathews and Simms had probably settled in to rest for the night by now. Simms had invited him over to watch a movie on the laptop he brought in country, but he had refused, insisting that he keep to his cover as much as possible. He would make a pre-planned stop at the café across from Abbud's little shop tomorrow, where he would put on a show of Jordanian hospitality to the two American researchers – it would give them a chance to speak without appearing as if they were trying to hide anything.

Omar glanced up at the sky without thinking, forgetting not to look for the drone, but stopped himself, putting his attention back on the dirt path along Highway 10. Once he was across from the bus stop, he sauntered across the road and sat on the bench, choosing this time to look as if he were examining the bus schedule glued to the wall of the small shelter.

A quick lean forward and his hand brushed the container superglued under the bench. No USB stick this time. No surprise there. This was the drop he used to communicate with the CIA, and the last time he loaded it was to pass along the attack plan for the embassy. CIA certainly had nothing to send him, since Mathews and Simms had already made contact.

After another minute or two pretend-studying the bus schedule, Omar rose and continued heading east for the next dead drop location. This one the Islamic State used to funnel him the latest intelligence information gathered near the embassy, and he still had to keep up appearances. If he failed to check it, and the person who loaded it for ISIS found its contents still there later tonight or in the morning, it might raise suspicions, or cause Akil to send a security team to check on him.

Back in Homs, Nusrat stepped into the living room and immediately averted his eyes. Akil was with his mistress again, and it was not proper for him to gaze upon her. "Excuse me, Sahib," he said, preparing to leave.

"It's alright, Nusrat," Akil said. Normally he would be very annoyed, especially since his conversation with Fatima had just begun moving towards a discussion of some very intimate acts later this evening, but he knew Nusrat would not disturb him if it were not important.

"A moment, my beauty," he said to Fatima quietly and he rose to cross the expansive living room's thick green carpet to speak to Nusrat. In his wake, Fatima looked after him with thinly disguised lust, her lips curved into a mischievous grin at what was in store for the evening.

"What is it?" Akil asked Nusrat, putting his hand on his shoulder and guiding him towards the office.

"I wanted to update you on Al-Amriki. He has begun his usual walk through the town, a bit later than usual probably because of your call. He appears to be stopping at his usual dead drop locations."

Akil nodded, pleased at the news. Nusrat was worth every penny he was paid.

"Excellent. Make sure he remains safe and arrives unharmed to our meeting. Are you watching the meeting location as well?"

Nusrat shook his head no. "Not yet, Sahib. It is too soon. We will begin surveillance an hour or so before we cross the border, if anything appears untoward, we will be able to return here long before you are placed in danger."

"Excellent," Akil said, adding in a firm, but quiet voice, "since all is well, barring armed men storming this house, you will leave me undisturbed until noon tomorrow." He did not want any more unexpected interruptions to disturb his time with Fatima tonight.

He knew her well enough to understand the look in her eye when she kissed him 'hello' after she had come home from another day of fruitless auditions in Damascus. Whenever her auditions went poorly, she sought sex to reassure her of her beauty, a high standard in the acting profession, even in Syria.

Nusrat understood immediately. "Of course, Sahib. I will inform the men on watch this evening, and leave immediately."

"Good. I will see you tomorrow then for our usual security update. We will have lunch while you update me. One o'clock tomorrow afternoon."

"Yes, Sahib. Good night."

Akil turned on his heel and headed back into the living room to find the pocket doors that separated the living room from the rest of the house closed. He slid them open, slipped through and closed them again. Once on the other side of the doors he thanked Allah under his breath that he had shut them again.

In the short time he had been gone, Fatima had decided to model her newest bikini bought this morning in Damascus as an added enticement, apparently changing right there in the living room. He saw in his peripheral vision the tiny shopping bag the flimsy bit of swimwear arrived home in, lying open on the floor before her, but his eyes were glued to her nearly naked body only meters away.

In the time it took for him to cross the room for a much better view and a hands-on inspection of exactly how the bikini came undone, he decided he had made the best possible choice in sending Nusrat away and having him put the guard force on notice not to disturb him until noon. When Fatima was like this, he knew he would need to sleep in the next day to recover.

Outside the living room, Nusrat returned to the small alcove adjacent Akil's office that served as his work area during the day. It was nothing more than a small table built into the wall of the alcove, and a power outlet, but it was enough space for him to stand and work on his powerful laptop. A latest generation Lenovo, built in China and shipped from a supplier in Germany, he had bought it in a Damascus electronics store earlier in the year.

He closed the laptop's lid, leaving the program running, and unplugged it from the house's power, tucking it under his arm and heading out of the house. As he walked toward the front door, he passed the pocket doors of the living room, doing his best to close his ears to the sounds of a passionate woman on the other side as he left the house. He would speak to the guards immediately. Akil would not be disturbed tonight for anything less than an armored platoon of infidels making its way down the street.

CHAPTER 15

"Good morning." Mathews said to the younger man having coffee at one of the plastic tables on the patio outside of Rashad's little café, offering him a friendly wave as he and Simms walked past to approach the front door to the café. It was another bright and clear day. The sun was well over the horizon, and the desert air was just beginning to warm from the cool of the night. Both men wore khakis with cargo pockets, T-shirts, and loose fitting, tropical weight, short-sleeved shirts that they left untucked to hide the pistols secreted into their waistbands.

"Hello!" Omar responded loudly, affecting the air of a well-meaning Jordanian who had just appointed himself genial host for his country. "Welcome to Ar-Ruwayshid, my friends." Omar rose to shake their hands. "You are studying the ruins to the east, yes? Many have, but we do not get many archeologists here anymore. You are most welcome."

"Thank you," Simms said. "My friend has been here for a few days, but I've just arrived."

Omar smiled widely. "Ah, well please join me for coffee." Both Mathews and Simms began to protest, but Omar insisted, waving them to his table, having carefully chosen the one farthest from the door to Rashad's little café. Both commandos assented as planned and joined him. Omar had already taken the prime seat with his back to the wall of the building, so Mathews and Simms slid into seats on either side of him, angling them slightly under the pretext of avoiding the sun, and keeping their backs to the wall as much as possible as well. Mathews took note of how they sat, and idly wondered if a more knowledgable observer would have noticed it as odd. Rashad appeared a minute later and Omar spoke rapidly to him in Arabic.

As Rashad headed back inside to fill the order, all three men lowered their voices to keep the conversation private. By prearrangement, Mathews and Simms watched for passersby on the street, and Omar kept an eye out for Rashad or any other patrons who might show too much interest in the three men. Fortunately, the patio area was devoid of other patrons for the moment.

"You sure doing this publicly is a good idea?" Mathews asked, keeping his voice down.

"Yes," Omar confirmed. "Remember, I was hiding from people like you, not the locals. They are a very peaceful bunch, and as far as I know, none of them works for ISIS. I've attended Friday prayers at the Mosque a few blocks over, and all any of the men ever talked about after the service were local issues like the need for government assistance with jobs and education for their children, and whether the Islamic State made any territorial gains nearby. They just want to raise their kids in peace and make a better life for themselves. This is a pretty poor town."

"I can see that," Mathews observed, casting his eyes up and down the length of Highway 10 stretched out before them, and the tired and worn exteriors of the homes that lined it. "God help these people if ISIS actually took any of eastern Jordan."

"Yes," Omar agreed. "Their brutality and strict conservatism is a pretty nasty combination. Fortunately, the strength of the Jordanian military and the 'Caliph's' focus on the mineral riches in northern Iraq and eastern Syria are keeping that from happening for now."

Simms was sure he heard the quotes around the word 'Caliph' when Omar said it. "Not a big fan of the so-called 'Caliph'?" he asked rhetorically.

"Hardly," Omar said with a smile, again thankful for the easy banter Americans usually engaged in. "His brand of Islam is not the one I learned and follow." Omar waited for looks of surprise from either man at his admission of faith, but neither man reacted with shock or even mild surprise.

Mathews did turn to look him in the eye. "May I ask a personal question?"

Omar nodded, wondering where he was going with this.

"Does killing a fellow Muslim, if need be, cause you any problem?"

Omar thought about that for a few seconds. "I can't say I've ever sat and had a long philosophical conversation with myself about it, but the answer is no."

Mathews' unexpected question made him think about the issue, and after a couple of seconds, Omar continued, "No more so that you might have a problem killing a fellow Catholic or Jew, if you happen to follow one of those faiths. You're a soldier, and your enemy's soldiers might follow many faiths, even your own. A person who commits a capital crime or makes war on you could be of any faith. If you're a police officer and you shoot a man threatening another person with a knife, or a gun, or a bomb, you shoot them to protect the innocent life. If you're a soldier and another country makes war on yours, you shoot and kill the enemy. As far as I'm concerned, a small organization that chooses to use terror as a weapon and justify its use through a misguided and extreme version of a religious faith, any faith, is a legitimate target of people like you and I who swore to defend our nation. I don't care if they are Muslim, Catholic, Jewish, or Hindi."

Rashad came out of café proper at that moment, bringing a tray laid with coffee, and a small pile of various sweet rolls, freshly baked by his wife. Mathews could smell the cardamom in the coffee and the cinnamon and sugar from the rolls and he began to salivate.

After Rashad had served them and withdrawn, Omar continued, Mathews' question triggering a swell of emotion and passion long buried as part of his cover.

"As I understand my faith, people that subscribe to the extremist views of organizations like al-Qaeda, the Islamic State, etc., are committing what is simply termed in the Holy Qur'an as 'unlawful warfare' or Hirābah as it's called under Sharia Law. In my view, it is the duty of every Muslim to stand up and oppose such criminals, and many have on social media or by joining the military as you have."

Omar took a quick sip of his cardamom-laced coffee and continued, "Also, that line they feed some of these young kids in the world about 'there is a war on Islam' is complete garbage. There is no such thing. There are several million Muslims living in the U.S., none of whom are being told they must surrender their faith and convert, or are prohibited from practicing their faith openly. Nor are they confined to internment camps – our nation already made that mistake during World War II with the Japanese. Jihadis would disagree and say I had been 'consumed by the 'Great Satan', considering me, a lifelong Muslim, an apostate and worthy of death, but they are the ones being led down a path that is far more immoral."

Mathews and Simms looked at each other and then at Omar with added respect and a deeper understanding of the CIA's man in ISIS. Like them, he was their nation's defender and would do what he must to protect it and their citizens from the evil that the Islamic State and organizations like it represented.

"How did the call go?" Simms asked to bring their meeting back on topic before taking a bite of a sweet roll.

"He'll be there tonight. 9 P.M.," Omar told him.

Mathews sipped his coffee, and added a little cream from the small bowl Rashad had left behind. "How big of a security force?"

Omar smiled. "I'm supposed to bring water and fruit for eight guards. Add Akil and maybe one or two others, and we're looking at a total of a dozen or so."

Simms frowned. "That's a tall order for just the two of us," he said pointedly, looking at Mathews.

"You know we can handle it," Mathews answered.

Undeterred by his officer's assessment, Simms said grimly, "It means the threshold for lethal RoE is a lot lower. We can't afford the risk of trying to stun all those guys quietly. One non-lethal takedown that isn't instant and we're blown."

"Lighten up," Omar told him with a smile. "We're in public."

Simms caught his meaning and leaned back, forcing a smile that seemed genuine to maintain the illusion of a less than serious conversation and choosing to add a leisurely arms-wide stretch as well.

"I hear you," Mathews told Simms. "We'll need to handle this a bit more forcefully than we planned to."

Omar looked from man to man. "Should we call this off?"

"No," Mathews said without hesitation, "we can do it, but your ass is going to be hanging in the breeze for a few minutes while we prep the environment to get to Akil and whoever he has brought with him. You sure you can keep Akil's attention?"

Omar considered that. "Yes," he said, nodding. "I'm sure I can." He reached out and topped off both their coffees, as a good host should.

"How long?" Simms asked, offering the cream to Mathews, who took it from him and splashed a little more into his refilled cup.

"About five, maybe ten minutes." Omar added thoughtfully, "He may have questions that might draw it out a little."

"Ten minutes or less?" Simms said searchingly, looking at Mathews.

"We'll just have to be quick," Mathews said.

"We need to be more than quick, boss," Simms responded, letting his face slip back into a serious look. "We'll have to be in two, maybe three places at once."

"Three places?" Omar inquired searchingly.

Simms nodded. "Yes. With eight or ten people on security, and one or two with you, you need to remember that the perimeter is going to be pretty big, and the ruins of the fortress create a huge obstacle, and an advantage."

Simms sipped his coffee again to try to keep up the illusion before continuing. Two Jordanian men had just rounded the corner of one of the side streets and had begun walking east toward the café.

"We'll have to eliminate everyone on the perimeter, and get close enough to where you are to complete the mission. While the fortress ruins give us cover and concealment to work with, they also obstruct our lines of sight."

Omar was not too concerned about Mathews and Simms killing Akil's security team. Every man was undoubtedly a staunch supporter of the Islamic State, or Akil would not have them protecting him, and Allah knew how many innocents they had killed in their time.

"But your airborne friend..." Omar began, his eyes automatically looking up to where the little RAVEN drone was orbiting. Mathews shook his head no, cutting him off.

"The RAVEN can help us see where the bad guys are, but we can't shoot them through a pile of stones. You could be on your own for a few minutes, if the bad guys figure out what's going on or we get into a firefight. What's your play for that?"

Omar thought a minute. "I can encourage him to flee and offer to cover his retreat, but he might want to take me with him..."

"Or shoot you," Simms added darkly. "He may decide you have too much information in your head once the bullets start flying."

Omar frowned at that. He had not considered that possible outcome in their earlier planning for the operation. "I guess I'll have to play it by ear. I may need to hold him there until you two get to us."

"How?" Mathews asked. "From what you've said, they check you for weapons. You'll be completely unarmed."

Omar smiled and explained his idea in a few short sentences.

Mathews nodded. "As long as you're sure..."

"It will work," Omar assured him, "as long as we set it up correctly. They will see what they expect to see. If not, I'm going to be relying on you two to be very good and very fast tonight."

Simms watched as the two men who were walking east along Highway 10 turn into the café's small patio area, chatting in Arabic.

"Voices..." he said in a low tone.

Omar immediately laughed aloud, and then continued in English. "No, my friend. You should not head into the eastern desert unprepared. I could be your guide for a very reasonable fee. I promise a safe return..." Omar's voice drifted off as the door to the café closed behind the two men. "I was listening to their conversation as they went by. They were discussing taking a trip into Amman so their wives could shop."

"We'll have you covered," Mathews assured him, nodding toward Simms, "but we'll need to spend a few more hours refining our plan. I'd like to actually visit the place today and do some onsite recon, but I think that's too risky."

"Think our friends back home would mind if we send the RAVEN on a little trip?" Simms asked hopefully.

Mathews considered that. "Nice idea, but we won't be able to command it real-time, and that leaves our friend here uncovered."

Omar frowned. "I don't need a nursemaid. To keep up appearances, I need to stay shut up in my shack, working to refine my plan. Akil expects my best work, after all."

"I'll clear it with our Uncle," Mathews said, "and make sure the RAVEN has the legs for the trip."

"Sounds good," Omar agreed. "For safety's sake, I'll prep a duress message on one of my burners, 'Allah's blessings upon you.' If anything goes wrong between now and tonight, I'll shoot that to you as a text message."

"I like it." Simms added, "If we get that, we'll head to your place immediately."

"Yes, but if you have to get mobile, just call me via voice and we'll coordinate a pickup as needed," Mathews told Omar.

Without warning, the café door opened and the two men came out carrying individual coffees and a sweet roll each. They mutually agreed on another table across from the trio and headed for it.

"Well, my friends," Omar said, slipping instantly back into his 'hospitable Jordanian' role, "I wish you luck in your studies." Omar rose and shook hands with both men again, then headed off, waving a greeting to the two men on the other side of the patio before walking east. Mathews expected he was continuing on to service his dead drops as usual.

"Nice guy," Simms observed, loudly enough that the two men sipping their coffee and talking animatedly over their sweet rolls could hear him without much effort.

"Yes," Mathews agreed. "It's always nice to meet people from different cultures. I've found the Jordanian people to be very welcoming since I arrived."

Both men finished the last of their coffee over innocuous small talk about desert archeology and land surveys that sounded good to their ears, at least, and then left the small café's patio area. Mathews took a quick glance at the two Jordanians as he passed, but they paid him no heed as the two men spoke rapid fire Arabic at one another, obviously engrossed in a serious conversation in the early morning.

Not seeing anything to concern him, he and Simms walked back to their safe house, keeping the pace brisk and taking a winding path through the little town to meet both their counter surveillance and exercise needs. They had a great deal of work to do once they returned home.

Nusrat counted himself fortunate, no doubt because of Allah's beneficence. As his driver pulled up to Akil's house, expecting to have the on-duty guards open the gate to allow the massive Land Rover Defender up the drive, he saw the silver BMW 335d belonging to Akil's mistress exit the drive and pass him. Recognizing Nusrat, Fatima even gave him a huge smile and a wave as she went past.

Nusrat's driver expertly maneuvered the Defender past the open gate into the drive, executing a three-point turn to point its nose toward the steel gate as it closed. Nusrat could see Akil standing before the house, obviously having just seen his mistress off, and expecting Nusrat to step out of the Defender.

"Good Morning, Sahib. As salaam alaykum," Nusrat said as he approached Akil, his lightweight Lenovo laptop in hand.

"Peace be upon you as well, my friend." Akil said genially, sated and well rested after last night's exertions with Fatima. "You're early," he chided Nusrat gently.

"I'm sorry, Sahib," Nusrat said sincerely, "but I have information you need to see."

"Oh," Akil said, curious. "Come with me to the kitchen. Fatima made coffee before she left."

Nusrat obediently trailed Akil through the entryway, past the stairwell to the upper floor and the now-open pocket doors to the living room, into the kitchen and its professional-grade appliances from Germany. Akil poured him a fresh cup of coffee.

"Shokran, Sahib."

Akil waved away his thanks. "It is no trouble, Nusrat. You are my head of security, but also a valued friend."

The unexpected praise surprised Nusrat and he smiled. "I am glad you think so, Sahib. I am pleased to have a friend like you on the path to Allah's victory."

Akil took a long drink from his coffee cup, before asking, "What do you have for me today?"

Nusrat immediately put down his coffee cup and opened his Lenovo laptop, placing it on the marble-topped island in the kitchen. "Al-Amriki is acting strangely."

Akil gave him a puzzled look. "Explain," he ordered.

"Instead of taking his usual walk and visiting the dead drops, he met with two men on the patio of a coffee shop in town today. The owner served them coffee and rolls. They spoke for nearly one-half hour."

"Oh?" Akil asked, arching his eyebrows in a 'why is this a problem?' look.

Nusrat took a deep breath to calm himself before explaining. "As you know, when we initially placed Al-Amriki in Ar-Ruwayshid, you were concerned that he be protected as a valuable member of the Caliphate. As such, we have used a variety of means to monitor him and his surroundings. We initially placed two trusted members of the jihad in the town to shadow him carefully, looking for anyone who exhibited undue interest in Al-Amriki – they saw nothing and after three months, we withdrew them, believing him safe."

Akil tilted his head with a 'get on with it look' on his face, his patience waning slightly, and Nusrat hurried on.

"During that time, they developed a very solid understanding of a typical day for Al-Amriki, one that was consumed with either work in his home, or twice daily walks to service the dead drops we established for him. Members of the jihad working undercover in Jordan ride the bus route back and forth between Ar-Ruwayshid and Amman every day to service the drops. In anticipation of your meeting, and that Al-Amriki requested meeting you at the old fortress, I prevailed on our reconnaissance section to fly the Shahed-135 over the fortress, and watch Al-Amriki for the day."

Akil nodded, not entirely sure where this was going yet, but recognizing now that Nusrat was being his usual thorough self. The Shahed-135 was an Iranian drone that the Caliphate had captured intact, along with its control equipment from an Iranian reconnaissance unit in northern Iraq several months ago. The unit had tried to flee the onrushing tide of the Caliph's fighters, but could not pack up their control equipment and the twelve-foot-long drone before the Caliphate's fighters captured them. Akil elected to travel to the site himself to see the captured equipment and the Iranian soldiers, all of whom were Shi'a.

Recognizing the importance of the cylindrically shaped drone with wings, Akil had ordered the handful of enlisted men's throats slit immediately, forcing the officers to watch as the unbelievers pleaded and begged for mercy, then gurgled and gasped for breath as their life pooled beneath their bodies in huge red lakes.

Noting that he had their attention, Akil promised the remaining officers that if they cooperated, they would not suffer. Fearful and well-motivated, the officers cooperated, and after two weeks, the Caliphate operators could handle the Shahed-135 without their help. Akil gathered the Iranian officers under the watchful eyes of his fighters, told them to pray and beg Allah to forgive them for not following the true, Sunni path of Islam, then ordered his jihadis to execute them. Satisfied that the Iranians now knew Allah's peace and mercy in a more personal manner, he ordered the Shahed-135 put to work immediately.

Using the drone in Iraq helped them win several victories in short order, solidifying some territorial gains along the Iraq/Syria border and helping the Caliph's forces defend against feeble attacks from the poorly led and trained Iraqi army in others. When it was not needed for direct battlefield support, the operators had orders to send the drone wherever it would serve the Caliph best, and that included taking orders from his director of operations. Naturally, his orders were always relayed by Nusrat, which allowed Nusrat to task the drone as needed to help keep Akil safe.

"So, my drone believes Al-Amriki is acting strangely?" Akil asked skeptically.

"Please look for yourself, Sahib," Nusrat replied, tapping the screen on the Lenovo and triggering the video playback.

Akil watched as a man dressed modestly in Thawb and pants walked along a roadside and turned left into the area before a small house with tables and chairs laid out. The video quality was poor, only black and white, and jittered constantly. Iranian drone technology left much to be desired.

"That is Al-Amriki," Nusrat told him, "we followed him from his safe house this morning."

The man sat at one of the outside tables, and the owner came out and served him coffee. A few minutes later, two men, obviously westerners based on their dress arrived, and Al-Amriki stood to greet them, appearing to invite them to his table.

Akil's eyes narrowed. "Roll that back to when the westerners appear," he ordered Nusrat. Nusrat tapped the screen again, and they watched the replay.

"It appears that the westerners were headed into the house before Al-Amriki stopped them," Akil observed.

"Yes, Sahib," Nusrat agreed. "It is a small, makeshift café run by a man named Rashad. His wife cooks and he and his sons serve the guests."

The video continued and Akil leaned in closer to watch it, adjusting the tilt of the laptop's screen to ensure he saw the clearest possible image. The proprietor was back, serving coffee and a pastry of some kind to the three men, all of whom were now seated at Al-Amriki's table. They spoke for nearly thirty minutes as they drank coffee and ate.

"It is difficult to read their expressions," Akil noted, "but their body language does not tell us much either. One man appears to have laughed aloud. Secret meetings are not often held in public." He was less concerned than when Nusrat had first arrived.

"Yes, Sahib, but I am concerned that a man of Al-Amriki's skills and position within the Caliphate would intentionally reach out to two westerners. Moreover, what are two westerners doing in Ar-Ruwayshid?" Nusrat's voice grew louder as he asked the last question, subconsciously projecting his concern more forcefully than he intended.

"Peace, my friend," Akil said, placing a hand on his shoulder as the video clip ended with Al-Amriki walking away from the table and heading further east along the road.

"Let us think this through." Akil continued, looking directly at Nusrat. "Al-Amriki is a very smart man; he has proven this many times. He also believes himself to be alone in the town, yes?"

Nusrat nodded.

"It would not surprise me that he would chose to initiate an encounter with two westerners to learn about them and what they are doing in Ar-Ruwayshid, rather than speculate. His cover there is well established; even some in the village can confirm his claim to be there on an infrastructure survey for the Jordanian government, yes?"

Nusrat nodded again, but was becoming concerned that Akil was talking himself out of questioning Al-Amriki's behavior, and he began to speak. Akil held up his hand.

"You raise a valid concern, and I will speak to him about it when I see him face to face tonight. Can the drone monitor him for the rest of the day?"

"No," Nusrat said. "It will be free tonight before we cross the border, but for the remainder of today it must be refueled and made available to support the expected battle at Raqqah. The Syrians have been moving troops into the area and the infidel airstrikes have been hitting several locations near the city. The local commander's needs must take priority, unless you wish to appeal to the Caliph..."

Akil shook his head as Nusrat trailed off. "No. The battle at Raqqah will be a tremendous victory for us, not just in terms of proving we can hold the Caliphate's capital city, but also for our social media campaign and the morale of the jihadis. I will speak with Al-Amriki man-to-man about this." Akil put his now empty coffee cup on the counter. "You are certain the drone will be available tonight?"

"Yes, but it must return to its base before sunset. Our Iranian friends only fitted it with daytime cameras, and we lack the technology to fit it with something more sophisticated."

Akil considered that. "Will you be able to monitor the border crossing and the area around the fortress before our arrival?"

"Yes, but only after the drone leaves the Raqqah area in the evening, and until seven-thirty or so. Sunset is shortly after eight, and it must land by then."

Satisfied that the Shahed-135 would be able to observe the area before his arrival, Akil thought the level of risk acceptable. After all, Al-Amriki was a proven member of the jihad, and his plans had resulted in many unbelievers learning the error of their ways. He also knew Nusrat would be suitably cautious during the trip.

"Not to worry my friend, I trust you to protect me if needed. Al-Amriki will explain his actions tonight, and if he has made an error in judgement, I will admonish him appropriately."

"It shall be as you order, Sahib. My men and I will protect you with our lives," Nusrat assured him.

"I am certain of this," Akil told Nusrat, his gaze steady, adding, "If Al-Amriki has betrayed us, which I doubt, Ghalib and I have already decided his fate, and you will see it done."

Nusrat nodded grimly, knowing Akil trusted him to see the harshest punishments carried out, and looking forward to disciplining Al-Amriki if he warranted it. "Yes, Sahib."

"What do you think?" Mathews asked Simms.

Both men, seated at the table in their little safe house, looked at the imagery the RAVEN had captured of the collapsed fortress called Qasr Burqu displayed on Mathews' tablet. Situated in the midst of the rolling hills of the Jordanian panhandle's northern desert, the ruin lay on the southeast corner of the seasonal lake. The whole complex sat in a shallow valley surrounded by broken ground, with low brush and rocky terrain, more reminiscent of the moon than anything else. Leading into the valley from each of the cardinal directions were rutted dirt tracks.

The lake itself was nearly 300 yards long at the moment, but Mathews could see from the watermark outline extending northwest that the lake had been, or could grow during the 'wet' season to, twice that. The lake, at least from the RAVEN's video, did not look like something he would want to drink from or swim in, appearing a uniform gray color, but he knew that might be just an artifact of the lighting conditions, or a view of the muddy bottom of the lake showing clearly through the water.

The old fortress, built on the southeast corner of the lake, was mostly lines and heaps of collapsed rubble that outlined what were the walls and ceilings now. The sole exception was the western tower, whose walls still stood. The entire structure was made of dark brown and ochre-colored sandstone. The lines and heaps of rubble, and tower covered a ten thousand square foot area.

"I think we need to do this very carefully," Simms observed, studying the image.

Mathews shook his head, "Really?" he asked rhetorically. Now was not the time for Simms' usual humor.

"I'm not kidding boss," Simms said, undeterred. "The cover is minimal. That will make this really tough."

"Yes, but I think we're going to have to adapt a bit more than usual on this one," Mathews told him. Doing what they had been discussing since the imagery of the site came in meant breaking one of the cardinal rules in special operations work. Each one of them would need to work alone on this mission, coordinating their actions as needed, rather than as a pair able to support one another immediately as the situation evolved.

Simms let out a deep breath, "Yeah. At least Cain gave us some good news."

"Yep. He's setting up the comms and everything else with his team. You want the inside or the outside?" Mathews asked.

Simms considered that. Each option had drawbacks as far as he was concerned. "I'll take the outside. I can set up here," he said, pointing a specific point about three hundred feet to the south of the fortress. "I'd prefer to be closer, but the terrain doesn't support that."

"And you'll need some space in case they find you," Mathews added.

"True," Simms said resignedly. "What about you?"

"Here, I think," Mathews said pointing to the image.

"You'll need to be totally radio silent," Simms said, staring at the point Mathews indicated. "One sound and they'll kill you."

"The same goes for you. I'll expect you to keep them off me if you can, but I'm not going to be able to support you at all." Mathews said.

Simms looked at him with worry in his eyes. "Don't sweat that. I'll be OK as long as I work quickly and they set up the perimeter the way we expect. Remember, Omar told us his security is all ex-military, so if they were trained well, they will be predictable and we should catch a break. As far as covering you is concerned, the south wall is going to make that a problematic. It's going to limit my sight lines."

"We'll just have to find a way," Mathews said confidently, then added, inspiration striking him, "I think I know how to stay out of trouble," and outlined his idea.

Simms considered his idea and nodded. "It's risky, but I like it." Simms reached out to tap on the tablet's display, zooming the image in. "Think that spot will work?"

Mathews leaned in to get a closer look, in spite of the extreme magnification, and then smiled. "Yes."

Mathews agreed with Simms assessment of the risk, especially since their plan counted on Akil's security doing exactly what they expected. If they did not, he and Simms had a contingency, but using that meant a very high probability that Omar would not walk away from the operation alive.

The final decision was his, of course. He could call it off now and they could simply let Omar lay out his plan to Akil and then let the Islamic State's next terror operation play out to keep Omar's cover intact. Balanced against the possibility of eliminating a senior leader of the Islamic State instead, or leaders if Akil brought someone with him, left Mathews with a tough call. As usual, he evaluated the gains and the risks he, Omar, and Simms were about to take, and made his decision quickly.

"Ok, let's go over the whole thing one more time," Mathews said, glancing at his watch. Omar would start his afternoon dead drop servicing in another hour, and the 'go mission' signal was Simms putting gas in the Range Rover at the sole filling station at the eastern edge of town along Highway 10. After that, they needed to recall the RAVEN and switch out its batteries early. It would need a full charge tonight.

CHAPTER 16

Akil stepped up into the armored Land Rover Defender to sit next to Nusrat in the rear seat, two of his bodyguards already occupying the front seats. The sun was very low on the horizon, and he had taken the opportunity to eat early, consuming the last of the chicken dinner Fatima had cooked for him in between their lovemaking sessions last night.

"So?" he asked Nusrat, who had his nose buried in the screen of the Lenovo laptop yet again.

Nusrat finished clicking through the images e-mailed by the Shahed-135 control team. "The area looks clear, both at the border and the meeting site, although the sun's position casts more shadows at this time of day," he reported.

"Are the fighters in place at the border?"

"Yes, Sahib. Their leader called me a few minutes ago. They are prepared for your arrival, and will hold the area if need be, Insha'Allah."

Akil grunted at Nusrat's last words. 'Allah Willing' indeed. "Then let's get going," he ordered the driver, a burly former member of the Iraqi Republican Guard.

As the man pulled through the gates of his home, the two escorting Defenders formed up with them, forming a convoy of three vehicles. As the lead and trailing cars slid into position, Akil asked, "How long?"

Nusrat answered immediately, knowing the answer from his research and anticipating the question, "An hour to the border, and another forty minutes or so to the fortress. We should arrive about twenty minutes before Al-Amriki does. That will give us time to secure the site and establish a security perimeter."

"Then wake me when we are five miles from the border," Akil instructed him, before making himself comfortable and closing his eyes.

In CTS, it was early afternoon, and Cain looked at the remains of his lunch sitting on his desk on the watch floor. He decided against a bite of the second half of his tuna sandwich, and snatched a couple of cheddar and sour cream potato chips instead. Every watch stander had their headphones on so they could communicate over the internal intercom. Cain used his mouse to tweak a few settings. In his right ear, he would hear only the internal intercom, and in his left, the external traffic, most of which was being routed through Mathews' and Simms' special iPhones.

"RAVEN orbit established over objective," Thompson reported from her drone desk.

A few seconds later, Thompson finished ordering her system to display the little drone's camera feed on the main monitor. Cain saw the image come up, the electro-optical camera showing them the growing shadows of a day ending in Jordan.

"When is sunset?" Cain asked on the open link.

"About thirty minutes," Thompson reported. "Want me to try the night vision now?"

"No, wait until twilight," he responded. "We don't want to inadvertently damage the camera now."

"Copy that," she told him.

Cain switched his microphone over to the external net. "Whiskey Base, this is Charlie One, we're ready here. Any last minute items?"

"Charlie One, Whiskey Base, negative. Everything is set from this end," Simon replied from Crane's office. They were watching the RAVEN's video feed as well, routed to them from Thompson's terminal over a secure link.

"Oracle," Cain said, using the call sign for the CIA watch center, where Walker was watching, "this is Charlie One, any objections to the mission plan?"

"Negative," Walker's voice replied. "As long as you think you can pull it off. Besides," Walker added, "the kid's earned it." The disappointment in his voice was obvious.

"Copy," Cain told him, keeping the satisfaction from his voice. The president had issued orders that Walker and the Director of the CIA were not happy about, but Cain needed to focus on what was about to happen.

Cain studied the image from the RAVEN, looking for any sign of human presence at the fortress, and switched back to the internal network. "Anyone see anything suspicious?"

Twelve pairs of eyes at the various watch center desks looked at the video feed, and after nearly two minutes, no one said a word. Cain switched networks again.

"Whiskey Four-Six, Charlie One. The objective looks clear."

"Copy that," Mathews replied, bumping along in the old Range Rover on the rutted dirt track two miles away from the fortress. Simms sat beside him, and Omar sat in the rear seat, still astonished at what they were wearing.

Mathews and Simms had donned their special armor, again wearing it beneath brown Thawbs, leaving their helmets in the rear cargo area of the Range Rover, along with the rest of their gear, and a few items Omar needed for tonight.

This time, both commandos had brought along their tactical radios from the 'care package' they brought back from the embassy, clipping them to the body armor behind their right shoulders, which gave their Thawbs an unnatural, hump-backed look. Laying between them on Simms' side of the front foot well and propped up against Simms' seat were two assault rifles of a kind Omar had never seen before. One had a longer barrel, and both had wicked looking suppressors attached.

"You were going to tell me about your rifles." Omar said to Simms as he tapped him on the shoulder, letting Mathews concentrate on his driving in the lengthening shadows.

Simms turned his head partially over his shoulder, keeping his eyes forward to look for threats, and raised his voice a little to be heard over the grit, gravel, and dirt being thrown up by the Range Rover's tires.

"They are Heckler & Koch M-8 assault rifles. 5.56 millimeter, 30 round magazines, and interchangeable parts for different missions. Change out the standard twelve-inch barrel for a nine-inch, and you have a compact carbine for personal defense. Switch that out for one of two twenty-inch barrels and the right optics, and you have either a sniper rifle or a light machine gun," Simms told him. Then he added, as any Special Forces soldier proud of his equipment would, "We can add suppressors to all the barrels except the machine gun one." The ability to fight as quietly as possible was something that was never overlooked in special operations.

"Wow," was all Omar could think to say. "So, what's the deal with the motorcycle helmets?"

"Those give us ballistic protection, built in radio communications, and integrated optics; thermal, low-light, and infrared. Wearing the Bluetooth headsets so we can stay in contact with CTS makes them a little snug, though."

Omar blinked; astounded at the capability their equipment gave them. "That's incredible. I'm betting all this cost a pretty penny," he said, angling as any American taxpayer might for what the price was.

"We don't ask," Mathews said over his shoulder.

"And we don't care," Simms added, "as long as it helps us complete the mission."

"Coming up on your stop," Mathews said, braking the Range Rover, and turning left about three-hundred yards away from the southern edge of the lake and the old fortress. After another fifty yards of driving, he found some brush to park the Range Rover behind as a precaution, turning in a one-hundred and eighty-degree circle first to point the car's nose back in the direction they came.

All three men stepped from the vehicle and Simms grabbed his rifle from the front seat, resting it against the side of the Range Rover before getting his pack from the cargo area and slipping its straps over his shoulders, then slinging his rifle at the ready. Drawing his CQC-7 combat knife from the sheath in front of his pistol as he stepped away from the Range Rover toward a small patch of bushes, Simms cut a four-foot-long piece of the scrub brush to use as a broom. He would use it to obliterate his tracks, another precaution that his training drilled into him.

Once he had everything, there was nothing left to do, except part ways. He and Mathews had already double-checked the gear and made sure both of their radios were working before they left Ar-Ruwayshid to pick up Omar a mile outside of town. Mathews and Simms looked at each other.

"See you later," Mathews told him, less than pleased about not working shoulder to shoulder with the man tonight, but recognizing he had little choice.

"Roger that, boss." Simms replied, equally displeased but professional enough to know that risk was part of the life of a Tier One operator.

Simms began hiking northwest, towards the southwest edge of the lake. In his backpack was the tablet and his iPhone. They had reprogrammed the tablet to allow CTS to command the RAVEN remotely, since Mathews and his phone would be too far away. His helmet hung suspended from the backpack on a carabiner using its internal nylon loop, which was designed for just such a need. He would not need the helmet just yet. The fading twilight was enough for now.

Mathews and Omar watched him hike off for a few seconds, before Mathews said, "You're driving," and reboarded the Range Rover on the passenger side. After a second's hesitation while he watched Simms hike off into the gathering darkness, Omar slid behind the wheel and led them back out toward the rutted path that lead to the fortress.

"Turn here," Mathews instructed Omar as they approached the rutted path again. Omar turned left, and they headed north, the old fortress less than five hundred yards away.

Over the encrypted Bluetooth link from his headset to his iPhone, tucked into a pocket of his armor, Mathews said, "Whiskey Four-Seven detached, designate Sierra."

"Charlie One copies," Cain replied, "we have him in sight."

In CTS, Cain watched the lone figure of Simms, now designated Sierra, making good time as he hiked north.

"Sierra, Charlie One. Area remains clear," Cain told him.

"Copy." Simms responded over his own Bluetooth connected headset.

"Sahib?" Nusrat said, gently putting his hand on Akil's shoulder. "We are at the border."

Akil came awake immediately, startled to find himself in the armored Defender instead of his own bed. He looked around bleary eyed for a few seconds, blinking to clear his vision as his mind caught up with his surroundings.

"Good." He pronounced once he was oriented again. Akil took a bottle of mineral water from the cup holder between them and twisted off the metal cap. After a long pull, he asked, "What does the drone tell us?"

"As of the last images thirty minutes ago, the fortress is clear and the border remains so."

"When will we get fresh images?' Akil asked, noting that the sun had just dropped below the horizon.

"We will not," Nusrat told him. At Akil's questioning look, Nusrat continued, "You will recall I told you that the drone's camera's do not function at night, moreover, during the battle near Raqqah today, the drone expended more fuel that expected, and it was forced to return to its base earlier than planned."

Still waking up, Akil did recall Nusrat's earlier mention of the drone's lack of capability, and he silently cursed it.

"Do you still wish to proceed with the meeting?" Nusrat inquired, seeing the look on Akil's face.

"Yes," Akil told him after a moment's consideration. Al-Amriki's next set of plans would deal a painful blow to the Americans, and he would not see the timetable delayed more than necessary.

Akil leaned left to look through the windshield between the driver and the bodyguard in the passenger seat, and saw the approaching checkpoint established by the soldiers of Allah.

Four vehicles and more than a dozen men manned it, some in the open, others near the vehicles. The men all carried AK-74 assault rifles. Two of the vehicles were Toyota trucks with mounted 12.7-millimeter NSVT Utyos machine guns with makeshift steel cupolas. The other two were a mixed bag: a Toyota Land Cruiser and a Nissan Frontier, both of which were worn with age and a hard life on rugged terrain.

While he did not see any evidence of them, he knew that the trucks likely held Russian 9K32 Strela-2 shoulder fired surface-to-air missiles, called SA-7 by NATO, to target low flying aircraft, and one or two of the ubiquitous Russian-made Rocket Propelled Grenades to deal with armored targets. More than enough to hold off an armed Syrian patrol, even if they appeared with light armored fighting vehicles supported by reconnaissance helicopters.

More importantly, Akil could see the hulking figure of Ghalib standing near one of the Toyotas, waving in the direction of Akil's Defender, having guessed he was in the second of the three armored four-by-fours.

"Stop and let him board," Akil ordered unnecessarily.

The driver was already slowing, having slewed the Defender closer to Ghalib. Once the Defender halted, Ghalib wasted no time in opening the passenger door and waving the bodyguard riding shotgun out. The man exited the vehicle, walked back to the trailing Defender, and boarded it.

Ghalib's twisted in the front passenger seat to offer his hand, and Akil leaned forward to take it. "It is good to see you again, my brother," Akil said. They were close enough not to offer the traditional, 'Peace be upon you' greeting.

"I heard we did well in Raqqah today," Ghalib offered. "The Syrians are no match for us on the ground, but the infidels continue their airstrikes, and I have heard of the coalition the infidels are trying to build with the 'Syrian resistance' as it calls itself."

"Good," Akil said. "I will be given the specifics tomorrow during the operations update. You will stay at my home tonight and join me for the meeting. I want to discuss the Caliph's plans for destroying the unbeliever's forces near Raqqah and the preparations for a thrust toward Baghdad with you and the other senior commanders. He is tired of the feeble Iraqi government and their infidel allies hampering the growth of the Caliphate. We will also examine the best ways to deal with this feeble Syrian resistance before it gets out of hand."

Ghalib smiled. "Excellent. I will need the men and material to commit to the campaign."

"You'll get them," Akil assured him. "We will take a page from the infidel's own history books, and leapfrog from city to city quickly. A strong series of victories will embolden our men and spur a surge of recruiting in Mosques throughout the world." The confidence in Akil's voice was unshakable, and Ghalib shared it, but he had to temper it with military reality.

"How will we hold the territory if my fighters do not remain in each city to solidify our gains?" Ghalib asked.

"The Caliph will be creating a force of Mutawa to enforce strict Sharia Law immediately after the conquest." Akil knew that creating an occupying force of Mutawa, or religious police, and stationing them in each city would free up trained fighters and avoid having combat resources wasted merely holding territory. In fact, he had offered the idea up to the Caliph, who approved enthusiastically. "You should be able to march on a new town or medium-sized city every week or 10 days."

"What of the infidel aircraft? Their sudden airstrikes cause materiel losses and demoralize my men," Ghalib noted.

"The Caliph has plans for them," Akil assured him. "We shall begin martyrdom operations against their airfields at once. Al-Amriki will be busy in his new position."

Akil checked his watch. "We'll be at the meeting site in about thirty minutes," he told Ghalib. "I'm sure you'll enjoy what young Al-Amriki has planned for our next overseas operation.

Ghalib grunted, not trusting himself to speak aloud, given Akil's preference for the man. As far as Ghalib was concerned, Al-Amriki had still not proven himself. If he could slow or stop the airstrikes, Ghalib thought he might change his opinion of the man, but it will take more than martyrdom operations to defeat all those aircraft.

"You ready?" Mathews asked Omar. They stood just outside of the ruined tower, Mathews with his M-8 assault rifle slung over his shoulder, its suppressor extending nearly eight inches above his shoulder, his black helmet dangling from one hand. The two men had finished preparing the site a few minutes ago.

Omar swallowed nervously. "Yes. How many operations like this have you done?"

"Like this?" Mathews asked. "None. This is definitely a first."

Omar smiled, "That's not confidence inspiring."

Mathews grinned in return. "Just play it the way we planned it out. Simms and I will cover you."

Suddenly, Cain's voice came over the link. "Whiskey Four-Six, this is Charlie One. Heads up. The Raven is north of you. We have a small convoy of three vehicles heading your way from the north. ETA to your location, less than five minutes."

"Whiskey Four-Six copies," Mathews said. He reached out to Omar, and Omar shook his hand. "Let's do this," Mathews said. "I'm going to get in position."

Mathews walked back into the collapsed tower, and Omar walked ten yards to the north, standing in the open, his hands away from his body, the Range Rover parked twenty yards away. He had no radio communications with Cain or Simms, so he would not be able to follow what was going on tactically, and he was unarmed. At that moment, he knew exactly what it meant to be bait. If they suspected anything, or saw Mathews or Simms, he was a dead man. He touched the Mont Blanc pen in his pocket for reassurance. He was unarmed, and would never be able to get in the Range Rover before Akil's guards shot him down, or worse, captured him. As he saw the lights of the cars crest the hill to the north and travel down the valley towards his position, he thought about his training and tried to stay calm, knowing that his actions in the next fifteen minutes would dictate the outcome of the mission.

Cain watched the cars get closer to Omar, and estimated the distance at less than two hundred yards. "Team, this is Charlie One. Target vehicles are one hundred and fifty yards away from the friendly. All units check in."

"Charlie Four-Six, ready," Mathews whispered from his position, his helmet on and the low-light systems activated.

"Sierra One, ready," Simms reported from his location, lying prone behind some low scrub less than one hundred yards from Omar's location. While Mathews and Omar had gotten ready at the partially collapsed tower, he had triple-checked his M-8. Its twenty-inch long-range barrel and its screwed-on one-foot-long sound suppressor were free of grit, and the AN/PVS-14 night vision optic attached to the paired sniper scope were in working order. He had even fired one test round at the top of the partially-collapsed tower to verify his elevation and windage settings on the scope – neither Mathews nor Omar had noticed as they worked. Peering through the sight, night turned into light and dark green daylight, and he could see Omar clearly, as he waited by the tower, hands in the open.

"Gunslinger, ready," said a female voice on the link, and while Mathews was grateful to hear it, he sincerely hoped they would not need her until the plan called for it.

"This is Charlie Four," Thompson's voice called out from CTS. "RAVEN drone holding north of the lake center, five hundred AGL. Confirm three target vehicles, now fifty yards from the friendly."

Omar could hear the engines of Akil's convoy, and he shielded his eyes with his left hand as the bright headlights washed over him, careful not to obscure his face too much. The lead Defender drove past him, close enough that the breeze of its passage ruffled the edges of his Thawb, and he felt the sand and grit it kicked up hitting his legs. As the second Defender pulled right up in front of him, stopping at a distance of no more than five feet, the headlights blinded him completely.

"Al-Amriki is early," Nusrat observed in the Defender. He raised a VHF radio to his lips. "Car Three, have your men secure the north side of the lake. Car One, let me know when your people are deployed."

Akil moved to exit the Defender, and Nusrat reached out to grab his arm, concern for his safety making him grip his superior's arm in a forceful way. "Please wait, Sahib, until my men have secured the area." Choosing to respect Nusrat's caution, and deciding that making Al-Amriki wait a few seconds would reinforce his superiority, Akil acquiesced. But then he had a better idea.

"Ghalib, step out and search Al-Amriki," Akil ordered.

"There is a weapon in the glove compartment worthy of you, Commander," Nusrat added.

Ghalib popped open the glove compartment and withdrew the weapon, beaming. It was a matte-black Desert Eagle .50 caliber automatic pistol. One of the most powerful semi-automatic handguns in the world, it weighed nearly five pounds. Its magazine held seven rounds that traveled at four hundred and seventy meters per second with an impact force of nearly 1,500 pounds-feet of energy. It was enough kinetic force to knock a three-hundred-pound man off his feet at the same time it blew a fist-sized hole through him. The only downside was that an Israeli company had made it.

Nonetheless, Ghalib pulled back the slide to make sure one of the half-inch diameter rounds was chambered and checked the safety before stepping out of the Defender. The Defender's driver remained where he was, ready to run down Al-Amriki if need be and then spirit Akil away from danger.

"Good evening, Al-Amriki," Ghalib said menacingly over the steady sound of the Defender's idling engine.

Omar swallowed his sudden fear at seeing Ghalib so unexpectedly, and found his voice. "Good evening, Commander Ghalib."

In CTS, Thompson saw a large man get out of the vehicle near Omar and zoomed the RAVEN's camera in on his face quickly, holding it for a few seconds, and then pulled it back so they could clearly see the twenty yards or so around Omar. They could not hear anything yet, even though Mathews had locked his microphone open. They were too far away from his position.

"Any idea who he is?" Cain asked the watch standers. Heads shook no throughout the CTS floor.

Ghalib stepped forward and motioned with the Desert Eagle for Omar to raise his hands. Frowning at what at this point should be an unneeded precaution; Omar raised his hands and stood quietly as Ghalib searched him thoroughly. Finding nothing, Ghalib turned and nodded towards the Defender.

"Satisfied?" Akil asked rhetorically as Nusrat released his grip. Nusrat let him exit the vehicle, now that his men were deployed around the area and Ghalib had frisked Al-Amriki. It was not in Nusrat's job description to take chances with Akil's life.

Nusrat left his laptop in the Defender and followed his principle over to

Al-Amriki, drawing his own pistol, a .40 caliber Browning Hi-Power, from his shoulder holster.

"You are early, Al-Amriki," Akil admonished gently as he walked over to shake Al-Amriki's hand.

Omar bowed slightly out of deference as he took Akil's proffered hand. "I'm sorry, Sahib. I left early to ensure that I arrived on time."

"I see. Are you prepared to brief Commander Ghalib and myself on your planning for the operation against the American embassy?"

"Yes, Sahib. I have laid out the plans and the materials inside the tower." Al-Amriki motioned toward the entrance arch in the collapsed stone tower.

Nusrat immediately headed through the opening into the collapsed tower, the Browning Hi-Power in a solid two-handed grip, visually scanning it before Akil could enter. A small folding table sat beneath a battery-powered fluorescent lantern suspended by an eight-foot high telescoping pole. The light from the lantern was bright, and it illuminated the entire floor of the tower to provide a welcoming place for the meeting.

Two smaller battery-powered lamps sat on the table to provide additional illumination for the documents spread across it. In one corner, Omar's ISIS-issued laptop showed a piece of overhead imagery and some other windows, tiled one on top of another, which appeared to be documents. Next to it were three small bottles of water and a few pieces of fruit.

Seeing nothing dangerous, Nusrat released his two-handed grip on the Browning and waved Akil forward. Akil entered the tower, followed closely by Al-Amriki and Ghalib. "Why is your laptop here?" Nusrat demanded. "You should not have brought it." The water and fruit drew no comment, since in this case, Akil and his men were Al-Amriki's 'guests'.

"I had to," Omar explained. "I could not print the imagery or documents I need to show these men, and they are more secure if left on the laptop." Turning to Akil, he asked, "May I offer you and your men water and fruit? I know it has been a long journey for you."

Akil shook his head no. "It does not appear that you have enough for all of my people," he observed.

"I have more in the cargo area of my rental car..." Omar began, but Nusrat cut him off.

"The guards will wait. They have duties to perform."

Omar looked at Akil for confirmation, and the older man simply nodded.

"Shall I begin, then?" Omar asked.

"Please," Akil instructed. "Show us once again why you are a Senior Engineer of the jihad."

Simms was sweating a little, and while he could hear the Arabic in his ears via Mathews' open microphone, it told him little more than that things were proceeding as expected, since he heard no angry shouts or loud exclamations after Omar and the three Tangos entered the tower. Mathews' position was secure for now, and it was time for him to get to work. He had to act quickly.

"Charlie One, this is Sierra, ready for your cues."

"Copy," said Cain's voice.

Almost immediately after, he heard Thompson's soft feminine voice in his ear over the link. "Sierra, this is Charlie Four. Zooming out now."

Normally, Thompson would use the local data link capability of a more capable drone to downlink the locations of all the hostile targets directly into the computer system he usually wore. That system would then display all the Tango's locations in an augmented reality display on the visor of Simms' helmet so he would not need to search for them. This time, with the computer system back in the States, Thompson would need to maintain overall situational awareness with the RAVEN's video feed, calling out target location and priority, while Simms serviced the targets based on her cueing.

Back in Fort Meade, Thompson looked at the location of each of the Tangos holding the security perimeter and watched them, getting a feel for their patrol patterns, if any, and choosing which order would be best. Making a mistake here would blow the whole mission.

"Sierra, I think we need to work from the far side of the lake toward you."

"Copy," Simms replied, shifting his aim point.

"Two men near the Defender, northeast side of the lake."

Simms shifted his aim to the right. He could see both men standing near the Defender in the surreal green world of the low-light optic. One near the rear right bumper, the other about six feet in front of the Defender's left front bumper. "Have them," he reported.

Back in CTS, Thompson looked at Cain. He had to confirm the use of lethal force.

Cain did not enjoy this any more than anyone else would, but American lives were on the line, there and around the world, and his commander-in-chief had made that decision long ago. "All units this net, this is Charlie One. Mission is a go. Engage and eliminate."

Simms placed the aiming reticule of his scope just above the head of the Tango near the rear bumper, and inhaled. He let out half a breath, and squeezed the trigger.

The bullet left the muzzle at just under nine hundred meters a second and, because of the suppressor, the loudest sound was the M-8 rifle's action cycling—and that dissipated to silence beyond ten feet. It crossed the three-hundred-yard distance in less than three tenths of a second. The round struck just below the center of the back of the man's head, and the more than one thousand pound-feet of impact pressure pitched the Tango forward, causing the body to sprawl face down on the ground.

"Tango down," Simms reported as he shifted to the man to the left, in front of the bumper. The man had heard something, probably the body of his fellow guard hitting the ground, but his mind had not reached that conclusion yet.

Simms could feel the timer in his head counting down. Omar said less than ten minutes, and he needed to be done with this stage of the mission long before that. Two seconds later he had a good sight picture and took the shot, letting out his breath to breath normally again as he saw the second guard's body crumple in front of the Defender.

"Tango down."

"Confirmed," Thompson's voice said in his ear. "Shift west, repeat west. Two Tangos patrolling the west side of the lake in trail. Take the rear target first."

"Copy," Simms reported, shifting his aim again. He found the two Tangos walking south along the lakeside, one man about four feet in front of the other. Normally, it would be a tricky shot, but the angles were working in his favor.

Simms aimed carefully, letting the aim point hover at just the right spot as he watched the bobbing and weaving of the men's bodies as they walked over the uneven ground. He controlled his breathing again. There. The trigger pulled almost of its own volition. The round passed through the forehead of the first

Tango, exiting the back of his skull, and then entered the head of the Tango behind him just below the bridge of his nose. The round was instantly fatal to both men, and they dropped like marionettes with their strings cut.

"Two Tangos down," Simms reported.

"Copy," Thompson said over the link, impressed with the difficult shot. "Next Tango, in front of the vehicle, southeast edge of the lake," she called out.

Simms shifted again, and identified the Tango, controlling his breathing. His finger was just about to tighten on the trigger, when the man moved, walking west.

"Hold! Hold!" Thompson called out. "Looks like he's heading over to his partner for a chat. Simms watched as the target did exactly that. There would be no chance for a double-kill here. Both men stood facing one-another, and he would not be able to hit one without the other shouting out a warning.

Simms ordered himself to remain calm and controlled his breathing. If they kept this up for too long, it would blow the timetable, and the entire operation would come apart.

"Charlie Four, Sierra, where are the remaining Tangos?"

"Two near the entrance to the tower, two on the foot path to your east."

Simms quickly repositioned himself, using the night vision enabled telescopic sight to scan the path to the east. He found the two men on the outbound leg of their patrol on the path, one behind the other. They were close together, too close together to be absolutely certain one would not hear the other die – he would have to risk it.

"Sierra, engaging the two on the path to the east," he called out.

"Copy," Thompson said, not daring to suggest otherwise. He was on scene, and once the execute order had been given by Cain, decisions like this ultimately rested in the hands of the operator in the field. Her job was to provide overwatch and situational awareness. For this engagement, she would watch the pair near the south end of the lake for any reaction, while Simms' attention stayed focused on his targets.

Simms chose the trailing Tango first, knowing the lead Tango's initial confusion would give him an extra second or two to line up on him. He aimed carefully, leading his target just enough, and squeezed off the round.

At this shorter range, the impact of the round sounded like a wet, meaty 'thwack' and the Tango's head disintegrated, brain matter, blood, and bone striking the back of the first Tango's head. Out of reflex, the lead Tango turned to see what happened as he reached up to feel the wetness at the back of his head.

Simms' second round passed through the second Tango's wrist, shattering it into hundreds of tiny pieces no orthopedic surgeon could repair before it struck his head. Depleted of energy from the initial impact with his wrist, the round's impact stunned the man, tearing off much of the side of his face. He stood stock still for a moment before he fell to the ground, the shock and pain overwhelming his senses and rendering him mercifully unconscious. While the round had not killed him instantly, the ongoing blood loss from the head wound would seal his fate in less than an hour. Simms was satisfied, believing the man dead.

"Two more down," he reported, swinging the M-8's muzzle back toward the two men at the south end of the lake. They were still talking. Part of Simms' mind wondered what the hell they were doing having a casual chat on guard duty, but he squashed that line of thinking, concentrating on his mission.

After another twenty seconds, their body language seemed to suggest the conversation was ending. The first Tango turned on his heel and headed east again, toward the vehicle. As he started walking, Simms lined up his next shot. Breathe in, watch the sight picture, let out half, and squeeze. The M-8's action cycled again, and the Tango standing still dropped, the back of his skull blown out. "Tango down," he reported, shifting aim again.

The Tango walking back toward the car reached it, but had barely turned to look south before Simms' eighth round of the night found its mark, followed by another 'Tango down' call on the radio. "Charlie Four, are the last two still outside the door?"

Thompson expected the question. "Affirm. No other Tangos in sight. You're clear to move up."

Simms felt the clock ticking in his head, and worked quickly. He slung the M-8 across his back, and donned his helmet, his fingers automatically finding the recessed button to activate its night vision mode. He drew his silenced Sig Sauer P226, and began to walk towards the collapsed tower of the fortress, keeping the outline of the guard's Land Rover Defender between him and the entrance to the tower. In spite of clearing the area around him, he still held the pistol up in a two-handed grip as he looked for unexpected targets. Fortunately, the dead Tangos had turned off the Defender's lights and engine. "Whiskey Four-

Seven is moving," he reported.

Mathews heard the radio call from Simms, and knew it was nearly time. He had held perfectly still since the one Tango had entered the Tower, obviously checking for traps or other people before their targets and Omar came inside. Stealth was key now, until Simms could get into position. The president's mission orders were clear – capture if possible, kill if necessary.

He listened as Simms dealt with most of the bodyguards Akil had brought along, except for the two right outside the doorway to the tower, as Omar explained to Akil his latest plan. Since it was all in Arabic, he could not follow any of it clearly, but from tone of the words and the body language, the man Omar had described as Akil seemed interested and engaged.

The larger man, whom Mathews did not know but suspected might be a bodyguard, seemed much more gruff and confrontational, but he had left the massive semi-automatic pistol tucked in his belt.

The smaller, wiry bodyguard who had checked the tower out before entering was going to be a problem. He stood away from the group, his back to the corner near the entrance, and his pistol in hand, which would make engaging him later a problem. We should have put the card table in a better place. Too late now.

Once Simms was in position, they could move, but for now, Mathews had to stay silent and still. All he could do is listen to the radio calls.

"What do you think?" Omar asked, finishing his briefing, and waving expansively at the map, the imagery, and schedules on the laptop.

"It is a good plan," Akil observed. "I am particularly impressed with the means you found to access the compound."

"I'm concerned with the number of our brothers you need for this operation," Ghalib observed acidly. "Logistically, it's a nightmare. It will take weeks to move two dozen men into the city without the authorities knowing, especially after the operation against the hotel."

Akil considered his words. "Ghalib makes a valid point. How do we address this?"

"One of two ways, Sahib," Omar responded, "we either delay the timetable to allow us to bring the brothers we need in," he paused, seeing Akil slowly begin to shake his head, then continued, "or, we use one of our captured freighters."

"How?" Akil asked, puzzled by the suggestion. The Caliphate only had two cargo ships under its control, both based in the horn of Africa, moored in territory controlled by a small cell of former al-Qaeda fighters who had aligned themselves with the Islamic State quietly nearly a month ago.

"We can put our brothers on one of the freighters, disguised as crewmen. The ship can moor in the port, and our brothers can slip ashore during what appears to be shore leave. The ship can sail before the attack, and none will be the wiser."

"How will the ship sail without a crew?" Ghalib asked disdainfully.

Now Omar shook his head at the man's failure of imagination and reasoning. "The brothers will be extra crew, and the crew needed to sail the ship home will remain onboard."

"Customs?" Akil asked.

"You have access to passport manufacturing equipment. Print them passports and give them papers listing them as deckhands and machinists." Seeing their skepticism, Omar added, "The deception does not need to work for long."

"The command and control?" Akil asked, his military training kicking in.

"Cell phones. We can set it up the same way we handled the hotel attack," Omar responded confidently.

Akil stood thoughtfully for a moment, deciding that now was the time. Al-Amriki's plan was audacious, as usual, and the briefing on his latest plan had been mostly cordial. Al-Amriki's response to the unexpected change of subject would tell him much. It was an interrogation technique he learned in the Republican Guard.

"Yes, that would work," Akil told him; continuing without changing the matter-of-fact tone of his voice, "what I still do not understand is why you met with two westerners this morning."

Akil saw surprise in the young man's eyes and on his face. "Please explain that to me now, Al-Amriki."

CHAPTER 17

Omar was shocked Akil knew he met with Mathews and Simms, and it took every bit of his training not to take a step back from three men he knew would kill him very slowly if they believed he had betrayed them.

"Sahib?" Omar said, thinking the best approach was to plead ignorance for the moment.

Ghalib moved toward Omar, the Desert Eagle coming up. In the darkness, Mathews' mind went into overdrive, and he moved his M-8 slightly up and left, centering the sights on Ghalib's skull and tracking him. Simms had not called out that he was in position yet, so he hesitated. Taking the shot would precipitate an immediate firefight, and the odds were unbalanced. Mathews was milliseconds away from pulling the trigger and declaring the mission compromised when Akil reached out, putting a hand on Ghalib's arm. Ghalib stopped, the pistol pointed at Omar's chest.

"Answer me now Al-Amriki," Akil ordered calmly.

Omar looked at Ghalib, his heart pounding in his chest, half-wondering why Mathews had not fired yet, and he raised his hands in surrender. "Sahib, please," he pleaded, "I'm not sure how you know, but I saw the men approaching the café and decided to play the role of amiable Jordanian to learn what I could from them."

Akil stared at him, waiting for more. Given Ghalib's proximity, and obvious willingness to hurt him, Omar did not let him wait.

"They are graduate students studying the ruins east of Ar-Ruwayshid."

"How do you know that?" Nusrat demanded.

Omar looked at him, breaking his eye contact with Akil. "I do not. I am only telling you what they told me."

"Which university? What are their nationalities?" Nusrat demanded.

Al-Amriki looked from Akil to Nusrat and back, doing his best to ignore the gaping hole in the end of the pistol Ghalib held on him. Feigning nervousness in the face of such a threat was not a problem. "They said the University of Chicago. I presume both are Americans. Their English was fluent."

"Did they suspect you were an American? Your English is also excellent," Akil observed.

"No, Sahib," Omar told him, his voice shaking slightly under the stress, "I used only broken English with them and affected an accent." To Omar's eye, Ghalib remained unconvinced, as did Nusrat, but Akil had narrowed his eyes, seeming wary, but edging towards giving him the benefit of the doubt.

"Sahib," Omar continued, "If I did not approach them, then we would not even know that. I thought the risk worth taking so I could learn more about them."

"What else did you learn?" Nusrat asked, his mind already thinking of ways to verify what the Americans told Al-Amriki, and how best to get Al-Amriki out of Ar-Ruwayshid for his own protection, or to ensure that Allah's justice be done upon him if he were lying.

"Very little," Omar replied, "they asked about the best places to get supplies in the town, and if I knew anyone in the town who might want to serve as a local guide. I volunteered my services, naming an unreasonable price. They bargained with me, but I would not go low enough for them, and I left."

"He lies!" Ghalib sneered, thrusting the Desert Eagle forward, as if wanting to impale Omar with the weapon.

"Leave him alone!" Akil told ordered, still uncertain.

Ghalib looked back to Akil, surprised, and stated flatly, "He cannot be trusted. Kill him now."

"Sahib!" Omar began to protest. Akil waved him to silence.

After several seconds, Akil made a decision. "Al-Amriki, you will be coming with us tonight."

Omar let his surprise show as Akil continued. "You are one of the jihad's most valuable planners. If the men you met today are more that you think, then you will be safe inside the Caliphate and you will continue your valuable work for us."

Akil stepped closed to be sure Al-Amriki could see his eyes. "We will also speak more of this. If we find out that you have lied, or are working for the infidels, then you will face Allah for judgement. Either way, I want to know where you are for the next few days while Nusrat discovers if the two westerners are what they have claimed to be."

Putting his faith in Mathews and Simms, Omar said the only thing he could. "It will be as you say, Sahib. Nusrat's inquiries will prove that I am loyal to Allah's jihad and the rightful Caliph."

Akil considered him, and motioned to Ghalib to lower his pistol. Ghalib elected to pretend he did not notice Akil's gesture. "If you are, and they are American students, we will investigate their families. Perhaps they will pay much for their sons before we kill them for daring to set foot upon soil that rightfully belongs to the Caliphate."

Akil turned to Nusrat, "Have some of your guards remain behind when we leave," he ordered. "They are to watch this area from a secure location to the north for any sign of the Jordanian military or others. If Al-Amriki has lied to us, they will no doubt come to this place to find him. Have the men at the border checkpoint send vehicles to retrieve them."

"That is unnecessary," Nusrat responded, his ego urging him to show Akil how thorough he was. "I have a small back up unit nearby. They will watch and report back."

Mathews saw the man nearest the entrance key a radio and say a few words in Arabic. Oh, shit. Is he checking with the guards on the perimeter?

"They are on their way, Sahib." Nusrat told Akil with a satisfied look on his face.

"Very well," Akil told him, again pleased by his chief protector's preparedness.

"I shall brief them when they arrive," Nusrat told Akil, then headed out through the arched entrance to the tower.

Outside, Simms had just made it to the right rear bumper of the Defender to the south of the collapsed tower. Kneeling in the darkness behind the vehicle's rear wheel and body, he paused a moment to make a radio call. "Whiskey Four-Seven in position." He peeked around the Defender's bumper and his helmet's optics showed him the last two guards standing on either side of the tower's arched entrance. He was about to raise the silenced Sig Sauer to sight in on one of them, when a Tango came out of the tower's doorway, turned right and walked toward the Defender parked just to the north of the entrance.

"Four-Seven, new Tango in sight, exiting the tower and heading for the vehicle to the north," Thompson called out dutifully.

"Copy," Simms whispered softly, not taking any chance, even with the distance and the helmet on, the two guards at the doorway might hear him.

"Four-Six, I'm in position. Two Tangos on the doorway, a third at the vehicle to the north. Ready to engage."

Mathews heard the call and waited. The bigger Tango still had a pistol pointed at Omar's chest.

Akil noticed that Ghalib had not yet lowered his pistol. "Ghalib, step outside for a moment," Akil said, tilting his head toward the doorway. "I wish to speak to Al-Amriki."

Ghalib nodded, finally letting the pistol drop. Frustrated at Akil's refusal to deal with an obvious traitor, he snatched a pear off the small table, and walked out the doorway quickly, taking a savage bite out of the piece of sweet fruit as he walked.

"Another Tango exiting the tower," Thompson called out.

"Four-Six, the odds are getting shitty out here," Simms reported quietly. He was starting to wish he had the chance to swap out the barrels in the M-8 before running toward the tower. He considered switching from the pistol back to the rifle, but decided against it. Aside from the potential of breaking noise discipline, at this range, with the scope attached to the rifle and his helmet on, he would be shooting from the hip with the rifle, whereas the pistol gave him the advantage of a solid sight picture to work with and the advantage of the helmet's full field of view.

Simms watched the big Tango head in the same direction as the first did. The Defender was about fifteen-yards north of the tower entrance, and the first Tango had the left rear door open, obviously doing something inside the passenger compartment.

"Nusrat," Ghalib called out as he approached the Defender.

"Yes, commander?" Nusrat answered him, leaning back out of the open door of the Defender.

"What are you doing?" Ghalib demanded.

"I am sending an e-mail to certain sources I have in Jordanian immigration. I want them to tell me what they can about the two westerners Al-Amriki met at the café."

"Do you trust Al-Amriki?" Ghalib asked.

Nusrat thought Ghalib's tone suggested the proper answer would be no, but answered him as a professional, rather than let his personal feelings enter into it. "The circumstances are not damning, but they are worthy of investigation. Akil believes him to be trustworthy, and his efforts to support the jihad are well known. I will withhold judgement until my investigation is complete."

Ghalib frowned, sure in his gut that Al-Amriki could not be trusted, and pulled open the driver's door of the Defender. He had a weakness for the sumptuous leather interior and the rugged capabilities of this vehicle made by the infidels in the UK. He would need to acquire one before the Caliphate conquered those islands.

"How long until the others get here?" Ghalib asked, discarding the half-eaten pear in the dirt and wiping his hand on his pants before caressing the leather driver's seat, avarice in his eyes.

"A few more minutes. I had one of the units at the border follow us in, but wait ten miles away in case we needed a quick reaction force," Nusrat told him.

In the ruins of the ancient tower, Akil stepped forward and grasped Al-Amriki by both shoulders, looking into his eyes from a distance of about one foot. "Have you told me everything about the Americans?"

Mathews was sweating, and his heart was hammering in his chest as the anxiety of the moment seized him. Simms was outnumbered four-to-one outside, and any untoward noise inside the tower would alert the two guards. Now, their prime target was literally in arms reach of a CIA officer, and he needed to make a decision.

Omar looked into Akil's eyes, breathing deeply now that the immediate threat of Ghalib was gone. "I have told you all I know," he promised.

Akil watched Al-Amriki's pupils carefully, his cultural heritage and long experience with men looking for any sign that Al-Amriki was lying to him. For a moment, he thought he saw a flash of something, but perhaps it was just a trick of the light from the lantern above them. He released Al-Amriki and turned to walk away.

Omar held Akil's gaze, trying to think of nothing except the loyalty he had shown to the Caliphate, but knowing in the back of his mind that Mathews was nearby, and that by now, Simms was too. As soon as Akil turned, he moved, throwing caution to the wind and placing his faith in Mathews to protect him.

Omar leapt forward a pace, using his right foot to whip kick Akil's leg behind the right knee, collapsing the joint forward at the natural bend. As Akil's torso leaned back in response, Omar wrapped his right arm around Akil's neck, catching Akil's carotid artery against his bicep and closing off his windpipe. Omar knelt, using his body weight to pull Akil farther off balance, and down to the ground.

While the takedown was quiet, it was not totally silent, and both guards outside the doorway heard the unexpected noise and entered the tower, AK's at the ready, screaming for him to release Akil.

Mathews saw the guards enter the tower below him, and he did not hesitate. Omar was unarmed and vulnerable, with only Akil's body between him and the guard's bullets. Mathews shifted the M-8 until the red aiming reticule of the ACOG sight rested over the head of the nearest guard, and he pulled the trigger.

The silenced three-round burst from the M-8 blew the man's head apart from a distance of less than twenty feet. He shifted again, and the second guard followed the first into oblivion, his head similarly destroyed.

"Four-Seven, keep them away from the tower! Objective secured," Mathews called out over the link. He dropped the rifle, allowing it to hang from its sling as he hit the quick release on the harness suspending him in the darkness of the upper level of the tower. He landed hard on the tower floor, but used his jump training to avoid injury, keeping his feet together and rolling when he hit.

Omar was still struggling with Akil, and Mathews rose to a kneeling position, bringing his rifle back up to put the still warm business end of the suppressor against the back of Akil's head. The unmistakable feel of warm steel and what it represented against the back of Akil's skull made him stop struggling immediately.

Mathews had to give Akil credit for guts. Instead of staying stock still, petrified by the feel of a gun to his head, Akil slowly turned his head toward Mathews. His eyes grew large and his body rigid as he saw the featureless, smooth front of the black helmet and the wicked looking, futuristic rifle. The man seemed like an evil Djinn who had appeared from thin air.

Taking advantage of Akil's sudden shock, Omar ordered Akil to roll onto his stomach and remain silent. Akil obeyed without protest, and Omar got on top of him, twisting one of his arms into a joint lock and setting his knee firmly in the small of Akil's back to keep him pinned and under control.

Mathews backed off a pace and knelt, keeping the rifle pointed at Akil, but paying attention to the doorway, looking for threats. With his free hand, he pulled a thick roll of silver duct tape off his harness, tossing it to Omar.

Omar used the roll of tape to quickly gag and bind Akil, not caring how much of the floor's dirt got caught in the gag, while Mathews covered Akil and the doorway. They both heard the shots starting to ring out outside the tower.

Outside the tower, Simms was not overly pleased with the situation. The two Tangos near the Defender had heard the shouted warning from the two guards in the tower, and immediately stuck their heads up.

As they did so, Simms reasoned that Mathews would handle the two guards and keep Omar safe, but he needed to eliminate the remaining two Tangos. He raised the Sig Sauer, lining up the larger man's head in his sights quickly. He just started to squeeze the trigger when the man moved. Worse, the round he fired missed low, ricocheting off the top edge of the driver's side door.

Both Tangos reacted immediately, pulling back to the rear of the Defender, using its huge frame and bulky armored body as cover, keeping him from getting a clear shot. Gunfire erupted from the left side of the Defender, but the shots were well wide of Simms position, passing harmlessly over the black surface of the lake.

The next thing Simms heard was Mathews' call out and warning over the secure link. "I've got two Tango's at the rear of the vehicle to the north. No clear shot," Simms replied. "Charlie Four, any options you can see?"

Back in CTS, Thompson was cursing under her breath about the lack of armament on the little RAVEN. Under normal circumstances, she would have command of a fully armed drone, likely an MQ-9 REAPER, and just one of its Hellfire missiles would make short work of that vehicle.

"David?" she asked over the internal link.

Cain did not hesitate, and made a radio call. "Gunslinger, this is Charlie One. Say ETA to objective area."

"Charlie One, Gunslinger, ETA twenty minutes. We're on the south end of the orbit."

"Copy," Cain said, shaking his head in frustration. "Whiskey team, twenty minutes for Gunslinger support."

Nusrat looked at Ghalib as he reloaded his pistol. "We must get to Akil."

"Yes," Ghalib agreed, "but how? We cannot see the gunman, and your sentries are not coming to our aid."

Nusrat pondered that. "They are likely dead. It seems you were right about Al-Amriki. He is the lapdog of the Infidels." Nusrat considered their situation, and saw few options. The support unit would be here soon. "We cannot let them escape. Our fighters are only minutes away. We must hold them here."

"Agreed," Ghalib said.

"Ready," Omar reported. He had trussed Akil up like a prize calf in record time; ankles, elbows, and wrists all wrapped with multiple layers of tape. Mathews stole a glance at Akil, who lay on the ground with his head to the side; his mouth taped securely shut. He was past his shock at the sudden change of fortune, and his eyes were full of hate and anger at his betrayal.

Mathews reached into a pocket of his Thawb and threw a small case toward Omar. Omar caught and opened it, withdrawing the small syringe. He tore at the shoulder of Akil's Thawb, ripped it open to expose his triceps, and plunged the needle in without hesitation, thumbing the plunger. A few seconds later, Akil's eyes lost focus, and then fluttered closed. The sedative would keep him unconscious for eight hours or so.

As Akil fell toward unconsciousness, Omar scrambled over to the table, packed up the laptop, maps and other documents, stuffing them unceremoniously into the waiting backpack. Next, he reached under the table, feeling for and then ripping his CZ-75 pistol from the duct tape holding in place. The pistol was a last-ditch backup that he told Mathews and Simms about, and now it looked like he would need it to escape rather than hold Akil at gunpoint until Mathews could scramble down from his hiding place. He flicked the safety off without conscious thought.

"Can you carry him?" Mathews asked.

Omar looked at Akil's unconscious form. "Yes."

"Good," Mathews told him, "use a fireman's carry so he's protecting your back. That should give his friends out there pause if they get a bead on you."

"What are we going to do?" Omar asked.

"Help is coming, but it's twenty minutes away. I want to break contact toward our support. Simms and I will cover you, so you can get to my Range Rover. Then we board and we are out of here."

"Four-Seven, what are we up against?" Mathews said.

"I've got two Tangos out here using a vehicle for cover, no clear shot," Simms reported.

"Are you secure?" Mathews asked him.

"Affirm. They don't know where I am. I think these guys are trained. They aren't 'spraying and praying'."

"Copy that," Mathews told him, now more certain than ever that they should fall back if they could.

In CTS, Thompson was watching the drone feed intently when she saw another vehicle come into camera range from the north, and she swore. "Whiskey team! Heads up. Another vehicle to the north. Looks like a technical. Mounted machinegun and gunner, unknown number of Tangos onboard."

Things had just gone from bad to worse. "Four-Seven, eyes open, fall back to the vehicle on my order. Cover from the driver's side."

Mathews pointed his M-8 skyward, and fired one round, blowing out the overhead lantern whose glare had hidden him in plain sight in the shadows above.

"Kill those lights!" he told Omar, motioning toward the lights on the table.

As Omar doused the small lights, throwing the entire tower interior into darkness, Mathews moved toward the open doorway, moving to the left and using the tower's solid walls for cover. He just needed the proper angle. There.

"Four-Seven, break contact now!" he ordered Simms as his finger tightened on the trigger. Two quick shots blew out the Defender's headlights, plunging the area in front of the tower into darkness, and he kept up a steady rate of controlled suppressing fire, giving Simms cover as he moved toward their Range Rover.

Outside, Nusrat and Ghalib instinctively ducked as they heard the impact of the shots and the shattering of glass and plastic from the front and along the left side of the Defender.

"They are killing the lights to move in on us!" Ghalib shouted, leaning around the Defender and firing two shots in the direction of the tower.

The sound of the Desert Eagle's fire was close to a cannon as far as Omar was concerned, and while one of the rounds ricocheted off the tower's thick stone exterior, the second .50 caliber slug passed through the open doorway, and bounced around inside. Mathews and Omar plastered themselves to the bare ground and waited for the round's kinetic energy to dissipate, while Akil slept through it. Miraculously, none of them were hit.

"That's it," Mathews exclaimed, "we are leaving! Four-seven, you in position?"

Simms had used Mathews' cover fire to move behind the Defender he was near and toward the front of Mathews' Range Rover, which Omar had left pointing south for their eventual escape. He was opening the exterior doors on the driver's side when the Desert Eagle's shots caused him to hit the deck. "Affirm. Doors open on the driver's side," he reported.

Mathews got up from the bare ground, moving away from the tower's open archway and toward Omar. "Get him up. When I open fire, you head for the car. Don't stop, and stay right of the centerline of my car so Simms can cover you. Move when I say."

In CTS, Thompson was watching the technical get closer, looking at the distances and trying her best to estimate the truck's speed. "This is Charlie Four, four minutes to contact on the vehicle to the north."

Time was running out quickly. Mathews readied himself and waved Omar forward. Omar bent, hoisting Akil with a grunt and throwing him over his shoulder in a firefighter's carry. Omar moved forward under Akil's extra two hundred and twenty pounds with effort, and knew that if it were not for the adrenaline running through his veins, he would not be able to carry the corpulent man.

Mathews reached back with his left hand to touch Omar's chest and hold him in place. He had to synchronize this for Omar to have a chance. "Four-Seven, Omar is coming to you with Objective Stone, watch your fire."

"Copy," Simms replied over the link.

Mathews grabbed at Omar's Thawb, pulling him along as the signal to go. Mathews kept walking, staying in a crouch until he reached the right side of the doorway, leaning around it to open fire. He felt Omar brush past him with Akil over his shoulder as he exited the tower, turning left toward Mathews' Range Rover.

Mathews flicked the M-8's fire selector to semi-automatic, and began squeezing off rounds at one second intervals, using his night vision helmet optics and the ACOG sight's aiming reticule to fire as precisely as possible. His helmet optics showed him flickers of movement behind the Defender through its glasswork, but his rounds ricocheted off the obviously armored vehicle with no effect. Mathews kept up the fire; rear fender, left rear glass, and left rear wheel; all in sequence, and then mixing it up once or twice to ensure he kept the Tango's heads down.

Omar reached the Range Rover, and the CIA operative popped the lift gate and unceremoniously threw Akil inside as Mathews continued to fire, slamming the lift gate closed before heading for the driver's seat.

A few seconds later, the M-8's chamber locked open on the empty magazine. Mathews went through the reload drill with an efficiency born of six-days-a-week practice for the last three years. He thumbed the magazine release to eject the empty thirty-round magazine and replaced it without conscious thought, releasing the bolt with his free hand a moment later.

Mathews saw the massive frame of a large caliber pistol and part of a Tango's arm reach around the Defender as he squeezed the trigger again, his sight picture currently on the glass of the left rear cargo area. He shifted his aim, but the round fired before he rested the ACOG's reticule on the Tango's arm, and the 5.56-millimeter bullet lanced into the armored glass window.

The previous impacts had weakened the strong polycarbonate, and the twelve-hundred foot per second impact of this round shattered it, throwing shards of glass and metal fragments from the frame in all directions. Some hit Ghalib's exposed hand and the sharp pain caused him to pull his arm back behind the Defender again, the Desert Eagle still firmly in his grip.

Mathews fired eight more times before Simms called out after Omar boarded the Range Rover, "Stone and Omar on board. Fall back now." Mathews did not hesitate, but rose in one smooth motion and ran like a deer, holding his rifle across his body in a two-handed grip, trusting his teammate to cover him as he ran for the Range Rover.

Simms was ready. While Mathews was getting Omar into position for his movement to the Range Rover, Simms took a few seconds while he was laying prone next to the Range Rover to holster his Sig. He unslung his rifle, making sure to stay prone, and then tossed his helmet in an arc through the open rear door of the Range Rover, where it landed on the far side of the rear passenger compartment's floor.

Simms watched through the night vision equipped telescopic sight as Mathews ran, taking a sharp angle away from the tower to clear his line of fire. After the last two-round volley from the Tango behind the Defender, he guessed what would happen when Mathews broke cover. Simms controlled his breathing and kept his right eye glued to the night vision augmented telescopic sight.

Simms saw the Tango's arm reach around the frame of the Defender again, the pistol held in a steady grip. He pointed it toward the tower, the Tango obviously intending to return fire after Mathews' fusillade. Mathews' motion must have caught the Tango's eye, and Simms saw the terrorist shift his aim to shoot at the running shadow in the dark, his head automatically leaning to the left so the large man could track what he was shooting at and form the proper sight picture. I guess he's not as well trained as I thought, Simms mused.

The telescopic sight's aim point found the location he wanted, and Simms' brain automatically ordered his hand to squeeze at the same rate his finger contracted to ensure a well-placed shot. The copper-jacketed round covered the distance in two-tenths of a second and entered Ghalib's left eye, breaking through the bone behind the socket, its built-up kinetic energy liquefying the left hemisphere of his brain and tearing an exit wound the size of a grapefruit in the back of his skull.

Nusrat was less than four feet away, and had turned to see if Ghalib had been hurt when the window shattered. He heard a meaty smack, felt a wet spray on his face, and Ghalib's massive body collapsed, falling backward away from the Defender. Even in the darkness, he could see the inky pool of black spreading beneath his skull. The commander of the jihad in Iraq was no more.

Mathews crossed to the passenger side of his Range Rover and ran until he reached the rear passenger door. He wrenched the door open and stood behind it, using the glass, steel, and aluminum of the door as cover, leaning left around it and sighting in on the Defender.

"Get in!" he ordered Simms as he opened fire again, peppering the Defender's body and glasswork. Without waiting for word, Omar started the Range Rover's engine with a roar as Simms boarded, slamming the rear door shut and rolling the window down as quickly as he could.

Once he had room, Simms faced backward on the seat, leaning out the window to train his M-8 on the Defender again, telling Mathews, "Get in boss!" Mathews did not hesitate, knowing Simms had him covered, and opened the front passenger door, clambering in and shoving the rear door shut. Once he was in, he ejected the nearly empty magazine from the M-8 and rammed home a fresh one.

Back in CTS, Thompson saw the technical getting closer. "Whiskey team! Evac now! Threat vehicle arriving on scene in two minutes!"

With everyone onboard, and Akil unconscious in the cargo area, Mathews shouted, "Get us out of here!" at Omar who immediately gunned the engine, sending the Range Rover bouncing over the uneven dirt path, its supercharged V-8 accelerating the two ton four-by-four quickly.

Nusrat was still staring at the bloody misshapen head of Ghalib when he heard the sound of the traitor's car racing away. His training took over, and he rose, placing his life in Allah's hands as he left the cover of the Defender to approach the tower entrance, bracing himself to find the corpse of his friend.

When he entered the tower, disappointment and expected sorrow turned to absolute rage. The overturned table and the three lights scattered on the ground were the only objects inside the tower. Akil's body was gone. The bodies of the two guards—Allah curse them for failing to protect Akil—were still there, lying where Omar and his American murderers left them. Scanning the scene, Nusrat decided that if Akil was dead, the infidels took his body for identification; if he was alive, they wanted to interrogate him. Nusrat knew Akil would prefer martyrdom rather than being an animal in a cage, and if he were dead, he deserved a proper burial facing Mecca.

A minute later, he heard the sound of a vehicle approaching from the north, and he retraced his steps and exited the tower. It was one of the Toyota trucks they had passed through at the border; its mounted 12.7-millimeter NSVT Utyos machine gun and partial steel cupola a visible menace even in the dark. The driver guided the pickup toward him, its headlights washing over him before it halted. The driver had rolled down the window and was about to greet him when Nusrat cut him off, speaking in rapid fire Arabic to the driver and jihadi on the machine gun.

"Infidels have taken a leader of the Caliphate! They must be stopped!" Nusrat gestured south, past the tower as he climbed into the rear bed with the machine gunner. "They are in a vehicle fleeing towards Ar-Ruwayshid! In Allah's name, hurry!"

The Toyota's driver mashed the accelerator to the floor before he could set himself, and the momentum threw Nusrat past the gunner and towards the lift gate. When he regained his balance, he stood, clapping the jihadi on the Utyos machine gun on the shoulder, "Let me, my brother. I will help you deliver Allah's justice to the infidels tonight." The man acquiesced, leaving the machine gun to Nusrat, and stepped forward to rap on the roof of the Toyota's cab. The man in the passenger seat handed up an AK-74 through the cab pass through to the truck bed and the former machine gunner readied it.

Nusrat checked the Utyos, its ammunition belt, and the sights before gripping the weapon and curling his finger around the trigger. For Akil's sake, Nusrat swore to Allah that he would free his friend and kill the infidels. Failing that, he would ensure his friend was martyred for the good of the jihad.

Omar had the Range Rover up over fifty miles an hour and Mathews thought the ride could not possibly get any rougher. The vehicle was one of the most capable off-roaders in the world, but its age and lack of quality maintenance over the years were not helping the suspension cope with what Omar was doing to it.

Mathews could hear the undercarriage working to stabilize the heavy four-by-four, and he and Simms were being bounced around like rubber Super Balls since they did not dare put on their seatbelts in case they needed to return fire or exit the Rover quickly. Only Akil got to sleep through it all. Mathews estimated that they were a couple of miles from the old fortress, and the gap was opening fast.

"Charlie One, Whiskey team is enroute to LZ Alpha for extraction, objective Stone onboard," Mathews reported.

"Whiskey team, Charlie One copies. Be advised that the technical stopped and picked up one Tango from the fortress, they appear to be in pursuit."

Shit. "We've got a tail," he said for Omar's benefit. He and Simms still had their helmets on, but Omar heard him clearly over the sound of the Range Rover's stressed suspension and the dirt and debris kicked up against the car's underbody by the tires.

"Ghalib or Nusrat?" Omar asked.

"How the hell should I know?" Mathews answered.

"Ghalib's a big guy, the one who left just before I jumped Akil," Omar told him.

"I think he's dead," Simms said after a moment's consideration. "I put a round through his head when he," gesturing at Mathews, "was running for the Range Rover."

"Then that's probably Nusrat and some of the Caliphate's fighters. We should have guessed he'd have a backup team nearby," Omar said, frustration in his voice.

"Just floor it," Mathews told him. "Maybe we can outrun them to the pickup point."

"I hope this thing can handle it," Omar observed, pressing the gas pedal closer to the floor.

Mathews watched the terrain ahead through the night vision system in his helmet. The rutted path was rapidly disappearing into the desert as the Range Rover carried them south. They had travelled this ground on the way to the fortress earlier, and he knew that they had another five miles or so of rougher terrain to go before it flattened into the vast expanse of Jordan's eastern desert.

"Charlie Four, how far to the LZ?" Mathews asked.

"Eight miles," Thompson's voice replied.

"Distance on the pursuit?"

"Two miles, roughly. They don't appear to be closing yet. Keep up the pace, and angle about five degrees left." Thompson told him.

"We're not planning on doing any sightseeing." Matthews responded, before relaying her instruction to Omar.

"Gunslinger, Whiskey Four-Six, we're going to need you soon."

CHAPTER 18

The MC-130W Dragon Spear drove through the night air over Jordan with a steady throb of its four Allison T-56-A-15 turboprops, their combined twenty thousand horsepower easily allowing the modified tactical cargo plane to slice through the air at a steady two hundred and fifty miles an hour. The Air Force major commanding the aircraft adjusted the trim minutely to compensate for the fuel they were burning off, holding the aircraft at five thousand feet while continuing his instrument scan.

The major piloting the jet-black painted plane heard Mathews' radio call and goosed the throttles before the mission commander in the cargo hold asked for it. He did not even think of reaching for the radio button on his yoke; Stewart would handle that. His job was to drive the aircraft; it was her job to manage the mission crew and equipment in the rear.

Senior Master Sergeant Rachel Stewart was a sixteen-year Air Force veteran who had joined the Wraiths more than a year ago. In that time, she had flown more interesting missions than her last husband, an F-22A Raptor driver who had thought that just being a fighter pilot was enough to make a marriage work.

On board the Dragon Spear, she was responsible for the reconnaissance systems and the weapons employment, and she took a perverse amount of pleasure, mostly because of the divorce, in telling the pilot of the MC-130W where to drive the plane. All of her operators in the back were seasoned Airmen, with a minimum of eight years of service, and she had handpicked every one of them.

Her standard-issue gray aircrew helmet, which insulated her from the sound of the Allison turboprops and was covered with a group of stickers, one for each flag of every country she had flown over, was comfortably fastened under her chin. Out of habit, she moved the attached microphone to within one finger's width of her mouth before gripping the plastic box on the cord that connected her to the cabin interphone and the tactical radio net. The twelve-foot-long cord allowed her to walk back and forth behind her people's positions in flight, seeing what they saw, and supporting them as needed. Stewart felt for the first switch with her right thumb, and keyed her microphone, "Whiskey Four-Six, Gunslinger. We're here for you. Can you identify?"

In the Range Rover, Mathews turned to Simms, "Beacon time."

Simms reached under his Thawb and fished in one of the armored vest's pockets. After a few seconds, he extracted a small, clear plastic domed object with a metal base. He flicked the small switch on the side, which did not seem to do anything, and put his arm through the window, slapping the device on the roof of the Range Rover, where the magnetic base held it in place. Simms nodded at Mathews.

"IR beacon lit. Gunslinger, identify," Mathews called out.

Aboard the Dragon Spear, Stewart leaned over the shoulder of her sensor operator. The infrared optics in the pod under the left wing saw the telltale one-flash-per-second of the infrared beacon Simms had just attached to the roof of the Range Rover. Invisible to the naked eye, the beacon easily marked them as a friendly to the mission crew onboard the MC-130W. Her operator, listening to the tactical radio net, reached out and tapped the vehicle on his screen.

"We have your beacon, Whiskey Team," Stewart reported.

"Gunslinger, Charlie Four, threat vehicle due north of Whiskey Team's car, about two miles back," Thompson called out from CTS.

"Gunslinger copies," Stewart responded. She pressed the second switch on the hard-plastic box to address her sensor operator. "Where's the hostile?"

The man zoomed the powerful camera out a little so he could keep an eye on Mathews' four-by-four and slewed the camera north a couple of degrees. Stewart saw the pickup clearly, and the mounted heavy machine gun in the bed.

"Whiskey Four-Six, we see your pursuit."

Mathews looked at Simms. Simms shrugged, knowing it was Mathews' call. Mathews recapped the situation quickly in his mind. They were at least two miles ahead of their pursuers, and they were not being fired on at the moment. Under the rules of engagement, he had to try to break contact first.

"Charlie Four, how much farther to the LZ?" Mathews asked.

"Seven miles," Thompson responded.

Mathews leaned over and glanced at the Range Rover's speed. At this rate, they would hit the LZ in eight or nine minutes, but they would need at least fifteen in total to allow the MC-130W to land, and get them on board, and take off again. Mathews knew once the Dragon Spear was on the ground, she was a slow, lumbering beast, and letting that technical within a mile would expose the entire crew to an unnecessary risk. That was not an option.

"Gunslinger, you're cleared to engage," Mathews said.

Aboard the MC-130W, Stewart issued an order to the weapons team. "Target the technical, engage with Griffin."

The two sergeants on the weapons consoles began the launch procedure, one running the brief checklist as the other uncaged the laser designator in the pod next to the camera and marked the technical with its invisible beam. The male sergeant running the list selected the point detonation option as part of his arming checklist. The AGM-176 only had a thirteen-pound warhead, designed to limit collateral damage, but it would be more than enough for the technical. In seconds, the forty-five-pound Griffin missile was armed and ready to leave its launch tube under the right wing of the MC-130W.

"Ready to fire," he reported.

"Target lit," the woman reported.

Stewart had moved to stand behind them, checking the status displays as they worked and double-checking that they had the proper vehicle lit for the engagement. "Clear to engage," she told them over the interphone. Then, to warn the flight deck what was about to happen, she said, "Aircraft commander, mission commander, firing Griffin on hostile ground target, in three, two, one, now."

The airman on the weapons console reached up and flipped up the red cover off the firing control, and punched it once. "Weapon away," he announced, per protocol.

Stewart switched over to the radio net. "Whiskey Four-Six, shot out!"

Two miles behind the Range Rover, Nusrat was holding onto the machine gun for dear life as the Toyota's driver raced over the bare desert, chasing the headlights of the vehicle in the distance.

Above them, in the pitch-black night sky, the AGM-176 shot from its tube launcher and its rocket motor fired. The bullet-shaped seeker head immediately acquired the spot of moving laser light that its electronic brain knew was a target, and its four stubby wings unfolded from its body. The computer brain issued a series of commands, and the wings pivoted to tip the missile over and let the reflected laser light become centered in its electronic eye. As the laser light rose and centered, the brain issued an order to reduce the angle of the wings, and three out of the four wings obeyed. The fourth did not. The airflow over the still-canted wing caused the missile to dip lower, and the computer tried to compensate, issuing new commands. The missile's flight path became erratic, bobbing up and down, rather than traveling a smooth arc that adjusted as needed to track the target vehicle.

Nusrat saw a flash of something above them. He strained in the darkness to make it out, but saw nothing. Suddenly, there was an explosion fifty meters in front of the Toyota. Nusrat ducked instinctively, and the Toyota's driver swerved left away from it. Nusrat made the connection instantly. "It's the Americans!" he shouted. He should have known they would have one of their drones nearby to help that traitor Al-Amriki. "Swerve! The drone should only have one or two more missiles!" he screamed at the driver. The jihadi behind the wheel did not need any more encouragement, and he slewed the wheel back and forth in what he hoped was an unpredictable pattern as he mashed the gas pedal to the floor.

Aboard the Dragon Spear, Stewart was flabbergasted. "What the fuck happened?"

"Unknown," the male sergeant reported. "Running diagnostics." Stewart did not make him stop the diagnostics or order him to re-engage. They only had three Griffins left, and if they had an electronic fault, they would just be wasting rounds. Besides, the friendlies on the ground had time and distance on their side, and they were not in any immediate danger.

"Target vehicle is driving erratically," the female sergeant said, adding, "for all the good it will do them." It just was not possible to evade a functioning missile once the laser painted the target.

Stewart switched to the radio link. "Whiskey Four-Six, engaged target with zero effect. Weapons malfunction. Consider us Winchester for two mikes."

In the Range Rover, Mathews shook his head. 'Winchester' was a term aircraft used when they were out of usable weapons. The term 'Magnum' meant they had weapons available for use. "Copy," he replied tersely.

"Whiskey Four-Six, Charlie Four, come left five degrees for the LZ."

"Copy," Mathews called out, relaying the direction to Omar before turning around, to look behind them for any signs of their pursuit, wrapping his left arm around the seatback to steady himself.

Omar had the Ranger Rover running flat out across the open expanse of desert, and with his headlights on, he knew he could handle the vehicle at this speed without any problem. He angled left to follow Mathews' direction. The partially buried boulder came out of nowhere.

Omar saw it, and turned the wheel farther left to avoid it, counting on the Range Rover's ground clearance to allow the Rover to pass over it cleanly, but their luck ran out. The bottom four inches of the left front wheel's strut assembly smashed into the boulder at more than sixty-five miles an hour. The impact sheared off the sharp top of the boulder, and sheared off the bolts holding the strut to the wheel. The left wheel immediately collapsed and the Rover's rear slewed to the right.

Omar stayed off the brakes, turned the wheel right to counteract the skid, and the Range Rover slid more than sixty feet, taking a dangerous list to the right before coming to a stop, its engine still running. Mathews thought it a minor miracle that the Rover had not rolled on them. "Out!" he shouted once the Rover stopped moving.

He and Simms scrambled out of the vehicle, Omar hot on their heels.

"Now what do we do?" Omar asked; a panicked look on his face.

"Charlie Four! Gunslinger, our vehicle is disabled! We need immediate cover!"

Nusrat was swaying with the driver's erratic back and forth pattern, doing his best to watch the sky for any sign of another missile launch from the drone, and the movement of the vehicle they were chasing by the motion of its headlights. He saw the lights sway and then swerve violently to the left, then stop.

"We have them!" Nusrat shouted, leaning down to smack the side of the truck. "Go faster! By Allah's Will, we will bring justice to these infidels!" The driver heard him and waved out the window and he stopped weaving the Toyota back and forth and made a bee-line for their prey.

Aboard the Dragon Spear, Stewart was apoplectic. "How long on the diagnostics?" she demanded of the sergeant on the weapons console. The man consulted the system readouts before answering.

"It's only forty-five percent of the way through the tests!"

"Interrupt the diagnostic and fire!" she ordered.

The man turned to her, "I can't. The system just started a test on the interface to the missile electronics from this console. If I interrupt now, the system has to re-boot to initialize. It will be faster to let it complete. Call it a minute and a half, maybe two."

Stewart wanted to order the man to reboot, but he was her expert on the Griffin and she would not discount his experience with the system. The ground team would have to make due for two more minutes.

"Whiskey Four-Six," Stewart radioed out, a resigned look on her face only an experienced professional can achieve in the face of lethal consequences. "It will be two minutes before we can fire again."

In CTS, Thompson and Cain looked at each other. Cain just shook his head, keying his microphone. "Whiskey Four-Six, Charlie One. No other assets available. You're on your own until Gunslinger can support you." Cain wanted to swear for a long time, but like the men and women on the MC-130W and on his watch floor, being professional mattered now, more than ever.

Simms looked at Mathews. "We need to get ready, boss."

"Suggestions?" Mathews asked him.

"The car's angled the right way," Simms observed.

"Roger that," Mathews replied. "Omar, get Akil out of the back and get him behind the right front wheel. The engine block and wheel will give you some cover. Don't shoot unless I tell you to, and stay in cover."

"What if they hit the gas tank? Won't it explode?" Omar asked.

"That shit only happens in the movies," Simms said disdainfully. "What about me?"

"Grab cover by the rear wheel," Mathews told him, wondering where he was going to find cover.

"No," Simms said, adding, "I've got the long gun. I'm going to flank them." Before Mathews could object, Simms grabbed his helmet and sprinted off at a ninety-degree angle to the damaged Rover. When he was a hundred feet away, he dropped prone and set himself up. He could see the pursuing Defender's lights drawing closer. The angle was bad for a shot, especially given the speed the Defender was traveling, so he settled for using the telescopic sight's mil markings to estimate the range – just under one mile and closing.

Mathews stood still, watching Simms race off in the darkness, worried that he might lose another teammate. Simms had no cover and only the dark of night to conceal him. If they saw him at all, or saw a muzzle flash when he fired, he was a dead man. Mathews looked out across the desert and saw the lights getting closer. He ran for the rear wheels of the Rover. *Hopefully, they want Akil enough to hold off opening fire when they get here.*

"Less than a mile," Simms called in.

"They should want their pal back, so wait for the green light. We need to buy Gunslinger time," Mathews told him.

"Copy that."

In CTS, Cain stepped down from the raised platform his watch floor desk was on, moving a few steps closer to the large display screens on the other side of the watch stander's desks, giving in to the psychological urge to be out there with Mathews and his people to help them fight off the inbound Tangos.

On the MC-130W, Stewart had leaned over the weapons NCO's shoulder to see the diagnostic's progress on the screen, close enough that he could smell the lotion she used on her skin. "Sixty percent," he said unnecessarily.

Nusrat could see the Rover now, headlights still on, lighting the desert in front of it, and clearly marking its location. "Do not fire on them immediately! I will give them the chance to return our brother unharmed, and meet their fates with dignity."

The Toyota's driver slowed the truck and stopped it when its headlights lit the scene well enough to give them all a clear view of the damaged Range Rover, its left wheel obviously collapsed. Nusrat looked carefully at the scene as the three jihadis took aim, but held their fire. The driver and passenger opened their doors and took cover behind them, pointing their AK-74s at the Range Rover, while the machine gunner stayed in the truck bed.

"I've got one heavy gunner and one Tango in the truck bed, one each at the driver and passenger doors," Simms called out.

"Confirmed," Thompson echoed, looking at the RAVEN's camera feed.

"Stay frosty," Mathews said, reaching up to touch one of the controls on the side of his helmet. The night vision mode turned off, which had become useless in the bright glare of the truck's lights, and left him with a clear view through the visor of his helmet.

"Al-Amriki! I know you have Akil! Surrender him to us now and we will send you to Allah quickly!" Nusrat called out in English.

Mathews turned around to look at Omar, opening and closing his hand like an alligator's mouth. Omar caught his drift – keep him talking.

Without sticking his head above the Rover's hood line, Omar shouted in English so Mathews and Simms could keep up with the conversation, "Why should I trust you?"

Nusrat smirked, "You should not. You have betrayed the jihad and us! I swear before Allah and his Prophet, blessings be upon him, that you all will die quickly and painlessly if Akil is returned to us unharmed. Do it now!"

Omar did not reply for a few seconds, considering his words, and Nusrat's lack of patience got the better of him. "Perhaps your American commandos have more courage, coward! Bring him out and die like men."

"Gunslinger, where are you at?" Mathews asked.

"Not there yet," Stewart's voice answered him.

Shit. "Four-Seven, stand by to engage. Get the machine gunner first," Mathews ordered Simms.

"Copy," Simms said tersely, concentrating on his sight picture and keeping his breath under control.

Nusrat would not tolerate any more delay. "In Allah's name, destroy them!" he shouted, squeezing the trigger on the machine gun. The rounds stitched the Range Rover as he swept the weapon's muzzle left and right, a footlong gout of flame lighting up the front portion of the Toyota.

Simms did not wait for another order. He let out half a breath and squeezed the trigger. The round whizzed by Nusrat's head as he swept the weapon right during one of his passes.

The other jihadis all began peppering the Range Rover with fire from their AK-74's. Rounds shot through the Rover's body, piercing the gas tank, fuel and coolant lines, and tires, all of which went flat. Omar crouched farther down behind the right front wheel, trying to make himself as small as possible as he prayed to Allah that the fire would not penetrate the engine block. Mathews knew it was suicide to try to return fire now. He squatted down as low as possible behind the right rear wheel, keeping himself back a few inches to let the rear differential provide some additional cover. He had flicked the M-8's selector to three-round burst, but he needed to wait until they reloaded to have any chance at all.

Simms was trying to get a bead on the machine gunner's pattern of movement, and gave it up as a lost cause for the moment. The man was moving too erratically for a clean shot, and the improvised steel shielding around him was decent cover. Instead, he shifted to the truck's driver, who was holding agreeably still. Deep breath, let out half, and squeeze.

Nusrat saw the driver's head explode in front of him and he kept firing, not sure how Al-Amriki and his American dogs had managed to kill one of them under such withering fire. He risked a quick glance down at the ammunition box and saw that he still had more than half left, and he keep the machine gun's trigger pressed, hammering away at the Range Rover.

The jihadi behind the passenger side door was focusing his fire on the rear of the Rover, drilling holes in the rear lift gate and the right rear panels when his AK-74's chamber locked open on an empty magazine. He ejected the spent mag, and reached into the Toyota to grab a spare off the dashboard.

Mathews heard the fire slacken, and decided to risk it. He stood up and stepped forward in one smooth motion, looking for targets, his years of training for combat taking over. He saw movement to the left of the glare of the truck lights, brought the M-8 to his shoulder, and fired as soon as the red dot of the ACOG sight settled on the dim silhouette on the other side of the passenger door.

The jihadi on the passenger side of the Toyota was just ramming the fresh magazine into the AK-74 when the three rounds from Mathews' M-8 ripped into his torso just right of his sternum. His right lung was punctured in two places, and every rib above the mid-line fractured. The last round punched through the last half-inch of the right atrium, and it gushed blood. The impact of the rounds and overwhelming internal pain that followed caused the terrorist to lose consciousness immediately, and he collapsed. The rent in his heart would cause him to bleed to death internally in less than a minute.

Mathews shifted targets quickly, not seeing any other movement, only the headlight's glare and the flame from the mounted machine gun marching towards him, and knowing he only had a second or two more. His finger tightened on the trigger again, and three rounds lanced into the right headlight, blowing it out. The rounds continued through the headlight's housing, ricocheting within the engine compartment, tearing a hole in the radiator and the oil filter. Coolant and oil began to pour from the engine, but for now, those were the least of terrorists' worries.

Mathews ducked back behind the Rover as Nusrat shifted fire more quickly, seeing an opportunity to kill one of the infidels. Mathews barely made it back behind the Rover's wheel, flattening himself to the ground as the red-hot 12.7-millimeter rounds sliced through the Rover's bodywork, passing inches over his head as they embedded themselves into the dirt, kicking up little puffs of loose soil.

Simms had lined up on the last terrorist in the open, and squeezed the trigger. Nusrat saw the man in front of him in the truck's bed fall, blood gushing from a horrendous head wound, and he knew he was alone now. He kept the machine gun's trigger down and kept scything fire back and forth across the vehicle that the cowardly infidels were hiding behind, dumbfounded and angry that they seemed able to kill his men with impunity, no matter how many rounds he fired.

Onboard the Dragon Spear, the NCO on the weapons console stabbed the launch button viciously, angry over having to watch the gun battle live on the infrared image and unable to do anything about it for so long. "Shot out! Danger close!" Stewart yelled over the link. Mathews heard the call and froze where he was, putting his trust in the crew on the MC-130W. 'Danger close' meant incoming fire that would be uncomfortably close to a friendly force's location.

The Griffin missile left its launch tube in the same manner as its errant brother, tipping over and arcing down towards its laser-designated target. This missile had no mechanical or other faults and homed in on the rooftop of the Toyota.

Aboard the MC-130W, the female NCO could see that the ground team had eliminated the other three Tangos and used the trackball built into the console to shift the laser's aim point from the roof to a spot in the truck bed, just behind the machine gunner's feet.

The Griffin dutifully altered its course slightly, and hit within three inches of the point of coherent light. The thirteen-pound fragmentation warhead detonated on contact. Instead of a bright fireball characteristic of larger warheads, it was as if a kid had lit a firecracker inside a cigar box. There was a small flash, a huge puff of smoke, and the sides of the truck bed bowed outward as if hit with a hammer as the pressure wave expanded.

Nusrat never knew how he died. The fragments from the warhead assaulted his body, penetrating it in more than a dozen places, and ripping through his heart, lungs, liver, and throat. The pressure wave followed instantly, smashing him against the mounted machine gun and its surrounding steel plates, crushing his body hard enough that his torso flattened to half its normal diameter and smashing his head like an overripe pumpkin. His lifeless corpse slid down to the floor of the truck's bed, smoking and bloody.

As soon as the crump of the pressure wave faded, Mathews got back on his feet, quickly raising his M-8 and peeking out from behind the bullet riddled-Rover. He could not see any targets, only the thin wisps of smoke rising from the Toyota's bed.

"Area looks clear Four-Six," Simms reported, scanning the truck with his scope.

"Copy," Mathews told him, "cover me." Mathews broke cover and moved quickly to the truck, staring through the sights of his M-8, looking for unexpected targets. He checked the passenger side Tango first, tossing the dead man's assault rifle out into the night, then looked into the truck's bed. The two broken and mutilated bodies told him all he needed to know about their condition. He ran to the driver's side, saw the head wound, and tossed the AK-74 away.

"Clear," he announced.

"Coming to you," Simms called out now that Mathews had confirmed the truck's occupants no longer posed a threat.

"Omar!" Mathews yelled, working his way back to the front end of the Rover, "you OK?"

Omar did not respond and Mathews quickened his pace, rounding the front end of the Rover at a jog. He found Omar bent over Akil's inert form, his hand pressed tightly over the upper right portion of Akil's chest. "He's been hit."

"What about you?" Mathews asked, seeing the growing pool of blood on Akil's chest under Omar's hand.

"I'm fine." Omar told him, the shock of first time close combat still on his face. Mathews was pleased to note that in spite of that, Omar still had enough awareness to treat a wounded man.

"Gunslinger, Charlie Four, this is Four-Six, are we clear?" Mathews called over the link.

"This is Charlie Four, no signs of hostile activity." Thompson reported back.

"Gunslinger, nothing in the immediate area." Stewart called out from the MC-130W.

"Gunslinger, we need you down here now for CASEVAC," Mathews said. "One Category One."

Aboard the Dragon Spear, Stewart's lips formed a grim line. CASEVAC meant casualty evacuation, and a category one casualty meant they had minutes. "A/C, mission commander," she said over the aircraft intercom, "we need to be on the ground now for CASEVAC, one category one victim. Original LZ is scrubbed."

"Copy that," Major Schaeffer responded. "Can they mark the LZ for me?" Schaeffer knew he could put the modified Hercules transport down practically anywhere, but it would help if they could give him a point on the ground to aim for.

"Four-Six, can you mark a good start point for us?" Stewart asked.

"Affirm," Mathews reported, triggering his helmet's night vision optics again. He looked up, barely able see the outline of the MC-130W above them, as he heard Simms run over to stand next to him. Mathews began to scan the desert floor for the flattest stretch of desert he could find.

Simms had donned his helmet again and stood next to Mathews looking over the terrain. "From there by that large pile of scrub to up here?" he motioned, the arc of his arm describing a flat expanse that would run more or less right toward them.

"Looks good," Mathews agreed, "let's get to it." Both men started at a run, heading away from the Rover.

"Charlie Four, help us out with the distance. We need to be three-thousand feet from the Rover."

"Copy that," Thompson said. It took them three minutes to cover the distance at a dead run. "You're there," Thompson reported.

Mathews and Simms were breathing heavily, but hardly winded, the physical fitness requirements of being a Wraith meant both men ran four to five miles a day, sometimes with fifty-pound packs. They quickly cracked two green chemical lights each from pockets on their assault armor and scattered them in twenty-five-foot intervals in a line to mark the start of their makeshift runway. The MC-130W was rough surface capable, and it did not need a pristine paved surface to make a safe landing, it just needed enough distance to stop in time.

On their run back, the two commandos spread out and threw two more green chemical lights at fifteen-second intervals, bounding the first one-thousand feet of the desert runway north and south, and making the whole thing appear as a 'U' from the air.

Once Mathews and Simms were back at the Rover, Mathews called in. "Runway marked, but we have no smoke. Look for the chem lights. Wind northwesterly at five knots."

Stewart acknowledged the information and passed it to the pilot. Major Schaeffer finished flipping the night-vision goggles attached to his helmet in place, as did his co-pilot, and he banked the aircraft into a twenty-five-degree right turn. Three-quarters of a way through the turn, he saw the 'U' that marked the start of his runway and he put the aircraft into a shallow dive, pulling the throttles back to reduce their airspeed.

On the ground, Simms began helping Omar with Akil's wound. The small first aid kit in the Rover had taken at least one round from the machine gun fire, and it took a minute to find some undamaged gauze four-by-fours and tape. Simms withdrew his CQC-7 combat knife and cut off a huge section of Akil's Thawb, crunching it up as an additional bandage, and wedged it in under Omar's hand. He secured it with the four-by-fours and tape, then put Omar's hand back on top of it. "Keep the pressure up."

Like all the Wraiths, Simms was trained as a paramedic, but without additional equipment and supplies, there was little more he could do for now.

With a solid thump, the MC-130W dropped onto the desert floor, fifty feet inside of the 'U' formed by the glow lights. Schaeffer's co-pilot dropped the throttle to idle, reversed the pitch of the props on the four big turbofans, and smoothly slid the throttle forward again to full power. The reverse thrust of the props slowed the MC-130W from one hundred and sixty knots to thirty in less than forty seconds.

Schaeffer could easily see the three men in the distance by the wrecked Range Rover, and as the co-pilot reset the throttles, he taxied the modified cargo plane towards them. When the plane was one hundred feet away, he pulled the left engine throttles to idle and jammed on the left brakes, letting the power of the right pair of engines pivot the aircraft smoothly so it was facing back the way it came.

"Drop the ramp," Schaeffer ordered the crew chief as the aircraft completed its pivot, "and give them a hand with the casualty."

Mathews squinted reflexively as the MC-130W's turbofans threw up clouds of loose dirt and debris, but the helmet protected his face and eyes. Omar covered his face with his arm.

"Give me a hand with him," Simms instructed once the Dragon Spear's engines dropped off to idle and the cloud of dirt diminished. Simms slung his M-8 and reached under Akil's arms to lift him. Omar reached under Akil's knees, and together the two men lifted in unison.

As they headed for the plane, the little RAVEN drone flew low over their heads at twenty feet, its motor cutting out just as it approached the lowered cargo ramp. The drone flew onto the cargo ramp, and the upward slope of the ramp brought it to a halt in only a couple of meters.

Mathews escorted them to the back of the MC-130W, its clamshell rear cargo doors opening before them to reveal the red-lighted interior of the cargo area. Mathews could see the trailer box that the mission crew worked in, where they controlled the camera and weapon systems near the front of the aircraft, its power and data cables snaking across the roof of the cargo space to connection points at the wing roots.

The remaining twenty feet of the forty-foot cargo bay held ten jump seats along the left side, and six canvas litter beds stacked two high along the right wall. A steel worktable stood in the center, and a series of three open topped cargo boxes ran in a straight line toward the edge of the cargo ramp. The steel planning/worktable had storage for tools, weapons cleaning kits, and other supplies. The cargo boxes were empty black shells that could hold anything. In this case, Mathews knew the standard loadout for the Spear meant ammunition containers in the box closest to the ramp, 5.56 by 45 millimeter and .40 S&W rounds. Next came six hard plastic Pelican storage cases with M-8 rifles and their various components, all stored vertically for effective space management in the middle box. Last, in the box closest to the table, there was miscellaneous gear like body armor, radios, batteries, and two spare helmets.

The crew chief, wearing his Nomex flight suit and flight helmet, waved them aboard, the aircraft's suitcase-sized trauma kit in his hand. Simms and Omar put Akil in one of the canvas litter beds near the cargo door, as Mathews trailed them up the ramp, stopping briefly to scoop up the drone with his free hand and bring it aboard. He had not made it half way when the ramp began to lift, and the upper clamshell door began to descend toward it.

The crew chief gave Simms the first aid kit, and said something into his interphone headset that Mathews did not catch over the sound of the four Allison engines throttling up to takeoff power. Mathews set the drone down in front of the seats on the left side of the aircraft, and then walked over to the litters.

Simms threw his rifle on the upper litter, laid the kit on the floor next to Akil and tore it open, pulling out an IV bag and administration setup before cutting the sleeve of Akil's Thawb open from wrist to shoulder with his CQC-7 knife. Omar stood back, and both he and Mathews gripped the edges of the upper litter as the MC-130W raced down the open desert, bouncing and shaking before the nose rose up at a twenty-degree angle and they were airborne.

With the Dragon Spear airborne, Mathews flicked the safety on his rifle to safe, cleared the chamber and laid the M-8 on the upper litter, then did the same with Simms's rifle before replacing it. He also took off his helmet and laid it next to them, and pulled the Bluetooth headset from his ear. The phone's signal had been lost as soon as the MC-130W's cargo doors closed.

"Do you need a hand with the IV?" Mathews asked.

Simms was already swabbing Akil's arm down and tying off the rubber tourniquet. "Nope, I've got good veins here." Simms slid the needle into Akil's flesh in one smooth motion and taped it in place with the white roll from the kit, then connected the plastic tube from the liter-sized plastic bag. "Hang this," he said over his shoulder to Mathews, holding out the bag of fluid.

Mathews took it, laying it on the upper litter for a moment before grabbing the roll of tape and securing it in place. By the time he was done, Simms was well into taking Akil's blood pressure and pulse. When he was finished, Simms put the tips of a stethoscope to his ears and listened to Akil's heart and lungs.

"Well?" Omar asked.

Simms turned to look at Mathews, finally pulling off his helmet to speak. "His pulse is 98, pressure is one-oh-one over sixty-five, but his lungs sound clear. I want to add some additional bandages to the entry wound and keep an eye on him, but he should be stable enough for an hour or two. We need to get him to a trauma center."

Mathews went forward, heading for the trailer, and opened the trailer's access door to find Senior Master Sergeant Stewart sitting in her seat behind her small team, all of whom were facing her and talking. She stood as he came over to shake her hand.

"Thanks for the help, sergeant," he told her sincerely. "My people would be dead if it weren't for you and your people."

"I think you were holding your own, sir," she told him with a smile that acknowledged his appreciation for their effort.

"I need to be on comms," he told her, and she handed him a set of headphones and a microphone they kept on standby for observers and as a backup in case someone's helmet equipped system broke down.

"Top switch for the radio net, bottom switch for the aircraft intercom," she told him.

"Charlie Four, Whiskey Four-Six, we're aboard the Dragon Spear and exiting the area, but Objective Stone is wounded. We have him stabilized, but we need to get him to a trauma center. Options?"

In the CTS, a small cheer erupted from the watch team when Mathews' voice came over the link, since the last thing Cain and his people saw courtesy of the RAVEN was Mathews and the team boarding the Dragon Spear, and its subsequent takeoff. Hearing his voice confirmed their safety, and strangely, it mattered more than what they saw with their own eyes.

"Whiskey Base, Oracle, what can you give me?" Cain asked Simon and Walker.

"Wait one," Walker said, but Simon beat him to it. "Whiskey Four-Six, this is Whiskey Six Actual, fly to Cyprus. Your destination is RAF Akrotiri. The Brits will be expecting you. They will have a helicopter ready to fly Stone to the USS America. Its trauma team will be standing by."

The America was the lead ship of the new class of amphibious landing ships. She carried an embarked regiment of U.S. Marines, all their armored vehicles, and enough aircraft to land them on any beach in the world and secure it. "Copy that," Mathews said. "Will the Jordanians let us clear their airspace?"

"Affirmative. We set it up through their defense attaché. The Jordanians let the Dragon Spear into the country for two days of joint exercises with the proviso that the aircrew be allowed to do a night navigational exercise over the eastern desert prior to leaving Jordanian airspace."

Mathews smirked at that. Simon had not told him about all the details of Operation Railroad in case something went wrong, but he was pleased the Jordanians had cooperated. He could even see from the amused glint in Stewart's sea green eyes as she listened in that she appreciated the subterfuge as well.

"Well done to you, Simms, and the Spear's crew," Simon told him, adding, "General Crane is already writing up the classified justifications for the medals."

Stewart's wide smile and the mission crew's high-fives echoed Mathews' feelings. "Thank you, sir."

"You've earned it. Our British friends will see to it that you and Simms get on a commercial jet to London, and then you can fly the rest of the way back via the pre-planned route. We're having a set of passports made for you at the Cypriot consulate. The tickets will be pre-paid."

"Copy that," Mathews told him, looking forward to the flight home and seeing Kristen.

"Whiskey Six out."

"Safe trip home," Cain replied, "Charlie One out."

CHAPTER 19

The people on the Airbus A380 from London to Denver laughed, talked, watched the inflight entertainment, drank, and ate; completely oblivious to the world Mathews knew. They might read about it in some news story in the New York Times or see it on CNN, watching the talking heads question the worth of risking American lives in intelligence gathering or military operations, but you never really gained an understanding of it until you swore the oath and chose to serve.

In fact, the story he had just watched on the in-flight entertainment system embedded in the seat in front of him from CNN international about the on-going fight against the Islamic State was light on facts and heavy on speculation and opinion, primarily because there were few facts to work with unless you were actually present during the latest battle near Raqqah – and getting a reporter and camera crew that deep into Islamic State territory was not safe or practical.

Mathews shifted his own headphones to a more comfortable position and stared out at the blue sky and the world below from his window seat in the A380's coach section, his thoughts dwelling on the dichotomy to pass the long flight. Simms was out cold, having fallen asleep about two hours after departure, his earphones clamped to his ears, and a blanket over his chest and legs in the aisle seat across from him.

In one sense, Mathews believed news stories and the pundits' opinions were important to the national dialog about how America chose to deal with organizations that chose terror as a weapon. On the other hand, they often implied or stated criticisms about the means and methods used, most times without all the relevant facts, just information or anecdotes culled from faceless people, often with agendas of their own, be they inside or outside an administration—who always spoke 'off the record'.

The resultant stories were often a mish-mash of a few out-of-context facts mixed with speculation, rather than comprehensive looks at how an operation was developed and then eventually played out, since most of its details were classified and never would become fully known. Mathews knew that their right to tell those stories and be critical was a freedom he fought to protect, and he was proud to do so, but he found it frustrating when such stories appeared and the best efforts of professionals like himself were cast as malicious or improper actions hidden behind a cloak of government secrecy.

Mathews shook his head at the Catch-22 presented by the need for government and the military to keep secrets and the press's right to publish, then leaned back in his seat knowing he would not find a balanced solution to that problem in seat 54A at thirty-eight thousand feet over the Atlantic Ocean.

The upside was that during his career, he had lost count of how many civilians had thanked him for his service when they found out he was an officer in the navy. Most never asked, unless they were veterans, what he did in the Navy, they just said 'thank you'. The veterans said it with a knowing look in their eye that communicated their greater understanding of military service; but he was always grateful for every one of his fellow citizens who ever said it and took the time to shake his hand.

Those memories and the knowledge that he had done his best to serve them helped him to stay motivated and ignore the 'hot-air' from critics or pundits that never had the full story about operations he had been involved in during his military career.

He glanced at the moving map on the bulkhead display a few rows up from his seat to see that the aircraft had crossed the eastern coast of the U.S. near Maine. *It's good to be home again.*

Knowing he was back inside U.S. territory allowed him to finally relax, and he muted his in-flight entertainment system's sound, closed his eyes, and drifted off to sleep for a few hours, safe in the knowledge that inside the U.S., the FBI and local law enforcement carried the burden of identifying and dealing with terrorists.

He awoke as the massive A380 touched down in Denver, and his thoughts turned to himself instead of his duty. He would need to call his parents, buy groceries, and pay his bills again like a 'normal' person in America. It was always a little strange to come back to the peace and stability of the United States after a mission, especially one where he had been in combat.

The transfer to the Gulfstream G280 was uneventful, Colonel Simon had arranged for both he and Simms to be met at the exit of the Jeppesen International Terminal and whisked by car across the airport tarmac to the G280, one engine already idling, the smell of burning jet fuel heavy on the light breeze. Simms settled in and promptly fell asleep again. Mathews hardly noticed the takeoff, or the short flight to Wraith Base, his thoughts occupied with seeing Kristen again.

He wanted to hold her, feel her warmth and her curves against him again, smell and feel the softness of her skin, and try to repair the damage he had caused to their relationship he caused in his grief. Thinking of her, Mathews resolved not to waste time if he could, because he knew, in the back of his mind, that after some time on leave, he would need to take up the duties of a team commander again, leading his men through the regular training cycle, and inevitably, Simon would come to him with another mission.

Mathews stared out the window of the Gulfstream G280 as it completed its approach and began to flare out for another landing. He and Kristen had returned on the same jet from San Francisco, just before Simon assigned him to ROGUE SENTINEL and sent him to Jordan. He could tell from the small nick in the leather of the seat in front of him, something he noticed right after he subconsciously sat down in the same row of seats the two of them occupied on that flight.

The main gear of the G280, whose call sign for this mission was MIDAS-25, touched down gently at 125 knots, and Mathews felt the thrust reverse and saw the wing flaps split to deform the airflow and add more braking power. The seat belt tugged at him as the aircraft slowed, but he barely noticed. His eyes saw it all, and he felt the aircraft's movements, but his mind dwelled on Kristen, and the inevitability of a conversation he had long avoided.

Mathews felt the G280 turn, bringing his thoughts back to the present. It turned again, finally rolling into the vast hanger at Wraith Base to park among the other aircraft assigned to the 152nd Joint Special Operations Unit. He rose, stopping to shake Simms, who seemed to be able to sleep on any plane, awake. The sole cabin crewmember dropped the boarding steps, and Mathews led Simms out of the plane.

Both men walked down the G280's boarding steps into the familiar sights and smells of the aviation hanger at Wraith Base, where a small deputation awaited them. Crane and Simon greeted both men, along with David Cain, who had flown in earlier in the day. Simon's military trained K-9 Zeus stood next to his master, his tail wagging, sensing the friendly atmosphere.

After some handshakes and pleasantries, they all walked to the passenger elevator for the short trip down to level seven, where General Crane led them to one of the secure conference rooms.

They took their places, General Crane naturally sitting at the table's head, flanked by Simon, who sat at the computer keyboard and mouse to his right, and Cain on his left, since they were the next most senior men in the room.

Mathews and Simms took the adjoining seats on Simon's side of the table, subconsciously choosing to sit alongside their senior officer. Zeus sat in a corner near the door, panting easily, their self-appointed sentry, his ears twitching back and forth between the hallway outside and the conversation inside as his dark brown eyes watched the men around the table while they talked.

"Did Akil survive?" Mathews asked. He and Simms had not received any mission updates since they helped load him onto the haze gray colored MV-22B Osprey for the trip to the USS America under the care of a navy doctor and two corpsmen.

"Yes," Crane told them, leaning forward in his chair at the head of the table to snatch a hard candy from the clear glass bowl in the center. Since it was no longer good for anyone's career in the military to smoke even the occasional cigar, given the stringent physical fitness standards, he had developed a mild candy habit. "He's been moved to an 'undisclosed location' by our friend Mr. Walker over at CIA."

"Have they gotten anything useful out of him?" Mathews asked.

Crane shook his head, "Not that the CIA has shared with me, but I'm sure if they do, they won't be shy about sharing, even though they'll launder the source of the information cleaner than a mobster's income."

Mathews and Simms were not quite old enough to actually remember the FBI's war on organized crime in the 1980s, and while they were educated enough to get the reference, they were not sycophants, and did not do more than smile slightly in appreciation at the reference.

"How about Omar?" Simms asked.

"Mr. Walker did share that Omar will be awarded an intelligence star from the CIA for his mission. The president will be informing him of that in person today," Crane told them.

"Nice," Mathews observed, looking at Simms with a sly grin. "Pity no one signs us up for meetings with the president." The sarcasm tinged with envy in his voice was mild. Mathews certainly did not begrudge Omar the honor. The man had sure as hell earned it, but like all military members, he had just enough pride in his work and a big enough ego to want to see his actions rewarded too.

Simon looked at Crane, who nodded, letting his operations officer spill the beans. "You two will be going in about three weeks," Simon told them, "and we'll be throwing in a meeting with the SECDEF and the Chairman too."

"Sweet!" Simms observed, as he reached out to bump fists with his officer, glad the brass did not overlook him and Mathews.

"You'll both also be awarded the Silver Star by the SECDEF during that meeting," Crane added, and their eyes widened in surprise.

"Thank you, sir," Mathews said for both of them. He did not think that they had done that well, but one does not argue when command nominates you for a Silver Star.

"You've earned it boys. Well done." Crane rose and the other military men all came attention around the table. "Carry on," the general said, reaching out to shake Mathews' and Simms' hands one more time before heading for the door. He gave Zeus, who rose to a sitting position when the men stood, a scratch behind the ears on his way, shutting the conference room door behind him, leaving Simon, Cain, Mathews, and Simms alone with their four-footed sentry.

"Sit down, men," Simon ordered. "We've still got to do a more complete debrief, which is one of the reasons why Mr. Cain came out from the east coast to join us."

"Well, for that and the tour," Cain said as he got comfortable again, and they all shared a quick laugh.

Once they were all seated, Simon gave Zeus a hand motion order to lay down, then used the computer built into the conference table to activate the microphones in the room, and bring the mission CONOP, intelligence briefing, and links to all the Raven and Dragon Spear video up on the conference room's video display.

The formal debriefing ran for nearly four hours as Mathews and Simms recounted their actions from the moment Simon put each of them on board the Gulfstream in the hanger seven levels up, until they landed at RAF Akrotiri. While they recounted the mission, often referring to the videos and intelligence package, the microphones listened while Simon and Cain took notes and asked questions.

Once the two commandos had it all out, the two senior men consulted their notes. Not surprisingly, they had a few follow-up questions, and then it was over.

"You two gentlemen are on two weeks leave as of now, barring national emergencies." Simon said as he rose, dismissing them for some well-earned time off.

Simms and Mathews began to stand when Simon did, ready to come to attention, but the colonel just waved them down. As far as he was concerned, they had both earned a reprieve from strict military protocol for one day.

The door closed behind Simon, and it was just the two of them and Cain. Mathews could see that Cain had something on his mind.

"I'm really sorry we couldn't have done more for you out there," Cain told them, looking both men in their eyes, the sincerity in his voice obvious.

Mathews shook his head. "You and your people did a lot for us, Mr. Cain."

"David, please," Cain told him, as usual expressing his preference to be on a first name basis with the men and women he worked with, in spite of his colonel equivalent civil service paygrade.

"Absolutely," Simms agreed. "Without the experts you've got at NSA to make all our comms work, and without Thompson handling the RAVEN for us, we could have never gotten the mission accomplished and gotten back alive."

"What will you do with it?" Cain asked with a smile, obviously referring to the RAVEN still aboard the MC-130W in transit to the base.

"Once the Dragon Spear and her crew get back tomorrow night, I'll paint some silhouettes on it," Simms said.

Mathews smirked at Simms' idea, but he did not object. After all, painting Victory Tallies on ships and aircraft dated back to World War II. "What will you use?" Mathews asked.

Simms thought about it for a minute and said, "Miniature Islamic State flags seem appropriate, one for each of the Tangos at the fortress, and one overlaid with cell bars for Akil's capture." His smile grew wider as his spur of the moment plan grew fully formed.

"Sounds good," Mathews told him, "and I'll make sure the Dragon Spear crew chief adds a pickup truck to the one-thirty." That occasioned a broad smile from Cain and Simms.

"They've probably already added it," Simms said dismissively. "You know how ego-centric those Airedales are."

"You turned your phones in, right?" Cain asked as he rechecked his notes.

"Yep," Mathews confirmed. "We turned them off and put them in Faraday bags while we were enroute for Cyprus. The Dragon Spear team has them aboard."

"Good," Cain said, checking one of his notes. "I'll make sure Colonel Simon gets a precautionary forensics analysis run on them before they are completely wiped and prepped for their next use."

"Afraid we brought home some malware?" Simms asked, feigning an affronted attitude.

"Not on purpose, of course," Cain said, amused at Simms' play-acting, "but we'll want to check them anyway. They were connected to a network in another country for quite a while. They might have picked up something."

"Anything else?" Mathews asked, anxious after the long debriefing to take a shower and change his clothes before he went to Kristen's apartment.

"No," Cain said, shaking his head. "I just need to find a tour guide now."

Simms chuckled. "I'll be happy to show you around, Mr. Cain. Just let me grab a quick shower."

Mathews left them to it, shaking Cain's hand and thanking him again for all his help before heading straight to the elevator and his quarters.

Mathews approached his quarters, looking forward to the hot shower, laid his hand on the doorknob, and hesitated. He could smell her. Kristen usually wore a very small amount of perfume when she visited him, and he knew she was inside before he turned the knob.

The lights were out in the kitchen, the only illumination coming from two candles on the breakfast bar, set between china that she brought from her place – he recognized the pattern. The smell of a roast permeated the air, and most importantly, she was there.

Sitting in the living room in his easy chair under a lamp reading what looked like his most recent copy of Guns and Ammo, Mathews thought she never looked better to him.

Her blonde hair was up, pulled back into the cute ponytail he liked, and the green sleeveless dress she wore hugged her figure just enough. The next thing he knew, he was half way across the living room and she was in his arms. The hug was leisurely, but he held back a little on the kiss, worried that his nearly twelve hours in planes left him smelling and tasting less than his best.

"Are you OK?" she asked anxiously, looking at his face and chest, and running her hands up and down his arms.

"I'm fine," he assured her, "Better now that I know you were waiting for me." Mathews looked into her eyes, wanting to be sure she could see the meaning in his next to words. "I'm sorry."

Kristen slid her hands back up his arms to hold his face, returning his look. "It's OK. I love you."

Mathews hung his head as his eyes watered, and she hugged him harder, putting her hand on the back of his neck. After a minute, when she felt his arms relax a little around her, it was time for another question.

"Was the mission very bad?"

Mathews pulled back from her a little and looked at her again. The warmth and acceptance he remembered before their argument was there. "It could have been much worse, but we managed to meet the objective in the end."

"Good," Kristen said.

Mathews could see in her eyes that she knew he could not tell her all the details, but he also knew she understood the need for secrecy.

"How much longer before that roast is ready?" he asked, the smell of the roasting meet made him salivate a little, but he knew that now was not the time for food.

She smiled invitingly, expecting he wanted her if there was time before dinner was ready. "Another half hour or so," she said, a husky edge to her voice as the thought of his skin against hers flashed through her mind.

"Good," Mathews said, taking her hand and guiding her to the small couch in the living room. Once they had sat, he took a deep breath and let it out, looking at her.

"I want to talk to you about Sam," he said simply.

Her eyes widened at this unexpected development. "We can talk as long as you want," she told him sincerely, gripping his hands and looking deeply into his eyes. "It happened. It wasn't your fault."

"I know that now," Mathews said. "I just never expected..." he trailed off, breathing deeply to choke off the swell of emotion so he could finally get it out, looking down at their clasped hands. "...I never expected that with all the training, all the time we spent together as teammates, all the missions we went out on, that..."

"It's not your fault," Kristen assured him again as he trailed off.

"I went out on that mission looking for revenge. I wanted to make them pay for his death."

"I know," she said softly, and he could see the understanding in her eyes now. An understanding he had come to later than she had.

"While I was out there," Mathews continued, "in the heat of the moment, I put Simms at risk..."

Kristen started to speak again, but Mathews shook his head, plowing on. "...I almost killed a deep cover CIA agent too. All because I wanted someone to pay for Sam's death."

"You didn't..." Kristen started to ask.

"No," Mathews assured her, "I didn't. The guy is fine. We actually ended up working with him to do something pretty important against some long odds."

"Then it all worked out." Kristen said.

"Yes, but Sam is still gone," Mathews said bleakly, the image of Sam's lifeless body in his mind again.

"Yes, but nothing you did or did not do could have changed that," Kristen told him confidently.

"All he had to do was ask!" Mathews wanted to control his voice better, but the despair and anger at himself and the situation bled into his voice, the words coming faster and louder as he spoke. "He was more than a member of my team for three years. We were friends. We trained together, we went out on nine missions together and he should have come to me. We would have helped him."

Mathews tried to control himself, and he sat there, his hands in Kristen's, not wanting to say it, because saying it finally made it real in a way that could not be ignored. In the end, he knew he had no choice but to face it.

Mathews swallowed hard, the tears threatening to stream down his face as he forced his voice into a more conversational tone. "He didn't have to kill himself."

Kristen hesitated for a moment, then reached up to hold his face in her hands and look into his eyes. Mathews saw the acceptance and warmth in her gaze and reached for her.

He held her close to him, eyes closed, smelling her scent again, and breathed deeply, controlling himself as best he could. Mathews' eyes were watery and his next few breaths were ragged from the loss, the uselessness, and the waste of a good man. Kristen held him tightly, waiting.

Mathews knew the statistics from the mandatory training he had to attend as a team leader. The number of yearly suicides among special operations forces were the highest in the entire United States military. The way the military and the families looked at it, one suicide was one too many. Sam's had been one of more than a dozen in the last six months.

The stress of long deployments, sudden combat situations, and a cultural need to be seen as tough and unyielding in the face of every situation, of any situation, often led to a complete lack of outward signs. One day, a man would be telling jokes in the mess hall after a tough training session, and the next, he was found in his quarters with a fatal gunshot wound to the head.

Sam was due to report in for the team's usual morning workout and had never showed. As his commanding officer, he had gone to his quarters to wake Sam, intending to deliver a good-natured ribbing for sleeping late along with assigning some extra duty to ensure the entire unit knew that there were consequences, even if you were personal friends with the CO. Instead, he had to call the base guard force to unlock the door after two minutes of steady pounding on the door of Sam's quarters failed to gain a response.

Sam's body lay where he chose to do it, at the foot of his bed, a photo of his parents in one hand, and his personal sidearm, a .40 S&W Sig Sauer in the other.

Mathews read the clinical report of the scene from the base medical officer when it hit his desk in the team room two days later, the words on the page not coming close to the sight of the blood and brain matter splattered over the foot board on the bed, and the rug, and the side of Sam's face.

He had agonized over writing the letter to Sam's parents, not knowing what to say because Sam had not confided in anyone that he was feeling depressed or suicidal. Mathews snuggled his chin closer to Kristen's neck in a wordless apology as he recalled snapping at her when she tried to help him find the words to comfort a man and a woman who would soon bury their child. The arguments had grown more frequent after that night.

Mathews decided that tomorrow morning he would report in to Colonel Simon and request a temporary extension to his leave to speak to the base psychologist. He needed to talk this out with a professional. General Crane had spoken repeatedly about the need for anyone under his command to feel free to ask for assistance, whenever they needed it, no matter what the subject, and assured every member of his command that having the courage to seek help if they needed it was the mark of a professional and warrior.

Kristen rubbed his back gently as Mathews raised his head to put it next to hers. He hugged her fiercely. For now, Mathews decided it was good just to hold her. Soon, they would sit down and eat. He would tell her more about Sam, and she could tell him about what she had been doing while he was on the mission. Mathews looked forward to sleeping near her again, and to keeping her warm and safe in his arms tonight.

"Sweetheart?" Kristen asked gently.

Mathews wiped his eyes with one hand before reluctantly releasing her, kissing her cheek gently as he pulled back. "Yes?"

"Why don't we talk more while we eat?" she invited, rising and leading him toward the kitchen.

"That sounds like a great idea." Mathews told her, anticipating the meal and the days ahead. When he had finished grieving and his leave was over, Mathews knew that Wraith Team Four would need their commander, and that he would lead his team out on another mission.

AFTERWORD

Now that the story is told, please remember that we ask our nation's warriors to do tough jobs, in difficult environments, far from friends, family, and loved ones.

While we honor their sacrifices and their perseverance on our behalf before our nation's adversaries, it is a sad fact that too many of our men and women in uniform take their own lives every year as a result of stressors, be they combat related, or those involved living life in the 21st Century.

It makes no difference what branch of the military they serve in. In 2018 alone, 321 active duty servicemembers in the U.S. military committed suicide – the highest number in at least six years. In civilian life, it is a leading cause of death in the U.S. – 47,173 people in 2017.

The military has made great efforts in training NCOs and officers to actively look for signs of suicidal thoughts or intentions, and ensured unit commanders foster duty environments that support members suffering from combat related or personal stress. In spite of the assistance available through many venues, the sad fact is that we will continue to lose young men and women who chose to serve and protect us to suicide every year.

If you know someone who is showing the warning signs (https://afsp. org/about-suicide/risk-factors-and-warning-signs/) or has stated that they want to commit suicide, call the National Suicide Prevention Lifeline at 1-800-273-8255, 911, or your local emergency medical service. Making the choice to save a life takes only one phone call. Be a hero for a hero, before it's too late.

ABOUT THE AUTHOR

Tom Wither served his country for more than 25 years as a member of the United States Air Force, spending his entire career as a member of the Air Force's 25th Air Force, and its predecessor organizations, the Air Force Intelligence, Surveillance, and Reconnaissance Agency, the Air Intelligence Agency, the Air Force Intelligence Command, and the Electronic Security Command. In his most recent assignment, he provided authoritative technical advice and direction on intelligence collection, analysis, and production processes and techniques that underpin the operational employment, and acquisition of, Air Force space and cyberspace capabilities.

During his career, Tom served as an intelligence analyst at various locations throughout the world, including Japan and Saudi Arabia, and is a veteran of the 1991 Persian Gulf War. He has been an Intelligence Analyst, Senior Intelligence Analyst, and Special Projects Officer. Tom has also worked with a wide range of organizations within the intelligence community, including elements of CIA, DIA, and NSA, certain Under Secretary of Defense for Intelligence managed special activities, and the Defense Advanced Research Projects Agency. He has led analytic teams and spearheaded the design and implementation of unique intelligence processing and storage systems supporting Air Force space and cyber operations during Operations ENDURING FREEDOM, IRAQI FREEDOM, and NEW DAWN.